I'll Look After You

Meghan French

MEGHAN FRENCH PUBLISHING

My dog, my best friend, was beside me as I wrote every word of my first four books, but only by my side when the first was published.

This book is for him, so that my Gryff can be forever immortalized not just by me, but by everyone who reads this, so that everyone can know of his goodness for all eternity.

To my protector, my snuggle buddy, my best friend. The mightiest of hunters and the babiest of spoons. The biggest lovebug and the bravest boy in all the land.

Thank you for everything you gave to me. I will never stop loving you.

Content Warnings

Some of the following content warnings may be viewed as spoilers. However, your mental health is important to me, so please take care.

Depression

On-page depictions of panic attack

Stalking

Nonconsensual photography

Severe Mental Illness, off-page

Mentions of coercive control and emotional/financial abuse

Contents

1.	Alicia	1
2.	Alicia	12
3.	Warner	19
4.	Alicia	43
5.	Warner	55
6.	Alicia	64
7.	Alicia	70
8.	Warner	83
9.	Alicia	91
10.	Warner	101
11.	Alicia	115
12.	Warner	122
13.	Alicia	129
14.	Warner	135
15.	Alicia	144

16. Warner   151

17. Alicia   161

18. Warner   175

19. Alicia   182

20. Warner   186

21. Alicia   196

22. Warner   201

23. Alicia   209

24. Warner   213

25. Alicia   216

26. Warner   223

27. Alicia   226

28. Warner   238

29. Alicia   247

30. Warner   269

31. Alicia   287

32. Warner   297

33. Alicia   302

34. Warner   322

35. Alicia   332

36. Warner   338

37. Alicia   344

38. Alicia   351

39. Warner   361

40. Alicia   374

41. Warner   381

42. Alicia   387

43. Warner   397

44. Warner   408

45. Alicia   416

46. Warner   421

47. Alicia   436

48. Warner   443

49. Alicia   448

50. Warner   453

Epilogue: Alicia   462

Acknowledgements   468

About the author   471

Also by Meghan French   472

CHAPTER ONE

Alicia

"Low battery," a robotic voice speaks over the pulsing music in my ears. I internally curse myself, having forgotten to charge my wireless headphones overnight. I urge my feet forward; I'm not even halfway through my six-mile run. I can run without music, but my carefully curated running mix helps me keep time without having to pull up my timing app on my phone. I know if I make it to the ice cream stand on North Avenue Beach by the time I reach the end of the next song, I'm on pace.

I suck in a deeper breath when I realize I'm probably about fifteen seconds short of my target pace, and the guitar riffs fade. *Dammit,* I think, lengthening my strides. I'm more distracted today than I realized. I pride myself on my typically unflappable sense of pacing, and the ice cream stand is further away than I'd like it to be at this spot on my playlist. At least I don't have to dodge a lot of pedestrian traffic to reach it. No one else is crazy enough to be on the jogging path when it's twenty-one degrees out.

I'm a creature of habit, so a little thing like the weather isn't going to interrupt my most sacred of routines. Running is as much of a physical workout for me as an emotional pressure valve, allowing me to sift through my mental and emotional state as my feet hammer the pavement, my midfoot striking in time with the cadence of my thoughts.

I round the back of the stand and rejoin the path, now facing the opposite direction as the pounding of my feet carry me back towards my apartment. The wind is sharper, blowing against my face, and I tug my gaiter higher over my mouth and nose. The waves from Lake Michigan lash angrily at the shore. I lengthen my strides further right as my headphones decide to kick the bucket, Taylor Swift's voice dying abruptly. I'm left with the sound of wind whistling through my ears and the thoughts running through my brain.

As exciting as my mental imagery is, thoughts of the mail I brought in last week after work creep in instead. I release an audible sigh. I long ago learned that if the same thought pops into my head three times or more, it needs addressing. This is only the second time the issue has come up, so I don't have to address it to comply with my internal rules, but I have a feeling it will pop up soon again anyway. I might as well get it over with.

As I cross the street, I'm nearly run over by a massive silver minivan turning right on red to get into Navy Pier. I gasp, using my palms to push off the hood of the car before it screeches to a halt an inch away from my legs. My heart thunders and I stare in shock at the driver and passenger, who at least have the grace to look as equally shocked and chagrined.

The driver mouths "Oh my god, I'm so sorry," at the same time the woman in the passenger seat jolts to life, rolling down her window.

"Are you okay?" she asks breathlessly. Three small heads peek out behind her, all displaying various stages of surprise and fear.

"It's fine. I'm fine," I hold up my palms in a placating gesture. "You didn't hit me."

"I'm so sorry," the man driving the van blurts out. "I didn't see you. I didn't expect to see anyone out in this weather!"

I shake my head, mumbling, "It's okay," and resume my run. No need to ruin that guy's day by yelling at him in front of his family. The look on his face says he was chastised enough. I roll my shoulders, shaking off the adrenaline coursing through me at the near miss. I blow out a few deep, diaphragmatic breaths, letting go physically and emotionally from that interaction.

By the time I make it back to my apartment, I'm back to my emotionally regulated state. My lungs are screaming, and my face is raw from windburn, but the run charged me in the way it always does. I plug in my headphones while I ready myself for a particularly warm and steamy shower, all thoughts of the mail unpleasantness wiped neatly from my brain.

I should have known better.

"Jackson said he didn't care, as long as I'm happy, but I want this to be as much of his day as it is mine. It *is* his day, it's our day. I hate how everyone treats weddings as the bride's day." My best friend, Amy, is on a roll, which means she's at peak anxiety, discussing wedding planning on our lunch breaks. "I mean, I love peonies, but they just don't *go* with the other flowers we've selected!"

I smile while chewing a bite of my Greek chicken wrap. Amy continues rambling on, which she will do until she gets all her thoughts out of her head, at which time she will take a breath, and then I can finally say my piece. It's how our friendship has always worked, and I don't mind the extra time to collect my thoughts. Amy's word vomit can be helpful, because sometimes what she seems stressed about is not actually The Thing she is anxious about, so the extra ramblings allow her to sort through her own thoughts and get to the actual matter at heart. Today, though, I suspect the real stressor really is wedding flowers, which makes me smile.

Not that I want my friend to be stressed out, but stressing about flowers is such a relief compared to the usual stressors for the last several months that I'm grateful for small problems (not that it feels small for Amy, clearly). Amy and her fiancé, all-star shortstop Jackson "JJ" Jeffers, have been through the wringer lately. Several months ago, JJ's estranged and unstable mother confronted him and Amy outside his home. She demanded money to pay off gambling debts and brandished a gun, which *allegedly* misfired, grazing

JJ's arm. The worst part of it, as if those events weren't bad enough in themselves, was that JJ's mother had been gambling on sports, and, more specifically, her son's performance. There was a whole investigation, where there was a very real risk of JJ not only losing his job but destroying his reputation and all hopes of a future hall of fame spot. Luckily, the investigation cleared him and he's remained on the Chicago Foxes since, but it was a stressful time for the whole city, if we're being honest. JJ is beloved by all. So, yeah, if Amy is stressed out by wedding flowers, I'm happy for her.

"Ames, think back to the weddings you've gone to in the last few years. Actually, think about Elizabeth's wedding." Amy's cousin got married a few months ago in New York. "What did her wedding flowers look like?"

Amy pauses, taking a bite of her salad and chewing thoughtfully. After about a minute, she admitted defeat. "Honestly, I can't remember," she says, scrunching her nose.

"Exactly. You're the only one who is going to remember the flowers. So choose what makes you happy, whether it 'goes' with everything else or not."

"Yeah, but you know the media will be all over the wedding and want photos after." Through Amy, I have learned not only of the ruthlessness of Chicago sports media, but the rabidity of its fans as well. There's even a whole website devoted to the love lives of the Chicago Foxes and other local athletes. I understand her hesitation.

"You know Sean and Mariah will carefully curate all photos provided to the public," I say, referencing JJ's agent and publicist. I know I've got Amy where I want her when she breathes a deep sigh of relief.

"You're right. Thank you," she whispers. "I'm going to add in the white peonies because they make me happy."

"'Atta girl," I praise. I'll make sure to remind JJ of my contributions to lowering Amy's stress levels next time he grumbles about losing Amy to another brunch and bitch session we hold with our friends, Danny and Tim.

Our lunch break is interrupted by a light rapping of Eva's knuckles on the open door of my office. Amy and I are huddled together at my desk. My office isn't much bigger than hers, but I tend to keep mine a little more organized, which allows for a clear desktop we can use as a lunch table.

"Sorry to interrupt," Eva apologizes. "Our directors meeting ran longer than anticipated, so I would have emailed this, but I wanted to make sure you got the message right away. When you are done eating, Alicia, would you mind popping by my office? No rush, please finish your lunch."

"Oh, sure," I reply with as much composure as I can muster. My wrap turns to ash in my mouth. I like Eva; she's kind and incredibly good at her job. She's a team player and even though she holds a higher position, she never minds working down in the trenches with the museum educators like Amy and me.

Normally, as a museum educator, a lot of my work is behind the scenes, especially because I work with older students. My preferred population is high school and college-aged individuals, which means they're pretty independent if I have to step away or leave them to their own devices. I end up guiding them in their research or planning intellectually stimulating field trips for more niche groups. Amy, on the other hand, works with the littles, preferring an elementary school-aged population.

Eva gives me a small smile as she walks away. Setting my wrap down, no longer hungry, I take a fortifying breath.

"I'm sure it's nothing," Amy soothes, but she's not fooling anyone. For the last year, the Chicago Museum Association has been talking about cutting programming, due to a reduction in funding from the state. We've tried to make up the difference in private donations, grant approvals, and creative rearranging of the budget, but we always knew those weren't long-term solutions. I can't help but feel the meeting with Eva will be the axe coming down on my neck.

"Maybe," I say, unsure if I'm trying to convince Amy or myself. I roll my shoulders back, trying to release the sudden tension. Amy reaches across my desk to squeeze my hand.

"We'll figure it out if it is cuts," she supplies gently. *Easy for her to say,* I think. She wasn't invited to Eva's office, but it doesn't mean she is safe from budgetary repercussions. However, Amy officially moved in with JJ when they got engaged a few months ago, so she no longer has to worry about making rent or the vague threat of eviction if she is let go. I immediately feel ashamed of myself for thinking Amy losing her job wouldn't be stressful for her. I know it would be, although the real-life consequences for each of us are vastly different these days. I give her a wan smile.

"Yeah, you're right," I acknowledge. We're in this together. "Distract me for the rest of lunch. Did you find a dress for JJ's gala?"

Now that the holiday craziness has faded away, JJ's new charity foundation, Game of Hope, will be hosting its first fundraising gala at the Humanities Museum. His charity raises money for local organizations hoping to prevent and eradicate childhood neglect, abuse, and other traumas. Knowing how sparse the CMA's funding has been lately, I love the idea that his foundation funds already-existing organizations, rather than trying to create his own. There are a lot of good programs out there, but securing enough funding is always a battle.

I gently rap on Eva's office door twenty minutes later. It's a little ajar, and as she calls out to invite me in, I brace myself for bad news. I close the door entirely and take a seat. Eva's office is bright and sunny, one of the few in the planetarium with windows, as her office is located on the main floor of the building, a stark contrast from the basement closets Amy and I work out of. Eva has never been one to flaunt her elevated position, though, and I know she's been working tirelessly to advocate for all museum programs, mine included.

"Alicia, you know I respect you and your time, and I know how busy you are and how much stress these budget rumors have on everyone, so I'm not going to beat around the bush. I really feel that the directors looked at everything from as many angles as possible. The work arounds we put in place a few months ago were only a stopgap. If we continue like this, we'll hemorrhage money worse than we already have been. That necessitated some cuts, and unfortunately, with the declining enrollment from your student population, we must cut most of your programming." Eva winces as she delivers the news. My eyes prickle with unshed tears as I force myself to take a deep breath. "I'm so sorry, Alicia. We can only afford to keep you on part time. I know that likely changes a lot of things for you and you'll want to consider all your options. I would hate to lose you, though."

I nod, fighting a losing battle with my tears. I let them roll slowly down my cheeks but otherwise maintain my composure.

"We have put off the cuts as long as possible, but unfortunately, they need to take place by the end of next week," Eva continues gently. I nod, feeling like a bobblehead, but not trusting my voice even if my mouth could form the words. "Please know this is in no way a reflection of your performance or how strongly the CMA values you. I wish there was more that I could do," she tells me, and despite feeling the gut punch of losing half of my job, I recognize the sincerity in her eyes.

I leave Eva's office, forcing air into my lungs and drying my tears on my sleeve, giving her assurances I'll think about staying on part time. I make my way back down to my office in the basement and manage to get there from years of muscle memory, tears blurring my vision. Amy's office is the first in the small hallway of offices, and her door is open. I attempt to walk past hers, noticing her pacing anxiously back and forth, wringing her hands. It would almost be comical, given the tiny size of her office, if I weren't so distracted by the maelstrom of emotions swirling inside me. She takes two steps, then turns around, takes two more, and returns, pacing a tiny march across the limited open space in front of her desk. She takes one look at my face as I walk by before she crosses the room, pulling me into her arms. That's all it takes for the dam to break.

I sob into her shoulder, unable to put words to what I'm feeling, so I sit in it instead. Amy kicks her office door shut, giving me the privacy I need to feel everything, so I do. Disappointment, sadness, anger, betrayal, grief. Hurt, embarrassment, and anxiety. I pride myself on being in tune with my emotions, but right now, I am feeling *so much*.

"We'll figure it out," Amy promises, squeezing me tighter. She doesn't ask what happened because she already knows, or at least understands the gist of it. She doesn't ask for an explanation or try to solve anything. She knows me well enough to know I just need the release. There will come a time for planning, but that isn't right now. As I continue to quietly weep on my best friend's shoulders, I'm comforted by the presence of another emotion, rising from deep inside of me.

Love.

CHAPTER TWO
Alicia

I let Amy convince me to let her drive me home. My eyes are red and puffy and once I finally stopped crying, a deep exhaustion hit me. Our friend, Tim, works nearby and agreed to drive my car home for me, telling me he'll swing by my apartment tomorrow morning to bring me breakfast. I know Tim usually reserves his Saturday mornings for relaxation with his boyfriend, Danny, so his offer to change his plans last minute sends another pang of love and gratitude through me.

Amy offers to stay the night with me, but I know I need some time to myself, so with many assurances that I'll call her if I change my mind, I send her on her way once she drops me at the front of my building. After collecting my mail, I trudge up the four flights of stairs to my apartment. The elevator has been broken for about two weeks, with no repair date in the foreseeable future. I love the location of my little apartment in River North, but the building itself is in a bit of disrepair. The stairs are narrow, forcing me to hug the wall as Brady, my twenty-something neighbor, ambles down them, giving me a bow that makes his gray fedora wobble precariously on his head.

"M'lady," he says as he shuffles past me, tapping the brim of his hat.

"Hi, Brady," I say, fighting a slight smirk at his elaborate greeting.

When I make it into my unit, a tiny one-bedroom overlooking a busy street, I want to pour myself the biggest glass of wine I can find and collapse on my couch. Instead, I make a decision that future Alicia will thank me for, chugging a large glass of water before hopping in a steamy shower in an attempt to wash the day away. I should have known, given the way it started, that today was going to be complicated and challenging. I wonder darkly to myself if I should have let the van from this morning hit me. Not enough to do any real damage, but enough to garner me enough sympathy to *not* have my job half-stripped from me.

When I do finally collapse onto my couch, admittedly with said wine glass in hand, I relish the silence. Say what you want about my dilapidated apartment, but it's quiet, especially for a Friday night. I blow out a breath, take a large gulp of my tempranillo, set my glass down, and close my eyes. For the next hour, I sit, occasionally sipping my wine, and just *feel*.

I learned a long time ago that my quality of life is so much better when I don't try to control my emotions. I used to bottle them up, stoppering them in public, forcing myself to "get it together" to avoid feeling my emotions–or at least displaying them to others. It was only when I realized how damaging that was to my mental health that I could recognize by actually sitting in my feelings, it allowed me to gather myself so much more effectively.

The change from controlling or even denying my feelings wasn't an easy one, but one that I committed to fully once I experienced my revelation. I once read, "Don't control your emotions. It only leads to suffering. Feel them, feel them deeply, then when you are done, let them go." It took some time, but after a few years of practice, I am finally able to experience my emotions without boundaries, and my life has been all the better for it. A clever side effect of this practice was a massive boost of confidence and a solid sense of knowing who I am. Don't get me wrong, just because I feel all emotions doesn't mean I express them to everyone or everywhere, but I solidly know myself.

So, for the next hour, that's exactly what I do: feel my emotions. I sift through each feeling, sometimes with my eyes closed, examining each and letting it pass through me like water through a sieve. Sometimes, a stray tear falls, and I allow it to trickle down my cheek without wiping it away. *That is grief*, I notice. After several minutes, great, heaving sobs overtake me, wracking my body. I clutch a couch pillow and allow the cries to overtake me. *This is pain.* I sit in it. Eventually, my cries turn to small whimpers as I pull in deep, shuddering breaths. *Hello, anxiety.* I cycle through each feeling, turning it over and over in my mind, letting it run its course, and letting it go.

By the time I crawl into bed tonight, I mostly feel tired. I'm under no illusions that I'm done feeling the hurt from today's news, but I'm confident come morning, I'll be better able to figure out a plan to move forward.

As promised, Tim shows up in the morning, Amy and Danny in tow, laden with coffee, donuts, and Danny's homemade espresso martinis in a large glass jar. My eyes burn from yesterday's tears, but I offer my friends a genuine, albeit small, smile.

"Thank you for coming. You know I love you guys," I say, pulling the door open wide. Danny wastes no time pushing into my kitchen to make drinks, pausing briefly along the way to press a soft kiss on my cheek.

"Nowhere else we'd rather be, babe," Tim promises, handing me my keys and telling me where he parked my car.

Amy squeezes my arms when she pulls away from the hug she gave me upon entering. "How are you holding up?"

"I'm managing," I tell her honestly. "Donuts will help."

Over the next hour, I replay my conversation with Eva and do some problem solving with my friends. My savings aren't a total mess, but I'm not sure how much longer I can afford to live at my current apartment on half my salary. My place isn't the Ritz, but I am paying for a premium location in my favorite part of the city, close to the hustle and bustle of the Loop, affording me a convenient commute to work most days.

Danny's got a mind for business and finance, having invested in several of his own small businesses over the years, but his face after looking over all my finances is grim.

"It's not terrible," he starts. "But if you're going to go down to part time, you're going to need to make some serious lifestyle changes. You'll probably have to move and maybe get rid of your car; maybe both. Or pick up a second job."

I cringe at the idea. Working for the CMA is my dream job. I love helping high schoolers navigate potential career paths. I love helping to design research projects with less red tape than I would in the "real world." I love having real conversations with people passionate about learning. The thought of giving that up makes my stomach hurt.

"What about revisiting your crafting business?" Amy suggests.

Years ago, I toyed around with the idea of opening a small side business, selling my paper crafts on the side. As it stands now, half of my already small living room is devoted to my hobby. I've got a filing cabinet filled with an array of cardstock, myriad stamps and embossing supplies, and no shortage of paints, glues, and scissors. A dinky, wobbly table holds my Cricut machine, my pride and joy. Under the table, I store several types of vinyl and whatever blanks (craft surfaces like shirts, water bottles, glass ornaments, etc.) strike my fancy. I've invested a lot of time, money, and effort into my creative pursuits. At the time, I elected not to sell my creations, instead gifting items to friends and family. I felt unsure about monetizing my hobby, worried that it might suck the joy from the activity and add unnecessary stress to my life. Now, I may not have much of a choice.

I sigh. "I guess that's as good of an option as any," I admit.

"Income from that as a supplement can be good, but given that revenue stream may not be consistent, you may not want to rely so heavily on it. You might need to make cuts still," Danny prods. I know he's right.

"I have to give Eva an answer soon, since the cuts will take place after next week." I take a sip of my espresso martini and moan at the balanced flavors. Danny grins; he knows he made it perfectly.

"What would make you happiest?" Amy asks around a bite of chocolate cake donut.

"I can't imagine leaving the CMA right now. I want to see it through, at least for now. And since it's not like I have another gig lined up, continuing on seems like my best option. I guess I'll supplement with crafting." I say with a shrug, even though my decision is anything but flippant.

"We'll support you any way we can," Tim promises.

"Ugh, I'm exhausted dealing with all of this. Can we please talk about something happier?" I insist. "Let's talk about the gala or something."

Danny and Tim are joining us at JJ's gala; he bought several tables and Amy promised we'd all sit together as a group. My mind drifts to how I can revamp some of the dresses hanging in my closet to make them a little more gala-friendly. Amy walks to my kitchen to refill her drink, absentmindedly sifting through the pile of mail on the counter as we discuss some of the silent auction items JJ was able to secure for the event.

"What's this?" Amy asks, holding up a pale green envelope with my name, but not my address, on it.

"Hmm, I don't know, I'll check it out later," I respond, feigning ignorance and ignoring the way my stomach bottoms out. I must do a good enough job, because Amy seems satisfied with my response and sets the envelope down on top of the rest of the pile. I hadn't noticed it in the stack of junk mail and bills when I gathered my mail yesterday, but I had been sufficiently distracted. Had I noticed it, I would have immediately thrown it away, along with the growing history of similar notes taking up space in my garbage can and landfills across Chicagoland.

CHAPTER THREE

Warner

*S*hit.

My flight into Chicago from Atlanta was delayed due to weather. I should have anticipated that, given January in the windy city, without fail, lives up to its name. This time, I have an ice storm to thank for my delays, but at least I made it in. Four hours late. But it's better than a cancellation and having to miss my teammate's first event for his brand-new charity. JJ and I aren't close, but this is a big deal, and my whole team will be there.

I run around my penthouse, pulling my socks on and sliding my feet into my shiny black Oxfords. Paired with my smoke gray three-piece suit, I look good and appropriately dressed for tonight's festivities. My sister Eden convinced me to lace my shoes with narrow blue laces, instead of the standard black, and I must admit, she was on to something. Last week, she bought me the laces in the exact blue of the Foxes uniforms, begging me to swap out the original laces for a bit of "flair." Eden is always trying to add a bit of her own flair to my life. I'm not ungrateful; it's her way of taking care of me when I'm away from my family nine months of the year. Her flair has exploded all over my place in Chicago: a digital picture frame where she's always updating photos of her little family, plant pots spilling over with whatever flora she has shipped to me, shot glasses from her business trips across the country. I think she knows without these touches of flair she foists upon me, my apartment would be a relatively bare bachelor pad.

I like where I live. Admittedly, I paid a lot of money for an interior decorator, and she did a great job, but without Eden's help, my pad would feel a lot less personal. When I left at the end of the season this fall, I barely closed the place up. I pay one of the clubhouse attendants, Stephen, to come by regularly to water my plants and run my cars for a few minutes in the connected garage to ensure I'm not met with dead batteries when I return in the spring. River North, the neighborhood where I live, is not exactly a convenient location for Stephen to get to, but he assured me he had no problem doing it. I have no problem paying him extra for the inconvenience. I'd rather have someone I trust entering my sacred space as opposed to an impersonal company. I've been burned by too many people wanting a piece of Warner James The Athlete to turn over my keys to some random employee.

My phone dings, my car service telling me they have arrived at my building. I pull on my overcoat and lock up. Unlike some Chicago penthouses, mine does not take up the entire floor of my building. While I can afford it—the Foxes pay me well, and my agent negotiated an insane contract for me two years ago—I had the self-awareness to know I probably function a little better with neighbors surrounding me. The top floor of my oversized building is divided roughly into thirds, with my unit taking up slightly more of the floorplan than the other two. The Parkers, a husband-and-wife legal team specializing in corporate law, live down the long corridor. Mrs. Chan, a widower, lives on the other side. Her husband was some sort of investment banker who died decades ago. While I am friendly with my neighbors, we don't socialize together, but we do keep an eye out for each other. It's just the way I like it. I have my privacy, but I don't feel too isolated.

As I take the elevator down to the ground floor, I mentally chastise myself for not getting my shit together enough to invite a date to this event. I honestly forgot about JJ's Game of Hope gala until he sent a group text to the team last week reminding us. I was able to get a flight out but forgot about the whole *plus one* thing until I was actually on the airplane. These events are always more fun with a date: dressing up, having a beautiful woman on my arm, hopefully building the sexual tension all night, all culminating in a night of passion wrapped up in each other. Then, hopping on a plane to return to my off-season home in Georgia. I know tonight will still be fun, but seeing as most of the female company tonight will likely have their own dates, I know I'll be going home alone. It's not terrible; I'll likely be exhausted anyway from traveling and socializing. It's one thing to hang out drinking with your friends and teammates. It's another being at a charity event, especially in

Chicago, when you are expected to be "on" all the time. I'm sure there will be no shortage of photo opportunities for random Foxes fans who will have bought tables in the hopes of running into JJ, his teammates, and other local celebrities.

Don't get me wrong. I love the fans. I know without them, I wouldn't have a job. But there's only so long you can answer the same questions ("Do you think the Foxes will go all the way this season?", "Are you ready for spring training next month?" and the occasional "So…, are you here with anyone?" The last question I don't mind so much.) with a smile on your face as you pose for infinite photos and hope you gave the fans what they're looking for. It can be exhausting. I think JJ knows this, given how much he's been texting the team to express his gratitude. The man is clearly nervous, hoping the night goes well, but I know it will. Between the attention from his family drama last season, to the fact that he is genuinely loved by this city, to the backing of his brother and agent to bring in additional donations of cash and auction items outside Chicago and the Foxes organization, there's no way this night won't be a complete success.

By the time the car drops me a few miles away at the museum, I'm only a few minutes late. Fashionably late, as Eden would remind me. JJ really has gone all out for his first event, and the press has shown up in droves. As I step out of the car, cameras flash in front of my eyes. Time to get my game face on. I give them a smile and wave. Hayden Oliver, our first baseman, is unfolding himself from the town car behind me. I'm surprised to see he elected not to bring a date either. At least we can hang together rather than third wheeling it through dinner.

"Hey, James," he says, pulling me in for a back slapping hug. Oliver is typically serious and focused; tonight is no different. Sometimes I wonder if he has a frown quota he must meet each day. He's not exactly grumpy, but he rarely cracks a smile.

"Oliver," I say, embracing him back. We walk together to the museum entrance, and I briefly wonder how inconvenient this is for the actual residents who live near the Humanities Museum trying to drive up and down nearby streets.

"No date tonight, Warner?" a woman with pink hair and a microphone asks, surprise lacing her tone. It's not unusual for Oliver to show up solo, as he tends to be pickier about his time and whose company he spends it in, but I am rarely dateless. I offer a smile and a shrug in response but keep walking. I'm known to get around. My reputation doesn't bother me; it makes it easier to spend time in the company of gorgeous women without the expectation of a serious relationship forming. Sure, I've had my fair share of dates hoping to "fix" me by getting me to settle down, but I make my intentions clear with each date: it goes nowhere beyond one night. Besides, there's no fixing me, anyway.

Oliver and I make our way up the front steps and into a large, airy atrium, the location of tonight's events. Before we can reach the registration table, we're stopped by several groups of fans, asking for photos. They are dressed in black tie attire, so at least they aren't gate crashing the event. I'm hoping the team's presence will help JJ rake in more money.

JJ's ears must be burning, because at that moment, his fiancée, Amy, steps out from a room and makes a beeline to us. She looks beautiful in a green dress and gold bangles around her arms, which tinkle as she reaches up to pull me into a tight squeeze, followed by a similar one for Oliver next to me.

"Warner, Hayden, thank you so much for coming," she gushes. Her smile is radiant and genuine. It's comforting. Amy is one of those people that makes you feel important when she interacts with you; she's one of the most attentive listeners I've ever encountered, and I'm happy that JJ found her and is about to wife her up. She pulls us into the room she came out of, and I instantly relax.

This room is a private one with just a few tables, chairs, and an attendant on the outside to let us into the locked location. JJ thought of everything, and this room is proof: it's a quiet area where we can escape from the public for a bit. I shrug off my coat and lay it over a nearby chair. Some of my teammates and their dates are already in here. I make my way over to my fellow outfielders. I'm closest with Carter Perez and Matteo Cota, who typically make the starting lineup with me.

We catch up, sharing details from our offseason so far. The Foxes only made it to the first round of the playoffs in October before fizzling out, but it gives me hope for next season's performance.

It's only been a couple of months since I've seen my teammates, but when you spend nearly every day together for most of the year, time apart feels weird. Carter is telling me about a deep-sea fishing trip he took off the coast of South America when the man of the hour walks in.

JJ clears his throat and the conversation in this small room dies down. "I can't thank you guys enough for being here for me, not just tonight, but the last several months. It's been a real whirlwind."

I snort. Whirlwind is an understatement. I'm not sure getting shot by his own mother, triggering an official inquiry into JJ's integrity and performance, is best described by "whirlwind," but I see his point. Chicago never wavered in their belief in Jackson Jeffers, and while JJ is a humble guy who insists he didn't nearly die, the situation was serious enough to strike fear into all of us that our days sharing the field with the best shortstop I've ever played with might be over. I'm sure that's why JJ is getting choked up now.

"I couldn't have done tonight's event without you guys committing to showing up, and I can't tell you what it means to me." He clears his throat again, clearly trying to compose himself. He squeezes Amy's hand, then tries again. "I, uh, I…"

Caleb Andrews jumps in to rescue him. "What JJ is so eloquently saying," he says, slinging his arm around JJ's shoulders, "is that he appreciates you being here so he can rake in the dough for his incredible new charity. But he should know we'd all do anything for him, so he should have kind of expected this. It's the least we can do." He looks toward his best friend. "We love you JJ, and we're so happy for you." He turns his focus back on the rest of us. "Now open your wallets, you assholes. We're making this night a success for our man, Jeffers."

Say no more. The men and women around me clap and cheer before we all slowly trickle out to get drinks and appetizers while we peruse the silent auction items set up in nearby rooms. The tables consist of the usual items: gift certificates to local hotels, restaurants, and spas; guest spots on television shows; celebrity interaction events like golfing with JJ and other local Chicago athletes; dance lessons; autographed sports memorabilia...I walk through, peeking at each clipboard describing the item up for auction, looking for one with my name on it. After searching across two tables, I finally find it: Cooking with Foxes' Right Fielder Warner James.

I love to cook, and while I'm not a classically trained chef, I grew up with one in my mother. Mom has owned Squash Blossom, one of Atlanta's hottest restaurants, since as far back as I can remember. When I was younger, she was just starting out and Anita James wasn't a household name like it is now in Georgia. She's earned herself guest spots on national cooking competition shows, and rightfully so: she has a knack for perfectly seasoning each dish that comes out of her commercial or home kitchen. Nothing makes me feel more at home than my mom's meatloaf. An odd choice, I know, considering the plethora of gourmet dishes my mother is responsible for. But there's something about her meatloaf, mashed potatoes, and macaroni and cheese that makes the hardest days just a little bit better. When she ends the meal with her famous banana pudding ice cream, it's bliss. I'm convinced heaven consists of nothing more than a never-ending bowl of Mom's banana pudding ice cream.

So while I didn't go to culinary school, but I was raised in Anita James' kitchen, and that's almost the same thing. When I'm in a good mood, nothing makes me happier than making good food and serving it to people who appreciate it. Coordinating the date to make this dinner happen for whoever bids highest it will be a challenge with our travel schedule, but JJ assured me it would work. My publicist initially wanted to coordinate it with a magazine shoot, but I felt exploitative making my charity donation into a public relations move. Jacob, my publicist, is still a little salty about it, but ultimately respected my decision.

The value for my auction donation is listed as "priceless." I snort. I recognize my time is valuable, and I'll be absorbing the cost of the groceries, and the cooking will take place at the auction winner's home, so the cost is minimal, even if the menu I choose uses the most gourmet of ingredients. So far, there are two bids already, starting at $250. The second bid offered three hundred, even though the recommended minimum increment is $25. I smile. My mother's reputation has preceded itself.

I wander the auction tables, jotting my name and bids down on a few items, mostly related to my affinity for sports memorabilia. An autographed pair of Air Jordans would look great in my shoe display at my place in Atlanta. I make a couple bids on some local items as well: gift certificates for a local Turkish bath house and spa for when my mom and sister come to visit, a chef's table dinner at the newest Asian fusion restaurant in the Loop for a night out with my teammates. Sure, I could purchase these items on my own on any day of the week, but it's easy to get swept up in the contagious spirit of giving at an event like this. Game of Hope works on preventing and eradicating childhood neglect. It's not something I or anyone I know (aside from JJ) has experienced, but I know I'm lucky not to have experienced childhood trauma. You play with enough teammates in enough cities in the country and it's not hard to realize we're all walking around with some sort of baggage, no matter how privileged we are now.

A bell chimes, signaling the plated dinner is about to start. An event coordinator assures everyone the silent auction will continue after dinner as she ushers us into the nearby atrium. I find my assigned table, relieved to find I've been seated near Oliver; I guess it's easier logistically to stick dateless people together. We're seated with Caleb Andrews and his fiancée, Jenny, who looks fantastic. Jenny has been battling breast cancer for a couple years now, and things are finally looking like she's turned a corner in her treatment plan. She looks stronger than she did the last time I saw her, with more color to her cheeks. I suppose it could be her makeup, but she also seems a little more energetic as well, so I send up a silent prayer that these signs bode well for her recovery.

Amy seats herself between Jenny and Alicia, her friend from work. It took me several minutes to recall Alicia's name; I had met her during the season at one of JJ's many rooftop barbeques, but beyond our initial meeting, I haven't really interacted with her. She looks stunning in a red dress with a plunging neckline that shows off her delicate collarbones. Amy's friends Danny and Tim are here at our table as well. Both seemed like great guys when I met them, and apparently Tim strongly believes JJ is a spy instead of an actual baseball player. When I pointed out that he's watched JJ play multiple times, Tim insisted it was all just a clever ruse to maintain JJ's cover. I still haven't worked out whether Tim is joking. I take a seat, noting the two empty chairs at our table. One is for JJ, I assume, who is likely still working the room or getting ready to give a speech.

Dammit, I should have brought a date. JJ probably assumed I'd bring one, which is why there's an empty seat at our table. I cringe. It probably doesn't look good for him to have an empty seat at his table for his own charity event. I can't believe I was so thoughtless.

"What a night!" My thoughts are interrupted by the heavy plop of Samuel "Benny" Benjamin sliding into the open seat next to me.

Our manager's broad shoulders and wide smile enter my peripheral. Benny has one of those larger-than-life personalities; you can't help but instantly like him. His eyes twinkle and his cheeks are a little rosier than usual, hinting that the gin and tonic clutched in his fist is not his first of the night. Benny might have the right idea; I've been slow playing my own vodka soda, but this night could call for something more. My flight isn't until tomorrow evening anyway.

As if she can hear my thoughts, a server comes by offering wine. Normally, I'm not one to mix my alcohol, but the open bar is closed during dinner, so I accept the red she generously pours.

Conversation around the table picks up rapidly. Whoever designed the seating arrangements at this table (Amy, I'm guessing) did a great job; the personalities are a good mix and because the table is not just filled with Foxes, the conversation is an eclectic mix with little mention of work. This time of year tends to make me feel a little anxious. In a few weeks, we'll all be reporting to Arizona for spring training, which means I only have a few weeks left with my family and friends in Georgia before the grind of baseball season picks up again. I'm grateful for a night with my teammates where we can focus on anything but our jobs.

The night is filled with speeches from JJ and various directors of local children's charities expressing their support for Game of Hope before the emcee introduces the auctioneer for the night. Apparently in addition to the silent auction, participants can bid on higher-ticket items like cruises and other elite packages. I have no plans to bid on vacation packages; the fine print on so many trip packages makes traveling during my limited offseason difficult. It's easier to book my own trips and travel when and where I want, although some places are not as pleasant in the dead of winter. I guess I'll save my European travel for retirement.

The first travel package is a trip to New Zealand; Amy's eyes nearly bug out of her head when she hears all the amenities. I watch as she and JJ have a silent conversation with just their eyes. When JJ smiles and shrugs, it apparently is the green light for Amy to raise her paddle and bid on the trip. He is such a sucker for his woman; he'd do anything to make her happy. While I can recognize that with such love comes a great deal of happiness, when you tie your life to another person's, they get all your baggage as well. I'm not willing to subject another person to that.

After dinner and dessert, they open the floor for dancing. Oliver, Benny, and I head for the newly reopened bar instead and end up hanging there, leaning against the bar top and cracking jokes. I think I seen Oliver crack a smile at least once. After a bit, Caleb joins us, his face flushed from what I can only assume is some exuberant dancing with his fiancée. He wipes sweat from his brow and accepts the cocktail I hand him, taking a big gulp. Benny just raises an eyebrow at him.

"I'm about tapped out on dancing. Jenny didn't get the memo that this is the offseason; I want to *limit* my cardiac work, not exceed it." We all laugh, knowing that if Jenny is in the mood to dance, Caleb will spend the rest of his life dancing with her. She deserves nothing less. "I told her to come back to me when she's ready to sneak off to the bathroom or a coat closet for a different kind of cardio," he says with an exaggerated wink.

We all laugh, but I'm not sure Caleb's joking. I wouldn't put it past him. Hell, I wouldn't put it past myself, had I brought a date.

By the time the night is over, and people are trickling out of the ballroom, gathering any auction items they may have won, I barely remember to check on my donation. I'm not sure if I won anything I bid on, but I'm more interested in who won my item anyway. I sway a bit when I stand, looking around for Zahra, who Amy informed me is the coordinator of tonight's events. I guess those vodka sodas went down a little smoother than I realized. Benny, Oliver, Caleb and I stood near the bar for about an hour, casually refilling our drinks, before Jenny dragged Caleb off to who knows where. When he returned twenty minutes later looking significantly more rumpled than when he left, I knew not to ask any questions. We returned to drinking at the table, while Jenny returned to the dancefloor, hopping around and dancing with the girls.

I finally find Zahra and stride over to her. She swipes through the iPad she's holding, looking up details from all the auction items.

"Here it is!" she exclaims cheerfully. It's hard not to feel a little happy in response to her smile. "Looks like your item went for nine hundred and fifty dollars! Way to go, Warner," she says, touching my arm lightly. My ego swells, not just in response to her words, but the fact that someone spent that much money just for me to cook for them. "Looks like it went to a Daniel Knight."

I don't recognize the name, but I'm sure Zahra will reach out with their contact information later so we can set a date for the dinner. The donation included dinner for six people, so I'll need some time to shop and start cooking, which means it will need to be scheduled for an off day. I'm in no shape to begin planning anything right now, so I hope whoever Daniel Knight is, he's left for the night and doesn't want to try to figure out logistics right now. I give Zahra my number for coordination purposes, but if I'm being honest, I wouldn't mind if she keeps it for personal purposes either.

"James, you coming man?" Oliver shouts, holding my coat to me. More time must have passed than I realized while I was talking to Zahra. The atrium is emptied out except for workers cleaning up. The auction tables are bare, and the only guests left are those who sat at my table tonight. Even JJ and Amy have their coats on and are waiting on me. *Shit.*

I jog towards them, shrugging into my overcoat and preparing my body for the inevitably freezing weather outside. We agree to head to a dive bar down the street; no one is quite ready for the night to end. Amy's friend Danny catches up to me, his strides not quite as long as mine.

"Warner, I won your cooking dinner," he tells me.

"You're Daniel Knight!" I say, realization dawning on me. Danny nods. I'm swept over by a weird wave of relief. Cooking for Danny and his friends holds a lot less pressure than cooking for a bunch of strangers, even if they are Foxes fans. I'm not worried about the cooking; it's more the social aspect of living up to people's expectations that made me nervous to offer the auction item.

"Oh, sweet!" JJ chimes in. "Do we get to come?" He looks so excited that I'm sure it will crush him if Danny says he doesn't get to be one of the six guests.

"Obviously," Danny says, rolling his eyes. Danny and I exchange numbers with promises to coordinate a dinner party after spring training.

I pull the door to the dive bar open and wait for the rest of our group to pass through before following. I don't know how JJ and Caleb live in this city year-round. Don't get me wrong, I love Chicago. In fact, Chicago in the summer is the best. But there is no way humans are designed for Chicago winters with the way the wind whips off the lake and between the buildings.

I offer to buy the first round, with Benny, Alicia, and Danny offering to help carry drinks back to the tables Caleb and JJ are pushing together in the back. We're a rowdy group, but luckily there are only a couple of other patrons here this late. The bar itself is nothing special. It still has its Christmas lights up, colorful lights dotting the bar and ceiling. A mostly empty popcorn machine sits in the corner.

"What the hell is a hot toddy?" I ask after Alicia places her order next to me.

"Oh, it's perfect for tonight's weather!" Alicia gushes. "You should get one, too! It's whiskey, lemon, and hot water. Sometimes tea instead of hot water. It's so cozy and warm!"

I wrinkle my nose. "My mom calls that southern cough syrup." Alicia laughs, the tinkling sound carrying over the soft bar music. "I've still never had it because it sounds awful."

"Judge all you want," Alicia replies playfully, "but I'll be nice and toasty while you sip your shitty beer." The shitty beer in my hand is for Caleb, not me, but I see her point.

"Fine, I'll try your nasty drink," I tell her, then shift my attention to the bartender. "Make that two hot toddies."

"Three!" Alicia interrupts, throwing up three fingers. "I have a feeling Amy will change her mind and want one once we get back. She said she wanted white wine, but I know once I show up with a cozy drink, she'll agree my choice is superior." Danny laughs and nods in agreement.

It takes two trips to bring all the drinks to the table, now that we're ordering multiples for some people. Amy returns from the bathroom as I'm sliding into my seat next to Alicia, slapping down a round deck of cards.

"They have games on a shelf next to the bathroom!" Amy exclaims a little too loudly, and I wonder to myself if we really should have brought her two drinks.

Danny, JJ, and Tim groan in unison.

"Is everyone here prepared for Amy to kick your ass in this game? Because that's the only way these games end." JJ explains, and Amy looks triumphant. We all agree, and Amy deals the cards while explaining the rules of the game. After several rounds, most of which Amy wins, I see what they were talking about. I opt out of the next hand. Jenny saunters up to the bar and pleads with the bartender to start up the popcorn machine. Minutes later, tiny pops serenade us as Jenny wiggles in her seat with excitement. Food is probably a good choice; I have a feeling we're all going to be a bit wobbly by the time we stand.

"I'm going to have to remember this bar. I think my parents would love to come here when they visit if I still live in River North. Momma and Poppa Langley love them some dive bars," Alicia comments.

"You live in River North too? I'm about a mile away from here." I'm surprised. JJ and Amy, along with most of the Foxes players, live closer to the ballpark than I do. I assumed Alicia lived near them.

"For now, yeah," Alicia says sadly. "I think I'm going to have to relocate in the next couple weeks. My job just majorly cut my hours and rent in this area does not support a part time salary." She winces. Amy gives her a kind smile.

"You can always move in with us for a bit," she tells her friend.

"Thanks. I know. But there's no way I'm moving into JJ's condo so I can listen to you two having sex every few hours." JJ smirks but doesn't tell Alicia she's wrong. "I'll figure it out."

"You can stay at my place," I volunteer before my brain has a second to catch up to my mouth. Alicia just blinks at me. "I won't be using it till the season starts. That'll give you at least two months to settle in. And even if you're not out by opening day, the place is big enough to share. I don't mind a roommate. I'm in the Vandeveer building. Three bedrooms." I don't know why I'm trying to sell Alicia on the idea of moving into my place. I don't particularly care if she lives there or not. She's not exactly jumping at the idea either.

"Ooh, the Vandeveer? I've always wondered what that looks like inside," she says, without agreeing to anything.

"Anyway, it'd be great having someone there. I really don't mind you using the space. Someone might as well." Before I realize what I'm doing, I'm sliding my key off the ring and handing it to her. "I leave tomorrow afternoon for the airport, so you can use it any time after that."

Alicia cautiously takes the key from me. "Don't you think you'll regret this in the morning when you're sober?" I really don't think I will. It's not like Alicia is a stranger, really. She's connected through JJ, so if anything goes wrong, I know I'll be able to find her. JJ catches my eye and nods, silently reading my mind and confirming Alicia is trustworthy. "Are you sure?"

"Are you trying to talk me out of this?" I jokingly ask. She smiles; it's a good sign. "Just promise me you'll water my plants. I'm paying Stephen, the Foxes clubby, to go over once a week to water my plants and run my cars' engines for a few minutes, but I suspect it's a huge hassle for him. If you do it for him, you'd be helping us both out." She's still eyeing me warily, as if this deal is too good to be true. "My sister has gotten me at least a dozen plants in my house. I truly think she might murder me if they die."

"Lucky for you, I have a green thumb." Alicia smiles. "Only if you're absolutely sure."

"Yeah, I'm sure. I'll give you my number and I can text you the details later when we're both a bit more sober. But no rush to find a new place. Save up some money and deal with it only if a new place falls in your lap."

Before my sister met Xavier, her husband, she left an abusive relationship with hardly any money. Too ashamed to tell me or our parents what was really going on, she ended up living in a shithole apartment in a sketchy neighborhood before we found out and intervened. It turns out her ex was financially and emotionally abusive, something I later learned was called coercive control. I know Alicia is not dealing with anything remotely close to Eden's situation, but if I can prevent her—or anyone else—from an outcome like Eden's temporarily was, I will. I still carry a lot of guilt for being unaware of the realities of Eden's relationship until much later. She has repeatedly told me there's nothing to feel guilty about (*yeah, right*), and I know she's in a much better place now, but I still wish for a time machine to go back and eliminate my baby sister's suffering. So when Alicia agrees to temporarily move into my place, I'm happy.

The night is winding down, and much of the alcohol has slowly dwindled from our systems, but there's still enough there to make Benny's suggestion of greasy food sound like a good idea. Morning Warner will probably regret such fatty, salty food so late in the night, but he's already probably going to regret all the alcohol I've shoved through my system, so screw that guy anyway. Oliver peels away, opting for more sleep instead, but the rest of us traipse across the street to the 24/7 fast food joint promising greasy tacos, salty chips, and spicy salsa.

"Warner James, what are you doing here?" a clearly drunk stranger slurs. I'm used to people addressing me by my full name and fans not used to athletes living normal lives and eating shitty food. It's like when a kid sees his teacher outside of school for the first time. I flash him a smile, as do JJ, Caleb, and Benny. They're all prepared for the same fan interaction as I am.

"JJ Jeffers! Caleb Andrews! Holy shit, Benny too?" the man gapes, his friends behind him snickering at his fangirling. "But why are you here, Warner? They don't serve fried chicken here."

The air is suddenly sucked out of the room. An eerie silence descends upon the room.

Beside me, Alicia visibly stiffens, then slowly turns. If the situation weren't so serious, and unfortunately, relatively commonplace for me, I'd be amused by the Linda Blair parallels I could draw right now.

"I beg your finest fucking pardon?" Alicia sneers. The sniggering of the man's friends ceases immediately. Tension blankets the air and I feel everything in slow motion. Caleb blinks, not quite trusting what he heard. Alicia steps toward the man and his friends. The friends back up, but the original guy stays put. He may be drunk, but he knows what he said. I take a deep breath, not wanting to escalate the situation.

"It's not worth it, Alicia," I mumble. Because it's not. This guy, at the end of the day, is going to be a racist no matter what anyone says to him right now. The one who loses in this situation is the Black man, every time. Because if I escalate things, I'm the one arrested. And if I don't, I'm the one who lives with the comments burned into my brain anyway.

Alicia gently pushes me aside, stepping closer to the bigot and unintentionally placing me behind her. She jabs a manicured finger into his chest. "What, exactly, do you mean by your comment? Tell me, what, exactly, were you hoping to accomplish by saying that? And you!" Alicia rounds on his friends. "What, *exactly*, is funny about this situation?"

She is met with awkward silence before the man speaks again. "James, you need your girlfriend to defend you now?"

Before anyone can respond to his taunt, a fist comes flying from beside me and connects with the man's nose. Blood blooms instantly as he falls to his knees. Caleb stands over him, crowding his space. Everyone else seems to be frozen in place.

"No, he doesn't need anyone to defend him. But I'm going to anyway," Caleb sneers at the man cowering beneath him. Suddenly life seems to catch up and the scene no longer plays out in slow motion. The man's friends start apologizing, dragging him up to his feet. Caleb is panting. JJ is on the phone immediately, and when I hear him say Mariah's name, I know he's talking to his publicist, who likely will bury this story so deep it will never see the light of day. The offenders scramble away, apologizing profusely, saying this will never happen again. I doubt it. I have no illusions that the man somehow learned a lesson and is no longer a racist. The world isn't that simple.

"Sorry, man. I didn't want you to have to deal with that if there was something I could do," Caleb mumbles, shaking out his hand and returning to his spot in line like nothing happened. His knuckles are red, but he doesn't appear to be bleeding. JJ ends his call and, other than a single squeeze to my shoulder, also says nothing more about it. Benny offers me a small smile. Alicia is taking several deep breaths beside me. I don't miss the way her hands shake.

Later, as we accept the tacos from our server with words of gratitude and smiles, everyone else seems to have forgotten the incident. My tacos taste funny in my mouth. This wasn't the first time I've experienced a microaggression and reality dictates that it won't be the last. However, in my thirty years of living as a Black man, I've never experienced such an immediate, effective, and overwhelming show of support for me by others in response to it. I don't know how to feel right now.

CHAPTER FOUR

Alicia

I've been living in Warner's apartment–excuse me, *penthouse*–for a week now and I'm still not used to it. After the night of the gala, Warner texted me the details, including the address of his building, the code to the penthouse elevator, the names of his neighbors, and information on where to find his car keys. He told me I could park my car in a gated section of the parking garage reserved for residents. That alone was a huge relief. Free street parking in this area is nearly impossible to find and continually paying metered parking was taking a huge chunk on my already limited budget, especially since paying for a monthly parking permit was the first thing to go once my personal budget got slashed. The information Warner texted me wasn't much of a surprise, seeing as he told me he would do it. What was a surprise, however, was coming into a fully stocked fridge and pantry and a note from him telling me to please use all the groceries he bought for me.

Initially, I felt a little funny digging into the groceries. It felt like taking advantage of his already generous hospitality. But I figured the groceries were already purchased, and they would go bad if I didn't put them to use. I will make it my mission that once Warner moves back in, though, things will be split fifty-fifty. I told him so during a text exchange when he messaged to make sure I had everything I needed. He brushed it off and denied my request to pay for utilities while I am staying here. He's a stubborn man, but I'll wear him down eventually. In the meantime, I remain grateful.

Not having to pay rent, even for these two months before Warner returns, allows me a lot more wiggle room in my budget than I originally planned for, which is a huge relief. I opened my own Etsy store for my crafts, naming it A's Apothecary and Goods, but traffic and purchases have been slow. I know it's just growing pains and I'm confident I can turn things around with some creative marketing and hashtags. A huge piece of me, though—bigger than I'd like it to be—is relieved that my change of address brings another perk, in that mail from my previous address hasn't been finding its way to my new place. No more unaddressed little green envelopes to worry about.

Most of my belongings, like furniture and dishes, are in storage, and I was able to haul my clothes and crafting supplies to Warner's place in one carload. He told me I could have my pick of the guest bedrooms, which are located on the opposite side of the apartment than his bedroom. He left the door to his room open, his bed neatly made. I don't snoop in his room, but I do steal glances inside each time I walk by.

Warner's place is gorgeous. He either has a serious knack for decorating or hired someone who did. The penthouse has a modern, industrial feel, which suits his more masculine energy. It's a little lacking in personal touches, aside from some plants and one digital picture frame. If I didn't know better, I'd think I was staying in an immaculately decorated Airbnb rather than someone's actual, lived-in home. I take my plant watering duties seriously. The houseplants I brought over from my apartment mesh nicely with Warner's, although mine are housed in much quirkier pots and vessels compared to his standard–and probably expensive–shiny black ceramic. I don't have a ton of plants, only because I was limited on space in my old apartment, but the ones I do have all have names and personality traits as far as I'm concerned. Betty, my bird of paradise, stands sentry near the front door. I figured Warner won't mind that focal point since she is in a cream ceramic pot that goes with the rest of his decor. I brought my three monstera deliciosas, appropriately named James P. Sullivan, Randall, and Mike Wazowski, and scattered them throughout the apartment. James P. Sullivan is my largest and happiest plant; I would have been devastated if I couldn't bring him along. He's grown to twice his original size since I brought him home a few years ago. My pothos plants, Erma, Edna, and Evalyn, are tucked further into Warner's place, as they are housed in a teapot, a giant ceramic strawberry, and a pot in the shape of a human face. Somehow, I don't think Warner will find their quirks as charming as I do. His plants are stoic and majestic. They tend to fit his personality: a little enigmatic but beautiful nonetheless. My favorites are an enormous raven ZZ, a flourishing coffee tree, and a deep purple, almost black, towering orchid.

When I initially walked in and took stock of Warner's houseplants, I couldn't help but fangirl over them to him in a text. That was when he let me know he doesn't know anything about plants and they were all gifts from his sister, Eden. He doesn't know what he's missing. If I have my way, I'll teach him to chop and propagate his most beautiful plants to spread their joy to further corners of his house. Eventually, I'll win him over to the planty side of life.

I set up my crafting station in a corner of the bedroom I'm using and check my Etsy sales. So far, only one new purchase, but it's for a set of custom bachelorette refillable water bottles, so while it's only one sale, it's multiple items, which will boost my bottom line and hopefully increase traffic to my individual seller page once the reviews start rolling in. I feed the vinyl through my Cricut machine and set it to begin cutting out stencils for the bachelorette theme: Raising Hell Before Wedding Bells.

By the time I've finished weeding the design, applying it to the cups, and slathering on thick layers of the etching cream, it's grown dark outside the wide windows in my new bedroom. Time tends to get away from me when I craft. I wander into the kitchen and root around Warner's freezer for dinner. I'm not sure what was in there before he stocked up for me, but figure if he didn't tell me to steer clear of it, then everything in there is fair game. I select a plastic to go container of what looks like meatloaf and macaroni and cheese and pop it into the microwave.

Wandering over to Warner's enormous television, I realize I haven't watched anything since I moved in. Between getting settled and fulfilling A's Apothecary orders, I've had limited time for entertainment. I'm not big on television anyway, usually preferring to curl up with a thriller novel, but my love for trashy TV with Danny, Tim, and Amy knows no bounds. Warner stores his remotes neatly next to the wall mounted television, on top of a gorgeous cherrywood storage unit. I run my fingers over the smooth surface as I inspect the three remotes left there, trying to figure out which one to use. I almost miss the small yellow sticky note to the left of them, filled with a tidy scrawl indicating their functions and how to use each one. It turns out the small one is for Warner's streaming and casting device, the medium for his sound system, and the largest for his television. I don't need an entire experience; I just want to watch something mindless. Plucking the TV remote from the row, I follow the instructions to turn it on. It's simple enough, and I wonder if Warner doesn't watch television often, if he needs notes to help him remember how to turn things on.

The microwave beeps, alerting me to dinner, and when I open the door, I'm bombarded with the rich smell of butter, cheese, and seasoned meat. My mouth waters instantly. Popping the dish onto a ceramic plate, I bring my dinner to the couch. Warner's apartment is tidy, but he seems relaxed enough to not mind if I eat dinner on his couch instead of his dining table. If I don't spill, what's the harm?

I finally find a reality TV show interesting enough and settle in. I spear a small piece of the steaming meatloaf on my fork and am surprised to see a mound of mashed potatoes underneath. I audibly moan. Nothing goes better together than meatloaf and mashed potatoes. I haven't had meatloaf in years, though. It's not exactly a common item on restaurant menus, and I can't cook to save my life. Sure, I've mastered the occasional cookie recipe, but that's as simple as following directions step by step. I generally leave the cooking to Danny and Amy and stick to microwavable or excessively simple recipes.

This meatloaf, however, was worth the wait. I've never tasted anything like it. Perfectly seasoned, with onions that are not too big but plentiful enough to impart flavor, and fresh herbs, it practically melts in my mouth. I have to take a moment to close my eyes and savor this moment. I don't know where Warner got this, but I make a mental note to ask him and keep the restaurant's number on speed dial. I swipe my fork through the macaroni, preparing myself for disappointment. After the meatloaf and mashed potato combo, nothing can stand up. I'm pleasantly surprised when the buttery, cheesy goodness hits my tongue, and I release another dreamy sigh.

Danny, Amy, Tim and I have a standard for our favorite foods, particularly when they are prepared just right. We call them "Last Meal Good." As in, if we were on death row and had to select the last meal of our lives, we would choose it. High on my list are Jeni's brambleberry crisp ice cream (in a dish), a giant frosty glass of Dr. Pepper (with the little nugget ice), and Portillo's cheese fries. However, after this microwave meal I'm enjoying by myself, alone on Warner James' couch, in the middle of his somewhat cold and impersonal apartment, I know I need to rethink everything. Because there's no way this entire meal isn't going on my Last Meal list. I'm tempted to raid Warner's freezer for more of this exact meal tonight because, although I know I won't be hungry enough to eat more than this dish, I don't want the flavors to stop. I can't resist texting him. I need to find the origins of this dish.

Me

OMG, you have to tell me where this meat-loaf came from.

Warner

Are you raiding my freezer?

Me

It should have been the first thing I did when I moved in. Had I realized you were holding out on me, I would have.

I'm sorry, I have no shame. Please don't be mad. Tell me it's not some ultra-rare or

> ridiculously expensive meal you were saving for a special occasion?

Warner

> <laughing emoji>

> Not rare or expensive. Actually, it was free, considering my mom made it for me.

I close my eyes and cringe.

Me

> Please tell me I did not eat your mom's food. I'm so rude.

> If I was any good at cooking, I'd offer to re-make it for you, but that would probably be more of a punishment for you than stealing your mom's home cooked meal for you.

Warner

> Nah, don't worry about it. I'm in ATL with her for another week before I head to AZ for spring training. I'll get my fill of her cooking before I leave.

Me

> Again, I'm so sorry. But tell your mom it's incredible and if she ever opens a restaurant, I'll be first line for her meatloaf.

Warner

You might be a little late for that.

<link to his mother's restaurant>

Shit. Warner's mom looks like the real deal. The cover page of the Squash Blossom website shows her standing in front of her restaurant in full chef's uniform, arms crossed and holding a whisk. I recognize her from the photos that pop up in the digital frame in the living room. The Squash Blossom website leads me to Anita James' professional website. Before I realize it, I've taken my last bite of dinner and immediately regret not savoring it more. I was distracted by learning about Mrs. James' history. Warner isn't all that close with JJ, so I don't know him the way I know Caleb. In fact, the limited information I do know about him, I've gleaned from living in his apartment or snooping on Foxy Fanatixxx, the fan website devoted to Foxes players' love lives, which is hardly a reputable source.

All Foxy Fanatixxx tells me is that Warner is a bit of a player. I am not one to judge; I date around too, although that's largely fallen by the wayside with my job changes. I'll pick it back up when I feel like I've created enough backstock in my Etsy store to relax. Anita James' website tells me even less about her son, though. I'm not sure what I expected; it's her professional website. It's not like I'm stalking her personal social media. So, my landlord remains an enigma. I return to our text thread.

Online snooping done, I sink back into the couch, pulling a nearby blanket over me, and lose myself in the world of trashy television.

Three days later, I get a phone call from an unknown number. Normally, I don't answer unless I recognize the caller ID, but Warner told me his neighbors check in on him from time to time. I wonder if they might be calling to do the same for me. He mentioned he informed his neighbors I was staying at his place, but I haven't run into anyone yet.

"Good afternoon, Ms. Langley. This is Manny at the front desk of the Vandeveer. How are you today?"

"Oh, hi, Manny," I respond, a little flustered that someone from management is calling me. I hope I haven't broken some unwritten building code rule. "I'm good, how are you?" I pick at a particularly stubborn corner of the vinyl sheet I'm attempting to weed.

"Fantastic, ma'am, thank you for asking. I'm calling to see if you were home? A package was delivered for you, and it looks like it should be opened immediately upon receiving it. I can bring it up to you if you're here?"

A package for me? Very few people even know I live here, and I never get packages. I wonder if I addressed one of my Etsy orders incorrectly and it's being returned to me? I thank Manny and invite him up.

He arrives a few minutes later. I don't know what I expected, but he looks like a normal guy in a suit, although he's carrying a very large box with "KEEP REFRIGERATED" stamped on the outside. I guess I kind of envisioned him to be wearing a bellhop uniform, complete with a little red cap. I shake my head, reminding myself that Warner lives in an expensive, yet regular building, not an old-timey hotel. Manny deposits the box on the kitchen island. I don't know what the protocol is regarding my interactions with him, but I know I tip room service delivery people at hotels, and this is kind of like that, right? However, he refuses my offered tip, stating he's happy to stretch his legs and get out from behind the front desk. I give him a skeptical look, but he assures me *Mr. James* takes very good care of him, rendering tips unnecessary.

When Manny leaves, I double check the address listed on the box, and sure enough, it's correctly meant for me and contains Warner's complete address. I slide a sharp knife out of the block near the stove, slicing into the package's outer layers. Inside is a thick Styrofoam cooler, which I open to reveal heavy blocks of packaged ice. Underneath are at least a dozen plastic to go containers filled with familiar contents. As I'm pulling them out, a note flutters onto the counter. It contains large, swooping handwriting and a short message.

Alicia,

I'm happy to hear you've become a fan. Hopefully this will hold you over for some time.

Love, Anita James

I can't hold back my smile. Warner must have told his mom about my meatloaf theft. To have Anita James take time out of her busy schedule to make me my own personalized meals? More so than that, to have Warner convey my love of her cooking and likely ask her to send me more? My heart feels like it's ready to overflow.

I close my eyes, basking in the feel of this moment, wanting to cherish it and never let it go. Knowing words will never be enough to convey my appreciation, I open my text thread with Warner. With eyes filled with tears of gratitude and a wide smile threatening to overtake my face, I snap a picture of me holding the food containers, hoping Warner understands how much it means to me.

CHAPTER FIVE

Warner

My feet feel heavy as I trudge up the stairs to my bedroom. I just finished a grueling workout in the home gym I keep in my basement. All I want to do is fall into bed, saying fuck the shower, but there are some routines I know I can never break. I start the shower, allowing my bathroom to fill with steam. I'm not allowed to crawl into bed until at least eight o'clock tonight. Seeing as it's only four right now, I need to find something to occupy my time until then.

I purposely left my phone charging on my nightstand while I went downstairs to work out. My motivation was low and the last thing I wanted to do was exercise. I knew if I brought my phone, I'd use it as an excuse to dick around on it instead of doing what I needed to do. I mentally pat myself on the back for the choice. With spring training officially starting up next week, I'm in no position to miss a workout. Games don't start for a few weeks, so the next few weeks will be filled with team workouts, meetings, strategizing, press tours and photo opps, and plenty of downtime. Most players love spring training because it's less of a grind than the regular season. Especially early on in spring training, we hardly play for the entire game. Veterans are swapped out around the sixth inning or earlier for young guys just learning the ropes, leaving us free for most of the rest of the day. I'd rather have the grind of the regular season, as exhausting as that can be. My brain does better with limited downtime. I am a man who thrives on structure, a creature of habit. Spring training's looser schedule is a gift to some, but seeing as I don't have family in Arizona, the only people to hang out with are my teammates. I love them, but I'll have plenty of time to be with them during the regular season.

I stand in my steam shower until the water runs cold. I don't know how long I was in there; I must have lost track of time spacing out. I dry myself and walk to my closet to pull out a pair of joggers and a sweatshirt. Another one of the rules I have for myself: after showering, get dressed right away. I'm not the kind of person that feels like the world will end if I don't follow my rules, but I can focus better when I don't allow myself to be sidetracked by distractions. That's why I don't see Alicia's text until several hours after she sent it. I hope she doesn't think I'm an asshole for taking so long to respond.

I open my messenger app and pull up her thread. I click on the photo she sent, then zoom in further on her face. Her excitement is palpable. She is posing alongside the meals my mom sent her, chestnut hair tumbling over her shoulders. I squint, zooming in further on her face. Is she crying? Sure enough, her slate gray eyes are filled with tears. I'm a little embarrassed; having my mom send her a few meals isn't a huge deal. I mean, I know Anita James is an incredible chef, and I know better than anybody how good her meatloaf meal is. When I told Mom about Alicia's love of her meatloaf and asked if she could send a few more to her at my apartment, I knew she would oblige. I hope the gesture isn't too over the top in Alicia's eyes though. It's just food. My mom is a feeder; it's her way of showing love. But I hope I didn't make Alicia uncomfortable with the gift.

Me

> You're welcome. My mom loves to feed others.

Alicia

> I'll happily eat anything she sends me! If she ever needs taste testers–you know, someone to try new recipes on–just let me know!

Me

> Ha, will do.

I'm careful with my interactions with Alicia. I'm happy to take care of her and help a friend (okay, a friend of a friend). My history with women, however, makes me cautious of inadvertently sending a message that I'm interested in anything other than friendship.

Coming up in the minor league system when I played for Boston was its own unique experience. The game itself was largely the same, but the way we were treated at each level varied widely. One thing that was relatively constant was the female attention. I never minded the attention either. I've been told I'm an attractive guy, and it's a rare day when I turn down an opportunity for a date. Even though I've never meant to hurt anyone else, I haven't always been as clear or upfront about my intentions as I should have been, which led to a lot of inadvertent heartbreak. Over the years, I got better at letting women know that while I was interested in a date with them, the date was a singular instance, and that I had no time or availability for a relationship. Despite making that abundantly clear, sometimes the message I was sending was not always the message received.

I hope I never have to let Alicia down easy. She doesn't seem the type to become attached, but in an abundance of caution, I reread my texts to her, making sure nothing sounds too relationship-y. I think I'm good. I breathe out a sigh of relief and check the time. Only three more hours until bed. I'm so tired though, that I'd rather skip dinner and just head straight there now.

Worried that will fuck up my sleep schedule right before traveling, instead, I double check my suitcases are packed. I leave tomorrow night for Phoenix, giving me a few days to settle in before everything officially begins. I have lunch plans with my parents tomorrow. I shoot my sister a text, seeing what she's up to and if she has time to bring the kids over today. She assures me she'll be over with dinner soon.

Dressed and ready for them, I have nothing to do but wait. I flip on the television in my bedroom, turning it on to sports highlights, but it doesn't hold my interest. I return to my texts with Alicia, hoping to distract myself from the utter boredom that's been hanging over me like a cloud all day.

Me

How's work going?

Alicia

It's good, actually! Thank you for asking. I'm working on a new Etsy order right now, actually. I set up a little corner of the bedroom to work on my crafts and it's been perfect.

Me

You don't have to keep everything in your room. It's your place too. Feel free to spread out.

Alicia

I want to be respectful of your space.

Me

It's your space too. Besides, I'm not even there.

Alicia

Thanks, Warner. I really appreciate everything you've done for me.

I feel like I'm grasping at straws here. I've kept Alicia intentionally at arm's length, so I don't inadvertently send signals I don't mean to, but that means we don't really know each other that well and don't have too much to talk about.

Alicia's attachment is slow to load. Once it comes through, I see my own smiling face shining up at me, covered in vanilla ice cream, smooshed against Eden's smaller, equally messy face. We're both laughing. The photo is from my fifth birthday party, which means Eden is only three. I haven't seen this photo in years; my sister must have loaded it on the frame at some point this offseason. A flicker of warmth fills my chest as I gaze at our younger selves.

Alicia

<laughing emoji> No! I just meant I could see the resemblance!

Me

Luckily, I'm a slightly less messy eater these days.

Alicia

Don't lie. I saw the mess you made with tacos on the night of JJ's gala.

Alicia attaches a gif of the Beast from Beauty and the Beast chowing down on a bowl of cereal. I can't help the little huff of a laugh that escapes me. I needed a laugh today, even if it was at my own expense. I'm momentarily transported to that night in my mind. I remember the spark in Alicia when she jabbed her finger in that man's chest after he insulted me, and I'm filled with another little flicker of warmth. That night, as terrible as the moment was, I felt so protected, so valued by the people around me.

Alicia and I continue texting until my doorbell rings. I check the time and am stunned to realize we've been messaging back and forth for forty minutes, all awkwardness from the beginning of our conversation forgotten. Chatting with Alicia is easy. It's nothing more than it is. I don't find myself overthinking, nor do I find myself falling into the overpowering boredom I felt earlier today.

Huh, weird.

My sister's kids, Daisy and Dominic, fall through the doorway as soon as I open the door. Eden gives me a bright smile, shoving past me to set down bags of food on my counter before turning and swallowing me up in her embrace.

"Long day?" she asks.

"How did you know?"

"I just had a feeling. You're getting ready to leave tomorrow and it'll be a long time before you're back here. I know you. I know that overwhelms you."

"It doesn't overwhelm me," I insist. "It's just...daunting, I guess." Eden raises a brow, as if to tell me those are the same things, but she doesn't say anything else on the matter as she unpacks the food.

"Uncle Warner, can I sit next to you?" my niece begs, dancing around in her socks, sliding herself around the kitchen floor.

"Me too!" Dominic, never to be outdone by his older sister, copies her in every way, including her erratic dance moves.

"How 'bout I sit in the middle, and you can *both* sit next to me?"

Eden adopts a theatrical pout. "But then *I* won't be able to sit next to you!" she jokes.

"Mom, you always get to see Uncle Warner!" Daisy argues. Not true, but Eden doesn't dissuade her.

We eat family style, my kitchen table groaning under the weight of all the Thai food Eden brought over. On nights Xavier works late, Eden and the kids get takeout. If it's the offseason, they bring it over and we eat together. I spear a potato from Daisy's bowl of Massaman curry and pop it in my mouth; in return, she steals a stick of my chicken satay and takes a particularly aggressive bite. It's going to be a long baseball season, but I know it's this I'm going to miss most.

CHAPTER SIX

Alicia

The almost two months I've spent at Warner's penthouse have been a dream. Not only do I get to live in a gorgeous, albeit a bit masculine and empty space, but its location in the city is even more convenient than my old apartment. It's just a block away from my favorite running trails, and two blocks from Lake Shore Drive, which makes getting to work on the days I go in very convenient. I don't live that far from my old place, but the extra perk of free parking in the garage attached to Warner's building cannot be overstated. Normally, I'd have to walk several blocks to my car before starting my commute. In the winter, it's especially annoying, since I'd have to sit in my frozen car, waiting for it to warm up. I'm a girl who prioritizes her sleep; anything less than eight hours and my whole day is thrown off. So, cutting out the twenty minutes of trudging through the snow and sitting in the car, teeth chattering, really helps me start each day on the right foot. It's convenient when I swing by to pick up groceries too; I can buy more at once now that I can easily make multiple trips to the car.

As I'm bringing the last of my groceries in, I swing by to check the mail. Warner initially told me he stops the mail and forwards it to his house in Georgia during the offseason, but he started it back up again when I moved in. Most of it includes junk mail addressed to him, which I've organized neatly in a little pile on the kitchen counter. He returns home tomorrow from spring training, and the first game of the season starts later this week. He'll have two days of downtime before games, but he's already mentioned he'll be going into the ballpark both days to prepare.

I'm a little nervous about Warner's return. I know we get along great; we periodically text and have gotten to know each other a little bit better. It's always an adjustment, though, to go from living by yourself to living with someone else. I'm sure it will be fine. Warner's place is huge and we'll both be busy, but I hope I don't make him feel inconvenienced by my presence. I slide the thick stack of mail from his mailbox, wincing when I realize I must not have checked it in quite some time. I doubt he wants all of these random flyers and junk mail, but I feel weird about throwing them out without consulting him.

When I get upstairs to his unit, I toss his mail onto the island, along with the last of the groceries. I kick off my shoes and start unpacking all the food. I admittedly got more than I normally would. I feel the need to repay him for stocking up in anticipation of me moving in; it's only right that I return the favor. Not knowing what he prefers (beyond his mother's meatloaf), I kind of went a little crazy at the store. I could have texted him to ask, but I want to surprise him with this little kindness. I have a feeling if I let Warner in on my plan to stock his kitchen, he would have tried to talk me out of it. Little does he realize, acts of service are my love language. It's how I take care of my people, and now that we're roomies, Warner is one of my people.

I pull out the premade "Welcome home" banner I grabbed at the store and start to untangle it. It'll look perfect against the bookshelf, which is situated within the eyeline of the front door. He'll probably feel a little embarrassed; it's his home after all, and it might be a little weird to welcome him into his own space, but I thought it was cute and tossed it in my cart before I could talk myself out of it. I attach it with craft tape on the underside of one of the shelves and step back to ensure it's symmetrical. Pretty good for eyeballing it, I think.

I finish putting away the groceries and get started on sorting the mail. Rarely is there anything in there for me, but I always double check, just in case. I'm flicking through the mail, barely paying attention, when my eye is caught by the corner of a mint green envelope sticking out from behind a flyer for a local physical therapy clinic opening down the street. I suck in a shallow breath, then immediately chastise myself. I didn't leave my forwarding address when I moved out. Besides, the green envelopes that previously arrived in my mailbox never contained my address, so I know they never came through the mail. They somehow always just showed up.

I will my heart to slow its rapid beats, infusing my lungs with a fresh hit of oxygen. I don't want to move the physical therapy flyer, just in case. This is silly. It's not what I think it is. Whoever used to leave those letters in my mailbox is long gone. I live at *Warner's place* for goodness' sake. It's not like *they* know that.

Heart in my throat, I flick the therapy clinic advertisement to the side and stop breathing altogether. There, in the same thick, black scrawl as always, is my name. Alicia Langley. The envelope never says anything else, but still, I turn it over, irrationally hoping there might be a return address or some other identifying information on the back. There isn't. I set the envelope down and slowly back away from the island.

Part of me is in shock; I know that. How could he have found me? Very few people even know I moved. My landlord obviously knows, as do my friends. My family knows too, but they're all out on the West Coast. Most of my coworkers don't even know I moved. Now that my hours at the museums have been slashed, there's less time for socializing. I mostly hang out with Amy during any work downtime anyway, and she already knows.

I take a deep breath and close my eyes, moving my focus inward. I do a quick body scan, taking stock of my physical sensations and emotions. What I'm feeling is fear, which is immediately accompanied by anger—at whoever sent the letter and myself for allowing myself to be affected this way. I roll my shoulders and stretch my neck side to side, eliciting a good pop on my left side. I can't even enjoy the feeling of its release. *The only way out is through.*

I step back toward the envelope, steeling myself to open it. *This is ridiculous.* I'll just open it and get it over with. Just rip the corner and pull out the note. That's all there is to it. The sooner I do it, the sooner I can forget it even happened. Just slide your finger under the flap and rip it open.

Jesus Christ. It should not take this much of a pep talk to open a single envelope. But I know this isn't a regular envelope containing a regular letter. I blow out a breath and rip it open quickly. I find what I expect to find: a small, square piece of paper in the same mint green as the envelope, the ink from the message inside bleeding through to the other side. My fingers fumble as I unfold it before dropping it onto the surface of the island. The message is clear, concise, simple, delivered in all capitals in permanent marker.

ALICIA:

YOU MOVED WITHOUT TELLING ME.

DON'T WORRY, I FOUND YOU. THEY'LL NEVER KEEP US APART.

YOURS ALWAYS.

CHAPTER SEVEN
Alicia

I feel like my brain went offline for several minutes after receiving the note. Shaking my head, hoping to knock some sense into myself, I reach forward and it up. Destroying the evidence somehow makes me feel better, like I have some semblance of control here. After ripping it up, I scoop the tiny pieces into my palms and toss them unceremoniously into the trash. I close the drawer containing the trash can with my hip, pause, and think better of it. I don't want anything he touched near me. Tugging the drawstrings of the trash bag closed, I tie it off. The bag itself is only half full, but I take it to the hall garbage chute anyway, swiping the envelope off the island to throw it down the chute on my way. My name has never looked so ugly in those chunky block letters.

When I return to the apartment seconds later, I turn the deadbolt and lean against the door, breathing hard. I close my eyes, forcing more composure into my body. I press my shaky palms flat against the door, grounding myself. *It's just a letter,* I try to convince myself. The truth is, this reaction–my racing heart, sweaty palms, erratic breathing–isn't in response to the actual note. It's the meaning behind it. That despite the difficulty he should have had in searching for me, he (or she, I suppose) found me. I can't bring myself to believe that a woman would do this to another woman, so I've always called the letter writer 'he' in my head. I haven't been hiding, but I haven't exactly broadcasted my whereabouts.

I need to get past this moment in time. I turn on some calming music and lie down on the plush rug in Warner's living room. Closing my eyes, I start the neurogenic tremoring exercise Amy taught me years ago to relieve tension in my body. As my legs start to shake, I allow the movements to flow through me, cycling through wherever they need to go. My body knows what I need and where tension release is necessary; I just let it happen, taking deep, purifying breaths as needed. By the time I stretch my legs and stop the shaking ten minutes later, my muscles feel noticeably less tense, and my mind is a little more at ease. I stand and replace the trash bag in the kitchen, and move on with my day, finding that now that I've released my physical tension, it is a lot easier to push all thoughts of the letter and the mystery author out of my mind.

Getting out of bed the next morning to begin my long run of the week wasn't as difficult as I thought it would be, but as soon as I exit the Vandeveer, I'm filled with regret. The wind howls, cutting through my outer layer and whistling through my headphones. I take stock of the direction of the wind and run towards it, knowing by the time I make my out and back loop, the wind could change direction; this is Chicago after all. However, if the wind stays constant, at least it will be at my back when I need it the most.

I love running next to the lake. There's something calming about running near water even on the windiest days. Today, though, I'm feeling like I need a change of pace. Because it's the weekend, the sidewalks in the Loop, the business district of the city, are less crowded, making my run next to skyscrapers and parking garages a little more pleasant. I get to enjoy my run, the buildings serving to block some of the wind, without having to navigate the obstacle course that is commuters, pedestrians, and taxis normally in this area.

Crossing the bridge over the Chicago River steals the breath from my lungs. Without anything to block the wind coming directly off the lake, it whips around me. I suck in more air through my nose before I give up and switch to breathing through my mouth, never ceasing the relentless pounding of my feet. Who would have expected that Chicago in late March would be so beastly? I momentarily think of Warner and am happy for him that while he returns today, he does not have any games for a few days. The Foxes don't have a roof to their stadium, so inclement weather can really impact the games. Because there are so many games in the season, Major League Baseball tries not to postpone them unless it is absolutely necessary. I shiver, thinking of how

Warner will have to stand in right field, attempting to stay warm between plays. Arizona and spring training must have been nice for him. I turn up my music so I can hear it over the wind and almost–*almost*–regret signing up for the Chicago Marathon this fall. I have plenty of time to train for it, and I know the weather will only become more cooperative as I start my training plan. Days like this make me almost want to train on the treadmill in the gym in Warner's building, and running on the treadmill is the kiss of death for runners like me who need a change of scenery every few feet.

An hour and a half later, I make it back to the Vandeveer building, feeling lucky that the wind didn't change course and was at my back for the last four or five miles of my run. I wave hello to Manny at the front desk; between him and Rosalie, the other front desk worker, I'm feeling more and more at home here. I'll be bummed to leave once Warner comes back, even though he insists I don't need to move out. I haven't been looking for a place as consistently as I should. Sometimes I think of it and start looking online, only to become quickly discouraged by what I can afford, now that I'm working with half a salary. My Etsy shop is doing well, but it doesn't nearly make up for the money lost when my hours were cut. I'm slowly coming to the disappointing realization that I likely will have to find a new, full-time job. I've been resisting that idea simply because working as a museum educator for the CMA is my dream job, even with my hours cut.

There's something about working with high schoolers and college students to discover their passions and helping them translate those passions into a potential career that fuels my soul. Because Chicago's major museums are all connected under the Chicago Museum Association, I get more opportunities to work with students in diverse fields, compared to other cities whose museums would employ me only at a specific campus. Between the Field Museum, planetarium, aquarium, Museum of Science and Industry, the Art Institute, and the Humanities Museum, I get a good smattering of everything I could possibly want. The idea of leaving all that diversity is devastating, but I know I can't mooch off Warner forever. I got lucky meeting him and benefiting from his generosity these last few months, but it's time that I pick myself up by my own bootstraps and return to adulthood and self-sufficiency, even if it breaks my heart in the process.

I'm in a deep dive on my laptop, tabs open on my web browser for apartment listings, resumé writing support, and job openings, when the front door unlocks.

"Alicia? It's Warner," his deep voice calls from the front entrance. I forgot just how deep and soothing his voice is since we've stuck to communicating via text these last two months.

"Hey! I'm in the living room. Welcome back!" I say, rising from my blanket cocoon to greet him. "How was your flight?"

"It was fine. A little bumpy due to all this wind," he says, walking into the living room. We both glance outside his floor to ceiling windows, watching a few snowflakes swirl around. I shiver involuntarily, thinking about the long, steamy shower I needed to warm up after my run this morning.

Warner and I stand facing each other, a little awkward. I'm unsure whether I should hug him hello or not. We're not that close, but I feel like I should say or do something. He shifts his focus to the bookshelf behind me.

"Did you put that there?" he asks with a smirk, pointing to the shiny welcome home banner I hung there yesterday. I grin, happy he noticed.

"Yeah! I didn't know if you would be embarrassed by something bigger or if it would bother you that I kind of took over that space, but I wanted to welcome you back with at least a little bit of flair!"

Warner's eyebrows jump. He clears his throat. "No, uh, it's really nice of you to think of me," he says gruffly. Nice to think of him? Of course I thought of him; it's his house that he's let me take over for the last few months–free of charge! "My sister, Eden, tells me I need to put more flair in this place, too."

"Sounds like Eden and I would get along well. She's got impeccable taste in plants," I say, gesturing to the raven ZZ spilling out of its container. It might be time to repot that one soon. "I hope you don't mind that I've added my own plants to your collection."

Warner is touching the new leaf that unfurled from Mike Wazowski earlier this week, rubbing it gently between his fingers. The new leaf growth tends to be shinier and smoother than the duller, older growth, and I smirk, knowing I love rubbing the new leaves between my fingers as well. I can't help it; it's so soothing.

"She usually comes out during the season to visit a few times, so I'm sure you'll get to meet her eventually. She's one of my best friends." Warner's smile grows when talking about his sister. It's heartwarming to see. I get along with my own brother and sister, but we aren't incredibly close.

"Ah, well, I'm sure I'll be out of your hair by then," I promise. I know my presence is likely inconvenient for a man used to living alone. Warner's face is inscrutable.

"You know you don't have to move out just because I'm back, right? I mean, if you find a place you love, go for it. But I'm not kicking you out. Like I told you earlier, this place is plenty big enough for the both of us. I'm happy to have you here."

I smile. Perhaps Warner is being polite, but there's a sincerity in his eyes when he speaks that I can't help but believe. A weight I didn't realize had settled in my chest is suddenly lifted.

"As long as you're absolutely sure," I start. "But you have to promise to tell me if anything changes. You won't hurt my feelings if you need me to move out." Warner scoffs but agrees. His phone then rings, effectively ending our conversation. I step back to let him pass. He pulls his suitcase into his bedroom while answering his phone.

I turn on the oven to preheat it. Yesterday I picked up a half-baked Chicago style pizza from my favorite pizzeria. I can't cook like Warner is probably used to, but the least I can do is feed him some well-prepared food, even if I'm not the one doing the preparation. I wonder briefly if Warner is one of those athletes that is very regimented about his diet and hope that my welcoming offer of pizza isn't frowned upon. I guess we'll find out soon enough.

Forty minutes later, I'm pulling the pizza out of the oven, its cheesy goodness bubbling cheerfully in the center of the pie. Warner still hasn't come out from his bedroom. I'm not sure of the protocol here; will he be annoyed if I knock on his door, inviting him out for dinner? I creep over to his door and softly press my ear against it. I don't hear him say anything, so he must be finished with his phone call. I tap lightly on the door just in case. I don't hear a response. I knock a little louder.

"Um, hey, Warner? I don't mean to bother you, but I made us pizza for dinner. In case you wanted something to eat?" I hear rustling on the other side of the door before Warner opens it softly. He looks groggy and rubs his eyes, peering out at me. "Oh my gosh were you napping? I'm so sorry to wake you up!" I feel terrible; he must be exhausted from traveling and I can't even leave him alone the first hour he's home.

"No, I'm glad you woke me. I didn't mean to fall asleep. I sat down to unpack and must have drifted off. I didn't realize I was so tired." He steps out of his room and pauses. "It smells great in here. You said you made pizza?" His eyes light up and I no longer regret my dinner plans.

"Yeah, I got a Chicago style pizza from Alfredo's. I didn't know what kind you liked, so I got a sausage and pepperoni?" I ask hopefully.

"I eat any kind of pizza toppings. Except olives." Warner shudders dramatically and follows me into the kitchen.

The pizza cools on the top of the stove, steam wafting theatrically from the top. I pull out plates and silverware while Warner slides a chef's knife from the block on the corner of the counter, slicing large pieces. I tilt a bottle of tempranillo toward him, wordlessly seeking his approval.

"Sure," he says with a shrug, pulling down two red wine glasses from over my head. When he leans in to gently close the cabinet, I'm met with the woody-citrus scent of his cologne. It smells incredible, warm and comforting. I'm not surprised he has great taste in cologne; he's always impeccably dressed, even when wearing the joggers and fitted tee he's sporting right now. He must be one of those people that can pull off any look. I think back to the three-piece suit he wore the night of JJ's gala and confirm he probably looks good in everything.

Warner and I bring our full plates and glasses to the dining room table. We chat about the upcoming baseball season, our families, and my crafting interests. There's rarely a lull in the conversation, I'm pleased to discover. I wasn't exactly worried that Warner and I wouldn't get along, but we haven't been met with the growing pains of sharing a space like I thought we might. It comforts me knowing I won't have to rush in finding my own space.

He informs me that on game days, he'll rarely be home. I mention that I typically work mornings each week but sometimes will work full days for two to three days a week if one of my students has a special project or I have meetings scheduled later in the day. Conversation swings around to opening day on Monday. It's two days away, and Warner seems confident about the Foxes' chances of having a winning season. Last year, they made it to the postseason, but their winning run fizzled out in the first round.

"We seem a little more settled so far," Warner says. "Spring training ended on a high note, and I think we'll be ready to take on the season. It's gonna be a cold opener though," he says, glancing at the weather app on his phone and tilting the screen so I can see the forecast.

"Yikes, thirty-seven degrees." I shiver just imagining it. "I haven't been to opening day in Chicago. When I used to live in Los Angeles, I went to opening day once in high school for the Cougars and it was pretty cool. The energy was electric, even though they were never good while I was growing up," I laugh, remembering the yearly disappointment that was my hometown team.

"Yeah, they usually do a little ceremony on the field on opening day, celebrating accomplishments from last season for the guys who are still on the team. They invite the family and friends of players getting awards for the on-field celebration before the game begins."

"Who's getting awards this year?" I ask.

"Well, JJ Jeffers for his defensive performance last season, which isn't much of a surprise. The man's a beast." I'm not surprised either, although I don't remember Amy mentioning the award. I know she's planning on being there on opening day, and she mentioned both of JJ's brothers will be in town for the game as well, so I'm sure that's why. "There are awards for charitable works, which is going to Caleb Andrews for his pediatric cancer volunteering, and for offensive performance, too."

I'm not surprised Caleb is getting recognized for his volunteer efforts. After seeing what his fiancée is going through as an adult with cancer, Caleb seems to be a vocal supporter of pediatric on-cology programs.

"Who's getting the offensive performance award?" I ask conversationally.

Warner coughs, looking suddenly uncomfortable. "Uh, me," he says quietly.

"What? That's amazing, Warner! Congratulations! I'm sorry I had no idea!" I loosely follow the Foxes, now that my best friend has been with their star shortstop for the last year or so, but I haven't paid enough attention to know who their strongest player is. "Is your family coming to town for the ceremony? I can stay with Danny and Tim if you need the space here to put them up," I offer.

"Nah, they can't come in. My mom is filming a promo for a show she's guest judging, so my parents need to be in Atlanta for that. It's hard for my sister to get away during the school week; her kids are six and four years old."

No one is coming to Warner's ceremony? I know JJ will have Amy and his brothers there. Caleb will certainly have Jenny on the field with him too, and likely Jenny's family, as they are local to Chicago, too. Without someone there for Warner, his family's absence will be noticeable.

"It's not their fault," Warner assures me. "We weren't told of the award winners till last week, so it was hard for anyone to rearrange their schedules. I told them they didn't have to come." Warner is clearly uncomfortable with such recognition for his efforts, and I can't help but feel a pang of sadness for him. He insists it doesn't bother him, but I would feel incredibly lonely if I were in his shoes.

"Would you like me to come?" I ask quietly. "I know I'm not family or anything, but if you want someone on the field with you, or just someone there so you know you aren't alone, I'd be happy to come. No pressure either way."

"You're not busy?" The hope in Warner's eyes kills me. Of course he would want someone there. He deserves someone there to celebrate his accomplishments. He may try to downplay his disappointment at his family's absence on Monday, but the surprise in his tone lets me know he doesn't want to do this alone.

"Warner," I start, gently reaching over and placing my hand on his forearm. "I would be honored to be there for you." I give him a gentle squeeze, and he nods, clearing his throat again.

"Thanks, Alicia," he says quietly. "It'd be nice to have someone there."

"I'm happy to do it. If your sister isn't busy at that time, maybe I can video call her so she can watch?"

"That would be great. I know she would love it," he tells me earnestly.

We finish eating and I promise Warner I can clean up dinner. He's initially resistant, but when I promise cleanup is minimal and I'm more than capable of handling it, he acquiesces, agreeing to unpack instead.

I don't see him the rest of the night. I presume he fell asleep early, given how tired he was earlier. I pop onto my laptop in bed, placing a rush order that promises to arrive tomorrow evening. I fall asleep shortly after as well, feeling satisfied that at least Warner will have one friend there for him on opening day.

CHAPTER EIGHT

Warner

Opening day has arrived with predictably cold weather. I'm layered in moisture wicking long sleeves under my jersey. Before I head to the dugout, I'll grab a Foxes blue gaiter that connects to a head covering that will keep my neck, mouth, and ears warm under my baseball hat.

I've been at the ballpark for several hours already. I've completed my warmup, workout, and team meeting. Batting practice was cancelled due to the weather; no one complained.

JJ, Caleb, and I are herded to the hall that leads from the clubhouse to the dugout. Tanya, our events coordinator, reminds us that Caleb will receive his award first, followed by JJ, then me. We'll receive the plaques at home plate; after each award is given, the recipient will have a few minutes to take photos both for the press and with family there before moving aside for the next recipient. Yesterday, I shared Eden's contact information with Alicia; she promised me my sister would be able to watch the whole ceremony.

"Ready?" Tanya asks, putting on her beanie and tying the belt around her coat a little tighter. I pull the gaiter over my head and neck but leave the head covering off for now. Caleb jumps up and down in place; sometimes he acts like a little kid, but I can't blame him for being excited. Opening day, despite the weather, is always the onset of something new, full of promise and hope.

We step out of the dugout and onto the third base line to surprisingly thunderous applause. It's freezing outside and the game doesn't start for another forty minutes, so I wasn't expecting the stands to be full yet. They aren't completely packed, but there's enough people there cheering as the three of us walk onto the field that it more than makes up for the empty seats. I nod to Robin, our on-field reporter, as she tugs her scarf closer around her face. We've been instructed to meet up with her after receiving our awards so we can do a little bit of press before pregame stretching.

There's a cluster of people by the gate leading to the stands from the field. I recognize Jenny right away, looking fashionable in a long mauve puffer jacket and Foxes blue beanie. She waves excitedly to us as Caleb takes his place behind home plate. The MLB representative behind the plate speaks into his microphone, extolling Caleb's volunteer efforts and support of the local children's hospital. Jenny moves closer, angling her phone to better record the scene. As she steps aside, I catch sight of Alicia behind her, bundled in a bright pink faux fur jacket. Her nose and cheeks are rosy as she smiles at me, joy radiating out of her. She holds her phone up excitedly, pointing at it with her other hand, and mouths "Eden!" I nod, grateful she was able to get my sister's participation.

After Caleb and Jenny take photos, JJ receives his award and poses for pictures with Amy and his brothers. His older brother, Sean, who works as my agent, nods at me and quickly shakes my hand as I walk toward home to accept my own award. Alicia shuffles around, holding the phone so Eden can watch. I barely register the cold or the words the MLB rep is saying about my offensive performance last season. He hands me my plaque, adorned with a silver batter. I shake his hand and pose for photos with him. The photographer asks if I'd like photos with my family, and out of the corner of my eye, I see Alicia hand her phone off to Jenny, who holds it up to continue the call with my sister.

"I'm here!" She raises her hand at the photographer and beams. "Just one second!" She wriggles out of her coat and tosses it on the grass, rubbing her arms as she comes to stand by me. She's wearing a gray sweater under a number twenty-four jersey, matching my own. I'm stunned.

"Where'd you get that jersey?" I murmur, smiling for the camera as Alicia slides her arm around my waist.

"Ordered it Saturday night after you invited me here. I had to represent!" She is practically glowing with pride. An unnamed emotion swells in my chest.

"You did that for me?"

"Of course! I'm so proud of you, Warner!"

I hope I don't look as dumbfounded as I feel, or the press will be disappointed in these photos. I hardly know Alicia, not nearly enough for her to feel proud of me, right? The photographer signals he's gotten the shots he needed, and Alicia runs back to grab her coat, shivering as she puts it on. I barely have enough time to say a quick hello to my sister before I'm being shepherded toward Robin for a pregame interview.

We end up winning the game one to nothing. I scored our only run off Matteo Cota's RBI double. It's not the flashiest game of baseball, but a win is a win, and it feels great to start the season on a high note.

"Undefeated, baby!" Kyle Crawford, today's starting pitcher, crows when we get back to the clubhouse. He pitched a great game and his excitement is contagious.

"Let's keep it rolling!" Tyler Edwards, our catcher, sings, turning up the speakers blasting Bad Bunny. JJ is walking around, handing aluminum bottles of beer to everyone, making multiple trips back and forth to the beer fridge kept in the locker room. I gladly accept mine, only briefly wishing it was the hot toddy Alicia introduced me to in January. I'm only just now getting feeling back into my fingertips due to the cold. The hot shower after the game helped, but I have a feeling the cold that chilled my bones for hours on end today will take some time to fully dissipate.

"Yeah, O'Reilly's?" Elijah McClintock suggests, shouting to be heard over the bass. He's met with a chorus of cheers from most of the guys. He looks toward me and raises a brow.

"Yeah, sure, I'll be there, too," I agree. McClintock slaps my hand in celebration while I check my phone. I'm still not dressed, but I want to touch base with my sister. Usually, her kids send me a video recording on opening day, wishing me luck. Seeing Daisy and Dominic's annual greeting always warms me in a way other things simply cannot. In addition to the video, which highlights Daisy's new loose tooth and Dominic's stuffed dinosaur, Eden sent a few texts.

Eden

Congrats again on your award! You looked great out there and your new roommate seems really sweet. I'm glad she was able to be there for you.

She's cute too. <winky face emoji>

Just sayin'. Don't roll your eyes at me. I know you're gonna do that as soon as you read my texts.

Anyway, I'm proud of you and really happy for you.

Woohoo! First win of the season! The kids will be so excited to hear their Uncle Warn scored the Foxes' only run! Love you, big bro.

I roll my eyes, despite Eden's warning not to. She knows me too well. Her texts came in over several hours, but since our phones aren't allowed in the dugout, I'm seeing them all at once now. In addition to her texts, I've got messages from several others, including my parents, Sean, and Alicia. I've got more texts from extended family members and friends all congratulating me or wishing me luck on the new season, but I'll answer those over the next few days. It's too much to manage right away, but I click open and shoot quick responses to Eden, my parents, and Sean. Alicia's message is a video recording of today's ceremony. It must have been recorded by Jenny or Amy, because Alicia is in the shot. I double click the video to like it, then download it to my saved files. I'll watch it later when I can hear the sound.

It's an hour after the game by the time I'm ready to leave the clubhouse. As I make my way upstairs with Caleb and JJ, each of us holding our new plaques, I'm surprised to see Alicia waiting for me in the lobby next to Jenny and Amy.

"Hey! Great game," she greets me. She's got her jacket off but is still wearing her Foxes beanie as her chestnut hair cascades over her shoulders. She looks cute. "I didn't know if you wanted me to stick around after so we could go home together or not? Jenny drove me here."

"Oh, cool. Um, yeah, I was going to go out with the guys for a few drinks. Not a lot, since we have a game tomorrow," I explain. I probably should have texted her that we usually go out as a team after opening day.

"No worries," she answers quickly. "I can just get a rideshare. I'll meet you back home, yeah?"

"You can come with, if you'd like?" She seems flustered.

"Oh, uh, I don't want to impose," she starts before Amy interrupts her, answering for me.

"Girl, we're all going. You're not imposing on anyone! Come with, it'll be fun!" That seems to be all the convincing Alicia needs as she nods slowly, picking up her jacket from a nearby bench, and following us out the door. I feel weird carrying my plaque, like I'm bragging about receiving it. I'm only carrying it because it didn't fit in my backpack. I shove it under my arm as we walk to my car in the player's lot across the street.

"Can I see your award?" Alicia asks. I hand it to her wordlessly, instantly feeling relieved that she's carrying it instead of me. She gushes about it, commenting on its weight and attention to detail on the little silver batter in the center. I didn't really pay attention to it. I'll probably just toss it in my guest room closet when I get home. I don't know what else to do with it.

Alicia slides into the passenger seat of my car when I unlock it. We ride together to the bar in relative silence, but the quiet is comfortable, rather than awkward.

Later, as we sit in the bar with my teammates and their families, I'm quietly thankful to have her here with me. It's nice to have a companion at these types of events, however casual they may be. It's nice to be able to laugh as a group, sharing a sense of camaraderie before heading home together. It's nice to not always feel so alone.

CHAPTER NINE

Alicia

The next several weeks pass by in a blur. Between my Etsy orders, starting my marathon training, working at the museum, and catching the occasional Foxes game, I'm exhausted. Social time with Amy, Danny, and Tim has evolved into a combination of wedding planning for Amy and JJ's upcoming day and an assembly line of weeding and cutting for my Etsy shop.

Tonight, my friends have come over to help with a large custom sweatshirt order for a men's golf tournament. Warner is out of town for a string of away games, so I don't feel like we're intruding upon his space by getting together here. It's easier to meet at his place (it still feels weird calling it "my" place, even though Warner insists it's mine as much as his these days); all my crafting supplies are here.

Living with him is easy—far easier than I thought it would be. He was right about how much time he spends at the ballpark during the day; the man puts in so many hours at work, it's no wonder he comes home exhausted. We usually hang out together on his off days if we aren't already committed to other things. We have breakfast together when we're both around, Warner sticking to black coffee only, while I consume my weight in bagels and cream cheese each morning. When we are together in the mornings, he typically studies the stock market on his phone or while reading the newspaper. It's oddly domestic and the way Warner looks in his black rimmed glasses while he reads the newspaper? A girl could get used to that sight. I couldn't tell you the first thing about investing, but Warner is a genius when it comes to it. He's intelligent and patient in trying to explain economics, but it's just something my brain has difficulty understanding. I'm a smart person, but my brain turns to mush when it comes to understanding the complexities of the stock market. Now, talk to me about structuring a lesson or activating prior knowledge for learning or the biochemical processes that go into running recovery, and I'm your girl. If I ever do decide to play around with some small investments, I'll probably just ask Warner's advice first and then do whatever he suggests.

Yesterday morning, we sat together at the dining room table, as usual, him sipping his coffee and reading the Wall Street Journal, me slathering as much onion and chive cream cheese as could fit on my blueberry bagel. He had looked at me in disgust, proclaiming my sweet and savory combination an affront to bagelkind until I forced him to take a bite. He begrudgingly admitted it was not as gross as it sounded, but I still couldn't get him to admit it was good. Whatever; I know I'm right.

When I checked my Etsy orders that morning, Warner jumped at the squeal I made in response to the golfing sweatshirt order.

He listened avidly as I explained how I was planning on designing, cutting, and ironing on the vinyl to custom make the twenty-five sweatshirts requested. It was a huge order, bigger than I normally get, and the thought of ironing that many sweatshirts made me a little nervous. There are machines out there that function like industrial irons, pressing and heating the vinyl onto the shirts in record time compared to an old-fashioned house iron, but I'm not at the point where I can afford that. I lamented the time it would take and worried I might not get the order shipped out in time.

This morning, I walked into the kitchen to see the exact industrial iron press I had shown Warner the day before, sitting on the island with a bow on it. He had already left for his road trip, and his phone was off when I called him. He was likely in the air on the way to his first destination, but I left him a voicemail anyway, gushing about my new present and thanking him profusely.

Now, with Danny, Tim, and Amy gathered around Warner's oversized island, we've worked out a system. Amy is manning my Cricut machine, supervising the cuts into vinyl. Danny and Tim are weeding the images, pulling out the unnecessary vinyl, leaving just the image requested. I'm working my new press, marveling at the speed in which my custom images are infused onto the sweatshirts. Not only will we finish the order tonight, in record time, but we're on track to finish within the hour, leaving us plenty of time to eat dinner and settle in for a night of trashy television.

Amy periodically leaves her post at the Cricut machine to attend to dinner. She's making vegetarian chili and cornbread, so the kitchen is filled with the rich smells of onions and peppers. I snap a selfie of the four of us working together and send it to Warner, thanking him again for my new gift. I can't get over how thoughtful it was. Not only will it make this order manageable, but it will also make all future orders so much simpler. Once this project is complete, I'll have to spend some time reorganizing the craft corner in my bedroom to fit the press. I want to be mindful that my craft supplies don't spill out of my room and into common areas; Warner has done enough already. I can't ask him to tolerate my stuff being everywhere.

Danny pulls the last of the vinyl on his sheet off and walks to the television to find something for us to watch. He holds up the little sticky note with instructions for the remotes.

"Okay, this is adorable," he comments, flipping on the television.

"What is that?" Amy asks.

"Directions on how to use the remotes."

"Why is that adorable? I think Warner forgets which goes where. He hardly watches television out here." Danny blinks at me.

"Alicia, this isn't for him to remember. He wrote this down for you." Danny brings the sticky note over to me, flipping it over. On the back is a little note saying *If you can't figure it out, just give me a call. Warner.* Danny reads it aloud, laughing at me. "He's not going to write himself notes to call himself!"

I laugh at myself. Warner really is that thoughtful, and here I figured he was just forgetful. I should have known better. I probably also should have turned the note over in the first place.

We settle in with our bowls of chili in front of the television, satisfied from a night of productivity. Once Tim finishes eating, he leans back on the couch and pulls out his phone, preparing to dive into his latest favorite hobby during commercial breaks.

"Okay, Foxy Fanatixxx, here we come," he says, rubbing his hands together greedily as the page loads. Tim is a whore for gossip, regardless of whether it's true or not. He loves refreshing the fan website every few days, regaling us with the who's who of local celebrity hookups, and debating whether the encounter happened the way fans reported it did on the website.

"Okay, here we go. This girl says she hooked up with Kyle Crawford a few weeks ago after opening day. Says she met him..." he pauses, scrolling further on the blog to find the pertinent information. "At a bar named O'Reilly's?"

Amy laughs. "We were all there after the game, but that doesn't mean Kyle went home with anyone. Any random girl could have seen him there and claimed he took her home."

"Excellent point," Tim says, raising his eyebrows. "Counterpoint anyone?"

I have no idea if Kyle Crawford took someone home that night, nor do I really have a vested interest in the information, but Tim is obsessed with this new game, and I don't have it in me to break his heart by not participating.

"Counterpoint: Kyle Crawford is a known man-whore. So, it's possible. Not that I'm judging," I add quickly. What Kyle Crawford, or anyone really, does in their spare time is their business.

"Hmmm...this girl writes that he's great in bed, and particularly skilled at dirty talk."

"I could see it," Amy and I both say simultaneously, then dissolve into laughter. I don't know the Foxes players the way she does, but I've been spending more time with the WAGs–wives and girlfriends–and sometimes even the players now that I'm living with Warner.

"We'll chalk that one up to a likely confirmed hookup," Tim says, glee written on his face. Danny just shakes his head, laughing under his breath at our antics. "Okay, next up...our very own Warner James!"

I don't know why I feel surprised to hear his name on the blog. Just because his name pops up on there doesn't mean he's hooking up with whoever wrote it. Case in point? Someone last year claimed they hooked up with Caleb Andrews, a statement so laughably improbable that no one considered it factual. Not only is Caleb so hopelessly in love with and devoted to his fiancée, but the date of this alleged hookup occurred while Caleb was on the road–on a series where Jenny accompanied him.

"Sexibunni23 claims she and Warner hooked up last weekend after connecting online. She says he invited her back to his place," Tim reads.

I snort a laugh. Warner has never brought a woman home since I've lived here. Not that he couldn't; I'd have no problem with that. In fact, I'd probably encourage him to do so because it will prove I'm not cramping his style. I haven't brought anyone home since moving into his place either, but that has more to do with how busy I've been, rather than an intentional choice.

"False. I'm the only woman who has been here since I moved in," I state simply.

"What am I, a dude?" Amy asks, offended.

"Okay, *romantically*," I clarify, then realize what it sounds like. "No, *no one* has been here romantically, myself included!"

"Ah, here! I needed to keep reading. Looks like she says Warner invited her over here, but she declined and instead they hooked up at her apartment."

I can't put my finger on it, but I feel weird about that. I'm not sure if the information in that post is true or not. Given that anyone can write in saying they hooked up with literally anyone, and no fact checking is done, all the information submitted there is more than likely untrue. But I can't help but think if it's true as it relates to Warner. Does he feel awkward bringing someone back to his place because I'm here? Maybe it has nothing to do with my presence, and he wants to safeguard his own privacy. Although if Sexibunni23 is to be believed (which, I tell myself, she probably isn't), Warner invited her here first, but *she* turned *him* down. And why does that elicit an unfamiliar feeling in my belly?

Later that night as I'm lying in bed, I can't help but think about that blog entry again. I really don't want Warner rearranging his life to convenience me—not that him sleeping with anyone would inconvenience me in any way. I hope he knows that. In fact, I should probably clarify with him, just in case.

Me

Hey, you know you can hook up with anyone at your place, right?

Three little dots pop up, indicating Warner is typing. Then they disappear, reappear, and disappear again. Finally, his message comes through.

Warner

Um, okay? Where is this coming from?

Me

Nowhere, I'm just saying I hope you feel comfortable doing so. If you wanted to. Don't let me stop you.

Warner

Okay. Is this your way of asking if you can bring someone back to our place?

I don't miss the way Warner always calls it "our" place even though it's his place.

Me

No, not at all! I'm not dating right now. I'm seriously saying it for your benefit.

Warner

I don't know what to say to that.

I'm not doing a good job communicating this but given that Warner's game just ended twenty minutes ago, he's likely in the locker room or on the bus back to the hotel. Neither situation lends itself to a phone call, so I continue texting.

Me

I'm just saying, I don't want to inconvenience you. I don't want you to change the way you live your life just because we're roomies now.

Warner

Noted. Same goes for you.

Me

Sounds good. But like I said, I'm not dating now.

I don't know why I feel the need to explain I won't be bringing someone home anytime soon, or to justify myself to Warner, but I can't help it. I set my phone aside, putting it on sleep mode so any notifications are muted until morning. That's enough texting for tonight.

CHAPTER TEN
Warner

This road trip was grueling. It's been ten straight days without an off day. All I want to do is get home and curl up in bed for a week to recover. When our plane finally touches down in Chicago, all I want to do is sprint to my car to get home sooner, but I just can't muster the energy. At least we came home with a winning record from all our games. The team is doing well, but it's still early in the season.

"Lee? I'm home," I call through the door as I cross the threshold. I've taken to shortening Amy's nickname for Alicia even further, cropping the Leesh down to Lee. I love referring to my friends and family by their nicknames. I don't know why, it's just something I've always done. Eden and Xavier are E and X, respectively. I affectionately called my niece, Daisy, Crazy Daze or CD for short. Dominic is Dom, sometimes Dom P. Most of my teammates go by nicknames anyway.

Alicia doesn't respond, but there's a note on the island welcoming me home and letting me know she went for a run. I admire her dedication to her sport. I enjoy running when I have the energy, although the thought of going for a run right now is aversive enough to make my stomach clench. Alicia's love of running is a little more extreme than mine, though. While I have no problem going out for a run for a few miles, Alicia's idea of a "short" run is five to six miles. On a good day, that's my max. She's a beast.

I grab a bottle of water from the fridge and force myself to drink it. I tend not to hydrate well enough on return flights to Chicago, preoccupied with getting home. Tomorrow is an off day, finally, but I don't want to spend it with a headache because I neglected to drink water today. As I'm tipping back the final third of my water, Alicia walks through the front door, a stack of mail in her hands. I'm glad she's responsible enough to regularly check the mail; it's the household chore I forget the most. Probably because there's hardly anything of value in there.

I lift my chin in greeting at Alicia as I swallow the last of the water. I haven't even taken off my coat or put away my bag. She kicks off her shoes and takes the water bottle I hold out to her, leaning against the counter. We've fallen into a familiar rhythm together.

"How was your run?" I ask her, sliding the stack of mail towards me and flicking through it. Just junk mail so far. I wish there was a way to tell our mail carrier to skip the grocery store ads and the newspaper flyers; neither Alicia nor I even look through them before tossing them in the recycle bin.

"Good. Now that it's starting to warm up, it's not such a struggle to get out there and get going. I don't feel like my lungs are being stabbed each time I try to catch my breath," she jokes.

I nod in understanding, picking up a light green envelope that's face down in the pile. Alicia chokes on her water, sputtering and slapping at her chest.

"You okay?" I ask, giving her a moment to gather herself.

"Yeah, wrong pipe," she gasps. She clears her throat and attempts to grab the stack of mail from me.

"I got it, just catch your breath," I tell her, but instead of regulating her breathing, her breaths become shallower and all color drains from her face as I flip over the green envelope. "Whoa, are you okay?" I slide the envelope, which has her name on it, but no address, toward her. That seems to be the only mail for her.

"Yep, I'm fine," she answers shortly, tossing the envelope into the trash without opening it. I raise my eyebrows at her. "What?" she challenges.

I'm as surprised by her curt tone as her actions. What she does with her mail is her choice, but I'm surprised she doesn't at least want to open it first before tossing it away. My curiosity is piqued, but it's her business, so I let it slide and say nothing else.

"Sorry," she mumbles.

"No apology necessary," I tell her honestly. "I've just never seen you react that way."

Alicia doesn't explain further, so I don't press. She's entitled to her own privacy, regardless of my own curiosity.

"Anyway, I'm probably going to head to bed soon. I'm exhausted." I give her a tired smile and start moving toward my bedroom.

"Warner, wait, I'm sorry. I didn't mean to be short with you," she says, lightly grabbing my forearm as I pass her. I put my hand on top of hers.

"I meant it, no apology necessary. Don't beat yourself up over it." She steps aside and lets me pass. I fall into bed and pull the covers over my head, where I remain until morning.

By the time I resurface the following day, Alicia is already cooking breakfast. She hands me coffee in my favorite mug, the one with the "stonks" meme on it; Eden got it for me years ago. The image is mostly faded from overuse, but it's my favorite because it's oversized and the handle is large enough for me to fit all four of my fingers through. I murmur my thanks to Alicia and sit down at the table.

I still feel groggy, and while I would like nothing more than to spend my off day in bed, fighting off this never-ending exhaustion, I know sticking to my routines will be helpful. Alicia slides in at the head of the table, her usual spot next to me, setting her plate of bacon and bagel in front of her. I give her a pointed look. She knows I think she overcooks her bacon; it's an affront to the pig who created it. It's practically black it's so burnt, but she insists it's better this way.

"Oh no, don't you be judging me this early in the morning, Mr. Flaccid Bacon," she warns. I choke on my coffee.

"I don't like my bacon *flaccid*," I correct. "I like it properly cooked–not burnt. I'm surprised you can even taste anything aside from ash when you eat that."

Alicia laughs good naturedly. There are plenty of delicious foods we can agree upon, my mom's meatloaf making the top of the list, but Alicia's taste in bagels and bacon are things I will never get on board with. The girl is an abomination in the kitchen.

"Look, Warner, can we talk about yesterday?" she asks, ducking her head as if she's embarrassed.

This again? I'm no stranger to replaying embarrassing moments in my head, but this seems excessive. I shake my head.

"Alicia, please stop worrying. It's already forgotten."

"No, it's not that. It's..." she seems at a loss for words. She doesn't explain further but stands and walks to the trash cabinet in the kitchen, pulling it open and fishing out the green letter from yesterday. She hands it to me without comment, and I'm relieved to find it was still on the top of the trash, so it's not gross.

"Do you want me to open it?" I ask, and she nods. The envelope has her first and last name on it in chunky block writing, but nothing else. I slide a finger under the back flap, ripping it open and pulling out a folded note on matching green paper. Before I unfold the note, I ask, "Do you know who it's from already?"

I'm guessing she does, seeing as she tossed it before opening it. I'm nervous to read the letter only because Alicia looks like she's about to throw up. "Do you want me to read it first? Tell you what it's about so you don't have to?"

She blanches. "I...have an idea what's inside. I don't need to know the specifics, but it's probably best that you know about it, now that we're living together." I have no idea what she's talking about, but I unfold the note anyway and flatten it on the table.

ALICIA,

WHY ARE YOU IGNORING ME? I'VE BEEN WAITING FOR YOU. I'M GETTING IMPATIENT-I CAN'T KEEP WAITING FOREVER. I CAN'T WAIT TO BE TOGETHER AT LAST.

YOURS ALWAYS.

"Alicia, what the fuck is this?" I stare at the writing, which looks to have been done in black Sharpie. When she doesn't respond, I look up at her and see her eyes filling with tears and immediately regret my harsh tone.

"I don't know," she whispers.

"Okay, it's okay." I reach across and pull her hand into mine. "Who sent you that?"

"I don't know," she repeats. She takes a deep, shuddering breath and attempts to compose herself. I say nothing more, giving her time to explain. After several moments, she seems able to talk again. "I've been getting them off and on for the last year and a half."

"What?" I practically shriek and Alicia flinches. I'm such an asshole. "I'm not judging you, Lee. I'm sorry; your answer just surprised me. Please continue." I rub my hand over my mouth, scratching at the stubble.

"I don't know what else there is to say. These letters just started showing up in my mailbox one day. They never have my address, so I don't know how they get there, but he clearly knows where I live. Always the same handwriting, never really much substance. For a long time, I just threw them away without opening them. But then they started coming here, and it's starting to freak me out."

Starting to freak her out? Jesus. I pinch the bridge of my nose between my fingers. I know this isn't her fault, and I'm not judging her, but I wish she would have told me sooner.

Yeah, and what would you have done about it, dickhead?

"How many have been sent here since you moved in?" I ask, not sure I want to know the answer.

"This is the second one." I hate how small her voice sounds. Alicia is bright, and sunshiny, and full of life and personality. I hate how this has caused her to shrink herself in any way.

"Do you think we should go to the police?" I don't want to tell her what to do. I know from experience when Eden was going through her challenges, telling her what to do only made things worse. She needed to come to her own decisions on her own time. It frustrated the hell out of me, because the decisions she needed to make were so easy for me, as an outsider, to see. But I understood the value in allowing her to make her own choices on her own timeline.

"And say what, exactly? Some guy is sending me mail that I don't want?" She scoffs.

"I don't know. Someone is clearly watching you. This seems like stalkerish behavior, don't you think?"

Alicia pulls in a sharp breath. "I don't know," she says yet again. I have to remind myself that just because this scares me, because I want to react in a specific way, doesn't mean I need to take it out on her. She's clearly scared too, although she doesn't look like she wants to cry anymore. "I don't want to think it's a stalker," she whispers and my heart cracks a little for her.

"C'mere," I say, dragging her chair closer to me so we're shoulder to shoulder. I put my arm around her shoulder and pull her into my body. Alicia and I have rarely hugged, but this moment calls for comfort. I rest my cheek on the top of her head and think for a moment. "It's going to be okay. We'll figure it out. Security here is great, and I'll talk to Manny at the front desk about keeping an eye on the mail delivery if he can. Does anyone else know about this?

Your parents or anyone?" I know she talks on the phone regularly with her mom.

"No. I was afraid if I said it out loud it would make it more real. I only told you because you live here." My heart breaks for her. Her earlier indecision makes a lot more sense, knowing she wasn't ready to admit the scope of the issue. "I'm sorry to drag you into this," she says after a pause.

"Hey, now," I say sternly. I grasp her chin and tilt her face toward mine, making sure I establish eye contact before I say my next words. "You didn't drag me into anything. We're friends. We'll get through this–whatever it is–together. I've got you, Lee."

When Alicia leans further into me, seeking out comfort, another piece of my heart breaks for her. She's been dealing with all this alone. All I want to do is relieve her of her burden, to fix this situation, but I have no idea how.

After several minutes, she sniffles and straightens up. I fold the note that's still sitting on the table and stuff it in my pocket. I want it out of her sight; I'm sure its mere presence is stressing her out. I'm not sure what to do with it, though. The side of me that's seen enough true crime shows knows that we should probably hold on to it as evidence, but the rational side of my brain agrees with Alicia: technically, there's nothing wrong with this note. No laws (that we know of) have been broken, and no real threats have been made. I'm pissed as hell that someone has dimmed Alicia's light, but that isn't a crime. It should be, but it isn't.

Once the note is off the table, Alicia seems to perk up a little. She clears her throat and goes back to eating her bacon. It's so crispy that on her next bite, a piece breaks off and flies across the table, leaving greasy little skid marks in its wake. I raise my eyebrows at her as she tries to suppress a giggle.

"You know, if you had cooked that a normal amount, that wouldn't have happened," I tell her with a smirk. She leans across me and pounces on the rogue bacon chunk, popping into her mouth with dramatic flair. We both fall into much needed laughter, lightening the darkness that had clouded the morning.

"Do you have plans for today?" she asks me. I was previously fantasizing about doing nothing, spending the day napping, but after this morning's excitement, I know I'll agree to do just about anything with Alicia if it'll help restore her mood.

"Not really. Wanna do something?"

"I was hoping to go for a short run at some point today, after I digest my breakfast." She pats her stomach and takes another sip of coffee. "I'll probably only do two or three miles today. Technically it's my rest day, but I think I need a run for my mental state more than anything. Any interest in joining me?"

I groan. Only Alicia would interpret a rest day as a "run a couple of miles" day. But I agree, knowing that if there is someone out there watching her, there's no way in hell I'll be okay with her running by herself.

"Yeah, I'll run with you, Lee. But we stop after two miles. I'm fucking tired."

"Promise," she says, holding up two fingers in a 'scout's honor' gesture. "Then we can veg out the rest of the day. Eat cookie dough, watch a movie, relax." I grin at her; that sounds much more my speed for an off day. Maybe tonight I'll turn on the gas bonfire I have on my patio, and we can sit outside together. At some point, we'll have to figure out what's going on with these letters, but that's a problem for a different day. Right now, Alicia is smiling, and I'll do anything I can to make sure it stays that way.

While I wait for her to be ready, I unpack from my road trip, throwing in a load of laundry while she cleans up her breakfast dishes. Alicia keeps up a steady stream of cheerful chatter, calling out loudly so I can hear her while sorting my laundry down the hall. She's talking louder so I can hear her, but she's not really pausing long enough for me to answer her questions or to comment. I don't think she even notices I'm not responding. I honestly don't know where she finds the energy. Must be the bacon. I walk back into the kitchen right as Alicia turns and calls loudly to me.

"Ooh, Warn!" she startles when she realizes I'm so close to her and smiles, lowering her voice. "I think I know the answer to this already, but do your plants have names?"

"Names?" I reply stupidly.

"Well, all of my plants have names. Like my monstera plants are all named after Monsters, Inc. characters. You know, the Disney movie?" She chatters away, again, not noticing I haven't had a second to answer her yet. She tugs me over to the nearest plant and pulls out a tiny white sign that I've never noticed before. There, in dry erase marker, she has written "Randall."

"Oh. No. I don't name my plants," I say, finally comprehending her meaning.

"That's so sad!" she pouts. "Did you know they've done studies that show if you speak kindly to plants while you're watering them, they actually grow better?" I didn't know that. She nods eagerly, excited about imparting this wisdom. "Yeah! And so, I find that if I name them, it just personalizes the plant's experience a little more. Plus, it's just more fun that way."

"Lee. Do you want to name my plants?" I ask, guessing where this is going.

"Can I?" she asks, wide-eyed and excited. I'm momentarily reminded of Daisy when she gets permission to stay overnight at my house in Atlanta or when we get to go to the park together. I nod. I truly don't care if my plants have names or not; I keep the plants because they make Eden, and now apparently Alicia, happy.

"Knock yourself out," I say, and she practically skips to her bedroom and comes out seconds later holding blank plant nameplates and a black marker.

"Okay, so I was thinking something like Edgar for this one," she suggests, walking over to the stalk-like plant with black leaves. It must be a joke that I don't understand, because she playfully rolls her eyes and explains. "This is called a raven ZZ plant. Edgar, for Edgar Allen Poe? You know, quoth the raven?"

"Ah," I say, understanding dawning. "Go ahead. I give you free reign to name all my plants. I might not understand all of them, but have at it."

She doesn't stick around any longer, as if she's afraid I'll change my mind. She checks back with me for final approval on all names, but she could call all the plants Warner and it wouldn't bother me. Before long, Alicia introduces me to Cubano the coffee plant; Clea, Calliope, and Cletus (all calatheas, I'm told); a tradescantia named Trevor; Khaleesi; several viney plants with names all starting with P; Frank the succulent (which I didn't even know I had); and Dahlia the black orchid. Along the way, she shows me the plants she's brought over from her apartment and tells me their names as well. I'll never remember all of them, but I guess that's what the little name tags are for. Eden would be so proud. Come to think of it, I'm not sure even Eden names her plants. I make a mental note to ask her the next time we talk.

By the time we finish with our run, which really didn't take long at all–Alicia is remarkably fast and was barely winded by the time we hit two miles–it's late afternoon and my stomach growls embarrassingly loudly on the elevator ride up to the top floor.

"Have you even eaten today?" she asks, narrowing her eyes on me. She knows I rarely eat breakfast, and I wasn't in the mood for lunch. My silence tells her all she needs to know, because as soon as we get inside our unit, she starts pulling out all the fixings for a sandwich. It's over the top and way too involved. I'll just eat a handful of cereal or something. I tell her as much, but she scoffs and otherwise ignores me, continuing to pile layers of turkey and cheese on top of wheat bread. I don't have the energy to fight her. Besides, I grew up with Anita James as my mother; I understand sometimes people just have a need to feed others. So, when she cuts the sandwich in half and slides the plate towards me across the island, I accept it with mumbled thanks.

It isn't until I take the first bite that I realize just how hungry I am. I end up eating the whole thing in minutes. Alicia levels me with a look of smug satisfaction. I hold my hands up in surrender and grumble that she was right, under my breath.

CHAPTER ELEVEN

Alicia

The silver lining of having your hours majorly slashed at work is that I can do fun things during the day with Warner, especially on days when I work from home for a few hours. After we shower following the run, we settle into the couch to watch a movie. He picks an action movie that barely holds my interest. It apparently doesn't hold much of his either, because when I peek over at him halfway through, he is sound asleep, head resting in the corner crook of the couch. I can't help but smile. He seems so tired lately, and he's spent his entire off day with me, just hanging out.

I was surprisingly impressed with his stamina on our run. He barely broke a sweat and had no trouble keeping my pace, despite a steady stream of grumbling about it. I know he's an athlete, but baseball players tend to employ more sprinting, rather than endurance running. It was good to get out of the house together; aside from the occasional drink together after a game, we rarely go out. Even then, it's usually part of a larger group. I enjoyed my time with him today, getting to know him a bit better. He humored me with the plants; I could tell he wasn't invested in the activity, but I bet his sister will be pleased when I eventually move out and leave all the little plant name tags behind.

The main character in the movie drones on about his need to protect the heroine, who is clearly badass enough to take care of herself. The man suggests he and the woman move in together, to give the illusion of falling in love and marrying, so their enemies believe she is under his protection. Some sort of mafia law apparently makes her untouchable if she "belongs" to him. This movie isn't that great, but it did spark a potentially great idea. I can't, however, bring myself to wake Warner just yet to share it with him.

He looks so peaceful lying there. His eyelashes are so dark and thick, and the way they fan over his cheeks makes me jealous. Some women pay good money for eyelashes like that. His dark chocolate skin looks gorgeous, peppered with a light coating of stubble from missing this morning's shave. His sharp jaw is softened a bit in sleep. He truly is a remarkable looking man, and I ogle him while he sleeps like the creep I am. After a few minutes, I get up to grab my laptop to get some work done. I answer a few emails and make a few lesson plan outlines for a field trip group I have coming to the Field Museum next week. Warner starts to stir as I close my laptop, finishing out my projects for the day.

"Hey sleepyhead," I greet as he rubs his eyes. It's adorable, like a little kid waking up from a particularly restful nap. He smiles at me and it's devastating. Warner's smile could stop wars; he doesn't even realize the power he possesses. I give him a few minutes to wake up before suggesting we order dinner. Warner knows my less than stellar reputation in the kitchen, and while he's got culinary skills, he doesn't seem to be jumping at the chance to use them tonight.

We settle on Mexican food and when Manny calls up to let us know the delivery has arrived, I offer to ride down to grab it, rather than making him bring it to us. I still feel weird about all the work Manny does for us. I know it's his job, but I've never been comfortable being waited on like this. I express as much to Warner before heading down to grab the food, and he insists he'll get it for us.

Over dinner, Warner is quiet and contemplative. No time like the present to dive right in, I guess.

"So, I was thinking…" I start. He meets my gaze but says nothing, letting me continue. "I don't know how much of the movie you paid attention to, but the guy was trying to protect the girl from the rival mob family, and he suggested they live together and make it appear that they're married so she received the protection of *his* mafia family, by extension."

Warner doesn't say anything, waiting for me to make my point. Apparently, he's not connecting the dots the way I need him to. Damn him for not being a mind reader. I have no idea how he'll react to my proposal, and I'm nervous to fully present it to him.

"Anyway, I know that was a movie, and you're not in the mafia–or at least, I hope you're not." *Get it together, Langley. Now is not the time for your rambling.* "I, uh, was thinking it might apply to maybe this letter situation?"

The silence I'm met with is deafening. I can't read the expression on his face as he slowly chews. I'm encouraged that it seems almost contemplative, although that might be projecting on my part. I wait him out, trying not to let the embarrassment I'm starting to feel show on my face.

"So, you want to get married...?" he asks, unsure.

"Well, no, not get married. But I thought maybe, since this guy said he was waiting for me and seems to have some sort of romantic or hopeful feelings towards me...I guess if he saw me in a relationship publicly with someone else, he might give up and move on."

Warner still says nothing, and I want to crawl under the table, mortified. I'm mentally making a list of all the things I need to pack so I can move out of his apartment tonight unless I can mercifully die of embarrassment before then.

"You want to date me?" he finally asks.

"*Fake* date," I clarify, then cringe at how awkward that sounds. "If this lunatic thinks I'm off the market, then he'll probably leave me alone, right? I know it's a lot to ask." I trail off, and when Warner still says nothing, I lose my nerve. "You know what, never mind. It's a stupid idea. I would never want to impose on you. Forget I even said anything." I push myself away from the table, readying myself to flee to my bedroom where I can hopefully succumb to death by mortification sooner rather than later. He reaches across the corner of the table, placing his hand on mine.

"I got you, Lee. I just need to know the details, the parameters of what we're working with. We need to be on the same page if this is going to work."

I blink at him several times, then heave a sigh of relief. I have no idea if this plan is advisable, but it's the only one I've been able to come up with in response to a year and a half's worth of inconsistent but unwanted letters.

"Okay, um, how do you want to do this?" I ask, unsure where to start.

"I guess just by making a few public appearances together. As you may know, um," Warner clears his throat, "I'm usually not photographed with the same woman more than once." He winces, then quickly adds, "I'm very clear from the beginning, and everyone I date goes into it knowing I don't have time for a relationship right now."

"Warn, I wasn't going to judge you," I tell him gently. "Will you be okay faking this relationship? Being seen with me multiple times? Holding up this ruse? I know you're busy. I promise I won't put more work on you than necessary. I'll do all the work."

"Fuck that," he grits out. I'm taken aback by his uncharacteristic vehemence. "Fake relationship or not, I'm not letting you do all the work. This will be fifty-fifty." I can't help but smile; it's such a Warner attitude to take. "We can go on public dates and attend some events together. What else do you think we need to do?"

"Would you be okay with me posting pictures of us on social media? I mostly have my settings private but seeing as how I don't know who is sending me this garbage, it could be someone who already has permission to see my posts."

"Yeah, that's fine. I rarely use social media, but if you want me to, I can post stuff, too."

"Let's play that by ear. Maybe a few dates and my social media posts will be all that it takes, and this guy will back off." Warner agreeing to this plan has got me feeling all kinds of hopeful. "And, uh, listen. I know you have an active, um, social life, and I don't want to get in the way of that, so if you can maybe just be discreet, I would appreciate it."

Warner tilts his head to the side for a moment, studying me.

"Are you asking me not to fuck anyone else while I'm fake dating you?"

Jesus.

"Well, when you put it like that...I just meant, if you want to go out with others, or meet other people..." I stammer.

"Lee, if we're doing this, we're doing it right. I'm not some animal that can't keep it in my pants for a few months to maintain your safety." He glares at me, and I realize how insulting my insinuation was.

"I'm sorry, I didn't mean to imply you couldn't control yourself or anything. I was just trying to make this as convenient as possible for you." Warner growls in response. Actually *growls.* I don't know what that means.

"I haven't been with anyone all season," he starts, and I feel momentarily triumphant that Sexibunni23 is a damn liar. "I won't jeopardize your safety if there's a chance this guy will take this seriously. Because I *am* worried about your safety, Lee." The look on his face is sincere, his mocha eyes blazing as he says it. "But I would ask the same from you. That if this is going on, we don't date anyone else."

I nod.

"I'm in it for as long as you need, Lee, but if at any point, you change your mind, whether it's because it worked, or you meet someone new, whatever. Just let me know. Okay?"

"Okay. If it becomes too much for you, too, we can call it off whenever you need, too," I promise.

"Let's do this," Warner says, flashing me another one of his devastating smiles.

CHAPTER TWELVE

Warner

The first thing I do after dinner is head to my room and slide my phone out from my pocket. I scroll through my contacts, finally finding the one I need.

When Zahra picks up, she sounds surprised to hear from me.

"Hey stranger," she greets flirtatiously, and I'm already feeling guilty for getting her hopes up. She had reached out to me during spring training to get me Danny's contact information for the auction dinner, not knowing I had another connection to him. We had chatted off and on over the weeks since, until I finally asked her out while texting during my last road trip. She had enthusiastically agreed.

"Hey, Zahra. How are you?" We make small talk for a bit before we get to the point of my call. "Look, I feel terrible about this, but something has come up. I'm going to have to cancel our date next weekend."

"Oh, no problem," she says, trying to hide the disappointment I can already hear in her voice. "Want to do a rain check for the next weekend you're in town?"

"Normally, I would. But, uh, I've met someone," I tell her. It's not exactly a lie but isn't totally the truth either. Regardless of how I categorize it, it is necessary. "I'm not sure how serious it is, but I owe it to her to give it a real shot. I'm sorry, Zahra. I never meant to lead you on."

She pauses before saying, "Warner, I'm happy for you. I mean, I'm a little disappointed for me, but I'm happy for you. I wish you all the best." Her tone is sincere, and I can't help but think that in another life, she would make me genuinely happy. I chase that thought away, reminding myself I don't have time to date, don't have enough of myself to continuously give to another person. But if Alicia and I are really going to sell this fake dating thing, then I really need to commit to it. Sure, Zahra would have been fun for a night, but Alicia's safety is on the line.

Not having much more to say, we end the call. I pace my bedroom, gathering my thoughts. I must admit, Lee's plan initially threw me for a loop. I don't date anyone seriously, and if I'm being completely honest, I'm worried that fact alone will make this whole thing very unbelievable to whoever this stalker is. I'm calling him a stalker. After breakfast this morning, I looked up Illinois laws regarding stalking and what classifies stalking or harassment. This person hasn't made an outright threat, so Alicia is right, there's little law enforcement can do at this point. Not satisfied with those limitations, I spoke with Manny when I picked up dinner tonight. He promised to keep an eye on the mail delivery and assured me he would let Rosalie know to do the same. He also gave me the business card for building security. I'm sure I already have their contact information somewhere in my unit, but it was a good reminder to inform them as well.

I pull the card from my pocket and dial the number. A dispatcher answers after one ring, which encourages me. I inform the dispatcher who I am, where I live, and what Alicia's situation is. She assures me building security will keep an eye on things. The dispatcher also reminds me there are security cameras in all common areas of the building, including the stairwells. I heave a sigh of relief, hoping that Alicia's physical safety will be maintained while she's in the building. I confirm the security cameras are being monitored twenty-four-seven, which they are, rather than recorded for later viewing, should anything happen.

Seeing Alicia's scared eyes when she showed me the letter opened old wounds from what Eden went through with her abusive ex years ago. I still remember just how panicked and out of control I felt when she finally divulged the situation to me. I know it's not the same thing, but knowing Alicia could be feeling even a fraction of the terror Eden did kills me. So, yeah, I was a little thrown off by her proposal, but I'm one hundred percent in. Whatever it takes.

After hanging up with dispatch, I pull up the Foxes Family app on my phone. The team family program director, Deb, strongly encouraged us to download it when we each signed with the team, but I've never used it. It was designed mostly for players' and staff members' spouses to use for things like signing up for the kids' room during home games, accessing the team social calendar for non-mandatory events, and checking out local amenities like recommended doctor's offices. It sounds like a great resource, but seeing as I don't have a partner, nor do I have family living in the city, it's not one that I've ever needed. As if to prove my point, the app prompts me to create an account prior to use. I'm sure Deb intended for us to make our accounts as soon as we downloaded the app, but I never did.

I quickly enter my information, verifying my account through the automated system and my Foxes' email, and find what I'm looking for: the team social calendar. It's color coded and well organized; I don't know Deb well, but every encounter with her has proven she's exceedingly organized and good at her job. The calendar only confirms my impression. Items in green are non-mandatory family events, such as a weekend visit to the aquarium. Those in red are required events; those are few and far between. There's one next month for The Foxes Foundation, the charity work the team participates in. Blue events are for spouses only (no children); orange indicates suggested events that don't seem to be organized or sponsored by the family program in any way, but are fun things occurring in the city that families may be interested in. I'm already overwhelmed. If Alicia is going to play the part of my girlfriend, I hope she finds navigating this less unwieldy than I do.

I click on The Foxes Foundation event. It's scheduled for two weeks from now at the Four Seasons hotel. I screenshot the information and shoot it over to Alicia via text. She might already be asleep for the night, but at least she'll have the information when she wakes up. However, a few minutes after I send it, I'm met with a loud squeal, followed by the patter of footsteps and light but insistent tapping on my door.

"Come on in, Lee," I say with a smile. She wastes no time bursting in here, phone in hand.

"Are you inviting me to the Foundation's gala?" Before I can answer, she plows ahead. "Oh my gosh, JJ's gala night was so much fun! I can't wait to do it again! I'll probably wear the same thing; are you okay if I wear red? If you don't want red, I can see if there are some good rental dresses or secondhand designer dresses somewhere?"

I chuckle, amused by her excitement and, yet again, images of Daisy's childlike wonder come to mind. "Yes, I'm inviting you. No, I don't care what color you wear, but since we're going to my event, you can take my credit card and get a new dress if you want."

Apparently, those were the magic words to get Alicia to stop rambling. I feel smug for the span of one heartbeat before she bursts into tears. *Fuck.* What do I do? What *did* I do to make her cry? Is this because she thinks I don't think she can afford it? Is this a pride thing?

"I'm sorry, Alicia! Why are you crying? I didn't mean to make you cry!" I'm panicking now. *Jesus, fuck.* Two hours into my fake relationship and I'm already making her cry. This is why I don't do relationships; I'm always fucking something up.

"No, it's okay," she waves me off. "It was just such a sweet, thoughtful gesture. I wasn't expecting it." She slaps her tears away with the back of her hands, fanning her face and looking towards the ceiling. "Warner, you really don't have to buy me a dress. But the gesture is appreciated."

"Fuck that. If you were my real girlfriend, I'd be doing the same thing. So, if you're not upset, let me do this. It'll make you happy, so it'll make me happy." I rarely spend my money on anything anyway. I have my investments, which give me a greater return than my already overinflated salary brings in. I might as well spend my money on something that brings someone else this kind of excitement.

"Are you sure?" she whispers, as if she's afraid I'm going to change my mind. I press my card into her hand and tell her to go nuts. The watery smile she gives me in return makes my throat feel oddly tight.

I've lived on my own for so long, Eden's been stable for a long time, and my parents have always been rock solid. Is this what it's like to really take care of someone else? I don't know what to do with this strange mix of happiness and pain that I feel in my chest. If this is what it takes to make someone so happy, I'll gladly do it.

At the same time, I'm sad for Alicia for what she's been missing out on for so long. A piece of my heart swells with pride knowing I can be the one to give this to her at a time when she's already scared and stressed.

CHAPTER THIRTEEN

Alicia

"**S**o, you're going with Warner to this event, he gave you his credit card for a new dress, and you're going out to dinner together next week? I knew he had it bad for you," Danny says around a mouthful of pizza. He holds his hand out to his boyfriend, wiggling his fingers. Tim begrudgingly slaps a twenty-dollar bill in his hand.

"What is this?" I ask, gesturing between them.

"When he bought you that craft press thing for your sweatshirt order, I called it, didn't I, Tim? I said he wanted Alicia." Tim nods solemnly.

"Okay, first of all, he got me that because he's a nice guy who just wanted to help a friend. Besides, it probably made his life easier knowing I'd fulfill the order faster with it so I wouldn't have craft stuff scattered about his apartment for so long." Danny's face is painted with a shit eating grin, which only makes me more insistent that things are not as they seem. "*Second* of all," I continue, louder, "we're not really dating. We just need to make it *seem* like we're dating."

"Yeah, you didn't exactly explain that part," Amy chimes in.

I brace myself. Besides Warner, no one knows about the letters I've received over the last eighteen months. As much as I want to convince myself that I haven't told anyone because it's not a big deal, the real reason I kept it to myself is because if I voice the situation out loud, it becomes more real. So sue me, I'd rather be a coward and bury my head in the sand. I mute the Foxes game we have on in the background. We've hardly been paying attention anyway, although Amy regularly shushes us for JJ's at-bats.

Ducking my head, I mumble, "So I've been getting these kind of, sort of stalkerish letters over the last year or so." I say it quietly, intentionally downplaying it.

"Excuse me?" Amy's eyebrows are practically fused to her hairline. I know she heard me.

I set my plate to the side, curling my legs under me on the couch. Worrying the hem of my sweatshirt sleeves, I focus my attention there as I tell my best friends about the little green envelopes and their disturbing contents. At varying points, Amy makes small noises of commiseration. When I finally finish, looking up at them, Amy's napkin is shredded to ribbons, Tim's mouth is hanging open, and Danny's eyes are wide.

Okay, not the reaction I was hoping for. I really was hoping one or all of them were going to brush it off, tell me it is nothing to worry about, and that I'm overreacting. The fact that none of them are doing that adds to my anxiety.

"Anyway, Warner and I thought that maybe this guy would get discouraged if he saw me in a very public, committed relationship. Which is why he and I will be playing that up for the cameras and the press not only at the gala next weekend, but when we go out to dinner on Wednesday." I'm met with silence from my friends. I wish I knew what they were thinking, if they think this is a colossal mistake that will blow up in our faces, or if I'm secretly a genius for coming up with this plan.

Danny finally blinks and comes back to life. "Okay, I support this. Even if it means I haven't won the bet," he says, handing back Tim's twenty.

"Tim, would you mind maybe writing a post on your favorite blog to get things started?" He snaps his jaw shut, replacing the shock on his face with one of absolute glee.

"Yes, I have been waiting for a moment like this!" he says, rubbing his hands together. "Where are you going to dinner? Dan and I can hit the bar, snap a couple "candid" photos and pop them online before you even get home. I'm going to be so good at this, just you wait and see."

His evil cackle is the levity we needed for the situation. I return the game to its normal volume just as Warner is rounding the bases after a home run.

"Don't think just because we haven't mentioned it yet that you're off the hook from hiding this from us for a year!" Amy's voice is anxious and high-pitched.

"It wasn't all the time. Sometimes there were months between letters!" I add softly, "I didn't want to say anything because I didn't want it to be real." Amy launches herself towards me and wraps her arms around me, nearly strangling me in the process.

Later, when Warner finally makes it home after the game, we're wrapping up our night as well. He looks tired when he comes in–he probably *is* tired after his incredible game going three-for-four tonight and being responsible for not only the winning run, but some insurance runs later in the game–but when his eyes lock on me after saying hello to Amy, Tim, and Danny, he perks up.

I don't miss the way Tim slides the earlier twenty-dollar bill from his pocket back into Danny's hands; I internally roll my eyes. Warner is just happy to be home; it has nothing to do with me.

"Ames, JJ is downstairs waiting for you. He said to tell you there was no point to him going home to an empty house if you're here. The man is gone for you," Warner adds, eyes twinkling. Amy gathers her things to leave, Danny and Tim following her and leaving us alone together.

"Looks like you had a phenomenal game," I tell him, matching his grin. "That warrants a celebration, unless you're feeling too tired?" I've noticed Warner tends to prefer going to bed or hanging out in his room after night games.

"Nah, I've got some energy, let's hang out. Tell me about your day," he says, sliding on to the couch, shifting the blankets I tossed there earlier out of the way. I walk into the kitchen to grab the glass bowl from the counter.

"We made cookie dough tonight. Want some?" I hold out the dish to him as Warner looks it over.

"Tell me you did not make that with raw eggs," he demands.

"It's cookie dough! That's how you make it!" I reply, appalled as Warner gags in response. "Okay, you are taking this food snobbery thing a step too far, insulting cookie dough. You're like an alien or something if you don't like cookie dough."

"I don't know, the idea of raw eggs is so gross that it overpowers all the good that cookie dough brings to the table. Blame it on my attempts to bulk up in high school. Our baseball coach had us drinking raw eggs for extra protein in the morning." I wrinkle my nose.

"Still, you're pretty judgey about my bacon–"

"That's because you're supposed to cook it, not incinerate it, Langley!"

"--and my bagels," I plow on.

"Okay, blueberries and onions do not go together as well as you think they do," he insists.

"And you hated my hot toddy until I made you try it and then you ordered yourself one–don't think I didn't see that!"

"Alright, fine, I'll agree that the hot toddy is good, at the right time and place, *if* I'm in the mood for it," he reluctantly concedes. "But you ruined the cookie dough by using raw eggs."

"Fine, more for me," I insist, laughing and turning my body and the bowl of gooey, raw eggy goodness away from him.

134

CHAPTER FOURTEEN

Warner

Admittedly, I have a lot of rules for myself. No caffeine after three o'clock unless I have a night game. Get dressed as soon as I'm done showering. Force myself to eat at least two meals a day, even if I'm not hungry. But there are certain days that I just know, when I wake up, I won't need them. I call these nice days. They're not perfect, but they're better than good days.

Today is one of those days. I don't know why; I rarely have an explanation for their presence or absence, but I take them for what they are: a gift. When I opened my eyes this morning, I could feel it. There was an energy in the air, or maybe just inside myself, that told me today was going to be one of those nice days. I felt lighter as I showered and brushed my teeth. And because I like to tempt fate, not always trusting myself that what I think is going to be a nice day is *actually* a nice day, I decided to start making breakfast before getting ready the rest of the way.

Normally, I skip breakfast in favor of intermittent fasting, especially when we have a night game the day prior. So much food is provided at the ballpark, but on night games, it's particularly over the top: lunch (usually at least three entree choices), post batting practice (typically a few entree choices, in addition to several pre-made wraps and sandwich options), and post-game (an enormous spread, often catered by a local gourmet restaurant), in addition to the plethora of snacks, smoothies, and prepackaged options that we always have in the clubhouse. It's rare that I'm hungry enough to eat breakfast; instead, I opt for black coffee while I read the business section of the newspaper.

Given how I woke up today, though, bacon and eggs sound like a great option, in addition to my trusty coffee. Walking out to the kitchen in my towel, I flip on the coffee maker. When it was just me living here, I used my single-cup coffee machine, but now that Alicia is here, I dug out my full pot drip machine. It takes a little longer, but it's worth it to be able to ease into the day, leisurely sipping coffee with her instead of having to constantly get up to make more, or, God forbid, only drink one cup.

I catch Alicia on the terrace out of the corner of my eye. Last night, she mentioned doing yoga out there in the morning before it gets too humid. She's been trying to add in more cross training now that she's started her marathon training program, and I must admit, I'm a lot more comfortable with her working out here than running around the city where God knows who can be watching or following her.

It's been a couple weeks since I found out about her little pen pal. While she hasn't received another letter since she showed me it, it's done little to ease my nerves about the situation. Never one to be satisfied in a gilded cage, Alicia hasn't changed her normal routines, and while it's hard to blame her for her decisions, I'm immensely relieved on days where I can count on her sticking closer to our place where her safety is better maintained.

She slides the terrace door open, rolled up yoga mat under her arm. I imagine her hair was probably tossed up in a messy bun when she started, but it's mostly escaped the confines of her hair tie now, falling in artful chunks around her face and down her shoulders. She stops when she sees me, and I guess it must be like seeing a wild animal cook breakfast. I can cook, I just rarely do it, and cooking breakfast is an even rarer occurrence. I realize, based on the look on Alicia's face, I have never made breakfast once since she's lived here.

"You haven't eaten yet, have you?" I ask her. She takes a few beats too long to answer; so much so that I double check to make sure she's not wearing earbuds and missed my question entirely. She gives her head a tiny shake and then finally responds.

"No, I haven't eaten. Warner James, are you cooking?" I could have done without the stunned incredulity in her voice.

"I can cook!" I sputter defensively. "You do know who my mother is right? She would have disowned me if I didn't know my way around the kitchen." I laugh at the scowl on Alicia's face. She sticks her tongue out at me but accepts the mug of coffee I offer her.

"I feel like your mother might have something to say about naked cooking, though. That's gotta be a health code violation or something," she mutters.

I glance down my bare torso, realizing she's right. I should probably throw a shirt on if I'm making bacon. I wince at the thought of bacon grease splattering up onto my stomach and concede Alicia is right. I shrug and retreat to my room to toss on a pair of athletic shorts and my favorite, threadbare Chicago Bears tee.

"Happy now?" I say to her, as I reenter the kitchen and start cracking eggs. She smirks in response and returns to whatever is capturing her interest on the open laptop in front of her. She looks up when I slide a plate containing her abomination of a bagel towards her.

"Just because I made it for you does not mean I condone the use of this flavor combination," I tell her, licking a dollop of onion and chive cream cheese off my thumb. She ignores my comment but shifts her computer screen toward me.

"Look at this, we're famous," she says. On the screen is what looks like a blog, or maybe a gossip website. There's a photo of us together from the other night, our first public fake date since we hatched this plan. Someone must have snapped it as we were being led to our table at the cavernous pan-Asian restaurant Alicia chose. I'm looking over my shoulder, my hand on her lower back, as I allowed her to walk in front of me. My full face is in the photo, while Alicia is only visible in profile. The caption declares "Warner James steps out with his new prospect on Wednesday night."

I'm rankled by the description. A prospect? I immediately hate that descriptor, as if Alicia is some sort of conquest, or worse, an object.

"What is this website?" I say, checking the address. "Foxy Fanatixx" glows in black and silver sparkles across the top of the page as I scroll up. It looks cheap and terrible, like the early days of social media pages in beta mode. The title of the article Alicia was reading, emblazoned above our photo, confirms just how cheap and terrible the website is. *Foxes' Outfielder Playing the Field with a New Woman.*

Alicia explains the website is a fan site of sorts, where people can submit celebrity sightings from around Chicago. While named after my team, it does not appear to restrict itself only to baseball players, although we seem to take up the bulk of the "reporting."

Chicago media is its own beast. Early in my career, I received media training, which my public relations manager refers to frequently at the beginning of each season. I've never been involved in a scandal, so I don't know why he stresses it so much, but I suppose he takes his job seriously. I momentarily think back to that night in January when Caleb punched that guy on my behalf, before promptly shoving the memory away. Today is a nice day; I'm not going to ruin it by ruminating on uncomfortable memories. In all my media training, however, I haven't been faced with a situation quite like this. I feel a little gross for dragging Alicia into it, and I'm about to tell her exactly that, when I catch the look on her face. Is she actually...*happy* about this?

"Lee, I feel like you're excited about this post," I start.

"Well, yeah, it's exactly what we wanted, isn't it? Now the public, and hopefully whoever is sending me these letters, will know I'm off the market. Now they can move on to someone else."

She's right. So why am I feeling so uncomfortable? I don't think it's the lie; I have no regrets there. I think it's the language surrounding Alicia and the comments below the article that have some choice words for her. I scan the short article quickly; there's no mention of her by name. I feel a weird sense of relief about it. The last thing we need is her trading one stalker for another.

"And you're okay with them talking about you like you're some sort of conquest?" I ask, incredulous. I'm used to the media taking shots at me, especially if my on-field performance is lagging, but Lee has never been in the public eye.

"I mean, the comments don't use the most flattering descriptors for me, but hopefully this article and this weekend's gala will do the trick. I do wish Tim made it seem a little less 'flavor of the week' and a little more serious, but I guess beggars can't be choosers," she adds thoughtfully.

"Tim? What does he have to do with this?" I say, returning to the stove to flip the bacon and add the scrambled eggs to my preheated pan. They sizzle more than I would like; I left the pan heating too long when I went on a deep dive on the Foxy Fanatixx website. Swearing lightly, I turn the heat down and begin moving the eggs around.

"Oh, I guess I didn't tell you. I asked him to be at the restaurant and submit the story to the website. Kind of control the narrative, you know?" she says around a mouthful of bagel.

"You're a schemer, Langley," I tell her, pointing the spatula at her. "Next time, give a guy a head's up or something. I'll smile for the camera then." I give her my fakest, cheesiest smile and she snorts a laugh in response.

Shortly after breakfast, I change to head into the ballpark. Wearing a collared shirt in and out of the ballpark is a requirement, so I select a short sleeved, linen button up and navy slacks. I slather on some sunscreen before walking back out to the living room, where I find Alicia sliding her laptop into her work bag.

"You going in to work today?" I ask her. I can never keep track of her work schedule. Some days, she doesn't work for the museums at all, other days she puts in a full day on campus followed by working from home on the couch at night. I suspect she's probably working more hours than she should, given how much her salary was cut, but she's devoted to her job and the students she serves.

"Yeah, I have a meeting at ten, so I'll probably stick around a little bit after and get some more hands-on stuff done for next week." See what I mean? Devoted.

"Are you and Amy coming to the game today?" It's a rare late afternoon game, which allows me to go in later than usual. Some guys find the three o'clock start times annoying, since it cuts into their mornings and nights, but it allowed me to cook breakfast at home for Alicia and me today, so I've got no complaints.

"I didn't really think about it. I'm sure she'll be there." Sometimes Alicia tags along with Amy to games to watch JJ. It's nice to see her there, to know someone in the stands is cheering for me personally, wanting me to succeed because they know me, not just because me doing well generally equates to the Foxes doing well, too.

"I can leave a ticket for you if you want," I offer. I don't know why I'm pressing the issue. It'd just be nice to have her there, I guess. "In fact," I say, checking my watch, "if you want, I can drive you to work if we leave in the next five minutes. Then you and Amy can drive to the game together straight from work and won't have to worry about parking two cars."

It's a lame excuse. The girls can park in the covered players' lot for the games, so they never have to worry about parking. All I know is that hanging out with Alicia eases my mind, and I'm having a nice day, so why not extend it? We don't live too far from the museum campus but spending a few extra minutes with her will probably elevate my already good mood, which means I'll likely play better. Just like Alicia, I'm devoted to my job, too. That can be the only explanation for why I'm pushing these plans.

"You don't mind? I don't want to inconvenience you or make you late," she hedges.

"Nah, you're good. I got you," I promise.

By the time Alicia exits my car at the staff entrance of the planetarium, I'm pleased to note my hypothesis has been confirmed. I hum along with the song on the radio, my mood significantly elevated.

"I needed this," Amy sighs as Adele tunnels her fingers through her blonde hair, fluffing the strands closest to her scalp before pinning them back. We're at Amy's salon in Lakeview East, getting our hair done for the Foxes Foundation event tonight.

Adele already put the finishing touches on my hair while Amy had her makeup done by Adele's business partner. I opted to do my own makeup to save some money, but Adele unsurprisingly spared no effort in making my hair match the timeless classic look of both my makeup and dress. I had shown her pictures of the dress, and she instantly understood my vision. A visionary herself, she pulled out all the stops (and quite a bit of hairspray) to make me look like a stunning, 1920s star of the silver screen. My full lips are painted in the deepest, most gorgeous shade of matte crimson. This morning, Amy and I had coated ourselves in a light, even layer of self-tanner, just enough to cover my less than stunning tan from my sports bra. Luckily, the tanner seemed to do the trick and now the dress will be the eye-catching focal point of my look tonight, rather than chunky, racerback tan lines across my shoulders and upper back.

I pull up the score of the Foxes game. They are still scoreless heading into the eighth inning. I try and fail to suppress a groan.

"Still scoreless?" Amy asks hopelessly from the chair next to me.

"Yeah," I sigh. "If this goes into extra innings, we'll definitely be late to the gala."

Adele makes one more pass of hairspray over Amy's blonde locks before removing the haircutting cape from her shoulders and releasing her to stand. She looks incredible. Unlike me, Amy has chosen to go with a muted lip color in favor of making her eye makeup the showstopper. Her large brown eyes are expertly coated in black along her waterline, while shimmery, silver-pink shadow coats her lids. Her false lashes add an extra dose of glamour; JJ is going to lose his mind. We snap a quick photo, which we send to Danny and Tim, then we pay Adele and head to our respective cars. If the game doesn't end up going into extra innings, I will have barely enough time to make it home to change before Warner comes back to pick me up.

At the stoplight waiting to get on to Lake Shore Drive, I turn on AM radio and flip through the stations, trying to find the game coverage. I find it just in time to hear the commentator announce, "And that's a walk off home run from Matteo Cota to give the Foxes a win!"

I release a sigh of relief and press a little harder on the gas once the light turns green, knowing the clock is ticking to finish getting ready.

Warner texts me as I'm pulling into the parking garage, letting me know he's hopping in the shower and will be back to change and drop off his bag before we have to leave. While the game didn't go into extras, it dragged on. Normally, scoreless games tend to move quickly, but of course, when the whole team has an event to get to, the baseball gods plan differently. Looking at the game recaps on the elevator ride up to the top floor, I see that despite the score, baserunners made it on in nearly every inning. It looks like neither team was able to seal the deal until Cota's two-run homer in the ninth.

I shimmy into my dress, careful not to mess up my hair in the process. I readjust my boobs; the structure of this dress lends a lot of support for the girls, which is great, because the back tends to dip lower than I'm used to. This dress is very much outside of the normal, more conservative cut that I typically get, but because Warner's budget allowed me to go outside of my "standard" options, I'm excited to try something new. With the rose gold fabric and black lace overlay, I pulled out all the stops tonight. If he's planning on wearing anything even remotely close to the suit he wore to JJ's gala, I'm in trouble. Just because we're fake dating doesn't mean I can't appreciate the eye candy that is Warner fucking James.

I work out a lot, not because I'm dissatisfied with my body, but because I love it so much that I want to take care of it. Running keeps my legs and stomach toned, and this dress shows off those assets well. I glance down at my right leg, visible through the high slit on the thigh and send a prayer of thanks to the inventor of self-tanner. After putting on my diamond pendant necklace, a college graduation gift from my parents, and my cubic zirconia earrings, I grab my black kitten heels and plop myself down in the dining room to put them on.

Warner walks through the front door and freezes, his eyes on me. I self-consciously bring a hand to my chest; at the time he walked in, I was bent forward, breasts practically on display, as I finished buckling the strap of my shoe. Straightening and standing, I fidget with my clutch.

He is still staring at me, and the look on his face is like the one I imagine I was wearing when I walked in on him cooking in just a towel yesterday. I practically swallowed my own tongue. I know he's an athlete, and I could tell from the way he fills out his shirts that he was incredibly toned and physically fit. Seeing him shirtless, however, showing off a lion tattoo on his chest, rivulets of water running down his defined pecs and across the ridges of his hard abdomen, altered my brain chemistry for a moment. I'd like to think I recovered quickly and played it off easily, but I'm pretty sure I'm lying to myself. Warner clears his throat.

"Wow, Lee, you look beautiful," he tells me sincerely. I beam at him. I'm glad we have the kind of friendship where we can compliment each other.

"Thanks, Warner. You bought the dress, so you really should be thanking yourself."

"It's not just the dress," he murmurs. Before I can say anything in response, he drops his backpack on the chair next to me and rushes off to change.

"Do you want me to grab a rideshare?" I call. His response is muffled from behind his bedroom door.

"Nah, I arranged for a car service. They should be here in ten."

When he emerges from his bedroom, I'm stunned into silence. The man can wear a suit; I knew that from JJ's event earlier this year, his three-piece gray number still fresh in my brain. Warner's style, however, is not limited to that one suit or that one night. Tonight, in classic black suit, black tie, and white button down, he is the picture of timeless elegance. His shiny black shoes click along the hardwood floor as he comes to stand near me, adjusting his tie.

"Looks like I'm not the only one pulling out all the stops tonight," I say, far breathier than I intended. His responding smile is genuine, if not a little shy.

"Come on," he murmurs, pressing his palm against the small of my back as we walk out his door, locking up along the way.

Mrs. Chan, Warner's widowed neighbor from down the hall, shuffles slowly towards us, making her way to the elevator. The entire ride down, she chatters at us, gushing over how glamorous we look and reminiscing about events she and her husband used to attend.

"You two make such a gorgeous couple," she continues effusively.

"Thank you, but we're not–" I stop short at Warner's warning raise of his eyebrows. *Oh, right.* We're supposed to be dating.

"Thank you, Mrs. Chan," he says for me.

I have got to get myself together. Tonight is not just Warner and me hanging out. It's Warner, Foxes star, baseball god, and attractive celebrity, and me, his alleged girlfriend, going to a team-sponsored event. All the earlier confidence imbued in me from this dress dissipates as I step into the black town car waiting for us outside the Vandeveer. *What am I doing?* Can we even pull this off? Warner looks positively delicious in his suit and what appears to be a fresh haircut; who would believe that we're together? I've never been one to struggle with self-confidence, but I find myself second guessing everything right now, including our harebrained scheme to convince Chicagoland we're in a committed relationship.

"Are you okay?" Warner asks, concern etched on his face.

"Yeah, just...nervous," I respond. It's not a lie, but only a fraction of the truth and turmoil swirling through my head. He nods, reaching across my lap to squeeze my hand. He doesn't say anything, but the small gesture grounds me and reminds me that however crazy this idea is, we're in it together. The ride to the Four

Seasons isn't long, but his hand remains firmly around mine for the duration of the drive.

CHAPTER SIXTEEN

Warner

I'm careful to step out of the car in front of Alicia so she isn't immediately bombarded with the press I spied from the window as we pulled up to the hotel. A few years ago, this event only attracted a small media presence, usually just some local sports bloggers and the occasional small blurb in The Chicago Tribune about the charity and the money raised. Seemingly overnight, it turned into a red-carpet event, complete with photographers, journalists and sometimes even fans lingering around the entrance, hoping to snap photos or scoop the next story about their favorite baseball players. The sudden attention makes my head spin if I think about it too much.

I hold out my hand to Lee, who takes it eagerly and uses it to help her step out of the vehicle. Her red lips stretch into a wide grin as she allows me to lead her toward the hotel entrance. The same pink-haired reporter from January accosts us on our way. I wonder briefly if she writes for Foxy Fanatixxx.

"Warner, who is this gorgeous specimen?" I pull Lee closer to me, feeling a sense of ick over the word "specimen," like she is the result of some weird science experiment. What is with the awful ways people describe this woman? They're not exactly insults, but they're certainly weird compliments.

"This beautiful *woman*," I say, stressing the word, "is my girlfriend, Alicia." I level the reporter with a hard stare. I'm sure Jacob would be annoyed if he were here, but my publicist can respond to any blowback from my less than friendly response. Whatever. I answered her question.

"A girlfriend?" she practically squeals. "Turning over a new leaf this season, James?"

I ignore her and Alicia falls into step with me as we enter the hotel lobby, thanking the doorman along the way.

"Wow, I'm a specimen now, huh? And here all this time I thought I was a human," she reflects facetiously.

"Right?" I ask, relieved she thought the phrasing was as rude as I did.

"Thanks for standing up for me back there," she says quietly. I give her hand another squeeze and smile softly.

"Always. I got you, Lee."

We make our way through the opulent lobby, the fragrance of fresh flowers overpowering all other senses. We are ushered towards a gilded elevator bank near the back of the lobby, which will presumably bring us to the ballrooms hosting tonight's event. I don't miss several hotel guests gawking at us along the way. I'm used to it, but I hope it doesn't make Alicia uncomfortable. If she notices, she doesn't comment. Her eyes are wide, taking in the lavishness of the lobby and elevators. While waiting for the elevator, we're joined by Benny, Caleb, and Jenny. Jenny and Alicia embrace, raving about each other's dresses, hair, and makeup. I smile, comforted by the fact that even though tonight will mostly be pretending, at least between Alicia and me, she will have friends here.

After disembarking the elevators, we are asked to pose for photographers in front of a Foxes Foundation backdrop. I hold Alicia close for the photos, following the photographer's directions, amazed at how natural it feels to pull her into my body. The scent of something bright and flowery infiltrates my nostrils and momentarily scrambles my brain. Alicia is so put together, so incredibly flawless. I can't believe so many people willingly believe she'd be with someone like me, but I take it as a win. The more convincing we can be, the better the outcome regarding her stalker, I tell myself.

After photos, Amy and Jenny pull Alicia away from me to join them and Elijah McClintock's wife, Hailey. They flounce off to grab drinks at the open bar. Elijah brings me a vodka soda before we're joined by JJ, Matteo, Caleb, and Oliver. I'm friendly with all my teammates but generally spend the most time with Matteo, my fellow outfielder. However, when JJ starts talking about our antics after his gala this winter, I'm surprised to realize how close he and I have become over the last few months of this season. I suspect all the time Amy and Alicia spend together has something to do with that.

"What do you think, James?" JJ says to me, pulling me from my thoughts. His piercing blue eyes are trained on me, as if he knew I wasn't paying attention. "Golf this Thursday when we land in LA?"

We have a road trip coming up next week, first flying to San Diego, then spending an off day in Los Angeles on Thursday before a three-game series there. We will then crawl up the West Coast for a few games in San Francisco and Seattle. It's a long road trip, and I'm filled with dread at the thought of being away for so long. I tend not to sleep as well in a hotel, but the prospect of an off day is comforting.

"Sure, I'm in," I tell them.

"Hell yeah!" McClintock cheers. "We've been trying to get you to go out with us for *weeks*, James."

I realize he has a point. I turned down invites a lot these last few weeks; I need to make a better effort to bond with my teammates. I give him an apologetic smile.

"Yeah, sorry. I'll get better about socializing," I promise.

"Here we go," Caleb groans, making eye contact with his fiancée across the room. She points at him, then the champagne flute in her hands, then back at him, not so subtly asking if he wants one. "Jenny is a sloppy drunk when she gets her hands on champagne," he explains, but the look on his face says he loves every moment of it.

"Those aren't just champagne flutes, Andrews," Matteo warns. "That's part of the fundraiser. Each one has a gemstone in the bottom. Most are fake, but a couple of the champagne glasses have a real diamond in them. Costs two hundred bucks a glass."

Caleb grins. "Fucking of course my fiancée would find the most expensive drink at an event with an open bar." His eyes shine with love for his woman, and I'm momentarily stunned to find myself wondering what a love like that might feel like, before reminding myself that I'm too busy to foster a relationship like that.

We make our way toward our dates just as Alicia is about to put down her information on the tablet held by the champagne server.

"You better be putting my name down on that order," I tell her, coming up behind her.

"It's two hundred dollars, Warner," she says, as if that's relevant. She's my date; if she thinks she's spending her own money at my event, she's got another thing coming. I pull the tablet gently from her hands, typing in my own information instead. She doesn't put up too much of a fight.

The server presents the tray of numbered champagne flutes to Alicia for her to pick one, while he explains that the number of the flutes with the real gems in them will be announced at the end of the night. Not a bad fundraiser, if you're not worried about your guests getting rip roaring drunk on champagne or choking on a gemstone, I think. Alicia must have the same thought because she sips her drink gingerly, mindful of the jewel in the bottom.

She pulls me aside after I hand the tablet back to the server. Amy and Hailey are debating which numbered glass they should choose as we step away.

"You didn't have to do that, you know. You already paid for my dress. I can pay for some things," she tells me quietly.

"I know you can, Lee. I didn't mean to offend you. I just wanted to take care of these things because you're here as my date," I explain, keeping my body a half step too close to hers, but it's loud in here. At least that's what I tell myself.

"You're not just paying because I lost half my job, and you feel sorry for me?"

"What? No," I tell her honestly. "This isn't about pity, Lee. I just think it'd be rude for me not to pay for my date's drinks tonight when I'm the one who invited her here in the first place."

I watch her shoulders visibly lower, losing their tension, and mentally chastise myself for not making that clear sooner. I should have known this would be a nerve-wracking night for her. I should have expressed that my desire to take care of her stems from a place of caring, rather than pity. I hope she doesn't think I pity her for this stalker thing either; I'm pissed at the situation, but I don't pity her. She's strong as hell, and while I don't want her to have to deal with what she's going through, I certainly don't think she's weak or incapable of solving her own problems.

"Tell you what: next time we go out for dinner, you can pay," I tell her, striking a compromise.

"Even if it's the falafel cart down on Rush Street?" she jokes.

"We'll be even if you get extra tzatziki," I tell her with a wink.

Besides, I'd gladly pay for that dress ten times over, based on how it looks on you.

Whoa. Where did that thought come from? I step back from Alicia, exceedingly grateful that the filter between my brain and my mouth is solidly intact.

Fortunately, the rest of the night progresses without incident, and no unfiltered thoughts cross the threshold of my mouth. A fan, someone not affiliated with the Foxes at all, wins the real diamond from the champagne glasses, but Alicia vows to turn her stone into a piece of jewelry anyway, even though it isn't real.

By the time we climb into the back of the town car waiting for us, Alicia is almost as tipsy as Jenny was before Andrews hauled her away. Alicia is a cute drunk. I haven't had the opportunity to see her like this. She's mostly herself, just amplified. She is easily excited about everything, emoting loudly to her friends. In the car, her voice volume is loud, and she giggles at the realization, covering her mouth with her purse.

"Thank you for inviting me, Warn," she sighs, clutching my arm and snuggling next to me on the bench seat. "I had so much fun, and everyone was so nice." I look down at her as she speaks. She's slouched more in the seat, clearly having drank more than I did tonight, and she looks smaller than usual in this position. Her slate eyes are wide with wonder, and I can't help but chuckle. She's just so *happy*, it's hard not to feel a little happier myself when I'm in her presence.

She stumbles a little when we cross the threshold into our unit. I reach my arm out in a flash to steady her.

"Okay, wrecking ball, let's get you out of these shoes and into bed." I guide her to the dining room table to sit in her usual seat. Sinking to my knees, I pull her feet toward me, unbuckling them one by one. Her ankle is dainty, small and warm in my palm, her toned leg smooth and tanned. A zing of energy connects my hand with her ankle.

"I feel like Cinderella," she exclaims as I pull off one heel, placing her bare foot on the floor and grasping her slim ankle in my hands.

"It's a little bit of a backwards Cinderella," I comment. Confusion colors her face. "Cinderella had the prince put the shoes on, not take them off."

"Oh yeah," she says. Our eyes connect for several seconds before she yawns and hiccups at the same time. Maybe Jenny isn't the only one who gets a little messy after champagne.

"Come on, let's get you in bed before you fall asleep at the table. Do you need help with your dress?" Knowing the state she's in, she might trip on the length of it before reaching her room. I escort her down the hallway as she mumbles something about needing to take off her makeup.

"Okay, do you want to get in your pajamas first?" I ask, envisioning water splashing everywhere. I imagine she'll be disappointed tomorrow if her dress gets soaked tonight.

"Let's just do makeup remover wipes," she says, emitting another loud hiccup and frantically grabbing at the back of her dress for the zipper. She locates it and starts unzipping. I immediately turn away as I hear the swish of her dress pooling at her feet.

"I'll go grab them," I say, trying not to sound as panicked as I feel. I stride off towards her bathroom, looking around for makeup remover wipes. I hope they're labeled, because I'm not exactly sure what I'm looking for. I'm happy to volunteer to lead the search for them though. I hope by the time I find them and return, Alicia will be in her pajamas. Opening the top drawer of the cabinet, I spy a purple package, blessedly labeled with its contents. I grab them and walk back to her bedroom, keeping my gaze trained on the floor, just in case she's not dressed by now. Thankfully, I find her in bed, covers pulled up to her neck, a dopey, sleepy look on her face.

I step over the dress she left in a pile on the floor, pulling out a wipe from the pack in my hand. I hold it out to her, and she takes it, scrubbing it across her face vigorously. She flips it over and repeats the process with the other side of the wipe.

"Did I get it all?" she asks me hopefully. *Absolutely not.* She's got dark smears under her eyes, and her lips still contain faint pink traces from her lipstick.

"Not quite," I tell her, pulling another wipe from the pack. I sit on the edge of her bed as she sits up. I'm relieved to see she has a T-shirt on. I gently swipe under her eyes with my new wipe, dragging it across her cheeks. I lightly pat at her lips before giving up. They might still be a bit pink tomorrow, but at least she doesn't look quite so much like a raccoon. We both sit there, gazing at each other. The moment feels charged, electric. Alicia's gaze dips to my lips, her eyes hooded. Then she lets out another loud hiccup, breaking the tension of the moment.

"Lee, you're a bit of a mess tonight," I tell her, glad for the interruption. "Stay right here. I'm going to get you some water. I need you to drink a bunch of it before you fall asleep or you're going to be hurting tomorrow."

She nods enthusiastically, eyes a little more alert than a moment ago. I waste no time bringing in two cold water bottles from the kitchen, along with a couple tablets of acetaminophen. She accepts them readily and noisily gulps down the water while I hang her dress on the hanger I find on the back of her door. I take the empty bottle from her, wish her goodnight, and turn off the lights on my way out the door.

What a weird night.

CHAPTER SEVENTEEN
Alicia

When I woke the next day, Warner was already gone. He had a day game on Sunday, after which the team flew out for their West Coast road trip. After being gone for almost two weeks, Warner comes back tonight. We've texted a few times during the trip. I found an updated article about us on Foxy Fanatixxx a few days after the Foundation gala. The accompanying photo was an official one taken in front of the backdrops they had sprinkled throughout the venue.

I suspect whoever posted the Fanatixxx update got the image from Amy's social media pages, where she posted photos of all of us from the night. Her social media profiles are less private than mine these days, but she's very careful about what she posts. I had sent the link to the article to Warner, but I find myself pulling up the photo of us from the event every few days.

I have to admit, we look fantastic. I'm grateful Amy invited me to get my hair done with her, because my hair remained in its voluminous, Old Hollywood waves all night. My makeup looked great too, which was perhaps the most surprising part of my ensemble. I'm not particularly skilled or interested in makeup; I can do enough to get by. I watched so many YouTube makeup tutorials in advance of the event and I'm pleased to see my efforts translate to what I was hoping for in the photos.

Even more than my incredible hair, makeup, and dress, however, is how I'm drawn to the photos because of the obvious dynamic between Warner and me. The way he took my hand and led me into the event, or pulled me in by the waist for photos? I wasn't surprised by the actions themselves. We are fake dating, after all; people expect that, and in a way, I expected a little of that myself, too. It would be weird if we *didn't* touch. What I didn't expect, however, was how natural it would feel touching Warner, or having him touch me. It's weird how normal it feels to be tucked into his side, or clutching his arm, or to be on the receiving end of his warm gaze.

Maybe the reason I keep pulling up the photo is because I'm trying to decipher whether it weirds me out that things like that are natural to us. I close out of my photo app, turning off my phone screen and shaking my head. I need to shake some sense into my brain. I don't need to be gazing adoringly at myself and Warner together. We played a role, and so far, it seems to be working. I haven't received a letter from my stalker in about a month.

I try to suppress the worrying voice in the back of my mind that tells me I've gone more than a month before without hearing from him, only to have him pop back into my life, wreaking havoc on my emotional state. I have to have hope that this will work, though.

"And if it doesn't?" Amy asks, eyeing me over her rice bowl. We're crammed into her tiny office, eating lunch with the door closed. Her office will smell like fried rice for the next few days, but she insisted it was worth it to maintain the privacy needed for this conversation.

"I don't know, Ames." I sigh out. "What else can I do?"

"Well, you can go to the police, for starters!" I groan loudly. We've been through this before and she knows it. "I'm seriously worried for you. This isn't normal."

"I know it's not normal, but what can I do? The police aren't going to do anything. He's not threatening me. It's not against the law to be a total creep." I'm not hungry anymore, the tension in this conversation, which I feel like we've had about a hundred times by now, chasing away any appetite I may have had.

"Look, I didn't want to say this to you, because I don't know that it's going to be helpful, but I think it needs to be said. I'm not saying this to scare you either," she starts, and I brace myself for whatever she's going to say next. She sets down her fork carefully, looking me in the eyes. Hers are shiny with unshed tears. "This is stalking, Leesh." I nod. I already know that. "I've watched enough true crime to know that stalking *always* escalates. It always leads to something else."

My heart plummets straight out of my body and through the floor. I've been trying to downplay this whole situation, because I don't want to admit that I am creeped out. I'm angry that this guy has gotten enough of my mental energy. But now, with Amy's words, I realize I am scared. It's not just discomfort, not just an emotion that I can shove down or downplay further. I close my eyes and take a deep breath. I don't want to sit with this emotion. Every cell in my body is bucking against the feeling, wanting to throw it away, outside of my body, to focus on something else. But I can't, because denying how I truly feel helps no one. *Don't control your emotions. It leads to suffering.*

Amy continues talking before I open my eyes. "JJ thinks you should talk to the Foxes security team and see what they think."

My eyes fly open at that. "Absolutely not. No way." I know she and JJ have talked about the stalker and my letters. JJ is the only one of Warner's teammates who knows our relationship isn't real.

"Why not? They're experts in these kinds of things." I give her a skeptical look. "Okay, maybe not this specifically, but they might have some advice or give you something to think about that we haven't considered before. I mean, if nothing else, they can keep an eye out for you when you come to games."

"No." My answer is firm. So firm, in fact, that Amy balks. I feel a little bad; she tends to take things more personally than she should. I soften the blow. "Ames, it's sweet of you to think of me. I appreciate your concern, I really do. But there is no way I'm involving the Foxes in this. It's bad enough I've dragged Warner into this already."

"I don't think you've dragged Warner anywhere he doesn't want to go," she tells me gently. I'm not sure about that. I've upended his life enough as it is, first by moving in, then by foisting this fake dating scheme on him.

I close my container, hoping Amy will take the hint that I am closing this conversation as well. She doesn't fight me on it. She knows me well enough to know that she's said her piece, and I'll reflect on it later. But that doesn't mean I'll change my mind.

"Want a bite?" I offer my spoon, loaded up with peanut butter chocolate chip cookie dough, to Warner, who is seated in the corner of his sectional, his preferred spot on the couch. I'm two cushions away from him, my bare feet propped up on his coffee table, while we watch another action movie. As usual, Warner picked the movie, and as usual, I'm barely paying attention, mindlessly scrolling on my phone.

He levels me with a look of disgust, a frown marring his otherwise flawless features. "Get that salmonella trap out of here."

"It doesn't have salmonella this time!" I insist, leaning over the empty cushions between us and shoving the spoon closer to him. "I made it with applesauce instead of eggs! Danny told me it was an easy substitute, and it totally tastes the same!"

Warner hesitates for all of one second before he grabs the spoon from my hand. Halfway to his mouth, he apparently has his doubts.

"You promise? You're not messing with me and secretly trying to get me to eat raw eggs?" His tone is so serious that I can't help but snort a laugh.

"Why would I try to get you to eat raw eggs?"

"To prove a point that it's not gross?" The spoon is still suspended in midair. A little fleck of the dough falls from the bottom of the spoon and onto his lap. He looks at it with disdain until I put him out of his misery.

"I promise, it's totally egg-free. No tricks. Want me to show you the applesauce jar I bought the other day to prove it to you?" I'm halfway off the couch when Warner acquiesces.

"No, I'll trust you...this time," he adds, shoving the spoon into his mouth. He groans in pleasure. "Shit, this is really good. I forgot how much I love cookie dough."

"Warner James," I say, shaking my finger dramatically at him, "have you been denying yourself cookie dough all this time when you actually love it?"

"I told you, the idea of raw eggs makes me gag," he defends.

"Is the rest of your family as big of food snobs? Is it because your mom is a world-famous chef?"

"I'm not a food snob, I just know what's good and what's gross," he grumbles as he lunges across the couch to steal another scoop of dough from the bowl in my lap. I grab the spoon and pry it from his grip as a bomb explodes in the movie playing in front of us.

"Get your own spoon!" I say as he watches me shove it back into my own mouth. He's lucky I'm even sharing this with him. Cookie dough was practically currency in my house growing up; you don't just give that shit away for free.

Warner heaves himself off the couch, muttering under his breath. When he returns from the kitchen with a new spoon, he seats himself closer to me, pulling the bowl of sugary goodness to rest on the cushion between us.

"Speaking of my family," he starts, almost hesitatingly, "my sister, Eden, usually comes out to visit me a couple times a season. Would you be okay if she comes out next week?"

"What? Of course! Why are you even asking me?"

"Well, because she usually stays here. I can put her up in a hotel though, if it's too much to have her here." Warner ducks his head, like he's almost afraid of my response.

"Don't be ridiculous, of course she can stay here! It's your house!"

"It's your house too, Lee," he starts, before I interrupt him.

"It's not. My name is not on any sort of rental agreement. I barely contribute!" It's not entirely true. We've settled on me purchasing groceries and maintaining a light cleaning schedule, despite Warner rarely eating meals at home and still insisting on a once a month deep clean performed by a professional. I'm still trying to fight against that, but he's just as stubborn as I am on that count.

Warner does that growl thing again, letting me know I'm annoying him. I don't care. Like I told Amy earlier today, I've disrupted his life enough; I'm not about to get in the way of some much-needed family time. Warner hasn't seen his sister since before spring training, and I know they are close.

"I'll see if I can stay with Amy and JJ or Danny and Tim," I say, scooping another spoonful of dough. Before I can get it fully into my spoon, though, Warner is ripping the bowl away and growling again. Seriously, is he some kind of werewolf and tonight is a full moon? What's with the growling?

"You're not going anywhere. Eden can stay in the third bedroom. The kids are staying home with Xavier, my brother-in-law, because they have summer camp. There's no need for you to leave." It's rare that I see Warner this serious, but between the grave look on his face and his incessant need to growl tonight, my resolve is waning.

"It's not just about the physical space. I can give you guys time to hang out alone," I offer softly.

"You're not going anywhere," he says emphatically, pausing between each word to really drive the point home.

"Fine. Jeez. You don't have to be all weird and growly about it," I say, grabbing the bowl and setting it back in its rightful spot between us. He says nothing in response, back to watching the movie with a satisfied look on his face.

After a few minutes, he reminds me I owe him dinner this week. He says it with a smirk on his face, so I can't tell if he's being serious or not.

"I do?" I wrack my brain, trying to remember if we made plans I forgot about. I even pull up my calendar on my phone when Warner's gaze returns to the television.

"Falafel cart at the very least. Extra tzatziki," he reminds me. *Oh, yeah.*

"How about I do you one better?" I offer. "Danny told me about this new French restaurant called Saint Agnes. Wanna try it? I can see if I can get reservations for Wednesday, since you have a day game," I say, referencing the Foxes schedule in the team app.

"Sure, that'd be great. Wanna try around eight o'clock?" he suggests. I pull up the restaurant website and easily make the reservation.

The group of high schoolers I've been working with are scheduled to arrive at the planetarium any minute, so I head to the lobby to wait for them. Chris, one of the daytime security guards, catches me along the way, to let me know construction is going to begin on the terrace outside next week. I already knew that information;

Eva had sent out an email to all educators letting them know. The railings along one side of the terrace overlooking Lake Michigan rusted badly this spring and need to be replaced. Normally, things like building construction don't impact me; the CMA has campuses throughout the city, so finding alternate space has never been an issue. The construction on the planetarium terrace, however, will impact my work, which is why the students are coming today instead of early next week. It's just weird that Chris, as a security guard, is the one sharing that information, since it has little to do with his job. I thank him anyway for the reminder.

The high school students who are participating in an advanced version of the STEM summer camp we offer for younger students arrive soon after. Each month, they take a plethora of meteorological data, tracking the impact of climate change on things like air and water temperature, wind speed, and barometric pressure. They took these readings each month last summer as well, so there's longitudinal data showing potential long-term changes over time. Amy even modeled a lesson after this project for the elementary students she worked with last summer and it was a hit. One day, we're hoping Amy's students will continue enrolling in the STEM summer camps until they become mine. It hasn't happened yet, but now that we've worked together for several years, we're hoping to experience it soon.

Marisol, an upcoming senior, is telling me how she wrote about her experiences to craft her college essay. She hasn't heard back on any of her applications yet; I know it's too early for that, but I'm confident she'll get in everywhere she applies. I said the same thing in my letters of recommendation she requested from me. Her excitement about her applications is palpable. She's hoping to be the first generation in her family to attend college.

With all of the craziness of the CMA and budget cuts, it's moments like today that I'm reminded why I've stuck around even after all the changes. When Marisol returns to her work, I slide my phone out of my pocket and shoot off a text.

Me

> Hey Warn. I just had a really cool moment at work and wanted to say thanks again for letting me live with you. It makes staying on at the CMA, and moments like today, possible. I appreciate you.

I'm a strong believer in spreading gratitude whenever you feel it. I whip out another text to Amy letting her know I appreciate her moral support over the last few months as well. She responds immediately with a gif of Michelle Tanner saying, "You got it, dude." I chuckle to myself. Several minutes pass, in which I assist various groups with their readings and interpreting data, before I get a response from my roommate.

Warner

> You're welcome. It's nice having you around.

Warmth spreads throughout my chest, but somehow it feels different from the feeling I got reading Amy's response. *Weird.*

When I make it home after work, I don't expect Warner to be there. He texted me earlier to let me know he was grabbing dinner with Hayden, Caleb, and Elijah since there was no game scheduled for today. I'm looking forward to a glass of wine and a bubble bath.

So, when I walk into Warner's place and toe off my shoes by the door, I'm surprised to see him sitting on the couch in the living room. He's perched on the edge of the cushion, like he's coiled and ready to pounce. Bent forward, elbows on his knees, he looks up at me when I enter the room. I can't distinguish the look on his face; it's almost like he's deliberately wiped it clean of all emotion.

"Hey, I thought you were getting dinner with the guys?" I ask, taking a seat on the other side of the sectional. Guess I won't be getting in the bath right away.

"I, uh, cancelled," Warner says, clearing his throat. "Lee, we've got to talk."

My heart rate instantly accelerates. No good conversation starts this way, but nothing prepares me for Warner leaning over and pulling a small, mint green envelope from his pocket. Forget my heart racing; I think it stops altogether. He gently places the envelope on the table in front of me, as if handling a bomb.

"I think you should open it," he suggests gently. Why is he being so gentle? I hate it. It's like he's afraid I'm going to lose it, or cry, or have some sort of a breakdown. I pull the letter towards me. It looks the same as always: mint green envelope with chunky block lettering, all capitals. All it says is my first and last name. But somehow, holding it in my hands, it feels different. Heavier. Maybe it's because the reappearance of the letter holds the weight of my disappointment. It shatters the illusion that this fake relationship between me and Warner somehow worked. I tear my eyes away from the note to peek up at Warner. The concern in his eyes makes me want to cry. He's become my friend over the last few months; I should never have dragged him into this. He doesn't need to stress about it.

"Lee," Warner's deep, soothing voice drags me away from my spiraling thoughts. "Do you want to open it? I can do it for you if you want."

It's such a kind offer, to spare me from the contents, that my nose tingles and my eyes prick with the formation of tears. His face softens as he gently tugs the envelope from my grasp. I don't stop him. He slides it open and unfolds the note. Fury flashes across his face before he glances up at me and schools his features into a neutral expression. His reaction alone is enough to scare me.

"What is it?" I say, ashamed to hear a tremble in my voice.

"You don't need to see this." He moves to fold the note back up, standing and turning away from me. Sudden anger spikes through me. I'm not breakable; I can handle my own shit. This is certainly mine—not Warner's—to deal with.

"Let me see it," I say, my voice sharp with resentment. I stand, reaching toward him, fingers outstretched, and when he hesitates, I channel my own inner Warner and growl at him in irritation. Surprise, and maybe a little pride, flits across his face, quickly replaced by wariness. He slowly hands the letter to me and waits as I unfold it.

ALICIA,

YOU'RE CONFUSED. YOU DON'T KNOW WHAT YOU'RE DOING WITH THAT BASEBALL PLAYER, BUT HE'LL NEVER GIVE YOU WHAT I CAN. THE WAY YOU LOOK AT HIM IS NOTHING LIKE THE WAY YOU LOOK AT ME. I'LL SHOW YOU.

YOURS ALWAYS.

It's the longest letter he's ever written to me. Four sentences. Forty-one words. But it's not the words that cause the breath to steal from my lungs. It's the photo that falls to the ground because my trembling fingers can no longer hold on to it. It lands face up on Warner's living room floor, its contents on display for me to see: me, from behind, running along the Chicago River last week.

CHAPTER EIGHTEEN
Warner

Alicia's knees wobble. In an instant, I'm around the coffee table, helping to guide her back on the couch. I don't know what to say or do, so I just sit next to her, my hand on her shoulder, waiting. When I'm reasonably assured she's not going to pass out, I lean forward and pick up the photo. It's clearly her, taken from close range, likely by someone just a few steps away from her. The photo was captured by someone behind her; it's clear the coward caught her unaware. I'm infuriated but now is not the time for my emotions. I need to make sure Alicia is okay. All I want to do is rain hell upon whoever this stalker is, but I need to ensure Alicia is breathing next to me, because she seems so frozen in this moment, that I'm not sure she remembers *how* to breathe.

"Breathe, Lee. You have to breathe," I instruct, turning the photo over. For some reason, it makes sense to remove the evidence from her line of sight. She pulls in a shaky, gasping breath. "Good girl. More. Keep breathing." I feel stupid and helpless telling her to breathe, but it seems to be working. I rub gentle circles on her shoulder, hoping to somehow soothe her with my touch.

Eventually, she starts to process everything aloud. She's trembling beneath my hand, shoulders shaking, but once she begins speaking, I realize she is not trembling in fear, but with rage.

"What the *fuck* kind of person does this? Follows me? Takes my picture? What do they want me to do–read their letters and fall in love with them?" I assume her questions are rhetorical. I don't have a response anyway. She continues raging, yelling about what a waste of oxygen, what a pathetic excuse for a human this stalker is. How his parents clearly never loved him, how he's never known the touch of a woman, how he is such a coward he wouldn't know what to do with her if they were to talk in real life. I don't disagree with her. I let her spill all her anger into the living room. She's like an open wound, unable to stop bleeding. Vitriol spews from her mouth as she rages against the disgusting, vile scum who is stalking her.

It's at this moment I realize that I've been, on some level in my mind, treating Alicia like a delicate thing. She is no delicate flower, she's a tigress. Powerful. Protective. Fierce.

Let it all out, sweetheart.

After several minutes, Alicia's rage dwindles, replaced by wracking sobs. I'd be alarmed if I wasn't feeling the same emotions myself. Frustration and fear war within her, culminating in body shaking tremors as she cries harder than I've seen anyone else cry. I shouldn't be surprised; Alicia experiences all her emotions to a heightened degree. She's in tune with herself and lets herself feel so deeply. I pull her into my arms, clutching her upper body to my chest and swinging both legs into my lap. Neither of us say anything else; she just cries while I rock her, and she clings to me.

It takes several hours for Alicia to fully calm herself. There are times when she is so quiet, I think she has possibly fallen asleep, only to feel her begin to softly cry against me once more. My heart breaks for her. I want to take all of this on instead of her, so she never has to feel an ounce of this again. I want to tell her she shouldn't run by herself again, that she should take more precautions, that she should have someone stay with her when I'm out of town, but I stop myself. Because there's not a damn thing different that Alicia should have to do. This sick fucker, whoever he is, needs to be the one changing.

When her cries dissolve into a series of yawns, I know she's hit her limit for the night. Never releasing my grip from her, I push to stand and carry her to her bedroom, lying her softly in bed. Her tired, red rimmed eyes crack my heart open a little more as she looks at me in gratitude and sorrow.

"I'm sorry you missed your dinner," she tells me apologetically. I shake my head.

"I'm not. I'm where I need to be. I'm going to get you some water, then you get some rest, okay? I'm not going anywhere. I'll be here all night." I've barely pulled her bedroom door shut before I'm pulling my phone from my shorts and getting to work.

My first call is to Manny, who is technically off shift tonight, he tells me. However, once I tell him the situation, he offers to come in to help figure things out. There's nothing he can do, but I thank him and fire off a call to Rosalie, who assures me she did not see anything out of the ordinary during today's mail delivery.

My next call is to building security. The dispatcher is hesitant to connect me to a supervisor without knowing details of the case, which I'm not going to divulge to just anyone. I tell her who I am, not bothering to do so with any modesty. I'm not one to throw around my name or my status as an athlete; I don't believe in doing that sort of thing unless necessary. I haven't found a situation in which it's been necessary until now, but it worked. The dispatcher connects me to a supervisor named Vincent. I explain our situation. Vincent promises to investigate the security tapes and call me back within the next few hours.

While I wait for Vincent's call, I dial Eric, one of the security team members at the ballpark. While technically not law enforcement, I'd trust Eric and his business partners with my life–and we often do, as they travel with us to all our road games. Eric advises me to have Alicia go to the police. While tonight's letter didn't include a direct threat, it's a clear escalation. He agrees that starting an official paper trail with the cops is a good start. He promises to increase the security presence around Alicia during games and events she attends. She's going to hate that. I make Eric promise that security will be as surreptitious as possible around her, not because I don't want her to know, but because I want her to feel as comfortable as possible. This fucker has disrupted her life enough as it is; I don't want her to feel even more off kilter by the presence of security at the ballpark too. Eric says he'll talk with his team in the morning, updating them of the situation and determining if there's anything else that can be done on their end. I thank him, recognizing that I'm very lucky to be able to know so many people who can help.

I pace the apartment waiting for Vincent's call, wracking my brain to figure out what more I can do. Eden will be in town next week; if nothing else, she can keep Alicia company when I'm gone at work.

Shit. Now I'm starting to worry that Eden could be unsafe if whoever this stalker is corners them when they're together. I take a few deep breaths and rationalize that if this guy is too much of a coward to directly approach Alicia, there's no way he will do it when she's with another person. I hope.

An hour later, my phone rings. I almost drop it in my haste to answer it, and Vincent's voice greets me.

"Mr. James. I was able to find the person I believe you're looking for on our surveillance tapes. Unfortunately, in all the shots from today, he's unrecognizable under sunglasses and a hat. He appears to be white, average height, large build. No other distinguishing features that I can tell from today's footage. However, I will personally be reviewing the security footage from the last several months to see if we can find other angles. I assure you, we will do everything we can to figure out who is terrorizing your girlfriend."

"Thank you," I say, my breath catching when he calls Alicia my girlfriend. *Oh, yeah, everyone thinks we're together.* "Do you have any idea how he is getting the letters in our box?"

Vincent clears his throat. "It looks like he had a key," he says, with the air of someone delivering bad news.

"*What.*" I don't phrase it as a question. My voice is deadly calm. "How is that possible?"

"Mr. James, I'm not sure, but please believe I will be having the handyman replace your mailbox first thing in the morning. I can personally deliver the new set of keys to your unit tomorrow."

I nod, even though Vincent can't see me. He clears his throat again, and I brace myself for whatever he's about to tell me next.

"Sir, because we don't know how he's gotten the mailbox key, it's possible he has access to more than just the mailbox." Icy fingers of panic sluice down my body. "I would recommend you replace all your locks. I can have one of my men stop by first thing in the morning to do so as well, if you'd like?"

"Yes. I don't care about the cost. I want the most secure locks, including on the terrace slider." I highly doubt this guy is going to Spiderman his way up onto my penthouse terrace and attempt to enter my unit from the outside, but I'm taking no chances.

"Consider it done."

After hanging up with Vincent, I put a dining room chair under the door handle of our front door. I bring my pillow, a few extra blankets, and a spare baseball bat to the couch in the living room. While my bedroom isn't that far from the front door, I'd rather be closer to it just in case anyone tries anything before the locks are replaced. I make one final phone call before allowing myself to drift off into a fitful, restless sleep. It's that phone call that once again reminds me why Samuel Benjamin is every player's favorite coach.

Chapter Nineteen

Alicia

I wake the next morning feeling hungover, despite knowing I hadn't had a drop of alcohol last night. My emotions were all over the place last night, and to be honest, they still are this morning. My head is pounding, my eyes are drier than the Sahara, and my throat is raw. I slept like the dead, though. Checking the time on my phone, I realize it's late morning and Warner is likely already gone for the day. That's probably for the best, since I'm not sure I'm ready to face him after the world's most epic meltdown last night.

I sit up in bed and take the next several minutes to close my eyes and meditate. I prefer to start and end my day with meditation, even if it's brief. I breathe in deeply, attempting to calm the emotions swirling inside of me. I perform a detailed body scan, taking note of any pockets of tension and visualizing my muscles relaxing. Finally, after a few minutes, I stretch and get out of bed.

I pad to the kitchen, planning to start the coffee maker before brushing my teeth. Halfway there, however, I freeze, hearing voices in the apartment. I experience momentary terror; no one else should be here right now. When I hear Warner's deep rumble, my body instantly relaxes. Wandering into the kitchen, I strain my ears to hear what he's saying.

"I appreciate you coming right away. Obviously, this couldn't wait."

"I completely understand your concern," an unfamiliar voice responds, followed by a whirring sound. My curiosity can't take it anymore. I poke my head out of the kitchen and into the front hall, where Warner stands, arms crossed, speaking to an enormous bald man. Behind them, a gray-haired handyman is drilling into the front door. Warner must catch my movement out of the corner of his eye, because he turns, his face softening when he locks eyes with me.

"I'm sorry, did we wake you?" he asks, walking over to me, his eyes filled with genuine concern. I must look like an absolute mess.

"No, I didn't know you were home. Why aren't you at work?" I whisper. Mindful of the men in the hall, I tug my sleep shorts further down my legs, attempting to cover up.

"I needed to be here for this. I'm replacing all the locks in here and we're getting a new mailbox key, too." I swallow, already regretting making him go to such trouble for me. There's no way he's coincidentally doing this the day after I received another letter. "Don't go looking guilty, Lee. I'm happy to do this. It needed to be done. Come on, I want to introduce you to someone."

I follow him back to the front hall, where he introduces me to the giant of a man hulking in the foyer. Completely bald, but in an attractive yet intimidating manner, with a nose that has clearly been broken more than once, tattoos covering the expanse of his thickly muscled arms, the man would be terrifying in any context other than standing supportively behind my roommate.

"Alicia, this is Vincent Coyle, head of security for the Vandeveer. Vincent, this is my girlfriend, Alicia Langley." I try to keep my facial expressions neutral, so I don't betray my surprise upon hearing Warner call me his girlfriend. He pulls me to his side by my waist. Like it did during photos at the Foxes Foundation night, it feels natural. Comfortable. Warner continues talking to Vincent, promising to share my contact information with him so I have a direct line to him, especially when Warner is out of town. My throat feels tight. It's too much, everything Warner is doing for me. I can practically guarantee no other resident of the Vandeveer has Vincent Coyle's personal phone number. I'm equally sure that Warner is paying extra for that access.

"Oh, it's okay, you don't have to do that," I mumble. "I'm sure I'll be fine."

"It's not a problem at all, Ms. Langley. Mr. James has informed me of your situation, and I can assure you, we're doing everything we can on our end to get to the bottom of this. In addition to replacing your front door access, we'll be adding additional security measures to the terrace door and penthouse elevators. Of course, we'll have to inform," Vincent checks his phone, "Mrs. Chan and Mr. and Mrs. Parker, of the elevator updates." Warner nods.

"All of this really isn't necessary, Warn," I start, discomfort prickling my skin. "I don't want to inconvenience anyone."

"Your safety is not an inconvenience." Warner's words hold a finality to them, and paired with the serious look on his face, I know there's no use arguing with him.

"I have to agree, ma'am. That's what we're here for," Vincent adds. Warner's gaze travels to Vincent, then back to me. His eyes spark with mischief as he pulls me closer to him, placing a soft kiss against my temple and squeezing my waist.

What. Just. Happened.

When I see Vincent's eyes crinkle into a smile, transforming his face from hard and intimidating to soft and squishy, I remember Warner is putting on a show. Selling the relationship. Of course. My face flames in embarrassment, not from the chaste little peck Warner gave me, but because for half a heartbeat, I thought it, too, was a natural, genuine action.

"I'm, um, gonna go make some coffee." I step backwards.

Warner winks at me. "Way ahead of you, Lee. It's already made."

"Oh. Thanks." I feel my cheeks flush further. What is wrong with me? I need to get out of here. Suddenly there isn't enough air in the front hallway. I turn the corner into the kitchen. As soon as I'm out of eyesight, I practically run to the bathroom under the guise of brushing my teeth. With the bathroom door shut firmly behind me, I splash some water on my face and take a deep breath, asking myself yet again, what is wrong with me?

Chapter Twenty

Warner

S hit.

I hope I didn't make Alicia uncomfortable by kissing her in front of Vincent. I don't know what I was thinking. I *wasn't* thinking. It just felt so natural to lean over and kiss her, to comfort her. We don't even touch each other as platonic friends. We haven't even talked about whether we're going to continue our fake dating plan, since it clearly hasn't been working so far. But when I saw her folding in on herself, getting nervous about people taking her safety seriously (as they should), I couldn't help it. I needed to assuage her guilt over allowing others to help her.

At least I played it off like it was an intentional, planned act to sell the relationship to Vincent. The last thing I want to do is make Alicia uncomfortable with her living situation, because moving out now, when she's at her most vulnerable, would be a disaster. I internally debate whether I should go after her and apologize or just let it go and pretend it never happened. Seeing as Vincent and his handyman will likely be here for a few more hours, I opt for the latter. I don't want to risk anyone overhearing anything they shouldn't.

I post up in the dining room, answering emails and staying out of Vincent's way while remaining near enough for him to find me if needed. Alicia eventually joins me, a mug of coffee in one hand and a plate of her disgusting bagel combination in the other. She doesn't say anything about the kiss either, so I guess we're both pretending it didn't happen. Besides, I rationalize to myself, it was a peck on the temple, barely more than a hug. It's not like I *really* kissed her; then we'd both be in trouble.

"Are you going to get in trouble for not being at work on time?" she asks, interrupting my thoughts. It's a good thing, too, because those were starting to go down a confusing path.

"Nah," I chuckle. "I talked to Benny last night. I hope you don't mind that I told him what was going on." Her eyes flash and she whips her head around, looking to see if Vincent and his handyman are within hearing distance. "Relax," I assure her. "Not everything. But he knows about the letters and the one you got yesterday. He knows I'll likely not make it to the ballpark today if they aren't done here in enough time. He's taken me out of the lineup today. They're going to call it right hamstring soreness and list me as day to day."

Alicia's eyes enlarge in panic. "You're missing the *game*? You can't miss the game!"

"I just told you, Benny took me out of the lineup. Missing the game is no big deal now."

"Wrong," she says flatly, pushing her plate away from her. "You can't do this. I won't let you rearrange your life for me, for this!" She spreads her arms wide, as if to indicate everything that I'm allegedly rearranging because of her.

"Lee, it's already done. I'm happy to do it. Benny is happy to do it. Please let us take care of you. We just want you to feel safe, to *be* safe. Besides, it's just one day. I'll be back in the lineup tomorrow and no one's the wiser."

"But you're pretending to be injured for me!" she hisses, stealing another furtive glance over her shoulder.

I laugh. "Okay, now that you mention it, I think my right hamstring *is* a little sore this morning." She narrows her eyes at me. "I should probably sit out for today's game. Don't want to make it worse or anything." Her mouth is pressed into a thin line of annoyance, but there's nothing she can do about it. I'm enjoying this because, at least right now, Alicia is safe and here with me.

"Don't be mad at me, Lee," I say, poking her in the ribs with my index finger. She squirms away from me.

"I'm not mad at you. I'm just...frustrated. Sad. Annoyed. Tired. Really fucking exhausted." I nod.

"Then take the day. Nap, relax, watch movies. Take a bubble bath. Do what you need to do to keep kicking ass and restart again tomorrow. But might I suggest you let your parents in on what's going on, at least a little?" I hate the idea of Alicia struggling through this mostly alone. I know Amy, Danny, and Tim are finally aware of the situation, but I feel like her parents should at least know some of what's going on. Eden and JJ are my only friends who know the full picture, fake dating included, and I've learned the hard way that not leaning on your loved ones can be painful and isolating. I have no idea what the Langleys know–about the stalking or even about me.

"Yeah, you're right," she huffs a resigned sigh. "I guess I'll call them today and fill them in."

"Do you want to make the phone call together? I can help," I offer and the look of hope and gratitude she gives me in response makes me want to hug her. One of these days, I'll get her used to asking for and accepting help from others.

Vincent clears his throat. He stands at the threshold to the dining room, phone in hand. "Ms. Langley, Mr. James. I'm sorry to interrupt. Do you want to see the footage of the man who put the letter in your mailbox? I have it here, although I'm not sure how much you'll be able to see. Perhaps you will recognize him?"

I watch the color slowly drain from Alicia's face. Her slate eyes are wide. I wish there was a way that only I could look at it and determine who the guy is, even though I know that's not possible.

"Yeah. Show me," she says quietly, but not weakly. I'm yet again reminded of her ferocity.

Vincent steps to the table, placing his phone down and pressing play on the video he's cued up. It's a black and white shot of the lobby in the middle of the day. The sun is streaming in from the floor to ceiling windows as people mill about. Together, we watch as a heavy-set man in a bucket hat and sunglasses walks to the bank of mailboxes and out of the shot. Vincent swipes and a new video appears. He clicks play again, and we watch the same man walk to the mailboxes, open ours, drop in a small envelope, and close it again before walking out of the shot. It's bold and confident, no sign of hesitation in the man's movements. He doesn't look over his shoulder or act suspicious in any way. For some reason, that infuriates me. Vincent was right, though. The man is virtually unrecognizable. He seems to be average height, and other than his weight, there is nothing remarkable about him. His face is obscured by the hat and glasses. No tattoos or other distinguishable markings are apparent.

I'm not surprised when Alicia murmurs, "I have no idea who that is." Vincent swipes again, this time to an isolated screenshot of the video we just watched.

"This is the best angle I've been able to get," he admits. The man's chin is tipped down, further obscuring his face. The isolated photo doesn't give us any more information than the videos. Alicia's disappointment is palpable as she slowly shakes her head no. "It's okay, Ms. Langley. You're doing a great job. I've been doing security work for more than thirty years; this isn't my first time dealing with a stalker, and unfortunately, it likely won't be my last. What I've found is that many stranger stalkers–that is, when the stalker is unknown to the victim," Alicia flinches at the term and Vincent softens his approach. "When people don't outright know who is harassing them, the perpetrator is often someone they had an innocuous form of contact with. Someone they stood in line next to at the bank, a neighbor they said hello to once, a former coworker they barely interacted with. I'm not saying that to scare you," he says, picking up on Alicia's shallower breathing. "I'm saying that it's not a surprise if you don't know him. That doesn't mean we're not going to do everything we can to continue to keep you safe." He stresses the word "continue," and I'm grateful for it. Alicia is currently safe, and if Vincent or I have our say, she will stay that way.

Vincent and his handyman finish sooner than anticipated. After rekeying the front door and reinforcing the glass slider locks, they installed an additional security system that should alert not only Vincent and his company, but the front desk and the Chicago Police Department, if the panic button is hit or the code is not entered soon enough after a breach. Vincent explained that breaches consist of shattered glass, manual breakage of the lock mechanisms, or disarming of the wired system on the terrace doors. When he took us around our unit, explaining all the upgrades, Alicia muttered something about overkill, but Vincent and I pointedly ignored her.

Now that he's gone, Alicia is pacing the kitchen, preparing to call her parents. They live outside of Los Angeles, so they are two hours behind us. It should be mid-morning for them. She explained both of her parents have worked from home since the pandemic, so reaching both at once should be simple enough, but it seems to make her more nervous.

"I don't know, there's something worse about telling my parents together. My mom will probably try to hide her panic while my dad will go into straight protector mode, and there's nothing either of them can do." She's probably right on a practical level, but she's forgetting the emotional support both can provide once they're fully apprised of the situation. She pauses her pacing, setting her phone on the island. I stand from the barstool I've been sitting on while watching her pace.

"You can do this," I tell her, rubbing her upper arms. She takes a deep breath, looking resolutely at her phone. She taps on her contacts, and I step away, allowing her some room to continue pacing if that's what she needs. She turns the phone on speaker, and it only takes two rings before her mother's melodic voice is answering.

"Uh, hey, Mom. How are you?" Alicia engages in small talk for a few minutes, and I try not to make it seem like I'm eavesdropping on their catching up. I pick at a stray hangnail on my thumb. Finally, Alicia comes around to the reason for her call. "Is Dad around, too? It's probably easier if I talk to both of you at the same time for what I'm about to say next."

Mrs. Langley immediately picks up on the change in her daughter's tone. "Is everything okay?" When Alicia doesn't respond, she continues, "I'm getting your father right now."

"Thanks, Mom," Alicia says, and I notice a slight wobble to her chin. I give her a small, supportive smile. She takes a few deep breaths, trying to compose herself.

"Okay, we're both here," Alicia's mother reports. There's shuffling in the background, followed by Alicia's father giving a quiet hello.

"You guys are on speakerphone, too. Warner is here with me. You guys remember me talking about my roommate?" Internally, I bristle at the title. I'd like to think we're more than just roommates at this point, but now is not the time.

"Of course. Hi, Warner," Alicia's mother says warmly. Alicia takes another deep breath, one I mirror myself, steeling myself to potentially have to take over the conversation. Alicia looks a little pale; I'm not sure her breathing is as regulated as she'd like it to be.

"Mom, Dad. I've got a bit of a problem here in Chicago," Alicia starts, then seems to regret opening the conversation that way. "I'm okay," she hurries to add. "But, um, for the last year or so, someone has been sending me letters." She pauses, tilting her head back to the ceiling and blinking back tears. I want to wrap my arms around her and protect her forever. Someone so kind and vibrant should not have to go through this. She spends the next twenty minutes filling them in and answering their questions. They responded as I would have expected, with concern and alarm, but Alicia wouldn't let them come visit and refused to agree to come home to them either. She's tired of having her life upended by this guy and I can't blame her. Alicia ends the call with promises to keep them updated, but did not divulge anything about our relationship, real or fake.

"Do you want me to cancel Eden's trip? I can have her come some other time, or stay elsewhere?" I offer.

"Don't you dare!" she responds with such vehemence that I know the subject is closed. "Warner, I'm tired of this asshole impacting my life. I don't want extra security, I don't want to change my marathon training, or my work hours, or my social life in any way! I want to have at least a little bit of normalcy. Please." Her plea kills me. I know she's right. Because while this stalker hasn't touched her or threatened her, he has upended her sense of peace, of normalcy. I want to do whatever I can to give that back to her.

"Okay," I agree. "I won't tell her to change her trip."

"And no more faking injuries, or going in to work late, or spending money on this situation!"

"Mmm," I hum, neither promising her anything nor disagreeing.

"I mean it, Warner!" Her eyes flash, but having Alicia annoyed at me is better than seeing the despair that was written on her face while talking to her parents, so I'll take it. Yeah, faking an injury to the public or missing work aren't habits I'd like to repeat, but I'll do it again if necessary. There's nothing she can do about how I choose to spend my money, though.

"So does that mean we're still on for Saint Agnes tonight?"

Alicia's tone is much more subdued when she responds. "I kind of forgot about it with everything going on. It would be nice to get out of the house and return to normalcy a bit," she admits sheepishly.

"Then we're on," I tell her with a wink. I can't help the sense of pride I feel in my chest at her responding blush.

CHAPTER TWENTY-ONE

Alicia

After finally shoving Warner out the door after noon, I took a bath and spent most of it meditating and sorting through my feelings. While I don't have a plan for dealing with the stalker, my emotions are organized enough where I feel like I can start to tackle a strategy moving forward. Starting with whether Warner and I are going to keep up this fake dating charade.

I don't have strong feelings on the subject one way or another. In a way, the lie is still convenient for me. I have no doubt it's only because of Warner's status that security personnel asked, "how high?" when Warner told them to jump last night. Would Vincent Coyle's phone number be saved in my phone if I weren't romantically or otherwise attached to Warner James? Doubtful.

On the other hand, I'm sure I don't fully understand just how inconvenient this lie is for Warner. It's bad enough I've encroached upon his living space. I know I'm messing up his dating opportunities the longer we keep this going. He's wasting time, money, and energy on me when I know he's got much better ways to channel those things. For those reasons alone, I'll have to call it off with him. I might as well talk to him about it over dinner tonight.

When we originally made the reservation at Saint Agnes, we factored in additional time for rain delays or extra innings. Considering Warner didn't even play in today's game, I shouldn't be surprised to see him home so early, but I am. With the extra flexibility in his schedule today, he suggests we arrive at dinner early to check out the bar and order some drinks. Apparently, it's a tradition the James family established once he and Eden were old enough to drink. Anita James enjoys the full restaurant experience, he explains with a chuckle. I rarely need convincing to try a new cocktail.

When we arrive and explain to the hostess we would like to grab a drink before our scheduled reservation time, she ushers into the dimly lit bar. Small glass bottles with flammable oil alight each high-top table and periodically dot the bartop. Rich dark wood paneling surrounds the intimate room and deep cobalt suede covers the high-backed bar stools surrounding the shiny bar. Gold decorative trinkets are interspersed across high shelves, scattered artfully among displays of fancy liquor bottles. Tasteful nude French art splays across the jewel toned walls. The entire place feels elevated, classy, sophisticated.

Warner pulls out one of the remaining bar seats for me. After I sit, he settles himself in the chair beside me, angling his seat towards me and handing me the bar menu. While we wait for the bartender to mix our drinks, we fall into easy conversation.

"I think I'm a little more settled about the situation. I took a lot of time to sort out my feelings today. I unpacked a lot, but I think I should have more of a plan now that things are escalating," I start, sipping the dirty martini the bartender places in front of me.

"*We* should have more of a plan," Warner corrects gently. I ignore his comment; what I really want to do is roll my eyes.

"Anyway," I plow on. "I'm not sure how to move forward, beyond what you've already done for me." I catch movement out of the corner of my eye. A blonde woman who looks barely old enough to drink at this bar is not so subtly trying to take a photo of Warner. The flash obnoxiously goes off, making her paparazzi attempts obvious. Warner is gracious and ignores it. I cringe. I'm feeling extra sensitive about nonconsensual photos these days. Warner must sense my discomfort; he moves his chair closer to me and angles his body in a way that mostly blocks my face from the woman's camera. I give him a weak smile and he leans in further, resting his arm on the back of my chair and blocking me fully from the offending shutterbug.

"Warn, you've been incredibly supportive to me, but I hate how much you're going out of your way for me. Last night and this morning were too much." My comment sounds full of innuendo, and my cheeks flush. Warner smirks. This conversation is going off the rails.

"I'm happy to support you," he says. Then, in a quieter voice only I can hear, "It's what friends do." I nod, preparing to make my case. I sip in another mouthful of gin before I forge ahead with what I came here to say.

"I know it is, but I feel like I've taken over your life. I feel like I'm not holding up my end of things here. You've done so much for me. Don't get me wrong, I am so grateful for you. But you're not getting anything out of this deal."

Another flash goes off, followed by a giggle from the blonde. Jesus Christ, does she have to be so obvious? Warner again ignores it but grasps my chin when I try to look away from his blazing gaze.

"I'm not getting anything out of this deal?" he asks quietly, almost dangerously. I've never seen him like this, and I can't place the emotion on his face. He's full of coiled intensity; he seems almost angry, but I can't understand why. "I told you, I like taking care of you, Lee. But don't tell me I get nothing out of being around you, making sure you're safe and looked after."

"But that's not your job," I insist quietly. "We don't have to keep doing this. I can't help but feel like I'm putting your life on hold, interrupting your routine. Invading your house and preventing you from dating, and–"

"Shut up, Lee." I'm stunned into silence. Warner has never said an unkind word to me; in fact, I don't think I've ever heard him say anything unkind or disrespectful to *anyone*.

After a moment, I sputter, "Warner! What–" My chin still in his gentle grasp, he interrupts me with a bruising kiss, the force of his lips so at odds with the tender way he holds my face.

I'm frozen in my seat wondering what is happening. Has Warner been body snatched? Have I been dropped into an alternate reality? My mind is whirring a thousand miles a minute, and I still can't make sense of his actions. He licks the seam of my lips and automatically, subconsciously, I open for him. My shoulders deflate as I relax into the most confusing, delicious kiss of my entire life. I don't understand what's happening, but my body is here for it. Goosebumps break out on my bare arms, and I repress a shiver of pleasure as his tongue lightly strokes mine. The commotion of the bar around us ceases to exist, all chatter and clanging of silverware muted in the background. Then, seemingly as abruptly as it began, Warner is gently pulling away, lightly sucking on my bottom lip as he retreats. I'm left breathless as the chaos of the bar springs back to life and into my consciousness.

Another camera flash goes off and it all makes sense.

Of course. Warner is still playing his part. And me? I'm not sure what I'm doing. I'm currently leaning toward him in my seat, cheeks flushed, eyes probably dilated, as if I'm desperately seeking another kiss. *Pathetic.*

I excuse myself, feigning the need for the restroom as I slide off my barstool. I wobble slightly as I get to my feet, inwardly cursing my body's complete and total malfunctioning in response to one measly Warner James kiss.

Chapter twenty-two

Warner

Eden's flight touches down ten minutes early, which means I'm just rolling up to the arrivals pickup at O'Hare when she walks outside, pulling her carry-on luggage behind her. I throw the car in park and practically leap out to get to her. It has been far too long since I've seen my family. I grip her in a tight bear hug, letting her warmth and familiarity flow through me. Everyone has their person, someone for whom they would bury a body, and Eden is mine. I know I'm hers too. Although, to be fair, she'd probably kill for her husband and kids, too.

"Warner. I love you, but I kind of need my lungs to breathe," she jokes, pushing me off her and rubbing her ribs dramatically. I take her suitcase and lift it easily into the trunk of my Range Rover. I can't help the smile plastered on my face. I needed her visit, and not just so there can be a buffer between the awkwardness creeping in on our apartment since I accidentally kissed Alicia.

Well, accidentally isn't quite accurate.

I couldn't stop thinking about her all day at work on Wednesday, but I brushed it off as nerves about her spending the day alone after receiving another letter and the photograph. What I couldn't rationalize, however, was the feeling I had walking in the door that evening and seeing her there. She's usually home when I get back from work, but somehow, this felt different. Then, when we were having drinks at the bar, I couldn't help but get closer to her. I wanted to blame it on the alcohol, but I was only half a drink deep when I started looking for excuses to get close to her, to touch her. She looked incredible, all tan skin and minimal makeup. Her lips looked positively edible; I haven't been able to stop thinking about them since she wore that damn red lipstick to the Foxes Foundation event.

Then she started spewing nonsense about me not getting anything out of our deal. I didn't wait to hear if she meant our friendship or this dating scheme, but I didn't care because it doesn't matter. I enjoy spending time with Alicia–I'm thrilled to be able to be there for her and support her in any way she needs, and I get a weird kick out of being able to protect her, even if she's not used to all the attention. The flare of annoyance I felt about her feeling like she was anything but fucking perfect was instant and the only thing I could think to do to shut her up was to kiss her.

So, no, the kiss wasn't accidental. And no, I still don't regret it.

Alicia came back from the restroom looking artificially spunky and happy and said nothing more on the matter, so I didn't push it. So now I've been stewing on it for two days and have no idea if I've made the most colossal mistake of my life, or if we're able to move past it and be friends. So far, I've taken her lead and pretended the kiss was just for that fan repeatedly taking our picture. It was annoying at the time, but it might just be the excuse I needed to play off the kiss as nothing more than reaffirming to that fucker out there that just because he ups the ante with his creepy amateur photographer skills doesn't mean we're backing out of our relationship.

Which brings up another issue. I feel like a piece of human garbage taking advantage of a situation that is so fucked up. Alicia didn't ask to be stalked. She didn't ask to be terrorized. And my fucking response is to want to feel her up? God, I'm such a selfish asshole.

To say that I'm relieved Eden is here to serve as an emotional buffer over the next several days is an understatement. I'm hoping her presence will chill me out and mellow whatever confusing feelings fake dating Alicia is bringing up. The good news is that despite the maelstrom of confusion I live in these days, my on-field performance has never been better. This afternoon's game resulted in a win, and I know my diving catch in the fifth is already replaying on sports highlights nationwide.

When Eden and I get inside, Lee is nowhere to be found. I feel a stab of annoyance, hoping she didn't change her mind about staying here this weekend. I meant what I said about her not being in the way. I offer Eden a glass of wine, which she readily accepts, and we walk out onto the patio to catch up. There's a light breeze that gently ruffles her hair. The summer sun is setting and the view from the terrace is incredible.

Eden is just finishing a story about Dominic and Daisy's summer camp adventures when I hear Alicia shut the front door. Immediately, I'm flooded with relief that she's still staying here, rather than falling back on her original plan to double up with Danny and Tim this weekend.

"Hey, Warn! I'm home," she calls, clearly unsure of where we are. "I picked up some pizzas. I wasn't sure if you guys had eaten or if you were wanting to go out, but no one hates leftover pizza, so I figured I couldn't go wrong."

Eden and I walk inside as Alicia is sliding the pizzas onto the stove. She tosses her purse on the counter and catches sight of us. She squeals, running over and almost knocking Eden over in her haste to embrace her.

"Eden! I'm so glad you're here! I've been so excited to meet you in real, three-dimensional life!" Alicia's excitement is genuine and contagious. Eden meets my eye when she's finally released from her grasp and smiles. I knew they would get along well.

"Thanks for grabbing the pizzas, Lee." I tell her softly. "Alfredo's?"

She fakes a scoff. "As if there's any other kind." She begins pulling plates from the cabinets and setting them on the counter. I uncork a bottle of tempranillo and pour a generous glass for Alicia, sliding it to her while she opens the pizza boxes. Tempranillo is her favorite to go with pizza. I move to the fridge to pull out the rosé Eden and I are drinking and top off our glasses. Eden's face is inscrutable; I quirk an eyebrow at her as if to ask her thoughts.

"Nothing," she murmurs, her face a picture of mock innocence. "It's nice that you know each other so well. I'm glad you're not getting too lonely in this giant apartment."

We eat at the dining room table, making plans to go to the Garfield Conservatory on Monday on my off day. Eden and Alicia insist it's the most gorgeous indoor greenhouse in the city and even if I hated plants, I'd have no hope arguing against them when they gang up on me. Which they unfortunately do next, as Alicia tells Eden that I'm barely paying attention to the precious houseplants she gifted me. I narrow my eyes playfully at Alicia for giving away my secrets, but I could never be mad at her.

"It's a good thing some of these plants thrive on neglect," Alicia points out. "Eden, tell me you name your plants." She has a gleam in her eye as she talks to my sister; Alicia is officially in her element.

"Name them?" Eden asks.

"Oh, yes. I name all my plants! Warner even let me name his plants!" I can practically see her vibrating with excitement; Eden might be her first plant friend. Eden has no idea what she's gotten herself into.

"Did he now?" Eden asks slowly, turning to face me, eyebrows quirked in amusement. I shrug.

"This one here is Khaleesi," she says, gesturing to a tall, sort of spiky topped tree in the corner of the dining room. Eden snorts, clearly understanding a joke that I don't get.

"I love it. Khaleesi the dracaena. Very clever." At my look of confusion, Eden rolls her eyes. "Dracaena, dragon? Khaleesi from Game of Thrones?" She sighs. "Alicia is funny as shit. I like her," she tells me. Then, turning to Alicia, "You should stick around."

The girls make plans to go to the games together this weekend. It will be nice for my sister to have someone to sit with in the stands. Secretly, I'm a little relieved Eden will be there as an extra precaution against anyone who might approach Alicia or make her uncomfortable. My sister takes no prisoners.

After dinner, Alicia insists she's too tired to have a drink with us on the terrace, opting to read in bed instead. We don't plan to stay up too much later; weekend day games require me to be at the ballpark early. I've barely sat down on the outdoor couch before Eden is eyeing me suspiciously. Her feet are propped up on the table while she spins the stem of her wine glass in her hand. She's the picture of relaxation, but the look she's giving me makes me nervous, like I'm a bug under a microscope.

"What?" I defend, shifting uncomfortably under the weight of Eden's examination.

"I see the way you look at that girl," she starts.

"What girl?" I feign confusion, but we both know who she's talking about. I also know my sister well enough to know where she's going with this conversation. She's been bugging me for years to settle down. I'm proud of my attempts to rebuff her thus far.

"Warn, you know who," she says gently. It's her gentle tone that alarms me more than anything else. It's quiet and almost...sad. "You care about her."

I'm conscious of my fidgeting now, but I can't stop. "She's my friend and my roommate. Of course I care about her," I say simply, hoping that will be enough for my sister to drop the subject. I'm grateful Alicia's room is the furthest from where we are sitting on the patio; there is minimal risk of her overhearing anything.

"Warner, *I'm* your friend. Matteo Cota is your friend. You've never looked at either one of us the way you look at Alicia."

"And thank goodness for that!" I quip, hoping my light tone is enough to distract from her scrutiny. My joke inadvertently tips my hand, though, because I don't deny the way I look at Alicia.

I've thought about it so much lately. Too much lately. About what it might look like if this thing between Alicia and me was real. The thought simultaneously thrills and terrifies me. It warms my heart until reality inevitably hits like a bucket of ice water thrown over my head. Alicia deserves so much more than anything I have to offer her. I rein in all thoughts of her as anything more than a friend.

"E, Alicia is good. Just pure goodness in human form. She deserves more than me."

She stares at me, eyes filling with unshed tears. "Warner, you are the best damn man I know. The best," she insists, but I know that's what sisters are supposed to say. I don't doubt her love for me, but she gets to see the highlight reel of my life, not the daily reality. If she spent day in, day out with me, she'd come to realize what I already know: Alicia is too good for me.

When I don't say anything for several minutes, Eden clears her throat. "Are you seeing anybody?" Instantly, I know that she isn't referring to my dating life, and my skin prickles with discomfort. I'm too tired to go down this road with her tonight.

"No, E, I'm not. And I don't have the energy to fight about this with you right now," I sigh out, draining the last of my wine. I've already had too much; I try not to drink a lot before a day game.

"I'm just saying, it might help you sort out your feelings about this fake dating situation you've gotten yourself into." She drops it at the look on my face. "I just want you to be happy, Warner," she says. "I'm not saying any of this to stress you out. I just want you to be happy."

CHAPTER TWENTY-THREE
Alicia

Having Eden in town for the long weekend was a perfect distraction. She was fun and friendly and so easy to get to know. We spent a lot of time together between going to games and out to dinner with Warner. She even agreed to go for a run with me, but as we got closer to Michigan Avenue, she insisted we veer off course, slow down and window shop instead. It was not exactly the workout I was hoping for, but it was exactly the kind of laughter-filled social event that I needed.

Getting to know Eden better allowed me to see Warner through a different lens. Warner James as a brother is sarcastic, playful, and relaxed. Each morning, we woke up early to drink coffee with him before he hustled off to work. Eden introduced me to coconut sweet cream, which she foamed over the top of my coffee. I don't know what she put in it, because of course it was homemade, but suffice it to say, I'm an addict. Each evening, we met up with Warner after his games and frequented some of the best gourmet restaurants Chicago has to offer. Warner and Eden both share a love of good food (no surprise there) but their passion for unique gastronomy extends to sharing their food experiences with those they love. The warmth and readiness in which they both included me in their plans was equal parts surprising and lovely. I was truly sad to see her go.

Now that Eden has gone home, though, and Warner and the Foxes are playing through a lengthy stretch of home games, I'm forced to face the reality of our kiss last week. We both refuse to acknowledge it to each other. But that doesn't mean I've stopped thinking about it. I swear, our kiss plays on a loop in my head a hundred times an hour. When it first happened, I thought it was real, until the camera snapped, which has me questioning whether my version of events is true. Was the kiss as passionate, as charged, as *real* as it felt to me? In the immediate aftermath, I could have sworn Warner's pupils were dilated and his breathing was heavy. By the time I returned from the bathroom, though, he was so normal that I convinced myself I had made it up. Am I gaslighting myself?

"So, what are your concerns then, exactly?" Amy eyes me over a forkful of salad. We're smashed in my office now, which is a little more cramped than usual. Extra meteorological measurement tools cover every available surface. In theory, I would find a new place to store all of it, as I prefer to keep my already impossibly small office neat and organized, but a water leak in storage closet B necessitated some emergency displacement of the tools. Amy's office is worse than mine, which is why we're eating in here.

"I mean," she continues, "Are you worried that living with Warner is going to be awkward now that you guys have kissed, or are you concerned about the kiss becoming more?"

I watch as a fleck of dressing flies off Amy's fork and lands on my keyboard. I swipe it off with my finger and wipe it on my napkin. Shit. Isn't that the crux of the issue? Because if the kiss was just for the public in the hopes the photo would make its way to the press, then things shouldn't be weird for us at home. But if the kiss wasn't playing for the camera, what does that mean? If it means Warner has feelings for me, or at least attraction to me, how do I feel about it? In spite of myself, I feel a grin inch its way onto my face.

Oh, no.

Does that mean I'm getting excited about the possibility of it being real—or real*er*—with Warner? That means things have the potential to get awkward. If I ignore the attraction, though, we can both carry on with our lives and our living situation. No harm, no foul. We'll just keep our hands and our lips to ourselves and tone down the heat that I've noticed forming between us. Warner doesn't do relationships. He's made it clear to everyone in Chicagoland that relationships are off the table for him. Hell, how many times have *I* heard him say he doesn't have the time or the energy for a relationship? I'm probably just misinterpreting everything. So, although it goes against everything I believe in, I'll stuff down these burgeoning feelings to maintain a comfortable living space.

By the time I come home later that night, I've convinced myself I don't like him. I blew the kiss up in my mind to be something more than it was.

I'm lying on the couch, Kindle in hand, when the key turns in the lock. I blow out a small breath, shaking my head at my nerves. This is stupid. This is Warner we're talking about. We'll be back to normal in no time.

The second Warner crosses the threshold and spots me on the couch, curled up with my book, he grins. It's devastating. I'm officially obliterated. Instead of grinning back in a normal, totally-don't-have-feelings-for-my-roommate sort of way, I stare frozen at him like a lunatic.

Because I totally have feelings for my roommate.

Fuck.

CHAPTER TWENTY-FOUR
Warner

I know the general effect I have on straight women. I've been told my chocolate eyes perfectly complement my dark skin. I work out regularly, and my job hones my body into prime physical form. I make dressing and grooming well a priority. My ego generally does not need inflating, especially not after today's call with Sean, my agent, who informed me he not only has a modeling gig all but secured for me for next season's Dior menswear line, but a potential for an audiobook deal as well.

"James, the audiobook deal is incredible. You just lend your deep, honey-toned voice to the recording studio for a couple weeks, and the ladies will be dropping their panties for you even more than usual," Sean had told me.

"Thanks for stroking my ego," I told him with a laugh. I'm interested in the deal, but only because it will help diversify my portfolio of career opportunities post-baseball. Some guys don't factor in that we won't be playing forever. I feel like I'm in my prime now, but that doesn't mean I will stay that way. I'm one career altering injury away from retirement, and while I hope the reality is that I won't retire for several years, with my body intact,

I want to ensure that whenever and however I finish my baseball career, it's with plenty of options to move forward.

I don't need Sean to tell me the effects my face, body, and voice have on the female population. I'd like to think I'm more than the sum of my physical parts, and most days, I like myself and my personality fine enough as well. So tell me why, when I smiled at Alicia tonight, she practically ran from the room to lock herself behind her bedroom door? I hadn't even said anything yet.

We had a great weekend with Eden, and other than seeming sad to see her go this morning when we loaded her up into my car to drive her to the airport before I headed into work, Alicia seemed fine. What changed in the few hours I was gone?

Knowing how much I value my own space, how much I treat my bedroom as a placid retreat, I'm reluctant to knock on Alicia's door and interrupt her peace. Internally, I debate asking her if she's okay for more than two hours. I'm restless with pent up energy, despite having just played three hours of baseball and completed my post-game workout. The look on Alicia's face haunts me; she looked almost scared of me when I came home tonight. She's got enough going on in her life; the last thing I want to do is add more stress to her already full plate, but the magnetic pull to talk to her is too strong. Three times already, I've walked to her door, intent on knocking to check if she's okay, and each time, I've talked myself out of it, not wanting to come off as overbearing or needy. Finally, I settle on the coward's way out and text her.

I heave a sigh of relief. Okay, just reading into things too much. I feel a little bit like an idiot, but at least now I know for sure. The three little dots that indicate she's typing appear and disappear several times before stopping altogether. I don't want to end on an uncertain note, so I decide to push it further.

I have little time to dwell on how pathetic I am. I need to scramble to get things organized now, but I'll make it happen.

CHAPTER TWENTY-FIVE

Alicia

I put in a full day of work at the museums today, which means I'm not getting to the ballpark until the sixth inning, by the time I made it home to change and freshen up. Warner had limited details last night on what time and where dinner was, so when I left for work this morning, I didn't know what to wear. Luckily, his text with the details came through a few hours later. The sundress I'm wearing will work double duty tonight: dressed down with tennis shoes, a denim jacket, and my hair up in a claw clip for the game and dressed up with some gold jewelry and wedge sandals for tonight's steakhouse dinner.

I get to my seat just as Warner runs off the field. I glance at the scoreboard with tonight's lineup. Warner will bat second this half of the inning. I'm seated next to Elijah's wife, Hailey, and Tyler Edwards' girlfriend, Carly. I've met them both several times and they are both kind and funny. I'm pleased to see they are not in their typical baseball attire either, indicating they'll be joining us for dinner.

"I'm glad I made it! I swear I was running around like a chicken without its head trying to figure out what to wear and to make it here on time! Warner only told me the dress code a couple hours ago!"

"I know, right? Normally we have a little more advanced notice on these team dinners," Carly agrees. "At least we don't have kids to arrange childcare for."

"Yeah, but Warner so rarely gets involved in these kinds of things that everyone is happy to see when he takes an interest in non-mandatory team events," Hailey points out.

"What do you mean?" I ask, not following.

"Just that Warner tends to keep to himself, you know?" I nod; I do, in fact, know. "Elijah said he's starting to make more of an effort these days, though."

"Yeah, he went golfing with a bunch of guys a few weeks ago," I report.

"It's nice that he's the one finally gathering the troops. Ty said Warner was so frantic last night trying to organize dinner tonight, trying to find a place big enough to hold us all at the last minute."

"*Warner* planned the team dinner? He told me Benny called it." I'm so confused, but, admittedly, I have no idea how these team events work. I'm the newest plus one to the team, even though it's just an act for the two of us.

"He told you Benny planned it? No way; Benny is way more organized than that. He would have at least given us two days' notice," Hailey snorts. I'm not sure why Warner would tell me Benny called the dinner when he did. Come to think of it, is Warner even allowed to call mandatory team events? Apparently he can, because everyone seems to be coming. I pause my thoughts to watch him absolutely crush a triple deep into the corner of left field. I'm on my feet screaming as the outfielder misjudges the hop of the ball, allowing Warner to slide into third half a second before the fielder flings the ball there. The Foxes were already winning, but Warn's triple allowed Caleb to score from second, adding an insurance run. I swear I'm screaming the loudest in the whole stadium, but I don't care. Warner deserves all the good things he's earned and I'll shout it from the rooftops if I need to.

After the game ends with a Foxes win, the wives and girlfriends all make their way to the waiting lounge where the guys will meet us once they finish their workouts, press interviews, and showers. I take the time to adjust my makeup, adding the deep red lip I've become so fond of since the Foundation gala, sliding gold bangles on my wrists, and switching out my shoes to strappy, heeled sandals I kept in my car. Amy finally joins us; she stayed at work longer and missed the game, but I'm glad I'll have a close friend to sit by during dinner.

Warner, Matteo, and JJ all come out of the locker room together. JJ rushes forward like an excitable puppy to greet Amy, pulling her close and assailing her with a deeply passionate kiss. It's a little excessive for a couple who just saw each other a few hours ago, but I'm happy for my friend. Warner catches me watching them and pulls me in for a hug of my own.

"You look beautiful," he murmurs in my ear, pressing a kiss to the top of my head before pulling away. My cheeks flame. I need to get my reactions under control, or no one will believe we're together. Amy catches my eye and gives me a surprised look, no doubt witnessing the slightly more than platonic kiss Warner planted on the crown of my head. I give her a look back as if to say, *see what I mean? What am I supposed to do with this?*

It's more than an hour after the game ends before we make the trek across the street to the player lot, so most of the fans have gone home or into the surrounding bars. I think nothing of it when we exit the building and a fan calls Warner's name.

"Warner! James, please! Please, I need your autograph!" The fan's voice reeks of desperation. Warner is usually happy to sign autographs for fans before or after games, but there's something about the level of anguish in this fan's voice that has the hair on the back of my neck standing up. Temporary iron crowd control gates are set up outside the building that houses the team locker room, making a narrow pathway for players and staff to cross the street to the parking lot unobstructed. This fan already has one leg over the barrier. Security is shouting for him to get back, but his cries are tormented. He *really* wants Warner's autograph.

Alarm bells are ringing in my head, but Warner is calm and collected. He grasps my hand tightly and pulls me behind him, putting himself between me and the fan.

"Please, Warner. You're my favorite player. Please sign my jersey!" I don't know if the fan is on drugs or is having a mental break; either way, he is unhinged and beyond desperate for Warner's attention. Security closes in on him and he drops his leg to the original side of the barrier, holding his hands up. He is gently but firmly escorted away, and I can suddenly breathe easier. It's only when Warner tugs on my hand that I realized my legs have stopped working. I allow him to gently pull me toward the car and tuck me in the passenger seat of his car. He buckles my seatbelt across me before I fully snap out of it.

"Do you have to deal with fans like that often?" I breathe. Warner is close enough to me that I smell his citrus and sandalwood scent; there's something comforting and warm about it.

"Like that? Not often. But that's why we have security. Nothing would have happened with Eric on top of things like that."

It only now occurs to me that while I'm the one with an official stalker, Warner and I might be dealing with a lot of the same things on very different levels.

At dinner, I'm pleased to be seated next to Amy on my right side and Warner on my left. He must notice I'm still a little shaky from the fan encounter when he covers my hand on top of the table. His hand is large and calloused but comforting. Instinctively, I brush my thumb along the outside of his pinky, letting him know I appreciate his grounding touch. The wink he gives me in response melts me on the spot. I have *got* to get a hold of myself. Warner is playing a part and I'd do well to remember my own role in this.

The rest of dinner passes without incident. I know Amy saw Warner and me holding hands, but she said nothing. I think she knows I'm trying to fight this as much as I can. I'm not prepared to move out. I have nowhere to go, so I have no choice but to suppress these annoying feelings of attraction for my roommate. When we get home though, it's harder to act natural. At least when others were around, I could distract myself with conversations to avoid making eye contact or touching Warner. Now that it's just the two of us, I'm immediately self-conscious. He has a night game tomorrow, so although he didn't drink more than a beer at the restaurant tonight so he could drive us home, it's not out of character for him to offer me a glass of wine when we get home.

He brings it to me as I'm settling onto the couch, pulling my favorite fluffy blanket across my lap. He lets out a soft chuckle but otherwise says nothing. He knows that having a blanket on top of me anytime I'm on the couch is more about comfort than temperature; blankets are a year-round feature as far as I'm concerned. Instead of taking his normal spot in the corner of the sectional, he sits closer to me, pulling my blanket-clad legs into his lap.

What is he doing? We don't do this. We're not the touchy-feely kind of friends. Or maybe we are entering a new level of our friendship and I'm just being the weirdo who can't handle it. The room suddenly feels too hot. Am I sweating? Warner is so close. He's got to be sweating, too.

"Is it hot in here?" I ask him, a small note of panic infusing my voice. I pull at the neck of my pajama tee, trying to get more ventilation.

"Hot? Um, no. Maybe you are because you're wearing a blanket when it's eighty-five degrees out, you weirdo?" I know I probably am being weird, but I am burning up. I toss the blanket off me but feel no relief.

"Why is it so hot in here?" I ask, frantically fanning my face.

"I feel fine. Maybe you're coming down with something? Do you feel okay?" Warner leans toward me and attempts to put the back of his hand on my forehead. I lean away. "Your cheeks are a little flushed," he points out.

"Jeez, you probably paid a billion dollars for this place, and your AC doesn't even work," I huff. Warner looks at me, genuine concern on his face.

He stands and walks to the thermostat. "Lee, it's a cool seventy-two degrees in here. Are you sure you're okay?" He walks back over to me and crouches in front of me, rubbing my arm.

"Maybe I am coming down with something. I should head to bed." I shove my full glass of wine at him, abandoning him for the solitude of my bedroom. I try to ignore the look of confusion on his face as I quickly retreat.

CHAPTER TWENTY-SIX
Warner

Alicia's being weird. I know it, and I'm pretty sure she knows it. And while there's only a small chance she is coming down with something, I suspect her reaction is really one of discomfort in response to my more frequent touching of her.

I couldn't help it. The way she hugged me after the game had me more fired up than my triple. The way she clutched my hand long after the scare of the rabid fan dissipated. The small circles she rubbed against the back of my hand as I held hers during dinner tonight. I know those things mean nothing to her, but they are starting to mean everything to me. Her soft, reassuring touches anchor me to the moment, reminding me no matter what's happening inside my head, I'm surrounded by people who love and support me. Because I do know Alicia loves me. She loves me the way JJ and Caleb and Matteo love me. Just not the way I want her to.

There's only so much longer I can keep telling myself touching Alicia is for the cameras only. I know it's for my own selfish reasons, but still, I can't seem to stop. I know she thinks it's for the benefit of the press and I feel terrible, like I'm taking advantage of her situation. She's doing this to stay safe, and I'm over here relishing in her soft touch.

I fall asleep knowing I'm an asshole.

The next morning, I decide to sleep in. I wake up around six when I hear Alicia leave the apartment. Knowing she likely is going on a longer run, I figure I can get a couple more hours of uninterrupted sleep.

I wake again around nine and am making coffee in the kitchen when she returns. She's obviously feeling much better. I knew her excuses about coming down with something last night were just that: excuses. I hate myself for making her feel uncomfortable.

I hand her a bottle of water, and she smiles her thanks. I need to get a hold of myself. Everything that she does lately turns me on or makes me want her more. I know she's not trying to elicit that reaction, but it's like I'm automatically drawn to her before my brain can stop me. She's not even aware of what she does to me. The way her chest heaves in her sports bra as she tries to regulate her breathing after her long run. The way she runs the tip of her pink tongue over her lip, catching a droplet of water left behind. The way her leggings cling to her lower body, leaving little to my very overactive imagination. I suppress a groan as she starts her post-run stretches. I need to get out of here before I say or do something I can't take back.

Touching Alicia was a bad idea. Getting closer physically under the guise of this fake dating charade was a bad idea. Allowing her to move into my house, to exist in my space, was a bad idea. Okay, maybe the last one is a bit of an exaggeration, because she really was in a desperate spot. But being so close to her, experiencing perfection in human form, and being expected to keep it to myself and pretend like I don't notice it, like I don't want to wrap myself up in her, like I'm not dying to know what she tastes like, is slowly killing me.

Yep, I need to get out of here.

"Warner? You okay?" She's looking at me like this isn't the first time she's called my name.

"Huh?"

"I asked if you wanted me to pick up more bagels today and you've kind of just been staring at me. Everything okay?"

"I got to go." I scoop up my keys and make a beeline for the door. I don't have to be at the ballpark for another three hours, but I can't stay here with nothing but Alicia, my lustful thoughts, and my raging hormones to act upon.

CHAPTER TWENTY-SEVEN
Alicia

"I feel like I'm losing my mind here," Warner's voice is full of anguish. When I don't hear a response, I figure he's on the phone and hasn't realized I'm home yet. It sounds like he's pacing his penthouse; I originally heard his voice in the kitchen, then in the living room. It's getting further away when I realize he's gone onto the terrace to continue his conversation. I kick off my shoes and slide my laptop out of my bag. I may be done at work for today, but there's always more to do. Amy asked me to look over some of her lesson plans for next week's STEM summer camp. She's taken on the brunt of my office responsibilities since my hours were cut; it's the least I can do to help her out.

I'm settling into the couch, staking a claim on the corner Warner usually occupies. Everyone knows that's the prime sectional real estate, but whenever we are both on the couch, I let him have it. It's his apartment, after all. I'm in the middle of responding to an email when Warner speaks again. He must have walked around the corner of the terrace earlier where I couldn't see him.

"She's being fucking *stalked,* E! Now is not the time!" I rarely hear Warner angry. I can feel the tips of my ears heat. He's talking about me. At this moment, it truly hits me how much I've upended his life. I knew it, on a logical level, even with the wonderful things he has done for me over the last several months, but hearing the agony in his voice when he talks about it with Eden makes it sink into my center. My drama is taking a toll on my friend. I hate this.

Warner steps inside the house and panic flashes across his face when he sees that I'm home. I see the exact moment he knows he's been caught talking about me. He flinches. He hastily tells Eden he needs to go, hanging up.

"Lee, hey, I didn't know you were home." He attempts nonchalance, stuffing his hands in his pockets.

"Hey," I respond, closing out of my email and gently lowering the lid of my laptop. "I'm sorry. I didn't mean to eavesdrop, and I didn't mean to put you through all of this. I'll start looking for places again."

"What are you talking about?" Warner walks towards me and looks like he's going to reach out to me before he thinks better of it, dropping his arm by his side.

"You've been nothing but generous and kind. I never meant to drag you into all of this drama. I can move out." I hate that tears are forming in my eyes. I've never minded crying; I normally embrace it. But I don't want Warner to see my tears and pity me. I blink back more moisture as I stand to walk towards my room. I'll pack a bag and see if I can stay with Danny or Amy until I can find a place.

"Lee, what are you talking about? I don't need you to move out," Warner's eyes are wide and panicked. He must be feeling awful that I heard his frustration with my situation. He again stops himself halfway to reaching out to me. It's then that I realize Warner is too nice to tell me how much my presence and our fake dating scheme is affecting him. He'll never ask me to leave, which is why it's even more important for me to go before things get more stressful. Dragging him into this mess was impulsive and stupid. I thought it would be a convenient way to stop the letters from coming without regard for the stress it would put him under. He's clearly been hiding just how terrible he feels about the situation.

He follows me to my bedroom as I try to get myself under control. "I'm so sorry, Warner. I never meant to hurt you," I repeat my apology, hoping he understands just how contrite I am for throwing his whole world out of whack.

"What are you *talking* about, Lee? You haven't hurt me!"

"I failed to realize just how stressful having me here would be on you, Warn. But you're so nice. You're *so* nice that you haven't told me just how frustrated you were getting. If I hadn't overheard you talking to Eden, would you have told me?" Realization dawns in his eyes.

"You didn't hear what you thought you did, Alicia," he says quietly, and I flinch at the use of my full name. "Lee," he corrects.

"Please don't go. I'm not frustrated about you living here, I'm not mad about the stalker thing. Well, I'm mad about it, but not at you. You being here is not an inconvenience, Lee!" I hear the same anguish in his voice that I did when he was talking to his sister and I can't make sense of it. His emotions are not matching his words.

"Then what are you upset about?" I ask gently, spinning around to face him.

"What am I upset about?" he asks quietly, almost as if he's asking himself. He says nothing for several more seconds before blowing out a breath. "I'm upset that I see you every day and I can't hold you the way I want to. I can't touch you the way I somehow need to. I'm upset that for years I've avoided relationships like the plague and now all I can think about is how one might look...with you," he finishes, even quieter than he started.

I feel like the air has been knocked from my lungs. My head took so long to process what Warner said, and then once it did, it stopped working altogether. My brain maxed itself out, short circuiting on his words.

"I never wanted to tell you because I knew you didn't feel the same. And you don't have to say anything; I'm already beating myself up enough that this fake dating thing is a matter of survival for you and here I am, reading into everything. I'm sorry, Alicia."

He turns to walk out of my room at the same time my brain decides to come back online. I grasp his wrist, spinning him back toward me.

"Lee," I say firmly.

"What?" His eyes are pained and confused.

"Lee. I'm not Alicia to you. Don't call me that. I'm Lee," I insist, belaboring the point. I step into his space. He stares hard at me, and I know the fire in his eyes is mirrored in mine. "And you're not reading into anything that isn't already written for us. This is not a one-way street."

Warner moves so fast I don't see it coming. His massive hands come up to frame my face, pulling me closer to him. He strokes my bottom lip with his thumb as he stares at me hard, as if he's trying to figure out if I'm real. If this is real. I don't blame him; my mind is somersaulting over itself, trying to figure out which way is up. I blink back at him before he pulls me roughly to his mouth.

If I thought our kiss at the bar a few weeks ago was passionate, it didn't compare to this. Nothing could have prepared me for what it was like to kiss Warner James for real. It starts intense and fervent, as if he had been waiting for this moment his whole life. My tongue matches his stroke for stroke. He backs me against the wall, mindful to place his hand between the wall and the back of my head, cushioning the landing before pulling back. He presses his forehead against mine as our chests rise and fall, trying to catch our breaths. The kiss both comes out of nowhere and is such a long time coming.

I feel a goofy grin stretch across my face. For so long, I had convinced myself that this attraction was one-sided, and in a span of minutes, Warner demolished any doubt that he wasn't feeling this, too. True, I have no idea what he's feeling, whether this is attraction or something more. But already this is so much more than I ever expected. I close my eyes briefly, intending to soak this moment in and commit it to memory. He groans and presses his body flush against mine so I can feel the outline of his hard erection against my low belly.

"Come on," he says, tugging my hand. His voice is raspy, and I delight in the effect I have on him. I don't ask where we're going or what we're doing, too afraid if I speak, I'll break the spell.

I allow him to pull me down the hall and into his bedroom. I've never been in his room for longer than a brief moment, never allowed myself to linger across that threshold into his inner sanctum. Sure, I've peeked in as I've walked by, but I never saw enough to really take it in. It's beautiful.

His bed is massive, much larger than a standard king. The comforter is thick and fluffy and cloudlike, the heavenly visual enhanced by its cream color. The headboard and footboard are heavy, masculine. A matching dresser sits on the wall opposite the bed under a massive television. An oversized navy armchair is angled in the corner between a nightstand and the window. A neat stack of books rests on top of the nightstand, his thick, black rimmed glasses perched on top. A cream throw is tossed artfully over the back of the chair. I spin slowly, taking in the massive space. He watches me for a moment before prowling towards me, suddenly predator-like in his slinking movements. I stand before him, an offering, trying not to tremble in my excitement.

He pauses in front of me but doesn't kiss me. His espresso eyes assess me, like he's not sure what he wants to do first. I'm about to say something, anything, to break the silence when he lifts me and tosses me easily onto the bed. I'm tall and thin, but muscular. Years of running have toned my body, but the effortlessness in which Warner threw me onto the soft surface of his bed has me feeling tiny. I can't help the giggle that escapes me both as I bounce on the fluffy surface and when he follows, crawling up my body.

My hands instinctively caress his arms as they bracket my upper body. Warner is in joggers and a T-shirt, leaving plenty of landscape for my fingers to map. I trace the topography of his forearms, his triceps, his biceps. He lets out an involuntary shudder before dipping his head and kissing me again, finally. While our first kiss tonight was frenzied and hurried, this one is slow, deep, and leisurely, but no less heated. He lowers himself onto his forearms, careful not to rest his whole weight on me, pulling us closer together.

We're in no rush. My hands roam the broad expanse of his shoulders and upper back as he angles his head, deepening the kiss. When I raise my legs, hooking my ankles together around his waist, it's like I flipped a switch in my previously polite, mild-mannered roommate. He becomes unhinged, groaning as his hands explore every inch of me he can reach. Our kisses return to their earlier frantic pace as he palms my breast roughly. I let out a moan, which seems to be his undoing.

"Lee, I need to see all of you. Please." He sits up, separating us only for the short span of time it takes him to pull me up briefly so I can pull my blouse off overhead. He stares down at my mauve lace bra and groans.

"I've fantasized about this so much, Lee," his deep voice rumbles before his lips latch on to my nipple through the thin lace. I tip my head back and let out another soft moan. Warner continues tonguing my nipple while his hand tweaks the other. I'm frozen in a pleasure limbo, taking it all in. My hands resume their exploration, sliding under the fabric of his shirt, admiring all the valleys and ridges of hard muscle. He kisses a line up the column of my throat and while I love it, I miss the heat on my breast.

"Warner," I gasp as his teeth scrape against that spot where my neck and shoulder meet.

"Yeah, baby. Tell me what you want," he urges.

"I want this off," I say, tugging at his shirt. He smirks down at me before pulling up to his knees to grasp the neck of his shirt and pull it over his head. I've seen Warner shirtless before, once, but I'm still unprepared for the glory that is my topless roommate. The lion tattoo on his right pec stares down at me, triumphant and proud. I can't help it; I bring my fingertips to it and trace its mane. Warner shivers, watching me with intensity. His own hands, calloused yet gentle, resume their own movements, rubbing down the sides of my ribcage and stopping at the waistband of my dress pants.

"Lee, you have no idea what seeing you in these pants does to me," he says, hooking a finger under the waistband and running it horizontally across my stomach.

"Tell me," I whisper, eager to hear how I make the great Warner James come undone. He grabs my hand and places it on the outline of his hard cock, already straining at the fabric of his joggers.

"How about I show you instead?" His dick twitches and I feel like a kid on Christmas morning. He's huge, which shouldn't be a surprise. Warner is tall and muscled, why should his cock be any different? I feel myself growing wetter at the thought of feeling him inside me–anywhere inside me–for the first time. He smiles like he knows what I'm thinking. Who am I kidding? He probably does; I've never had much of a poker face. I have a feeling I wouldn't be able to hide what he does to me even if I wanted to.

Satisfied I know what I do to him, he dives back down to resume peppering my body with open mouthed kisses across my chest and stomach. When he reaches my pants, he flicks the button open with so much confidence and practiced efficiency, I feel another gush of wetness in my panties. I'm not surprised he knows what he's doing. He pulls my zipper down with his teeth–with his teeth! --and I briefly wonder if anyone has died from being so turned on. All hydration in my body has gone to my panties. I already know it won't take long for him to make me come. I'm writhing underneath him, panting like a dog in heat.

"My greedy girl," he says, cupping me before pulling my pants down. "Lift," he instructs as he pulls them below my ass and tosses them God knows where. I don't care where they go. They're my favorite dress pants and I don't care if I never see them again. All I care about is getting Warner onto or into my pussy in any capacity he's willing.

"Warner, please," I whimper.

"I got you, Lee," he promises before running his tongue over my slit, still covered by my lacy thong. He hooks a finger through the wet gusset of my panties, pulling before letting it slap back lightly against my center. "I promise, I'll make you feel so good. You have no idea what you do to me. It's about time I returned the favor."

Before I have a chance to digest his words, he dives in, sliding my thong to the side and finally, finally, putting his tongue where I need it. He swipes it up my slit a few more times before lying his large body between my legs, settling in. He tongues me deeply, spearing himself at my entrance before focusing his attention on my clit. He nibbles the bundle of nerves before drawing it into his mouth and gently sucking and rolling it between his teeth, laving his tongue against it as he works. My back bows off the bed at the intensity and Warner snakes a hand to my chest, pushing me gently back down.

"That's my girl. Such a sweet cunt, I could eat you for breakfast, lunch and dinner," he tells me darkly, looking up at me while he continues to feast. He slowly inserts one thick finger, then another, continuing his ministrations on my clit. His other hand reaches up, working my nipple through my bra, plucking and pinching and pulling. There's so much sensation my brain doesn't know where to focus. I'm barely hanging on, my hands grappling in the comforter, trying to ground myself, to hold on, to do anything to withstand the onslaught of pleasure my nerves are undergoing right now.

"Let go, Lee. I got you," Warner promises yet again, and the echoes of his deep voice against my pussy finally push me over the edge. I fall, tumbling headfirst into the abyss of my orgasm. He never lets up, curling his fingers, flattening his tongue against my clit as he laps up all my juices and I scream and scream and scream.

When my legs finally stop shaking, he slows, gently pulling his fingers from within me. Sitting up, placing those talented fingers in his equally talented mouth and sucking them clean, he watches me. I swear, our chests heave in synchronized motion as we catch our breath. His beautiful plush lips glisten with my arousal as he leans back over me, kissing me, allowing me to taste myself on him. I groan, aroused all over again, or maybe still aroused, as he chuckles to himself.

Pulling back and brushing my hair behind my ears, Warner says, "You are so beautiful. I've dreamed of you coming on my tongue for weeks, but I could never have dreamt up something so perfect as your taste and your sounds."

I can't even verbally respond. I'm still coming down from the most intense orgasm of my life. My brain is still playing catch up when Warner leans down again, pulling my earlobe into his mouth before whispering, "I can't wait to hear what sounds you make stuffed full of my cock."

Warner

I'm not much of a liar. I wasn't lying when I told Alicia she is beautiful, or how much I enjoyed eating her perfect pussy. And I certainly wasn't lying when I told her I couldn't wait to hear her noises as she rode my cock. But just in case she has any doubts about the veracity of my words, I sit up and slide her panties off. Eating Alicia's pussy was incredible. It took every ounce of my self-control not to hump the bed the minute her salty sweetness hit my tongue. I need to play the long game here tonight, though, so my restraint a few minutes ago should serve me well. I have lots of plans for Alicia tonight.

"Baby, can you take this off for me?" I ask, pulling reverently at her bra strap. I have no idea what kind of lover Alicia is or what she likes in the bedroom. I have no doubt I'll do whatever she is into, but I know I need to proceed with an abundance of caution. This is crossing a line in our friendship, and while I'm ready to sprint to the other side faster than an Olympic track athlete, I'm not sure where her head is at. For weeks, I convinced myself her feelings toward me were nothing more than friendly, so for my own heart's sake, I need to make sure we're on the same page right now.

I shouldn't have been so worried. The enthusiasm with which Alicia rips off her bra and tosses it off the bed would make me laugh if I weren't so dumbstruck by the presence of her beautiful tits. Her perky pink nipples pebble under my gaze, making my mouth water. Of course Alicia is an enthusiastic lover; she does everything else with her whole chest. Why should this be any different?

"Warner," she says, crawling towards me on the bed. I think I die right in this moment. A naked Alicia crawling toward me? I almost lose it, and she knows it, judging by the smirk on her face.

"Yeah, baby?"

"Don't keep me waiting." She looks pointedly at my cock. He's making his presence known, tenting my pants and moistening the fabric with precum. She licks her lips, and I swear to God, I almost come in my pants like a teenager. Apparently, it's been a little too long since my dick got any action. I palm myself before standing and pulling off my pants. My dick juts out, proud and attentive. I stalk toward where she is kneeling on the bed. When I hit the edge of the mattress with the fronts of my thighs, she reaches out, grasping her fingers around my cock before guiding her mouth to it. I hold my breath as she licks the drop of precum beading on the head. I groan and she kisses the crown of my cock, licks the underside, and pulls back ever so slightly. She's teasing me and I simultaneously love and hate it.

"Lee," I warn, but she and I know there's nothing behind the threat. She could pull away for real in this moment and I wouldn't stop her. I look down at her, my powerful goddess. She's on her knees for me, but we both know who holds the real power here. She winks up at me before taking all of me deep into her mouth. My lungs expand in a feeble attempt to drag in enough oxygen. I fist my hands at my sides, not knowing if she will be okay with me touching her while she works. She pulls off me with a wet popping noise and gives me a confused look.

"You okay there?" she asks skeptically. I fold over her in ecstasy, not wanting her to stop but knowing I'd never force her to continue. She gestures to my hands and when I don't say anything, she pulls them toward her and places them on her head. My fingers spear through her dark hair as she resumes her licking and sucking, pulling me deep until I tap the back of her throat. I let out a long groan.

"Fuck, Lee. You feel so fucking good. Please don't stop," I beg. She moans around me, increasing the sensation. My hips buck involuntarily and she moans even louder. I take it as the green light to do it again, and once again, I'm rewarded with her noises of pleasure. This woman will be the death of me. Grasping her hair tighter, I whisper, "Tap my leg if it's too much," and fuck me, she tries to shake her head, as if the thought of tapping out is preposterous.

I start slowly, pulling my hips back and sliding partially out of her mouth before gliding back in. I feel her mouth relax around me. She tilts her chin, allowing me more access to her throat.

"Jesus, Lee. You are so good. You look amazing like this. I promise I'm going to worship you after this. You're doing so well, taking my cock down your throat," I praise. My compliments must spur her on, because she pulls me forward enthusiastically, fingernails digging into my ass cheeks as my cock slides further down her throat. Following her lead, I snap my hips faster, over and over. I watch Alicia's round, perfect ass on display as she's bent on her knees on my bed, sucking me off. She hollows her cheeks on the next thrust, and I practically fall over her. She is so fucking good at this. My fingers tangle in her hair as my pace becomes sloppier, matching the mess that is Alicia's face. Tears streak out of the corners of her eyes, smudging her mascara and drool pools on her chin.

"Lee, you look so fucking fantastic. I love making a mess of you." She groans around my length, and I know I won't be able to hold on much longer. I pull out of her completely and she pouts. I want to kiss that pout of off her; she's fucking adorable and sexy all at once.

"I want you to come," she whines. "I want to take care of you too, Warner."

"I want that too, baby, I promise," I tell her, using my thumb to swipe the saliva from the corner of her mouth before bringing my lips down on hers. "There will be plenty of time for me to come down this gorgeous throat," I say, bringing my hand around her neck and squeezing gently. Her eyes blow almost completely black, the gray barely visible as it's swallowed up by her pupils. I squeeze again and she lets out a whimper. I am going to really enjoy learning what she likes in bed. "I want to take care of this wet cunt first. Are you going to let me fuck it?"

She nods but quickly follows it with a verbal yes.

"Good girl," I praise, and Alicia's thighs squeeze together where she's kneeling. "You like it when I praise you?" I ask, knowing the answer already. She nods. She's been quiet so far, aside from screaming my name during her orgasm, so I feel the need to check in again. "Lee, anything you don't like, you can just tell me, you know that right? But equally important, I want to know all the stuff you love. I'll do whatever you want if it makes you feel good."

She swallows and hesitates for a heartbeat before saying, "Warn, I like it all. Bend me over the table, have your way with me, tie me up, spank me. I haven't tried everything, but I pretty much have liked everything I've tried so far."

Is this heaven? This must be what the afterlife is like. If heaven isn't this, then I don't want it.

I grin. "We are going to have so much fun together." I walk over to my nightstand and pull out a condom, tossing it on the bed next to her. "Come here," I instruct softly.

She scrambles off the bed and walks over to me, coming to stand in front of me. I grasp her chin gently, tilting it to give her a soft kiss.

"You are incredible." I glide my hands down her neck, over her delicate collarbones, and pause to palm her breasts. Her eyes flutter closed as I thumb her nipples. I love how responsive she is to me. I slide my fingers to the apex of her thighs. "As much as I want to bend you over the table and fuck you," I begin, Alicia's lips parting in anticipation, "I want to see your face when my cock makes you come again."

Her whimper catches as I pick her up by the waist and throw her gently back onto the bed. I don't know what it is about tossing her around like a ragdoll, but it's doing something to me. She's strong and athletic enough to handle it and she clearly likes it as much as I do. I crawl over her body, ripping the foil on the condom with my teeth as I do. She watches, fascinated, when I roll the condom down my length. I grip myself and drag my dick through her wetness.

"Still with me, Lee?" I check in.

"Yeah," she says breathlessly as I notch myself at her entrance. I push in an inch and the gasp she makes will forever be seared into my brain. My ego rarely needs inflating, but I'll savor this memory for years. I plan to revisit it whenever I need a good pick-me-up.

"You're so big," she gasps as I push in another inch. Yep, I'll remember that, too.

"You can take it," I assure her.

"More. Warner, please."

I give my girl what she's asking for, thrusting deep until I'm fully seated in her. I pause, giving her time to adjust. It's not my ego talking when I say I know I'm bigger than average; I don't want to hurt her. But like the champ she is, Alicia again hooks her legs around my waist, urging me to move. So I do. Thrust after relentless thrust, I snap my hips forward. I push in so deeply I press my pubic bone against her clit. Her breathless moan in response makes me want to do it over and over again, so I do. She's writhing underneath me, pulling me closer with her strong legs, scratching her fingernails down my back. I can feel her walls tightening around me. I didn't realize she was so close; just as I'm about to bring my fingers around to play with her clit, she explodes, screaming around me. I abandon the idea and continue my pace, changing nothing, while she rides her high.

"Yes, Warner!" she screams, her pussy rippling around me. I grit my teeth, wanting to withstand her pleasure so I can prolong the entire night. I mentally review the plays Mac, our bench coach, walked us through yesterday, pulling myself back from the edge of my own orgasm as Alicia comes down from hers.

When I feel her finally relax underneath me, I slide my arms under her torso and roll, flipping us both so she is now on top of me. I grip her hips gently, coaxing her back and forth slowly, silently urging her to find her own rhythm. She falls forward, slapping one hand on the headboard.

"Warner! It's so intense," she squeals.

"You're in control. Take what you need, baby. I want you to ride my cock until you come again."

"I can't," she whines.

"You can, and you will," I tell her sternly. She nods in agreement, moving her hands from the headboard to my chest. She swivels her hips, and my eyes roll back in my head. She whimpers again. "Bounce on my cock, Lee."

Alicia does as she's told, rising up and falling down, gravity assisting her in taking me deep. On each fall, her ass taps gently against my balls, and I edge just a little bit closer to nirvana.

"Warner, I can't," she whines again. She's tired. I reach up and pinch her nipple before replacing my hands at her hips, taking control of her movements again. "Yes, Warn, just like that," she chants as I drag her back and forth against my cock. The change in movement trails her clit across my pelvis.

"That's it baby. Give me one more. You're doing so well. Look at you taking my cock like the goddess you are. You are so tight, so perfect. Come for me." And fuck me, she does.

As her pussy flutters around me, I tighten my grip on her hips, dragging her on my cock until I explode too, pulsing into the condom. Alicia's perfect pussy milks me dry as her fingernails dig into my pecs. She collapses on my chest, spent and tired.

When we finally both come down, sated and sweaty, I wait for the post-sex clarity to eventually settle in. Any moment now, she's going to pull away from me, tell me this was a mistake, or a one-time thing. And when she does, I'll paste a smile on my face and pretend I'm fine when my chest inevitably cracks open.

246

CHAPTER TWENTY-NINE
Alicia

Lying on Warner's chest like this, I can feel his heartbeat slowing as we both come down from what was, without a doubt, the best sex of my life. I wonder if this is what sex with Warner always feels like, or if it's just different because we fought our attraction for so long. Whatever the reason, I felt so connected to him during the act. I still feel connected to him, although in all fairness, he is still technically inside of me. His fingers trace small patterns across my back as we lie together, listening to each other breathe. I wonder vaguely if I'm crushing his lungs or if the sweat sticking to our bodies is making him uncomfortable, but honestly, I'm too sated to move.

After several minutes, he clears his throat, and I take it as my cue that our post-coital cuddle is over. I roll off him and go to sit up, but he stops me by gently grasping my upper arm.

"Stay here," his deep voice whispers. "Just a sec. Let me take care of the condom. I'll be right back."

I'm so tired after a full day of work and coming down off our sex high that I don't fight him. I allow myself to sink into his pillows further. What are these things even made of? If I thought the comforter was made of clouds, these pillows must be made of angel farts or something equally fluffy. When he returns and I muse about the origins of his seraphic pillows, he tips his head back and laughs, a deep, rich, baritone. It reminds me I don't often hear his real laugh. Sure, I hear plenty of chuckles or polite chortles, but a true Warner James laugh? That will make you pause to appreciate your lot in life.

When he slides back under the covers with me, pressing a warm, damp cloth between my legs, I sigh. I wasn't expecting this level of aftercare; sure, cleaning me up is nice, but the way he settles in behind me after, dragging his fingers through my hair and pressing soft kisses against my shoulder and neck? It is more heavenly than his bedsheets.

Warner wraps his entire body around me, sliding one arm underneath my neck to wrap around the front of my chest. The other arm snakes around my torso after he pulls himself against my back and slings his top leg over mine. I never took him for such a snuggler, but I am not complaining. There is something so comforting, so safe, about being in his bed and in his arms.

We must have drifted off to sleep like that because I wake what feels like hours later, slightly more rested than earlier. Before my mind can whir to life, potentially overthinking everything that happened between us tonight, I stretch, desperately needing to move my arms and legs. Warner's thigh is no longer draped over mine, but he is still pressed against me, the hard outline of his erection digging into my ass. I giggle in spite of myself. The sound must rouse him enough.

He groggily opens one eye to peer at me. I don't miss the surprise briefly transmitting across his face at having me in his bed. I make my way to sitting, resigning myself to my fate that this was only a brief hookup. He pushes himself to a seated position too. I make to leave his bed when he places his palm in the center of my chest and pushes me back down to the bed and growls.

Ah, there's that Warner James growl. It's extra rumbly when it's laced with a few hours of sleep.

"Don't you dare," he warns.

"Don't I dare do what?" I taunt.

"You're not leaving this bed yet. I'm not done with you." He hauls me over him so that I'm straddling his chest, laughing. His arms band around my waist, preventing me from going anywhere. "The only place you're going is right here," he says firmly, pointing to his mouth. He releases the stranglehold he has on my legs and roughly shoves me further up his chest. I fall forward on a laugh, catching myself with my hands against the headboard. I get a feeling of déja vu as a familiar wetness slips from my center.

"Yessss," Warner groans, feeling it against his chest at the same time I do. "Get up here and let me have a taste of it."

"If you say so," I laugh agreeably. I straddle his face, and he pulls me forcefully down onto him. His moans reverberate against my pussy as his mouth gets to work. His hands glide up and down the backs of my thighs as his tongue traces every inch of me. My hips rock against him and his laugh vibrates through me.

"Good girl. Take what you deserve," he coaxes before diving back in for more.

I'm not surprised Warner is good at eating pussy. You don't earn that many dates, don't get that many rave reviews on Foxy Fanatixxx (even if some of them are fake), without possessing certain talents in the bedroom. Can confirm: five out of five, would ride again.

I clutch the headboard as he curls two fingers inside me. It must be a tight fit against his face, but he shows no signs of discomfort or slowing down. He smacks my ass and flattens his tongue against my clit, and I'm coming in no time.

"That had to be a new record for fastest orgasm," I tell him honestly when I finally roll off him. I'm rewarded with another booming laugh, and I realize making Warner laugh might be my newest addiction. I'm already jonesing for my next hit.

Warner stands and rounds to the side of the mattress I flung myself onto. His bed is so large that he has to pull one knee onto it to reach me still, but once he does, he pulls my legs toward him, sliding me across the surface until I'm back in his arms. He lifts me gently and walks with me to the bathroom, where he deposits me onto a small bamboo bench while he starts the water and we wait for it to warm up.

I look around in awe. I love the bathroom I've been using while staying at Warner's place. I have an active, devoted, and ongoing love affair with the bathtub in there. But I would drop the guest bathroom in a heartbeat to upgrade to Warner's bathroom. Palatial and pristine, yet not sterile, the white marble gleams. The hand towels look to be the softest, fluffiest sage green. Brushed gold accents adorn the double sinks. The deepest, loveliest tub I've ever laid eyes on is positioned diagonally in a corner of the room, between floor to ceiling frosted windows.

I shiver, the air conditioning forming goosebumps across my naked skin. Warner crosses the shiny marble floors and flips the switch that activates the floor heating elements. I'm pretty sure a whimper escapes my throat. I've never been a girl who needs a lot of luxury; I gravitate toward the simple things in life. However, after almost five months of living at Warner's place, I fear I am ruined forever. I've gotten a taste of the finer things in life, and you can peel me off these heated floors, kicking and screaming, to get me to give them up.

My thoughts are interrupted by Warner opening the linen closet I didn't even realize was there. He pulls out a ridiculously fluffy sage towel and deposits it into what looks like a very fancy garbage can. I have got to find out where he buys his linens or if he has a direct line to heaven's weavers himself.

"Come on, Lee," he says, gently tugging me to my feet and guiding me into the shower. He presses a panel on the inside shower wall and multiple heads spring to life, spraying streams of warm water out sideways from the walls and from another rainfall showerhead across from the one he and I are standing under. He presses another couple of buttons on the shower panel and steam gently hisses from a nozzle near the floor. Normally, I take baths to relax and showers to get clean. I may have to rethink a few things after seeing the way Warner showers. As if he can read my mind, he detaches a shower head and flicks it on, directing a spray of water across my breasts.

"What do you think about getting you a little dirtier before I clean you up?" My responding grin should tell him everything he needs to know.

He directs the stream of water between my legs. I'm still sensitive from my earlier orgasm courtesy of his mouth. And from the three he gave me last night–or is it still tonight? Either way, I squirm under the pressure; he flips the nozzle settings, and the stream sprays a little gentler.

"Bend over," he commands, and I almost slip in my eagerness to comply. Warner could tell me to do anything right now and I'd blindly follow, my desire to please this man is that strong.

I hinge forward slightly, pressing my ass into his lap, resting my forehead against my stacked arms on the wall. He directs the stream over my back, caressing me with the heated spray. He brings the shower head lower, one hand massaging wherever the water directs. My low back, my glutes, the backs of my thighs. Finally, he directs the spray where I need it most, causing me buck and flinch at the intensity. His deep chuckle sounds from behind me.

"Easy, baby," he soothes, bringing the thumb of his free hand to circle my center while the water sprays my clit. He plunges his thumb inside, wiggling it deliciously while I writhe and hump against the spray. "You are so beautiful, taking what you need. Once you come on my fingers I'm going to fill you up." He presses his hips against my ass, so I can feel his thick erection against me.

Words evade me, I'm so lost in the pleasure. This feels amazing, but I want more. I want more for Warner, too. I release one hand from the wall, reaching behind me to grasp his length, ready to jerk him off. My fingers brush the velvet skin of his cock before he pulls his hips back just out of my reach.

"Not yet. I've dreamed about having you in here so many times. So many times, I've fucked my fist to thoughts of you here with me, riding out your pleasure. I want to make it good for you. Come for me first."

I've had multiple orgasms in one night before. I've had a decent amount of sexual experience, and I'm not ashamed of it. I've had men play my body like an instrument. I've hooked up with my fair share of vanilla guys, too. But I have never been able to come on command. Until now. And maybe it's less of coming on command as Warner being in tune enough with my body to know when it's about to happen and preempting it with instructions. But it's also an equally likely possibility that Warner himself is commanding me, verbally coaxing out my orgasms, because the things this man does to my body is otherworldly.

I shake and scream around this thumb, the water maintaining a steady beat against my clit. My legs shake until they almost give out; Warner is quick to drop the showerhead to wrap his arms around my waist and hold me steady, pushing my chest back against him when my tremors subside. He presses gentle kisses against my neck and shoulders, murmuring small praises.

"You did so well, Lee. Are you ready for me?"

My eyes are still closed, but I crack one lid to see him rip open a condom foil. He rolls it on with one hand, the other roaming my body, my back still pressed against his chest.

"Yes," I whisper. I peek over my shoulder to glance at him. The raw hunger on his face is softened at the edges by some unnamed emotion. Being the recipient of Warner's worshipful gaze does something to me. I feel powerful, invincible, and so completely turned on that I'm sure he'll be able to slip inside me with just the tiniest of thrusts. We both stop breathing when he presses inside me, my hips tilted, his chest pressing into my back, arms wrapped around me. I'm both surrounded and filled by Warner and the sensation is a heady mixture of pleasure and safety.

He flexes his hips as he bottoms out inside me, allowing me to adjust to him one more time. I have no doubt I'll be sore tomorrow, not only due to his size, but the fact that I haven't slept with anyone in a while. Between not wanting to bring someone home to

Warner's house and the craziness of work, not to mention the stress from the continued letters, I haven't gotten off from anything but my own toys or fingers, and only when Warner is out of town or away from his apartment.

"Warner," I breathe, not sure what I'm asking for. He seems to know what I need before I do. He begins a slow thrust, pulling out almost completely before slamming back into me. If his arms weren't holding me against him, I probably would have gone flying towards the shower wall. The man is powerful in his movements. It adds an additional element to the way he fucks me, and I'm worried it's going to ruin me for whoever comes after him.

He continues a steady pace, pulling out and pushing back in, the relentless force at odds with the gentle pressure of his fingertips on my breasts, my collarbones, my throat. The only sounds are the ones from the water hitting our bodies, our heavy breathing, and Warner's skin slapping against mine. I twine my fingers around his neck behind me, pulling him even closer. In response, he shuffles us forward, until my body is pressed once again against the cool tiles of his shower wall.

He releases his hold against my chest in favor of a firmer grip on my hips. His thrusts turn faster, more punishing. It's all I can do to hold myself steady against the wall, fingers scrambling for purchase. He lifts and bends one of my legs, holding me open and changing the angle in which he hits me. He pounds into me, over and over, reaching that deep spot inside of me. I'm so close.

"This pussy is mine, Lee," Warner grits out. "You hear me? Mine." He sounds almost angry, and I love the feeling, knowing he's this unhinged for me. His fingers find my throat and give it a light squeeze, pulling me towards him, where he captures my lips in a bruising kiss. Gone is the gentle, careful Warner who makes my coffee each morning. In his place, a feral, brutal man thrusts roughly into me, taking what he wants. Both sides of Warner are so sexy, but this one might be the best. Warner unleashed is my favorite Warner.

"Yes, it's yours!" I cry out, so close to the precipice of my next orgasm. Maintaining his grip on my throat, Warner's other hand slides down to my center, strumming my clit. It's the final push I need to reach my release. He relaxes the pressure on my throat but keeps his hand there, no longer squeezing, as I scream and gasp and thrash my pleasure. Little white dots pop behind my eyes. He groans his release behind me, spilling into the condom and biting down hard on my shoulder. The pain and pleasure of the bite prolong my own release. My orgasm rolls on and on, my screams and moans on repeat. Finally, the last crest of the waves subsides, leaving me gasping for air. I turn my head, pressing my cheek to the cool tiles.

Warn pulls away from me, disposing of the condom. The warm water continues to fall gently on us from the overhead rainfall shower heads. My feet are planted in the additional spray from the handheld head he dropped earlier. He must have an industrial sized water heater; I'm surprised the water hasn't cooled by now. At the same time, I'm pretty sure only the most luxurious five-star resorts have showers like the one in Warner's home, so maybe he did shell out extra money for a bigger hot water supply.

The warmth of his body envelops me, pulling me from the wall and spinning me to face him. The gentleness in which he swipes the hair from my face makes my chest hurt. My sweet, tender Warner is back. Well, not mine, but still. I lean my forehead to rest against his chest. I press a kiss to the lion, to Warner's opposite pec, and between his collarbones. He strokes my back soothingly.

"Lee, you are so perfect. That was...incredible." I look up, taken aback by the reverence in his tone. His brow furrows when he catches sight of the bite mark on my shoulder. He traces it gently with a fingertip. "I'm so sorry."

"I'm not," I tell him with a soft smile, bringing my fingers to cradle his face between my hands. I pull him down gently for a slow, deep kiss. When we pull back, I say, "I loved it. It was hot."

He doesn't look convinced but doesn't say much more as he begins gently shampooing my hair. I try not to think too hard about how Warner knows to do such a thorough job washing a woman's hair. Who am I kidding though? I'd be a fool to think any of the things I just experienced with Warner were anything new to him. To be honest, they weren't new to me either, but they somehow felt different with him. Shoving the unhelpful thoughts out of my head, I remind myself to stay present in the moment. I refuse to be that person who asks, "What are we?" while we're still basking in the afterglow. Besides, I don't even know what I want us to be. I wouldn't mind a repeat of tonight's–this morning's? --activities, but beyond that, I haven't sorted out my feelings.

Warner and I take turns soaping each other up, washing every inch of each other. No words are spoken and none are needed. He steps out of the shower as I'm rinsing the conditioner from my hair. I watch through the fogged glass as he retrieves a towel from his fancy trash can holder and shakes it out. He wraps it around his waist without drying himself off. Rivulets of water sluice down his chest. I'm fully sated, yet I still want to lick it off, to trace their path with my tongue.

I turn off the water by the faucet handle but don't dare touch the panel on the wall for fear of messing it up. I push open the glass door to see him holding a towel out to me, a soft smile on his face as he rakes his gaze up my body. I've never been ashamed of my body, nor am I overly modest in my dress, so between my sports bras and running shorts, there's little of my body Warner hadn't seen before tonight. Now, he's seen it all, and the heat in his stare fills me with a sense of feminine satisfaction that he likes what he sees. I step towards him, allowing him to wrap me in the fluffy towel he pulled from the cylinder by the bathtub. It must be a towel warmer. I internally laugh at myself with how spoiled I am now and how difficult leaving Warner's house will be.

Once I'm cocooned in the towel, his strong arms lift me, carrying me back to bed. I don't know what it is about him lifting me or throwing me around, but I've never felt so small. I kind of love it. After placing me on the bed, he disappears. He returns several minutes later with a plate full of turkey sandwiches and a couple water bottles.

We eat in relative silence, smiling when we make eye contact over our food. I don't have much to say; I feel so completely relaxed and happy. He swipes some mustard from the corner of my mouth with his thumb and licks it off. My insides turn molten at the sight. "Lee," he warns, shaking his head with a small smile. "Don't give me that look if you're not prepared for me to act on it." My lips part, letting out a small gasp. I'm not sure what Warner's refractory period is, but the fact that he can go so frequently in such a short amount of time is both promising and exhausting. What have I gotten myself into?

After we finish eating, he brings the plate back into the kitchen. When he returns to bed, he slides in behind me, resuming our earlier position. Little is said, but I can't help the contented sigh that leaves my lips when Warner presses his own to my shoulder blade and settles in behind me.

I wake several hours later to the doorbell ringing. Warner rarely has visitors, and guests must know the elevator code to get up to the penthouse floor, so I know there's only a small pool of possible people it could be. Just as I am mentally placing a bet that the caller is Manny, Warner's deep voice sounds from the front hallway.

"Lee?" I roll over, feeling warm bed sheets behind me. Warner must have just gotten up to get the door. "Lee, Amy is here."

Shit.

I forgot she was coming over to work on her lesson plans today. Normally she calls first. I frantically look around for my phone before realizing I probably left it in the living room last night, and the battery is more than likely dead anyway. My towel and the comforter on top of my chest fall away as I sit up and reality sets in. I'm naked, in Warner's bed. In my *roommate's* bed. My *fake boyfriend's* bed.

Shit, indeed.

I scramble out of bed, frantically looking for anything I can throw on. Articles of clothing are strewn about the bedroom floor. Fuck it, there's no way I can figure out where all of yesterday's outfit is anyway. I grab Warner's T-shirt that was hastily tossed in the corner last night and pull it over my head. It's so large that the neck hole hangs loosely off one shoulder, but at least my legs are covered. I don't even want to know what my hair looks like. I didn't brush it after our midnight shower, so I guarantee it's a tangled, frizzy mess.

I mentally calculate if I can quietly sneak out of Warner's bedroom and into mine for a more appropriate outfit before facing my best friend. I crack the door. It sounds like Warner and Amy are talking in the kitchen, which means the coast should be clear for me to tiptoe back to my room, hiding the evidence of last night's activities, and Amy will be none the wiser. Not that I'm ashamed of what we've done; I'm just not ready to broadcast it, especially because Warner and I haven't even discussed it.

I miscalculate.

I know it as soon as I pull the door to Warner's room closed behind me and it lets out a large creak. I should have left it open, but the clothes all over the floor and the bedsheets looking like a tornado ran through the room were a dead giveaway to the sexfest that occurred inside. Amy pokes her head out from the kitchen at the sound and the devilish grin she gives me tells me I've been caught red-handed. I knew I'd never make it as a ninja or a spy.

She says nothing, just arches a very suggestive eyebrow, and takes a knowing sip from the mug in her hands. Warner walks out of the kitchen behind her, two mugs in hand, gym shorts slung low on his hips, his gorgeous body on full display. He grimaces when he catches me outside his bedroom, knowing full well we've been caught. He hands me my favorite mug filled with rich, dark coffee. I tug his shirt lower down my legs before giving up. It's not like Amy hasn't seen me naked before, and seeing as Warner spent a good chunk of last night with his head between my thighs, I'm not sure why I'm suddenly feeling shy.

"Um, I'm going to let you guys work. I've got to pack anyway. We leave for Denver tonight," he says. I don't miss the way his heated gaze trails over my bare legs. He looks like he wants to say more but stops himself. I nod and step aside, allowing him room to walk past me. As he does, he allows his body to brush against my arm. Glancing down at me, he throws me a quick wink before heading into his room. I breathe a sigh of relief; at least things don't seem awkward between us.

Amy catches the interaction but says nothing. Have I mentioned how much I love my best friend? Warner's door snicks shut and she turns, walking to the living room. I follow her, wondering briefly if I should get dressed first, but deciding against it when I catch sight of the clock and realize it's already 11:30. I rarely sleep in this much, even with a wonkier work schedule these days.

I plop onto the couch next to Amy, careful not to spill my coffee as I tug the blanket across my lap. I drag my laptop over from where I set it on the coffee table last night.

"I didn't really get a chance to look at your lesson plans last night like I had hoped," I tell her honestly.

"I don't doubt that."

I make a conscious effort not to respond to her comment. "Let me pull them up again." I can feel my cheeks heat under her scrutiny, even though I know I have nothing to be embarrassed about. It takes me several attempts to find the email with her attachments. I'm thrown off this morning and so far outside of my normal daily practices that my routine is galaxies away at this point. I missed my run this morning, I'm mostly naked and I'm sure I look crazy. Amy says nothing, but the pressure of her judgmental gaze eats at me.

"What?" I finally exclaim, when I can't take it anymore.

"I didn't say anything," she says calmly, sipping her own coffee, eyes narrowed at me over the brim of her mug. She's right, she didn't say anything, but she doesn't have to. She knows what she saw. What she's currently seeing.

Warner's door creaks again, and moments later, he reappears, pulling a small roller bag behind him. He's dressed in khaki fitted slacks and a light blue linen button down, black baseball hat on backwards. His shiny white sneakers gleam. His short-sleeved shirt shows off his toned biceps, which flex slightly as he tugs on his suitcase. His espresso eyes find mine as he lifts his backpack onto his shoulders. He smirks at me, and my fingers slip from my keyboard. I feel my nipples harden under his shirt and a quick flick of his eyes to my chest tells me he noticed. His smirk widens to a full-on grin. Bastard.

"I've got to head out. You ladies have fun. Don't work too hard." I'm jealous that he can be so nonchalant while I'm over here practically salivating over him. "Lee, I'll call you tonight when we get to the hotel. You should probably charge your phone." He gestures to my phone, where it's been sitting on the coffee table since yesterday evening. And with that, he walks out the door, locking it behind him.

It's approximately four and a half seconds later that Amy explodes.

"Okay, forget work. What the fuck happened last night?" she hisses. Apparently, she was biding her time, waiting for Warner to leave before she started the Inquisition. It's a good thing he left when he did; given how intensely her eyes are popping out of her skull, I'm worried she might have spontaneously combusted if she had to wait another minute longer. I can't help but mess with her.

"What are you talking about?" I respond, feigning innocence.

"Oh no you don't. You don't get to play all coy when I caught you sneaking out of Warner James' bedroom, barely dressed and looking freshly fucked as hell. Spill it." She levels me with a glare so intense I'm surprised she doesn't start shooting lasers out of her eyeballs.

I laugh at her reaction, then sigh when I think back on the memories of last night. "Okay, well, yes, I was freshly fucked. Am freshly fucked," I correct. "Last night was...wow..."

When I trail off and don't elaborate, she grows impatient, setting her coffee down. "Don't make me pry every detail out of you, Langley. Start from the beginning and tell me everything." She gestures wildly before picking up her coffee again and settling deeper into the couch, preparing herself to be regaled.

"You sure you don't want to work on this lesson plan?" I tease.

"Girl, don't make me call Tim and Danny in for backup!"

I take her threat seriously. I love our best friends, but the amount of theatrics–not to mention additional betting on whatever is going on between Warner and me–is not something I'm prepared for this early in the morning. Or late in the morning. Whatever. Like I said, my routine is all off today.

"Okay, okay," I grumble, but I'm just as excited to dissect last night's affairs with Amy as she is to hear them. "He was on the phone last night with his sister, I think. He seemed upset about the whole situation of having me here, and these stupid letters, and I just felt like I was upending his life too much. When he got off the phone, I offered to start looking for new places to live, which seemed to upset him more. Then he basically told me he didn't want me to leave, that he wanted to touch me and hold me and was frustrated that he couldn't. And when he went to walk away, I stopped him." Amy gasps, then sets down her coffee again to clap her hands in excitement. "Anyway, we kissed after that, and he pulled me into his bedroom...and ugh, everything was just so good!"

Her grin is so wide it's maniacal. "I'm so happy for you, Leesh!" She gasps loudly and points at me. "Um, what the fuck is that?"

My–Warner's–shirt slipped, the collar falling further down my shoulder and exposing his bite mark from earlier. I adjust the shirt, tugging it over my shoulder and blushing furiously.

"Is he a fucking vampire?" Amy's voice has reached a new pitch and volume. Maybe Danny and Tim aren't the only ones who bring the theatrics. I shrug. Amy continues pointing at me accusingly. "Details. Now."

The pot of coffee Warner made earlier is long gone by the time I finish telling Amy about last night's adventures. She's a great listener, commenting and nodding along enthusiastically. She adds in little tidbits of feedback, squealing and clapping like a teenager at a sleepover. As much as I play that I'm embarrassed by her over the top reactions, I love them. It's nice to have something to be excited about. Even with all of the crazy upheaval I've experienced lately, I still really love my life, but having something shiny, new, and exciting to share with my best friend brings it to a whole other level.

"So, what does this all mean? Are you guys dating for real now?"

"I don't know. We haven't talked about anything. Someone crashed our party before we had a chance to discuss everything." Amy has the decency to look sheepish, even though she was technically invited over.

"Okay, but what do you want to happen?"

"I'm not sure, honestly. I think it all came about so suddenly. I haven't really allowed myself to think that even kissing Warner for real was a possibility, you know? I thought he was doing everything for the cameras."

"You are so naive," Amy says, rolling her eyes at me. She's one to talk. She fought off her fiancé's advances so hard in the beginning of their relationship. Eventually, JJ wore her down and they're happier than ever these days, but for a long time, she resisted the idea of becoming serious with him. "Maybe some of what Warner is doing is playing it up for other reasons, but you can't fake the way he looks at you."

"Well, obviously he's attracted to me," I agree. "We had sex multiple times last night. But whether anything will come of it, who knows? Obviously, I'm attracted to him, too," I tack on at the look on Amy's face. "I just don't know if what we did last night was just letting off steam. Scratching an itch, you know? He told me he hasn't seen anyone since the season began, and he hasn't since we started this fake dating thing, and you know I haven't either. I just...don't know if we do anything more, if we're messing with the good thing we already have going, you know? Warner is amazing. He's kind and thoughtful and takes care of me, even when I don't need it. I'd hate to lose a friend and screw up my living situation just because we can't keep it in our pants."

Amy nods sagely. "But you like him, right? As more than a friend?"

"Yeah," I admit. "I just don't know if I like him enough to push for more and potentially ruin what we already do have. I still have a lot to figure out. I guess it's good the guys are going to be out of town for a bit."

"Only for a three-game series," Amy points out. I didn't realize it was a short road trip. Does that add more pressure to figure it out by then? Maybe. But if I'm being completely honest with myself, part of me is glad Warner will be back home in three nights. "So that begs the question. If he wants to have sex again, will you do it?"

I can't hide my sly grin. If Warner so much as brushes against me again, I have a feeling my clothes will spontaneously fall off. "If Warner wants any sort of a repeat of last night, I don't think I'd ever say no."

CHAPTER THIRTY

Warner

I've had a series of several nice days in a row. Even before that, though, I had several manageable days. It's enough to lull me into a false sense of security, so that when I have moments that are a little tougher, I find I'm harder on myself than I probably should be. At least that's what my old therapist, Roy, used to tell me. I feel like I'm exactly as hard on myself as I deserve.

So, when I wake up this morning feeling like absolute garbage, I brace for impact. As soon as I open my eyes, I know today is not going to be a nice day. I suspected as much last night, when I finally fell asleep, but my string of nice days fooled me into ignoring the signs. I'm paying for it now, but I know I must rely on my routines to ensure today doesn't get worse.

I was diagnosed with major depressive disorder when I was eighteen, but the truth is, I had been experiencing symptoms for years before I finally broke down and told my parents, who brought me to a doctor. Management of my symptoms has been a journey over the last twelve years. In the first several years, I leaned heavily on Roy and my family. I still rely on my family, but I haven't been a patient of Roy's since he retired and closed his practice five years ago. He offered to set me up with a colleague of his, but at that point, my symptoms were so well managed with diet, exercise, and regular routines, that I declined. Mornings like this, though, make me wonder if I should have taken his advice.

I'll always be depressed. When I was first diagnosed, I held out hope that I would "get over it," but years of therapy and patient education taught me that I can manage my symptoms, but I'll never shake this entirely. It's something I long accepted, but I can't help the pangs of annoyance I feel when I backslide on my symptom management.

So much frustration comes along with my depression. I have nothing to be depressed about: I have a great life. I have a successful career, with family and friends who love me. I make good money. I should be happy, and honestly, many days I am, but my happiness always exists with an undercurrent of exhaustion. That's why my regular routines are so important. I avoid my bed unless it's time to sleep, otherwise I would spend all day there. Some days I am just so *tired*. Of course, those are the days that sleep eludes me the most. I force myself to get out of bed and shower. I try not to skip meals, though I'll never be a breakfast eater. I get dressed; I stay active. All those things are very intentional. Everyone thinks I'm just committed to my job or I have quirks surrounding my routines. I wish I didn't have to do those things, but if I skip them, I'm met with a slippery slope of depression, numbness, and apathy.

Some days, my depression has me feeling so empty that it physically hurts. I lose all interest in anything that isn't lying in bed for hours on end, staring off into space, hoping to finally fall asleep. Other days, my depression has me so numb that I feel like I'm walking through a film set of someone else's life: the events still happen, but they don't happen to *me.* My symptoms also manifest in difficulty thinking, like I suddenly can't think as quickly as I used to. And on some really bad days, I experience all of those symptoms at once.

Today is not one of those really bad days. Yet. So, I force myself out of my hotel bed and into the shower. As the water streams down my back, I'm tempted to sit in the tub, letting the water flow down me until it turns cold. I know that's not helpful, but it's all the energy I have right now. I fight the urge to sit, and when I finally drag my clean body out of the shower, I have a text waiting for me from Matteo, asking if I wanted to grab coffee at a spot his friend recommended. I don't want to grab coffee, but I know I should. It's a good routine, and even though my mind and body are screaming at me to get back in bed and avoid the inevitable exhaustion of being social, I slide my feet into my sneakers and tap out a response, letting Matteo know I'll join him in five.

We got to Denver late last night, fresh off a win in extra innings at home. I told Alicia I would call her once I got back to the hotel, but JJ, Caleb, and Oliver dragged me out to a brewery they wanted to invest in; the brewery was staying open late just for them. The guys have been trying to get me to be more social, and since yesterday was a nice day, I decided to do it. I sent Alicia a text, letting her know of the changes in my plans, but she didn't respond, so either I sent it too late and she was already asleep, or she's upset with me. I feel like shit about it, because either way, I let her down.

I couldn't stop thinking about it all night at the brewery. I was distracted, constantly checking my phone for a response from her that never came. As much as the guys tried to pull me into conversation, I turned inward, allowing my thoughts to spiral. Sex with Alicia was incredible. It was everything. At the time, it felt so right, but now that she's not responding, I'm replaying everything in my head, trying to figure out if I said or did anything wrong. She told me she liked everything, and I believed her in the moment, but now I'm wondering if I was too rough, or too domineering, or just simply not that good.

I meet Matteo in the hotel lobby. He takes one look at me and says, "Hungover? You look like shit. You need this coffee more than me."

I grunt a response but don't tell him that I had only one beer last night. I must look like I feel, though. I trudge after him. He has no problem picking up the slack in conversation, chirping away about this coffee shop, the local girl he's trying to hook up with after tonight's game, and the stats from his favorite basketball team's performance in last night's semifinal championship round. I'm half-listening. I appreciate that he doesn't expect me to respond with more than some grunts and nods.

I mentally run through a list of five things I'm grateful for, an old coping tool Roy taught me that I use every day. Some days are harder for me to come up with five things than others. I scan the city sidewalk, desperate to find the good things. One: Matteo picking up the conversational slack. Two: no rain on this walk, since I don't have an umbrella. Three: a family that loves me, even though I haven't called them back when I should have. Technically, the piece about feeling guilty about not calling them back isn't allowed in Roy's coping tool rules, but it's hard not to attach some negative feeling to myself sometimes. Four: I'm about to get some caffeine in my system, which will be helpful since I estimate I got about four hours of sleep last night. Five: the little gasp Alicia made when I slid into her.

Thinking of Alicia's gasp sends me on another negative spiral. It's not lost on me that the purpose of that exercise is to ground me in the present moment and prevent spiraling thoughts, but some things can't be helped. I wonder if Alicia regrets her decision to sleep with me. The look on her face when Amy and I caught her sneaking out of my room yesterday morning is burned into my brain. Was it guilt at getting caught sneaking out? Or guilt for having slept with me? Don't even get me started on where things go from here. In one night, I may have simultaneously created a very uncomfortable, maybe impossible, living situation for myself while also losing a friend in the process.

"Dude, who pissed in your Cheerios this morning?" Matteo asks as he pulls the door to the coffee shop open for me, gesturing for me to walk ahead of him. My foul mood must be telegraphed across my face.

"Just need some coffee," I reply brusquely as I edge past him. The smell of vanilla and coffee beans infiltrates my lungs. It's a comfort; I've always liked coffee, but sometimes I prefer the routine of waking up with a warm beverage while I read the business section of the newspaper over the actual taste of it.

The coffee shop is bright and inviting. The summer sun streams in from the large windows, but the air conditioning keeps everything at a cool temperature. A large display case holds a plethora of baked goods: thick slices of iced sweet breads, oversized muffins spilling out of their wrappers, plates and plates of cookies, flaky croissants, pastries oozing fruit jelly, and a basket of assorted bagels. The thought of eating right now makes me want to throw up. I order a large black coffee and wait for Cota to place his order of a bagel, cream cheese, and latte.

Of course, the bagel makes me think of Alicia's disgusting blueberry bagel with onion and chive cream cheese. I want to smile but can't muster the energy. Matteo gestures to a small table in the back, one of only two that are empty. We weave our way over and sit down, coffees in hand. He places a placard with a little number seven on our table while he waits for his bagel delivery.

"Just hungover? Or something more going on?" I don't correct him on the hangover assumption. My teammates don't know about my mental health challenges, and I prefer to keep it that way. I'm an inherently private person anyway, and it's just easier this way. People tend to change their behavior toward you once they find out you're depressed.

"I'll be fine after some more coffee," I lie. Either Matteo doesn't catch the lie, or he doesn't find it worth the effort to challenge me on it, so he drops the subject.

"What are you and Alicia doing for the midseason break next month?"

"I haven't thought about it, honestly." It's the truth. Everyone thinks Alicia and I are officially together, so we're expected to make this decision as a couple. "Maybe we'll stick around Chicago."

"Last year, a few of us got a yacht and took it out on the lake. You're welcome to join us if we do that again. I was going to ask the guys about it today."

I nod. It's nice to be invited to things, but I have no idea what my energy levels will be like. It might be nice to just catch up on sleep the whole break. It's four days in mid-July. Usually, I fly home to Atlanta to see family, although I've also met up with friends in Vero Beach too. Now that Alicia is expected to join me in my plans,

I'll have to discuss everything with her. That is, if she even wants to talk to me now.

As if the universe knew I needed a win, my phone vibrates in my pocket right as a cafe worker delivers Matteo's bagel. Leaning over, I pull it out. The wave of relief I feel at seeing Alicia's name on my screen hits me like a ton of bricks. I swipe my phone open and pull up her message.

Lee

> Hey Warn. Sorry I didn't respond last night. We ended up going out to a new underground speakeasy in the Loop and time just got away from me. How are you? How was the brewery?

Emotion clogs my throat. Why am I feeling so emotional about a text from my fake girlfriend? I'm just relieved she's not upset with me.

Me

> It was good. Looks like a good opportunity for JJ. I'm sorry I promised I would call you and didn't. I hope you're not upset.

Lee

> Why would I be upset? I know you're busy. You have nothing to apologize for.

Me

> Thanks for understanding.

I do think we should probably talk about things at some point, though.

I swear I stop breathing when I see her last message. This talk could consist of Alicia saying everything is totally fine, or her telling me she hates me and is moving out. I wouldn't blame her; I took advantage of her vulnerable situation. I was supposed to be protecting her, not fucking her.

I don't mean we have to talk right now. Just whenever you're free. If you want to wait until you get home, that's fine too.

The idea of waiting that long sounds terrible. I'd rather rip the Band-Aid off and get it over with. Before I can formulate a response, two more texts come through.

I'm still sorting out all my thoughts, so don't feel like you have to get back to me immediately.

I had fun though, in case my texts weren't clear.

I glance up and see Matteo watching me carefully. I know he just saw a series of emotions cycle across my face, but he says nothing. I tap out a quick response, feeling about ten pounds lighter than I did when I walked into the coffee shop.

The rest of our road trip did not consist of any nice days. I had to force myself out of bed each morning and to eat before and after the games. I'm lucky that I'm usually able to lock it in for work–my pregame workouts, stretches, postgame work, and actual game performance are usually not as affected by my mood once I get started. It's getting the motivation to get started that is the hardest. Luckily, each day has gotten slightly, progressively better as I claw myself out of this depressive hole. By the time we fly home after three games on the road, I'm feeling mostly back to my normal self.

"James, you joining us at The Eight Ball?" JJ turns in his seat in the row in front of me on the flight home. "Ames, Caleb, Jenny and I are going. Maybe more people. You and Alicia should come."

"I'll have to talk with Lee. I don't know what her plans are." I don't want to commit her to something she's not interested in. JJ shows me his phone over his shoulder with his text string with his fiancée pulled up.

"Ames said Alicia was down if you were. It might be good for you guys to come out together, you know?" I know by the way he words the question and stares hard at me that he knows Alicia and I slept together. Of course Amy would have told him. And since JJ is the only one on the team who knows Alicia and I aren't dating each other, he knows why us sleeping together is a big deal.

He's probably right. Alicia and I haven't really talked about that night, although we've sent friendly, surface-level texts here and there this weekend. She wished me luck and congratulated me on wins. I checked in on her and asked about her day. I don't know if we're going to go back to pretending like that night didn't exist, the same way we initially pretended the first kiss didn't happen. I feel a tiny stab of disappointment in my gut at that, but I know going back to normal is better than allowing things to become awkward between us.

"Yeah, okay," I agree.

"Great. I'll tell Ames to pick up Alicia so you guys can ride home together instead of bringing two cars to the bar."

JJ is a great teammate. Insightful but never pushy. Devoted and caring without being overbearing. I'm glad Alicia's friend is marrying a good guy; spending my time with someone else during these social gatherings could be that much more exhausting.

When we walk in the pool hall, Amy, Jenny, and Alicia are already inside, standing around a table, leaning on their pool cues. A high-top table next to them holds two buckets of beer. The place is relatively empty. A few crusty regulars sit at the bar, but the three other pool tables are empty.

Amy and Jenny embrace their respective fiancés. I walk to Alicia, crowding her space as I lean toward her in greeting.

"Hey, Lee." I'm pleased to see a faint pink tint to her cheeks as she tucks her hair behind her ear. She doesn't step back.

"Hey," she says quietly. I love the small smile that surfaces on her gorgeous lips. Leaning further into her space, I pause, my lips inches from her upturned face. She sucks in a sharp breath as I linger there, taking in her fresh, flowery scent. Maintaining eye contact, I reach behind her and pull a cue from the rack behind her head. I step away, chalking up the cue as I walk away, breaking our small moment of intensity.

I can't help but laugh to myself. Alicia and I are going to be alright. The way her pupils dilated, and she licked her lips when I stepped into her space told me all I needed to know. She wanted me to kiss her. Disappointment flashed across her features when I walked away without doing so. She quickly schooled herself into a neutral expression, but I know what I saw, and I am elated.

"What the hell was that?" I heard Amy hiss to Alicia as I stepped around them. JJ catches my eye and smirks, having watched our entire interaction from across the pool table. Caleb, focused on racking the balls, misses the whole thing.

"Are we playing on teams or as individuals?" JJ asks, directing the attention away from Alicia's and my heated exchange. See? Great teammate.

"What about couples?" Jenny suggests, looping her arm around Caleb's waist. He wastes no time pulling her close. Jenny has a surgery scheduled for next week; if all goes according to plan, it will hopefully be her last procedure. Caleb explained the plan to us last week, knowing he may need to miss a game or two, depending on her recovery progress. I can't imagine the stress they are under; I don't know how they do it, but I guess they don't really have a choice.

We play a round as couples. Alicia looks like she's never played pool before. Her grip is too tight, and her stance is awkward. Amy finds Alicia's struggles hilarious. She giggles each time Alicia goes to shoot, and Lee just stares daggers at her. I decide to put her out of her misery and offer to help. Luckily, Alicia's ego isn't a problem, and she readily accepts my help.

Standing behind her, I pull her hips into a better position, slightly angled off to the side so she has some more room to work. It's technically the correct position, but I just made my life a whole lot harder, because now her ass is firmly nestled against my groin. Normally, I'd prefer it that way, but we're in public. My dick doesn't get the message because he starts to stir to life. Murmuring gentle instructions, I kick Alicia's feet slightly wider, helping her to stabilize her stance. Yep, this is not helping. I feel myself growing harder. Alicia shifts back and forth on her feet, causing her ass to rub across my lap. I close my eyes and try to talk my dick down from his semichub state.

"Bend forward," I instruct, and my mind immediately flashes back to my shower, where I gave her a very similar instruction in a very different context. I clear my throat. "Uh, just lean forward a little, and pull the cue," I wrap my right hand around Alicia's, pulling the stick further back. "Yeah, just like that." I clear my throat again at my inadvertently sexual comment. After adjusting her left hand, I help her pull the cue back and allow her to push it forward, taking her shot. The white cue ball smacks into the maroon seven she is aiming for, knocking it into the corner pocket.

"Yes!" she cheers, jumping up and turning to high five me. I step back after celebrating, desperate to put some distance between my now fully aroused cock and Alicia's ass. I take a seat at the highboy, watching Caleb line up his shot. Alicia steps between my legs, pulling the bottle of beer from my hands and taking a sip. I'm mesmerized by the way her lips mold to the mouth of the bottle. I can't tell if she's purposely being sensual or if it just comes naturally to her, but either way, I can't tear my eyes from her.

It's like that all night. Watching my gorgeous room-mate-slash-fake-girlfriend lean over a table, her denim shorts riding high on her thighs in the back of a dimly lit bar, is testing every ounce of self-control I thought I possessed. I feel like I'm watching her in slow motion, taking in every flick of her chestnut hair, enamored with the pure joy radiating from her as she laughs with Jenny and Amy. I excuse myself to the restroom, hoping getting Alicia out of my direct sight will allow me a small amount of control over my raging hormones. JJ follows.

As we're zipping up at the urinals, he laughs to himself. "It's funny, you know. Alicia has come here with me and Amy at least a dozen times. She has wiped the floor with us in pool every single time." He looks at me meaningfully. "Every. Single. Time. She's practically a professional."

"Interesting," I murmur.

When we return to the tables, it's my turn. I take my shot, knocking my ball in, before I resume my spot at the highboy table. Lee steps between my legs again, handing me a fresh beer.

"Nice shot, Warn." Her tone is light, but her eyes are full of heat. My damn cock stirs to life again. She goes to walk away and makes it one step before I yank her back by her belt loop.

"It's interesting," I say, pulling her flush against me as I stand. She leans back into my chest, relishing the contact as much as I do. I lean to whisper in her ear. "JJ just told me that you're actually good at pool, that you've never needed help the dozen or so times you've been here with him." I drag a knuckle down the outside of her arm and am pleased to see goosebumps erupt in its wake. I can only imagine her nipples tightening in response as well. "Did you suddenly forget how to play? Or were you perhaps looking for an excuse to press your beautiful body into mine?"

Alicia says nothing, so I pull her hips further against me, pressing the evidence of my hard erection against her ass. I breathe her in deeply, letting her flowery scent overwhelm my senses. She lets out a barely audible whimper and I chuckle as I let her go.

We both watch as JJ sinks his last ball into a pocket, winning the game for him and Amy.

"Let's play individually," Alicia suggests, avoiding eye contact with me. Amy and Alicia assign balls to each of us while Caleb reracks them. Amy insists she wants to still be on JJ's team, to allow for an even division of balls. Jenny breaks, scattering them across the table, but none go in. Lee lines up to take her shot. Before she pulls back her cue, she looks up, locks eyes with me, and releases, never breaking eye contact while she sinks her ball cleanly into the pocket.

Amy lets out a loud whoop in celebration before Alicia lines up her next shot. She repeats the exact same scenario.

Eye contact with me.

Sinks the shot.

This girl hustled me, and I can't even be mad about it. She misses her next shot so play shifts to JJ and Amy, but the game is pretty much a wash at this point. Alicia only has to make one more shot to win, and I haven't even taken a turn. I watch her in fascination as she leans against the table, advising Amy on which ball to aim for. Her long, toned legs are crossed at the ankles, her hip propped on the table. She's dressed casually in denim shorts and a tank top, but she's never looked sexier to me. Her hair hangs in a curtain as she leans over, pointing at one of Amy's balls.

"You need a napkin there, James?" Caleb says, sitting next to me and reaching for a beer.

"Huh?"

"You've got a little drool in the corner of your mouth." He smirks. "You haven't seen your girl in three days and you're salivating just watching her." He throws an arm around my shoulder. I shove him off, but self-consciously wipe the corner of my mouth, just in case.

The rest of the night continues in the same vein. Each time Alicia bends over to take her shot, my eyes are drawn to her ass if I'm behind her and her cleavage if I'm standing across from her. I'd feel like a pervert if she wasn't purposely positioning herself in front of me every time. I catch her adjusting her top once, pulling it a little lower as she leans forward, propping herself up on the pool table with her arms extended while I attempt to line up my own shot. Of course I miss. I don't know if she's distracting me because she knows I want her, or if she's just that competitive. Her cackle at my miss tells me it's a little bit of both.

I shake my head. I'm in so much trouble here.

By the time ten o'clock rolls around, everyone else seems as tired as I am. We have a night game tomorrow, which is helpful and will allow us all to sleep in. But based on the way Alicia has been taunting me all night, I have a feeling neither of us will be getting much sleep.

CHAPTER THIRTY-ONE

Alicia

Hours of foreplay at the pool hall leads to a charged atmosphere as Warner and I ride the elevator to the penthouse floor. My fingers tremble lightly as I type in the code to the top level. Warner wears a smug grin, so I know he sees my slight shake.

He says nothing as he unlocks the door, but nerves get the best of me. I was all boldness and bravado when we were with friends at The Eight Ball, but now that we're home, alone, my nervousness is settling in. We still haven't talked about the sex we had last week, and I have no idea how he feels about it. I could feel his erection press into me earlier tonight, but I don't know if Warner has talked himself out of another hookup in the hours since.

"Are you hungry? I can toss in a frozen pizza or something?"

"I ate on the plane," he says simply, throwing his keys on the small table beside the front door. He neatly tucks his suitcase under the table instead of pulling it to his bedroom to unpack.

I gesture to it. "Do you want to–"

"No, I don't want to put it away." Warner stalks toward me, closing the distance between us in a few steps. "I don't want to do anything," he pulls me flush against him by my belt loop, "except taste this beautiful mouth." He slams his mouth over mine. I open for him immediately. His hands transfer to my hips, pressing his pelvis into mine. I let out an involuntary moan and loop my arms around his neck. He kisses me fiercely, like he missed me in the three days he was gone. I kiss him back with equal enthusiasm.

He backs me against the wall of the front hallway, again ensuring his hand cushions my head from the wall. I lift a leg, hooking it around his waist and locking him against me, letting him know I want this–need this–as much as he does. A hand comes to my breast, palming me before pinching my nipple. I gasp in pleasure, and he repeats it on the other breast.

He reaches down and lifts my other leg. I lock it firmly around his waist, hooking my ankles together and sliding the apex of my thighs against his thick erection. He squeezes and kneads my ass, rocking his hips against me, giving me the friction I so badly need.

"Warner," I moan.

"I got you." He walks us back to his room and places me gently, reverently, on his bed. I'm almost disappointed at the missed opportunity for him to throw me around before I catch the heat in his eyes as he starts unbuttoning his shirt. Warner's biceps bunch as his fingers fly over his buttons. I bite my lip in anticipation. He towers over me, shirt hanging open, and I can't resist. I trace my fingers over the ridges in his abs and pectorals. The man is nothing but physical perfection and his body is begging for my mouth to be on it.

"May I?" I ask, sliding to my knees in front of him.

"Lee, baby, you can do anything you want to me. Take me out. Please."

I waste no time undoing his pants, letting them pool at his ankles. I slide my fingers into the waistband of his boxer briefs and gently tug them down as well. His heavy cock springs forward, almost smacking me in the face. My fingertips dance along the smooth skin of his shaft before fisting him gently. I lightly stroke a few times, teasing him, drawing out the moment before I pull him into my mouth. His responding groans tell me he's walking a tightrope of desire, trying to hold back. I cup his balls and tug; he falls forward, bracing himself on my shoulders.

"Lee," he warns. This is too much fun. I love the power that comes with unhinging Warner James. I lick a slow line from his balls to the tip of his crown. His head falls back in ecstasy, and he tightens his grip on my shoulders. I dart my tongue out, swirling around his head and capturing the bead of precum. He groans again, and I decide to put him out of his misery by pulling all of him—or as much of him as I can—deep into my mouth, still cupping his balls and circling the base of his shaft with my fingers where he's too big for my entire mouth.

"God, Lee, your wet mouth feels so good. You're so good—" he praises before cutting himself off on a gasp as I deep throat him. He shifts his hands onto my head, where he roughly grasps my hair, pulling it into a makeshift ponytail and tugging. I feel the resulting tingle all the way to my clit and moan to let him know I enjoy it. He gets the message, tugging roughly again. I reward him by taking him deeper. I gag slightly and he starts up a steady stream of praise, encouraging me to take him deeper, harder. His hips flex and my nose taps his stomach.

"Shit, baby, that's so good. Your throat feels so good." I redouble my efforts, spurred on by Warner's dirty words and encouragement. I hollow my cheeks while taking him deep. "Just like that, Lee. Just like that."

Tears stream from my eyes and I know my mouth is leaking drool. I'm sure I look a mess, but Warner doesn't seem to care. I look up at him just as he opens his eyes to look down at me. His eyes are filled with equal parts heat and adoration, and I've never felt sexier. I squeeze my thighs together, looking for any sort of temporary relief.

"Touch yourself," he commands. "I want you to get off while I'm coming down your throat." I waste no time unbuttoning my shorts and sliding my hand down my panties. Warner gently kicks my knees wider, a variation of his movement earlier in the pool hall. The additional space allows me more room to work as I glide my fingers through my own wetness.

"Pull your fingers out. I want to see how wet sucking my cock has made you."

I lift my fingers toward him and Warner leans forward to suck my arousal off my middle finger. The motion pulls his cock a little further from my mouth, but after thoroughly sucking my finger, he straightens and slams back into my throat. The movement is rough, commanding, and exactly how I like it. I moan around him, and he repeats the movement.

"Touch yourself," he instructs again. I slip my fingers into my underwear, swirling them around my clit. My jeans are tighter than I'd like in this moment, restricting the action to my clit, but between the feeling of Warner's cock in my mouth, his hands in my hair, and my own fingers between my thighs, I'm not sad about missing more contact. "Faster," he commands. I'm not sure if he means he wants me to suck him faster or work my own hand faster, but either way, I comply.

Warmth pooling in my low belly tells me I'm close. I can feel my inner thigh muscles tightening, a sure indication that I'm about to come. The thrusting into my mouth becomes more erratic, less rhythmic, and I know he's close too.

"Can I come down your throat?" he asks, his voice frazzled. I nod as well as I can with his enormous dick in my mouth and it's all the permission he needs. His initial pulse of cum into my mouth sends me over the edge, chasing my own release. I moan around him as my hips rock into my hand. We both continue thrusting, prolonging our own releases until our moans fade.

Warner pulls his hips back as I slide my hand out of my shorts. He helps me to stand. He brings his hands to my jaw, kissing me tenderly, no doubt tasting his own release on my tongue. He lifts me and gently places me on the bed, kicking his own pants off to the corner of the room.

At the sight of my red knees, he kneels silently, reverently, in front of me. He pulls my left calf into his hands, pressing soft kisses against my knee, before repeating the action on the other side. The thin rug in the bedroom did little to cushion my knees against the hardwood floors, but I don't mind. In the moment, I didn't even notice the pressure on my kneecaps.

"It's not even rugburn," I tell him as he continues his slow worship of my legs.

"It doesn't matter. You don't deserve to be in pain."

"Warner, I'm not in pain!" I throw up my arms, exasperated. "It's not even really that uncomfortable! You've got to stop treating me like I'm fragile." I roll my eyes. Warner rolls his right back at me but comes to stand in front of me.

"I like taking care of you, Lee," he admits, as if he's embarrassed. I feel my face soften at his admission.

"You do take care of me, Warn. And I appreciate all the things you do for me, more than you know." I bring my hand to his cheek; he leans into my touch. "I just don't want you to worry about me. I'm a tough kid. I can handle a little bit of roughness," I tell him with a wink.

"Oh yeah?" Playful Warner is back.

"Yes," I insist.

"Good," he says, pushing my chest back to the bed. It's gentle enough where I could prevent it. I don't. "Because this ass was teasing me all night, pressing up against me," Warner's hand creeps up my thigh and under the leg of my shorts. "And one orgasm is not enough to take the edge off."

I have to say, I wholeheartedly agree.

He climbs on top of me, nipping my neck while his hands roam down my body. He deftly tugs at my jeans, and I press my heels into the mattress to lift my hips, helping him wiggle them down my legs. He slowly peels my top off me as I slide my hands under his shirt that still hangs unbuttoned on his shoulders. He shrugs it the rest of the way off and tosses it aside, along with my shirt and bra.

Warner is a neat freak. He keeps his apartment tidy. Before bed each night, he does a general sweep of the place, putting everything away in its proper place. So the juxtaposition of neat freak Warner with this sex god, tossing clothing anywhere just to get it off our bodies, is a turn on in and of itself.

He rolls us, so I'm lying on top of him. I scramble up to my knees and roll my hips, once, twice, over Warner's hard cock. Impressive refractory period, indeed. He grips my hips and rolls me, gyrating, over his cock again before shaking his head rapidly, as if to knock some sense into himself.

"Condom," he gasps, reaching toward the nightstand. He can't quite reach, especially with me on top of him. I lean over, opening the drawer and pulling one from the box. I clamber quickly off him and remove my panties while he rolls the condom down his thick shaft. It's like we both can't wait until he's inside me. Our impatience is rewarded when he guides my hips back to straddle him. I rise up onto my knees before sinking slowly onto him, inch by torturous inch. It's been three days since we last had sex, and while that's three days too long in my opinion, I need to start slow and give my body time to adjust if I don't want to be walking funny tomorrow.

"You feel so good. This pussy was made for my cock. Look." Warner gestures to where we sit, connected, staring at it in awe. "Look at this wet cunt, swallowing up my cock. We look so good together, baby."

I roll my hips in agreement, no longer able to sit still. Leaning forward, I press my palms into his chest as I lift my hips a few inches. We both look down, watching Warner's sheathed cock slide out of me. He thrusts his hips up, pressing himself back in slowly, repeating the movement again. We both watch in awe, little sounds of pleasure escaping me.

I can't take the slow cadence anymore. "I need more, Warner," I whine, heavy desperation lacing my voice. "Please."

"I love when you beg for my cock, Alicia." He uses my full name, but I don't care when he's inside me. He picks up the pace, thrusting from below, and it's all I can do to hold on to his chest and enjoy the ride. After several minutes and one particularly deep thrust, he tosses me off him and hauls me to all fours. He spanks my right ass cheek hard before burying himself inside me again. I scream in pleasure. I asked for rough, and that's exactly what he's giving me, and I cannot get enough.

I slam my hips back, rocking into him, meeting him thrust for thrust. He wraps my hair around his fist and tugs my head back. Sliding my arms forward, I press my chest into the mattress, changing the angle he's hitting from inside and let out a long, otherworldly moan.

"Don't stop, Warner. Please don't stop. Right there," I chant between gasps.

"Play with your clit."

I comply, slipping my hand under my body and circling the bundle of nerves. It's not long before the tsunami of my orgasm is threatening to take me under. I can't form words, just incoherent moans. I'm so close.

"I know, baby, I won't stop." Warner knows I'm close, too. "Let go for me, Lee. You can do it. I've got you."

So I do. The waves of my release take me under. Warner keeps up his relentless place, hitting me repeatedly so deep inside, to that place I can only sometimes reach with my favorite vibrator. I pulse and flutter around him, my legs shaking, and still, he doesn't stop, doesn't slow. It's rough and dirty and exactly what I needed. I'm sobbing by the time my orgasm slows, tears streaking down my face. He presses in deeply and freezes, succumbing to his own release.

He slowly pulls out, collapsing next to me and pulling me to face him. He kisses my cheeks, the corners of my eyes, my lips, kissing away my tears while holding me close to him. The look of concern in his eyes almost breaks me. I blink away a fresh set of tears.

"It's okay, it was just intense. I'm okay. I'm not hurt, I promise." I've come to realize Warner is an internalizer. He feels his emotions just as intensely as I do, but sometimes he lets them eat him up inside. I don't want him worrying about me when there's nothing to worry about. He's already worrying enough with this stalker situation.

CHAPTER THIRTY-TWO
Warner

We still haven't talked about where Alicia and I stand on this fake-but-possibly-maybe-real dating situation. I'm a little afraid to rock the boat, but if I'm being honest, the whole situation has thrown me for a loop. I've never felt pulled to be in a relationship, not since I started my baseball career. As a college athlete, I was burned enough by people who I thought loved me, when they just wanted to get close to me for notoriety. Now that I'm in professional baseball, people wanting me for what I can do for them, rather than for who I am as a person, is amplified a thousand-fold. It's one of the major reasons I've avoided relationships. That, and I highly doubt once a woman discovers all the baggage that comes along with dating me, she'll want to stay, or worse, she'll stick around out of a misplaced sense of guilt or loyalty and end up miserable.

I like Alicia enough as a friend to want to avoid those options for her.

Alicia is so full of life. She is like living in technicolor. If she attaches herself to me, I have no doubt my depression will bleed over into her life, dimming her brightness like a ruined watercolor.

Her light has seeped into my life; all I want to do is avoid doing the reverse to her.

I hold her throughout the night. I can't get enough of her naked body pressed against me. Sure, I prefer her naked; she's beautiful and sensual. But in a nonsexual sense, feeling her skin on mine soothes me in a way I've never felt before. She makes small noises in her sleep, her fingers occasionally twitching where they lie curled by her face. On nights like tonight, when my insomnia hits me particularly hard, it's nice to watch her sleep, knowing at least one of us is at peace.

When we wake in the morning, Alicia more well-rested than I, she offers to make us coffee. Sitting up, she looks around the room, no doubt searching for the clothes I threw in every direction last night.

"Do you have a T-shirt I can throw on? I have no idea where my clothes are," she says with a devilish grin.

"I do, but I also got you something in Denver. Hold that thought." I rummage through my drawers to throw on a pair of basketball shorts before retreating to the front hall. I retrieve the suitcase we abandoned last night and tote it back into my bedroom. Lying it down, I unzip it and pull out the flattened bag on top.

"As much as I love seeing you in my shirt, I saw this in the hotel gift shop and thought of you." I hand her the bag, wondering at the last second if I should snatch it back, worried I overstepped.

"You got me a present? You didn't have to do that! I mean, I'll still take it." She reaches for the bag, wiggling her fingers. She pulls the silk from inside and holds it up. "Warner, it's beautiful. This must have been so expensive! You didn't need to get me anything."

The robe hangs delicately from her hand as she strokes her fingers adoringly over the smooth fabric. Deep blue florals scatter across the cream backdrop, the colors matching the hotel's color scheme.

"You don't have to wear it if you don't want to," I add, suddenly self-conscious.

"Warner, I love it," she tells me sincerely, scrambling up to her knees to drape the robe around her, cinching it with the tie at her waist. "You are so thoughtful. Thank you." She cups my face, placing a tender kiss against my lips. I would have bought her the whole gift shop to be on the receiving end of her gratitude.

She hops off the bed and saunters into the kitchen. I must admit, she looks good. The silky fabric stops halfway up her thighs, parting slightly as she walks. She looks over her shoulder at me as she heads down the hallway toward the kitchen.

"You don't always have to spend so much money on me, you know."

"I like doing it. I like taking care of my people. It makes me feel useful," I tell her honestly.

"Maybe next time just buy me a magnet." She winks.

Is taking care of someone else a kink? Because if so, that's mine. My love language is physical touch, but I give her acts of service only because it's what she likes. I love speaking her language. Seeing the way she visibly relaxes while simultaneously lifting her spirit? Yeah, that's my kink.

We continue our normal morning routine, Alicia checking her emails while I read the business section of the newspaper. The pot of coffee in front of us slowly dwindles. I think about asking her to make plans for the midseason break, but I chicken out. I don't want to make it seem like I'm pressuring her to determine our relationship just because we've slept together a few times. I also don't want to run the risk of changing things between us. She hasn't received another letter from the stalker in a few weeks, and I'd like to keep it that way.

It's time for me to head into the ballpark shortly after lunch. Alicia is sitting on the living room couch, her legs tucked up under her. Her laptop is set out, open, on the coffee table. Stacks of papers surround her; she is absorbed in whatever she is working on for the museums.

"Hey, Lee, I'm going to head out to work. You need anything before I go?"

She flashes me a bright, genuine smile. "I'm good. Have a great day!" She returns to her work and remains seated. All I can think as I walk out the door is that despite the incredible night I spent buried inside her, all I want is for her to kiss me goodbye.

I've dated my fair share of women, but I've never wanted someone in the way I want Alicia. Not only that, but I want her in my life outside of the bedroom–or shower, as it may be. I don't know how to grapple with that. What I do know is that I love the sighs she makes as I touch her, the way her chestnut hair spills over my pillow in the mornings, the laughs she expels so effortlessly when we share a meal together. In short, I want every part of her.

CHAPTER THIRTY-THREE
Alicia

The weeks pass without any more letters. I feel like I can finally breathe again. I'm not looking over my shoulder as much. There still is a small niggle of anxiety when I check the mail, but it seems that fake dating Warner has done the trick and gotten this guy to move on.

The last several weeks with Warner have been nothing short of magical. We made a few public appearances together, just dinners, nothing fancy, but it seems to be enough to keep the letters at bay. Beyond the letters though, nights with Warner are incredible. He treats me like a queen. He's been on a weeklong road series and returns tonight. I think we're both avoiding the conversation defining our relationship. I have a feeling we're both afraid to voice what we want, out of fear that the other person doesn't feel the same way. Warner is a hard read. I still can't decipher what he wants, or if this is all just elaboration on the fake dating front.

"Ridiculous," Amy says around a mouthful of biryani. We're at our favorite Indian restaurant for dinner. The guys won't make it home closer to midnight, so we're passing the time together.

"You know where my money stands," Tim says, spearing a piece of tandoori chicken from my plate. I smack his hand away, half a second too late. He triumphantly shoves it into his mouth as I scowl at him.

"Yes, we all know you have a vested interest in Warner's and my relationship," I say with a roll of my eyes.

"Betting aside," Danny interjects. "Warner is obsessed with taking care of you. He started buying you gifts long before this *plan* was hatched." He surreptitiously looks over his shoulder to ensure we're not overheard. "He agreed to exclusivity with you–real relationship or not. He comes home with little presents from every road trip. He wouldn't do that if he's not invested." Warner has been bringing me magnets from every away game series. It started as a joke, but now I really look forward to seeing what he's picked out for me every time he comes home. The fridge holds an eclectic mix of domestic travel destinations.

"That's just because he knows my love language is acts of service."

"Girl, do you even hear yourself?" Amy points her wine glass at me. "People don't just start speaking your love language for no reason. That's why it's not called a friendship language."

"You can love someone as a friend! There are all different types of love," I point out.

"Okay, then explain to me why you jerks haven't gone out of your way to provide me with words of affirmation?" Amy accuses, and I must admit, she makes a good point.

"Sooner or later, you're going to have to take the leap and have the conversation with him, Leesh," Danny says softly. "I know you're afraid of making things awkward or rocking the boat, but if you two are on totally different pages, it's better to know about it now before you get in too deep."

"You say that like I'm falling in love with him or something."

Silence meets me, all three of my friends pointedly not saying anything. Apparently, what I've been slowly realizing over time has been just as apparent to my friends. Shit.

When Warner arrives home, I'm sitting on the couch, streaming reruns of a workplace comedy Tim got me hooked on. He rounds the corner, exhaustion lining his face.

"Welcome ba–" I stop my cheery tone at the look on his face. "Are you okay?"

"Yeah, I'm fine. I'm just tired. I'm sorry, Lee. Do you mind if I just head to bed?"

"Yeah, of course. Do you need anything?"

"Nah, I'm good. Goodnight." He tries to slink off toward his bedroom, but something doesn't feel right.

"Warner, what's wrong?"

He holds out his arms, almost beseechingly. "Please, Lee. Not tonight. I don't want to talk about it." His voice cracks on the last syllable. My heart mirrors the sound. I let him go. I won't force him into any situation he doesn't willingly want to go, and that includes talking about whatever is going on tonight. But that doesn't mean I won't stand by his side and weather the storm with him. So I let him go, watching silently as he turns and walks away from me, quietly shutting the bedroom door behind him.

It wasn't quite the reunion I was expecting. He seemed fine when we were texting earlier today, but a lot could have happened between then and now. Maybe he really is just tired, and he'll feel better in the morning.

I turn off the television and make my way around Warner's apartment, turning off lights. As I pass his closed bedroom door, I swear I hear a ragged sob. That can't be right. Warner seemed tired but not upset. I strain my ears to listen. A muffled sniff sounds on the other side of the door. I tap it gently. He doesn't respond.

"Hey Warn? Is everything okay?" The noise stops. I hold my breath, afraid to make any sound that might cover up what's happening in his room. When he doesn't respond, I make the decision to turn the door handle and creep inside.

The lights are off, but the blinds aren't drawn. Moonlight filters in, along with remnants of city lights. I crack the door further and step inside. I'm quiet, but not so silent that he doesn't know I'm here. Warner is lying in bed, his back to the door. He's under the plush covers, but they aren't thick enough to hide the way his body shakes with his tears. I pad across the rug and slowly pull back the covers behind him, moving slowly enough where he can stop me if he wants to. He doesn't.

I slide myself into bed with him, pulling the thick comforter over my chest. I settle behind him, spooning him, and snake my arm across his chest. His breath catches but he grasps my hand tightly in his, pressing it against him.

I pull myself closer to him, wrapping my body around his, allowing us to sink into each other. We say no words. The only sounds are the occasional sniff and the echoes of our breathing. Eventually, Warner's breaths even out as he drifts off to sleep. I follow shortly after, and when we wake the next morning, we are still curled around each other.

His alarm beeps softly, rousing us from our slumber. He drags a hand down his face. He hits the snooze button and rolls toward me. Our knees knock together as we jostle for a more comfortable position facing each other. His eyes are puffy from last night's tears. I bring my hand to his face, gently caressing his cheek. I don't know what happened last night, but I'll wait for him to share if he wants to talk about it. I give him a soft smile and his face crumples.

"I got you, Warn," I whisper. I don't know what's going on, so I'm careful not to tell him everything is okay. He takes a shuddering breath, attempting to compose himself. He brings my knuckles to his lips, pressing soft kisses across them. Still, he says nothing. His alarm beeps again and he groans, silencing it.

I press a gentle kiss to his mouth before extricating my body from his. I enter his bathroom and start the shower before walking back to the bed, silently holding my hand out to him. He rises, placing his hand in mine. Wordlessly, we walk to the bathroom. He allows me to pull his shirt off, removing his pants, socks, and underwear himself. He slept in his travel clothes, which couldn't have been comfortable. I strip as well and follow him into the now steamy shower.

He immediately sits himself on the bench built into the far wall, the picture of exhaustion. I soap up a loofah and begin swirling it on his body. He closes his eyes, letting a small tear escape and blend in with the shower water. I press a kiss to the corner of his eye. He inhales deeply, taking the loofah from me and taking over his cleansing routine. I wash my own body while he attempts to compose himself. When we're done showering, he wraps a towel around his waist and leans on his arms on the counter, facing the sink. I busy myself drying off when he starts to speak.

"Lee," he croaks. I make eye contact with his reflection in the mirror. "I didn't want you to see me like that." He closes his eyes, tilting his face toward the ceiling. His vulnerability doesn't scare me. I step toward him, pressing my towel clad body against his back, wrapping my arms around his torso. Together, we take several deep breaths while I wait for him to continue.

"I'm depressed, Lee. It's called major depressive disorder. I've had it almost all my life." I press a kiss against his shoulder blade and squeeze him tighter, letting him know I'm still with him. "Some days are better than others. Last night was a bad night. I'm sorry you had to see that."

"Hey," I say sternly, grasping his arm and spinning him to face me. "You have done nothing wrong, so you have nothing to apologize for." I cup his cheek, and he closes his eyes, leaning into my touch. I wait for him to open his eyes again before I peer up into them. "I'm sorry *you* had to experience that. But this doesn't scare me, you know. I accept all of you, Warner."

I don't think anyone has ever said those words to him before, based on his reaction. He sucks in a sharp breath before his face collapses in despair. He doesn't shed a tear, though.

"Tell me what you're thinking," I whisper.

"That I shouldn't be depressed!" He spreads his arms wide. "That I have a great life! That I have nothing to be depressed *about!*" The anguish in his voice rocks me to my core, cracking my heart in two.

"Honey, surely you know that's not how depression works? Just because you have good things in your life doesn't mean you're not allowed to be depressed." He closes his eyes tightly and shakes his head. "Hey, look at me. You're allowed to feel however you're feeling, even if you don't have an explanation for it."

My tone is firm and brooks no arguments. When he doesn't respond, I tug his hands to follow me into the bedroom.

"Okay, we're both going to get dressed. I'm going to make a pot of coffee, and then we're going to talk. You can tell me as much or as little as you want, but you need to know that no matter what you tell me, I will still care for you, Warner. *I've got you.*" I stress the words he always tells me, hoping they will sink in enough for him to believe it. I shuffle him out into his bedroom, where I leave him to change.

I fill the coffee maker with fresh water and coffee grounds, flipping it on before getting dressed myself. I quickly brush my teeth and hair before returning to the kitchen. A few minutes later, Warner enters, dressed in basketball shorts and a T-shirt that shows off his defined arms. He sits heavily at the kitchen island, and I wonder briefly if he intentionally chose not to sit in our usual spots at the dining table. I slide his favorite "stonks" mug toward him.

"I don't know what else to say," he starts sheepishly. "I was diagnosed at eighteen. I used to go to therapy a lot in the beginning, but I haven't needed it in years. I tend to stick to certain routines. If I follow the rules I set up for myself, I can usually manage my symptoms."

"What kind of rules?"

"Getting out of bed immediately when my alarm goes off. Showering right away in the morning. Getting dressed as soon as I'm out of the shower. Working out every day. Watching my alcohol intake and eating relatively healthy. And never getting in bed until immediately before I need to sleep." I nod along with him as he ticks off his daily habits. They are all things I've noticed before, but I never attributed them to depression treatment. "Basically, I try to get momentum as soon as I get out of bed. It makes motivation easier on the harder days."

"What can I do to help?"

"What—to help?" He asks, confused. "You want to help?"

A flare of annoyance sparks in my chest, at war with the pain and sorrow I feel for him. How could I not want to help? Does he not feel like he's worthy of my help?

"No one's ever asked me that. Everyone just asks when I'll get on medicine." A beat of silence stretches between us. "I guess just helping me stick to my routines would be good."

"And you don't want to go on meds?" I ask, hoping I'm conveying curiosity rather than judgment.

"I don't know. I'm good at two things: sex and baseball. And if I get on meds, I can't guarantee both of those things won't be impacted."

"Okay, wait. Time the fuck out. Did you just say you were good at two things, as if sex and baseball are the only things you're good at?" I feel my temper rising and attempt to tamp it down. My annoyance with Warner's low self-image isn't going to be helpful.

"I don't know. I don't feel like that all the time. But on days like yesterday, it's hard not to let the self-doubt win."

"Warner James, you are kind, intelligent, generous, and thoughtful. What you do on the field and in the bedroom are only parts of who you are. I understand your concerns and I'm not trying to dismiss them. But you are more than the sum of your talents!" I'm breathing heavily, desperate for my words to sink in.

"Come here, Lee," he says, opening his arms wide. I step into his embrace. He holds me tightly against his chest and my arms grip just as fiercely back.

"If you want, we can go to the doctor together if medication is something you decide you want to try. And if you don't, I support your choice as well. I just want to support you." My words are somewhat muffled against his chest, but I know he hears them when he presses a hard kiss against the top of my head.

"Thank you, Alicia."

After Warner opened up to me about his depression, it was all I could think about. So many things start to make sense, the puzzle pieces of clarity finally clicking into place now that I understand the big picture. No wonder he always seems tired and treats his bedroom like his sanctuary. He told me he often skips breakfast due to a lack of appetite. The limits he places on socializing are due to exhaustion, rather than a stand-offish personality. I feel terrible for not picking up on the signs sooner, but I have to remind myself that this isn't about me.

I spend the rest of the day plotting ways to support my room-mate. The midseason break is coming up soon. Amy reminded me of the break in games earlier. I hope it will be helpful in allowing Warner to rest. Last year, JJ and Amy went to Telluride during the break. Warner hasn't said anything about traveling anywhere, so I don't know what he'll be doing with his off days. I'll ask him about it when he gets home tonight.

Warner's mom sent a new shipment of ready-made meals. Manny is kind enough to bring the box in for me, insisting this is part of his job. Suddenly, Warner's mother's gesture makes a lot more sense. If he doesn't have the energy to cook for himself, at least his mom ensures he has a homemade meal easily accessible. My heart melts a little for his family. He told me that while his teammates and coaches don't know about his depression diagnosis, the team doctors–and Warner's family, of course–are aware. I'm comforted to know that he's not fighting this alone. I wish he had told me about it sooner, but I'm glad that he's trusting me with the infor-mation now.

I finish up in Warner's bathroom and get to work researching. Reddit has a lot of useful posts on how to support loved ones with depression, and I've been scouring the posts for ideas. I go down a rabbit hole of mental health posts, but I consider it time well spent. Between a best friend with anxiety and a roommate with depression, my research will serve me well. As if Amy can hear me thinking about her, my phone rings. Her contact photo fills my screen.

"Hey, Ames. What's going on?"

"I need a favor." She gets right to the point.

"Okay, shoot."

"Okay, before you shoot down my idea, I got this discount code for a two for one special. And I know you're tight on funds with all of this going down at work, but I promise, I'll cover all the costs. Plus any accessories we may need. But I need someone to go with me because if I try to do this by myself, I'll talk myself out of it and probably end up regretting that decision. Because it is something I really want to do–"

"Uh, Ames, are you going to actually tell me what it is first?"

"Sorry, I'm just getting anxious about it."

I snort. "I know. I can tell."

"Okay, so you know how I've been looking at these wedding photographers?"

"Yeah..."

"Well, the one that I really like is actually offering a special on boudoir photo shoots and since it's a two-for-one and I'm too much of a baby to go by myself, will you do it with me?"

"A boudoir shoot? Hell yeah! It's been a long time since I've had lingerie to wear for anyone though. I'm pretty sure the one teddy I had is in my storage unit. When did you want to do it?"

"Well, that's the other thing. She's got an opening this Sunday. Are you free?"

"Yeah, but we'll have to cancel brunch with Danny and Tim. Worth it, but you know Tim is going to give us a hard time about it."

"Also worth it," Amy says with a laugh. "Thank you for doing this with me. I'm so self-conscious about it but I also think it could be fun."

"It will absolutely be fun. Here's what we're going to do. You're going to make a playlist of all the songs that will help you relax and feel sexy, and I'll check out this woman's website and see if I can come up with some fun ideas for themes."

"Wanna head to Antoinette's Closet tomorrow after work? I'm buying!"

"I will not say no to that!" Antoinette's Closet is a high-end lingerie shop on Oak Street. I've never been inside, mostly because I'd never be able to afford any of their gorgeous pieces, but if Amy is willing to drop the cash, I won't stop her.

"I'm going to put together a photo album for one of JJ's wedding gifts," she tells me shyly.

"Girl, he is going to love it. Make sure you include some tissues in the gift bag. He'll need it to wipe up his drool...or other fluids." Amy's resulting cackle convinces me she's no longer feeling anxious about the shoot.

After we hang up, I turn on the Foxes game. They end up losing and both JJ and Warner had mediocre games, but that happens. Baseball season is long, and they can't win all of their games, but I wish Warner could have gotten a win. After last night, I feel like he could use one.

When he returns home from the game, he seems subdued and quiet, but not as anguished as he seemed last night. He walks behind the back of the couch where I'm reading and kisses my head in greeting. He tells me he's going to put his bag in his room and then he'll come hang out with me.

"You wrote on my mirror?" he asks when he returns.

"You found my message! I thought having a little positive affirmation might be helpful if you're having a hard morning. Or night, as the case may be?" I lift my eyebrows in question. Earlier tonight, I scrawled *I am worthy of love just for being who I am* in dry erase marker on his bathroom mirror. I amassed a huge collection of positive affirmations in a file on my laptop earlier today and plan on changing the sayings daily. It's something small, but it helps me feel like I'm supporting him.

He doesn't say anything but comes to kneel in front of where I'm still sitting on the couch. He pulls my face into his hands and presses his lips against mine. "You. Are. The most. Thoughtful. Woman. I've ever. Met." He punctuates each phrase with another kiss, culminating in a deep, lingering kiss at the end.

When he finally pulls back, I say, "I didn't want to overstep, so if you don't want me to do it anymore, I won't. I just wanted you to know I'm thinking about you."

"Baby, I love it. It feels so good to know you're thinking of me."

"Yeah?"

"Yeah. Thank you."

"I got you something else. I know you rarely eat dessert, especially not this late at night. But ice cream always makes me feel better after I've had an emotional day. I got us stuff for hot fudge sundaes, if you're interested."

"That sounds great." I stand to start making them, Warner leaning back to allow me to pass. He grabs my arm before I can walk away. "Thank you, Lee. Really."

"You deserve it," I tell him, bending low to kiss him lightly. "Come on. You can tell me if you want Moose Tracks ice cream or plain old boring vanilla."

"Wow, I can tell which one you're going to choose." He rolls his eyes, but when we go to the kitchen, he chooses Moose Tracks as well. "What? I like peanut butter!" he defends in response to my raised eyebrows.

"Your mom will probably be embarrassed, but I don't cook, so you'll have to settle for store bought whipped cream and hot fudge sauce."

"I guess I can manage...for one night." He winks, and I'm so glad to see he's feeling a bit more like himself. I scoop out generous portions of ice cream while I allow the hot fudge that I heated in the microwave to cool just a bit. When I hand Warner his bowl, he pulls me forward by the sash of my robe. I'm in my pajamas, which consist of tiny sleep shorts and a tank top, but I've been wearing the new robe Warner got me every chance I get. I love the feeling of the smooth silk against my skin.

I come to stand between his widened legs. The heat from his hand warms my hips, but it's the heat in his eyes that has my thighs clenching together.

"I can't decide," he says, tugging at the tie, "if I'm glad I bought you this, or annoyed that it's covering you up."

I reach forward, swiping a large spoonful of ice cream from the bowl still in Warner's hand before replacing the spoon. "Guess you'll have to deal with it," I tell him saucily as I turn and saunter away from him.

I don't make it far before he pounces on me from behind, pressing me against the counter. He swipes my hair off my shoulder, pressing lingering kisses to my neck and gently nipping at the sensitive spot beneath my ear. He soothes the bite immediately with his tongue, tracing the shell of my ear next. A gush of wetness soaks my panties in response.

"I want to bend you over this counter, Lee. Show you how much I appreciate you and all you've done for me tonight and last night." I press my ass back into him, humming in appreciation when I feel his hardness pressing back. His hand cups my breast as he sucks on my earlobe.

"You didn't want your sundae?" I tease.

"I would rather eat you." His fingertips graze the bottom of my robe, and I lean obediently forward, resting my chest on the island and allowing him access to where I need him most. He slides my shorts and panties off before stopping himself. "Actually, I have a better plan," he says darkly before hauling me upright, spinning me around, and placing me, seated, on the island.

"Don't move," he instructs, stepping away. He comes back moments later carrying his bowl of ice cream and the dish of cooling liquid fudge. He sets them on the counter before sliding the sash of my robe out from the loops. "I think we can make good use of this."

He slides the robe from my shoulders and takes his time peeling my top off. "Lie back, arms overhead." He circles the island and binds my wrists together with the sash of the robe, looping the silky material over and over around my wrists before tying it tightly. "Doing okay?" he checks.

"Yes," I breathe. It's taking all my self-control not to squirm on the counter in anticipation.

"You've been so good to me, baby. I want to reward you. I want to devour you. I want to tongue fuck your cunt until you're screaming my name." He returns to standing between my legs and slides his large hand to circle my ankles, placing my feet on the island. He reaches by my head, sliding the bowl of fudge closer to him. "There's only one way to make this pussy even sweeter."

I watch, trembling in anticipation, as Warner stirs the sauce in its dish before lifting the spoon to drizzle a trail of chocolate across my chest. I hiss as it hits my nipples, the temperature hot but not enough to burn. The fire between my legs burns hotter. He drizzles a line of fudge down my stomach before dipping the spoon back in the bowl to gather more. He pulls it straight up, dripping the glossy concoction onto my bare pussy. A guttural moan releases from deep within my chest.

"I know, baby. You can't wait for my mouth on this gorgeous cunt. I see how you're dripping for me already." He whips his shirt off and bends low over me, drawing my nipple into his mouth. We both groan at the sensation. His tongue swirls around it until it's a hardened bud before switching to the other. "You've always tasted sweet for me, beautiful. But this is better than an ice cream sundae."

He skates his tongue down the chocolate on my abdomen. I strain against my bindings. I don't want to be released but I can't help but squirm under all the sensation. I'm so wet that I know I'm leaking chocolate and arousal onto the countertop. When he finally drags his talented tongue up my slit, I nearly jackknife off the counter. He chuckles before replacing his mouth on me, pressing my legs back into position.

"Mmmm," he hums. I'm breathless and dizzy as his tongue swirls around my clit, then penetrates me deeply. He suckles my clit, flicking his tongue over the same spot. Over and over. He squeezes my breasts, never stopping his assault with his tongue. He shakes his head, pressing his whole face into me, heightening the sensations one thousandfold.

"Warner!" I whimper.

"I got you, baby," he mumbles against me. "When you are this wet for me, it's my job to clean you up. You come to me, you understand?" I'm too lost in pleasure to respond. He slaps my clit with his hand. "You hear me, Lee? No one takes care of you like I do."

"Yes! No one but you, Warn!" I cry out, my orgasm cresting.

"Good girl." He thrusts two fingers deep inside me, hooking them slightly. He pistons his hand roughly, causing his fingers to tap, tap, tap repeatedly against my G-spot. The whole time, his flattened tongue maintains a steady, lapping beat against my clit. My orgasm rockets through me, exploding in wave after wave of pure pleasure.

"That's my girl," He soothes as I finally catch my breath. He pulls my arms in front of me, untying the sash and rubbing my wrists. "How are you doing, baby? Not too sore?"

"No, I'm so good, honey."

"Good. Because I meant what I said. I'm going to bend you over this counter and fuck you so hard, you'll remember just how crazy I am about you tomorrow."

My breath catches in my throat as he rolls on a condom. People say all kinds of things they don't mean in the heat of the moment. I won't hold Warner to anything he says in the throes of passion, as much as my heart wants me to. But try as I might, when he spins me, thrusts inside, and pumps his way to another earth-shattering orgasm for both of us, I can't help but wonder how much of his statement was just said in passion, and how much he really means.

CHAPTER THIRTY-FOUR
Warner

"**B**ut your eyes were ready to shoot lasers. I felt like I was watching a cartoon—like I could see the flames inside your eyes! I can't believe that guy didn't back down," I tell her as Alicia giggles, the sound so aesthetically pleasing I want to make it my morning alarm chime.

We're sitting up in my bed, Alicia with a towel wrapped tightly around herself, bowls of ice cream on our laps. Our original bowls of dessert turned into soup when we got distracted. After I fucked Alicia senseless, I gathered her up and deposited her onto my shower bench. I spent the next half hour kissing and cleaning every inch of her perfect body before bundling her up and tossing her into my bed. I love the way the covers poofed up around her as she landed. She looked so relaxed, so utterly satisfied, that I wanted to freeze the moment in time.

"I can't believe it either, to be honest. I wasn't sure what I was going to do next, but luckily, Caleb took the decision out of my hands."

"You could've taken that guy."

We're reflecting on the first night we really hung out together, the night of JJ's gala. We had met prior to that, at one of JJ's many rooftop barbeques, but the night of the gala was where we really got to know each other. It's also the night where my white teammates got a taste of what I experience on a regular basis. Alicia's expression sobers a little.

"Warner, I'm sorry you have to experience that. And I'm sorry if I overstepped that night. But I just couldn't sit by and let that guy spew his hatred. I hope I didn't embarrass you."

I look at her. I blink several times before I can respond. Who is this woman? And what did I do to deserve her? Not that I have her, really.

"Honestly? It was a relief that you and Andrews said something. It's exhausting dealing with that all the time, knowing that if I say or do something in response, I'm the Angry Black Man at best, but more than likely, the situation doesn't end well for me. And I probably won't change that guy's mind anyway. But having someone else, a white person, stand up for me, to another white person? Lee, I can't explain what a weight it took off my shoulders, even for just a few minutes."

She looks at me sadly. "Let me take on some of that energy for you, Warn. I know it's a lot to carry. You shouldn't have to carry it, but I know you don't have a choice. I can't pretend to know every microaggression, or even recognize them all the time, but I promise, when I see it, I've got your back, one hundred percent of the time."

"Thanks, Lee." My throat tightens with emotion. "I appreciate you and Caleb stepping up. And I'm sorry it's taken me so long to thank you."

She throws me a confused look. "You don't have to thank me for that. It's called being a decent human."

"No, it's more than that. I feel like I've always got my guard up, not just as a Black man in America, but as an athlete in the spotlight. I can't always respond the way I want to, and it puts a lot of pressure on me." I sigh. "I fucking hate fried chicken."

She snorts. "You're a food snob, so I shouldn't be surprised."

"Okay, first of all, it's not that good. It's hard to make it where it's juicy enough and not dried out without it drowning in grease!"

Alicia throws her hands up in surrender. "I don't have a strong opinion on it one way or another."

"Do you know that my last serious girlfriend was white too? In college. Her name was Josie. I was crazy about her." I wince, realizing I used the same words that slipped out to Alicia earlier tonight. "But one night, we were at this party, and everyone started playing a trivia game to see who knew their significant other better. It was a baseball party. My teammates were notorious for throwing the biggest parties on campus, so everyone was there. Josie was asked what my favorite food was, and she said fried chicken. I had never, not once, eaten that in front of her." Alicia sucks in a breath.

"We were all drinking, but I don't know. She was so confident in her answer, and the way she knowingly winked as she said it? At that moment, I just felt so alone. I was devastated. The woman I loved saw me as nothing more than a racist trope."

Lee sets her bowl on the nightstand and kneels on the bed in front of me. "Warner, that's terrible. I'm sorry your girlfriend sucked."

I try to make light of the situation. "Yeah, the only thing she could have said that would've been more wrong would've been raw cookie dough." I give her a meager smile, but she's not having any of it.

"I'm sorry you had to deal with that at all, especially from someone who was supposed to love and respect you." She pauses. "I hope you dumped her ass, right then and there."

I give her a small laugh. "I didn't. But that was the beginning of the end for us. I started seeing her in a different light after that, and everything she did after…well, it became apparent that she was only dating me for notoriety. For the status of saying her boyfriend was a baseball player."

"Gross. I hope she stabs herself in the eye every time she puts on mascara."

I raise an eyebrow at the speed in which she generated her hopes for my ex. "Remind me never to get on your bad side," I joke. Alicia snuggles in beside me, tucking her arm around my waist. It's not long before her breathing deepens and she falls asleep on top of me. I know it will be a long time before I can fall asleep. I have a lot to reflect on tonight.

I feel a weird mix of greed and generosity when I think of Lee. I want to hoard her, to know all there is to know about her, to keep her to myself and spend all my moments with her. At the same time, I want to show her off. I am so enamored with her, so proud of who she is, that I want everyone to know her goodness. I don't want to sing her praises, I want to shout them from every rooftop. I want the world to know the Lee I do: kind, selfless, loving, vibrant. After years of feeling numb, I feel so much with Alicia that I don't know what to do with a heart so full.

A few days later, I'm making coffee the next morning when Alicia joins me, pulling the sash on her robe tight as she walks into the kitchen.

"Morning, honey." She's started throwing that term around intermittently and I love it.

"Hey baby." If she can casually throw out terms of endearment, then I can, too. "Coffee?"

Instead of responding, she stands on her tiptoes to place a gentle kiss against my lips. Before she can pull away, I drag her closer, pulling her hips flush to mine.

"Or, we can go back to bed and I can worship you a little more before we have to get going with our day?" Placing her hands on my shoulders, she hops up, her legs circling my waist.

I kiss her deeply, cracking one eye open to make sure I don't bang into any walls on the walk back to bed. She squeaks when I grip her ass tighter. She shifts her mouth to my neck, planting open mouthed kisses across it. I harden immediately underneath her and walk faster to the bedroom. She grinds her hips against me and whimpers; I squeeze her ass again in response, urging her faster. She rocks again. I feel her wetness through the thin fabric of the joggers I threw on earlier. My cock is as hard as steel.

"Do it again, baby," I tell her as I sit on the edge of the bed. I trap her hips between my arms, urging her to grind against me and take what she needs. I bury my face against her breasts, licking and sucking and dragging my teeth against her soft skin. She tightens her grip on my shoulders as she swivels her hips, pressing her clit against my dick, chasing her pleasure. "You look so fucking sexy when you go after what you want. Take it, baby. Take what you deserve."

Her neck strains. I can see her pulse jump and I know she's straddling the knife's edge of her orgasm. I bring a hand to her perfect breast, sliding underneath her robe and pinch her nipple. She detonates, screaming my name as her orgasm washes over her. She continues riding me until the last dregs of it are wrung out and she collapses against my chest.

This might be my favorite version of Alicia. Cheeks pink, chest heaving, a slight sheen of perspiration on her forehead. She looks freshly fucked and I'm just getting started. I gently roll her off me and onto the bed.

I fish around in my nightstand for a condom. "How do you want me, baby?" I look up in time to see Alicia slide her robe all the way off her body and I pause my searching to enjoy the show. She smirks at me, knowing exactly what she's doing.

"I love me an unhinged Warner. I don't want you to hold back."

"Are you sure? I don't want to hurt you."

"I'm sure. I can handle it."

I've never torn open a condom wrapper so quickly. "On your knees. Let me see that ass I love so much." She scurries to the edge of the bed and does what I ask. I run my hands up the globes of her perfect ass, squeezing and kneading. I bend my knees and run my tongue through her folds.

"Ohhhh fuuuuuck." The guttural sound echoes across the bedroom as her chest collapses to the bed. I grin. I love the effect I have on her. I can't help it, I bend down and bite her ass cheek hard, then soothe the sting with my tongue. I'm immediately rewarded with a slick gush of arousal from her pussy.

"You like that, baby? You should see how beautiful your ass looks with my teeth marks."

"Warner, please," Alicia whines and I can't hold back a dark chuckle.

"I got you, Lee." Lining up at her entrance, I slam forward, filling her to the hilt in one thrust. Normally, I ease into her, but she told me she didn't want me holding back. I have to check in with her though. "Still with me? You okay, baby?"

"More," she begs. I pull my hips back until I'm almost fully released before pounding back in. She rocks forward on the bed a few inches with the force of my movements, and I pull her knees back toward me. She steels herself for more and I unleash, pushing in harder and deeper on each new thrust. She grips the sheets so hard her knuckles are white.

"You sure you're okay with this?" I ask as I lessen the intensity of my thrusts. "I don't have to go that hard."

"No, please keep going. I love it when you get that deep."

"Okay. But tell me to stop at any point," I insist, then pull back to resume my nonstop pounding. Her walls tighten against me, and additional moisture coats my dick.

"Oh god, I'm going to come," Alicia groans immediately before tipping over the edge again. She's strangling my cock, and I can barely hold on. I flex my hips a few more times before spilling my release into the condom. I collapse on top of her, rolling to the side at the last minute to avoid crushing her. She turns over, too, the two of us staring at the ceiling as we try to regulate our breathing. I know I'm trying to regulate my heart in more ways than one. Just then, I feel her snake her hand down to mine and wordlessly, she holds my hand.

This fake dating thing is killing me. The lines are getting blurred and I'm afraid to ask for clarity. I don't know if we should slow down on sleeping together or not.

"Hey, Lee," I whisper. "We should talk...about us." I cringe, hoping I don't regret bringing this up.

"Yeah, okay," she sighs. The way she says it makes me brace for impact, like I already know I won't like what she has to say.

"Maybe we should...it's not like I don't love fucking you, but if you don't want to do this, if this complicates things...or if...fuck, this isn't coming out the way I want it to." Leave it to me to fuck up a conversation this important. Alicia is silent, thinking.

"Let me ask you something, Warner. Are you pulling back because you don't want to do this anymore? Because if that's the case, I will respect your choice, and I won't fight you on it."

"No, Lee, that's not what's going on–"

She continues. "But if you're fighting this because you've caught feelings and you're afraid they aren't reciprocated, then dukes up, James. Because if you're offering it all, I'll happily take it."

The silence that blankets the room is deafening. I lean onto my elbow so I can look her in the eye.

"Wait, really?" She nods shyly. This beautiful woman, who has never been shy a day in her life, is suddenly self-conscious and I want to both kiss her for her foolishness and kick myself for making her feel that way, even for a second. "Lee, baby. I want it all."

Alicia's megawatt smile could have powered the whole city and I've never felt more grateful to be on the receiving end of it. I make an internal vow to do everything I can to have her smiling like that as often as I can.

"We're really doing this? Dating for real?" she asks, as if she needs to clarify one more time to be extra sure.

"Fuck yeah, we are. God, I've wanted to call you mine for so long, Lee." I pull her closer to me, kissing her deeply, imparting every ounce of my emotions into it, wanting her to feel just what she does to my heart.

CHAPTER THIRTY-FIVE
Alicia

"You know that saying 'ignorance is bliss?' Bliss is nothing compared to falling into Warner James' bed knowing he wants this–*all* of this–as badly as I do. Bliss is nothing compared to the feeling of falling for Warner, knowing that it's him who will catch me."

"Leesh, I am so happy for you!" Amy's eyes brim with tears as she drives us to the photography studio. "Also, it's about fucking time. I mean, Danny and Tim had you guys pegged for months!"

"We were a little busy trying to navigate the whole fake dating thing. Plus, you know, that teensy issue with the stalker?"

"Oh, we're joking about it now?" She glances at me out of the corner of her eye.

"I mean, I haven't gotten a letter in weeks, so maybe everything we've been doing worked." I shrug. "I hope," I tack on, not wanting to tempt fate.

"I hope so, too," she says, reaching across and squeezing my knee. "I'm really glad everything is working out for you. I've been worried about you, you know."

"Thanks, Amy," I tell her sincerely. I want to tell her she had no reason to worry, but after the stresses of the last six months or so, I'm glad to have her on my side. She throws the car in park, and we climb out, grabbing our bags loaded with outfit changes and accessories.

"I forgot to tell you. I added one more costume change. I brought a sexy librarian outfit, too."

"JJ is going to lose his mind!"

Amy's smile is devilish. "I know, I can't wait."

Denise, the photographer, was incredible. Between her makeup and styling tips and pose suggestions, I'm confident our photos will be flattering and sexy. She told us she could finish editing the photos within two weeks, but possibly sooner. I'm not exactly sure what I'll do with my photos. I know Warner would love to see them, and while I'm happy to watch the man salivate over what we did today, I also loved the boudoir photo session for what it was for me. It ignited a fierce sense of self-confidence and a renewed love for my body. I know Amy was feeling herself, too, and I couldn't be happier for her. As we were wrapping up, my phone vibrated with a message from Warner.

Warner

Hi baby.

During the photoshoot, Amy and I occasionally picked up the other's phone and snapped some candid shots to have on our own devices. I wasn't planning on sharing them with anyone, but she took an amazing shot of me lying upside down on the bed. My eyes are painted a smokey gray-green, my lips slightly parted as I play with a long string of pearls around my neck. The swells of my breasts are just visible in the black lacy bra I'm wearing. In the official shots taken by Denise, my legs are lifted straight in the air and crossed at the ankles, showing off my thigh-high stockings, garter and towering stilettos. The closeup Amy took captures me before I dragged the string of pearls through my teeth; she also got a great shot of that as well.

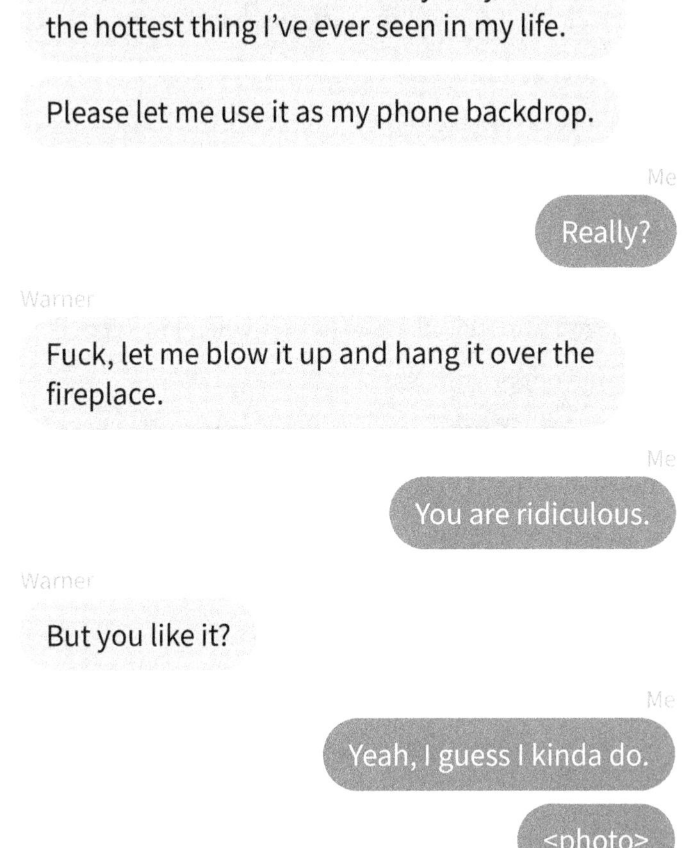

I wasn't originally planning on sending the follow up photo, but I like the idea of pushing my sometimes too serious and uptight Warner over the edge. When he doesn't text back immediately, I wonder if I've pushed him too far. The pearl necklace between my teeth left little to the imagination. His face suddenly fills my screen, video calling. I don't even get a chance to greet him before his voice echoes throughout Amy's car.

"Woman, do you know what you're doing to me? I can't walk around the clubhouse with my dick this hard!" I giggle, then pan the phone over so he can see Amy sitting behind the driver's seat, head tipped back and laughing. "Shit. Hi, Amy. Sorry you had to hear about my dick."

"Hi, Warner." She wiggles her fingers at the phone before turning on the car.

"Uh, do you want to call me back later when I won't make a fool of myself in front of your friend?"

"Don't worry, Warner. It's not the first time I've heard about your dick, and it probably won't be the last," Amy tells him through wheezing giggles.

Warner points his finger at me through the phone. "You, Lee. You are trouble."

"So, what you're saying is that you're going to add those photos to your digital frame in your living room?"

"Absolutely not. Those photos are for my eyes only." His tone is only half-serious.

"Oh, come on, I left plenty to the imagination," I tease.

"Lee baby, lucky for you, I have a very good imagination."

After a few more teasing jabs, he hangs up with promises that he'll call me after tonight's game. The team is in Atlanta but flies home after the game tonight. Warner's family has been attending his games the whole series and the effect on his mood is noticeable. He seems lighter, happier. I'm happy for him.

"Warner was right; you are in trouble," Amy tells me as she pulls away from the curb outside the photo studio. I feign a look of pure innocence. "Make sure you tell me once you tell Warner you're in love with him."

I blink at her.

I love the juxtaposition in our relationship. How Warner strips me bare each night and we allow ourselves to do filthy things to each other, only to lay ourselves emotionally bare afterwards. The sex is phenomenal. But the mornings after, where we share our truths and tumble deeper into whatever this is? That is life altering.

And for better or for worse, those life altering moments add up to one indisputable truth: I am completely, irrevocably, and undeniably in love with Warner James.

CHAPTER THIRTY-SIX
Warner

When I finally made it home from Atlanta, Alicia was already asleep but was in my bed. I had asked her earlier to sleep in there even when I'm not home. I know how much she loves the comfort of my bed, but I also secretly love the comfort I get knowing she's there while I'm gone. I slipped the latest magnet out of my pocket and onto her nightstand. She must have heard the click of it landing on the surface, because she started to stir. I felt bad waking her up, but I was also happy to see her. The sleepy smile she gave me warmed me so thoroughly I wanted to check to make sure the air conditioner was still working.

We spent several hours tangled in the sheets before falling asleep wrapped around each other. Today is an off day for the team and Alicia told the CMA she was going to take the day off too, so I'm thrilled we get to spend the day together. I know she's going to want to go for a run, which is not my most favorite way to spend an off day, but I'll do it for her. I have plans to take her to the Chicago Botanic Gardens later.

This morning has the makings of a great day, so I relax my rules for myself. When brushing my teeth, I smile at the new affirmation

Alicia has written on my mirror (*"I deserve time for myself by tending to my own needs without guilt or apology."*). I bring our coffee mugs to bed and slide back under the covers. It feels good to break a rule (my cardinal rule at that) and not have to worry about the repercussions; it feels good to know Alicia is by my side, even if things get hard.

She wakes after a few minutes. I'm scrolling on my phone when she sits up. She leans over and kisses my cheek.

"Morning, my love."

"Morning, baby. Coffee is on your nightstand. I thought we could go to the botanic gardens today if you want."

She narrows her eyes at me. "Are you just planning things so you don't have to go on a run with me?"

I laugh. "Not entirely, but if I can kill two birds with one stone, I'm going to do it."

"Fiiine," she groans. "I'll do my run tomorrow. You're lucky I knew this was going to happen and shifted my long run to yesterday." She hums in appreciation at the first sip of her coffee and shimmies her shoulders. I call it the Alicia happy dance; she does it when she's really excited about whatever she is eating. When I saw Eden this weekend, she sent me back with a few mason jars of the homemade coconut creamer Lee loves. Because we fly charter, the typical TSA liquids rules don't apply to us, and E took full advantage. Lee tips her head back and closes her eyes. "Ah, that's the good stuff. Tell your sister to just mainline it to my veins next time."

"She had me bring three jars of it back. They're in the fridge."

"She's the best! Thank you, Warner."

"You don't have to thank me. I like taking care of you. It makes me feel useful."

She carefully sets her mug on her nightstand before turning her body to face me fully. "What other things make you feel useful?"

I shrug, my response noncommittal.

"Come on, Warn. What's that shrug about?"

"I don't know. Sometimes it feels like my life lacks purpose. My job isn't important."

"How can you say that, Warn?"

"I guess I just feel like I'm not doing anything profound with my life. That's why taking care of you, protecting you, feels so good to me, I think."

She wraps her arms around my waist and settles her head on my shoulder. "Warn, your job is important. *You* are important." When I shrug again, she continues. "If you're really that set on adding an element to your life, maybe there's a hobby you can pick up. Go golfing more or something."

"Maybe there's a charity I could get involved with?"

"Sure, if that's what's interesting to you. But not everything in your life has to have a deep and meaningful purpose. Sometimes your purpose is just to be happy—and that's okay. Sometimes I think you put so much pressure on yourself to live up to these arbitrary expectations, you know? I'm all for everyone working to better themselves, but do it because you want to, Warner, not because you feel like you have to. It's not a moral failing to want to have fun without it having a higher purpose."

I sigh. "You're right." I press a kiss to the top of her head.

"I know I'm right. I'm always right," she says, flicking my nipple.

"Now you've done it!" I growl at her, pushing her back and climbing on top of her. She squeals and giggles as I tickle her sides, burying my face in her neck and laughing along with her.

We spend hours wandering the Chicago Botanic Gardens. We grab lunch at the cafe on site, then stroll the wide pathways, taking in the colorful blooms and bright flora. Birds of all sizes chirp loudly, a cacophony of noise the soundtrack to our walk. Alicia's hand has been firmly in mine for most of the time we've been here. She only pulls away to take photos or to stray near the edge of the path to take in some small detail on the nearby plants.

She snaps a selfie of us standing in front of large purple flowers twining their way up a wooden trellis. She tells me they are clematis, but I don't know how she can tell them apart from the purple ones in a bushy clump over by the pond. The backdrop is stunning, and it's one of my favorite pictures of us yet, only because Alicia's eyes are crinkled in such genuine happiness that I want to remember this moment forever.

"Send me that one."

"Why? So you can have a more appropriate phone background?" She bats her eyes at me.

"No, I'm adding it to my frame app."

"You really don't have to add pictures of me to your digital frame. I know you use that to share photos with Eden and your parents."

"Lee, I've been adding photos of you to it for months. I'm not going to stop now." Her mouth pops open, and my mind is infiltrated with thoughts too dirty for public.

"No you haven't," she says in a disbelieving tone. I hand my phone to her, where the selfie she just sent me has finished uploading. The screen is filled with photos from the frame, all time stamped with when I uploaded them.

"Hmm, maybe you *aren't* always right!" I say triumphantly, nudging her shoulder with my own. She sticks her tongue out at me and hands me my phone back. We keep exploring, traipsing through the fruit tree orchard. Bees buzz lazily around us, pollinating the buds.

"The midseason break is coming up in a couple weeks. Did you want to go somewhere?" I ask.

"You don't already have plans?" I shake my head. "It would be nice to do something together. I've been wanting to ask you about it but didn't want you to feel pressured to do something with me."

"Lee, listen to me." I pull her into a hug. "You don't pressure me. We can do whatever we want. I'd love to spend the break with my girlfriend." She smiles up at me.

"Well, now that I'm *officially* your girlfriend, it might be nice to do something together. Did you have something in mind?"

"Matteo invited us to rent a yacht on the lake with him if we stay in town. I guess a bunch of guys did that last year and it was a blast. But if you want to travel, we can do that, too, but it would have to be somewhere relatively close. We only have four days."

"Staying here would be fine. I'm good with anything."

"Let's stay here then. I can take you out to dinner each night and show you off. Then I can bring you home and have you for dessert." I wink at her as she tips her head back on a laugh.

"That sounds great to me."

CHAPTER THIRTY-SEVEN
Alicia

There's something to be said about the security that comes with falling asleep and waking up to the person who occupies your thoughts. Warner and I slipped from fake dating into real dating so seamlessly that even I have to occasionally stop and shake my head, wondering if this is real. It always is.

Being with someone so honestly is refreshing. Warner knows my challenges, and I know his. We are each other's support when the other is struggling, but to be honest, neither of us seem to be struggling as much these days.

The problem is, sometimes that security–the one that rocks you peacefully to sleep each night in the arms of your partner–also can lull you into a false sense of security, right when you least expect it. It's this shattered sense of security that leaves me grappling for peace and struggling for air after I bring the mail up to our unit after work.

A quick glance through the mail in the lobby had me sighing in relief. It is only when I get upstairs that I realize the small green envelope whose presence I was dreading, was, in fact, tucked neatly between two pieces of junk mail. I missed it in my initial sweep, and it floats to the ground as I walk to the recycle bin in the kitchen. Suddenly, there's not enough air in the apartment. My organs feel like they're being crushed by a vise. There's a gradual ringing in my ears.

I don't know how long I stand in the kitchen, staring at the mint green envelope on the floor, gasping on the last dregs of air in my lungs. It could have been minutes or hours. What I do know is that Warner comes home from his game, walks into the kitchen, and stops mid-sentence.

"I'll call you back, Sean." Warner's words float to me from a distance, as if I experience it underwater. Despite knowing, on some level, that Warner is in the kitchen with me, I still flinch when he touches my shoulder. He comes to stand in front of me, blocking my vision from the offending envelope. I blink several times. His touch, his presence, while initially jarring, seems to be enough to snap me back to reality. My lungs finally fill completely at the same time my knees buckle.

"Easy. I got you, Lee." Warner guides me to a stool at the island. I can just make out the corner of the envelope peeking out from behind the countertop. Warner must notice, because, after flicking his eyes over to it briefly, he positions himself again to block it from my sight. "I need you to breathe, baby."

I didn't realize I had stopped breathing. I gulp in gasping breaths as the tightness returns to my chest. He exaggerates his own breathing, silently coaxing me to lengthen my inhales and exhales.

"Good, good," he murmurs soothingly as I finally calm my lungs. He rubs his hands gently up and down the outsides of my arms, timing the movements with my breathing.

Maintaining his stance in front of me, he slides his phone back out of his pocket. With one arm continuing his soft strokes up and down my arm, he taps a few icons with his thumb and brings the phone to his ear. I barely hear his conversation, clipped words and a demanding tone I've never heard him use before.

Suddenly, I'm seated in the dining room with no recollection of how I got there. Vincent Coyle is standing in front of me, blue latex gloves covering his hands. The overhead lights in the dining room glint off his bald head, and I'm struck with a sudden urge to laugh hysterically. This hardened, badass version of Mr. Clean is just as shiny as the cartoon advertisement. I can't suppress the giggle that escapes my mouth. Warner, standing beside him, flicks a worried glance at Coyle.

"Is this still the panic attack?" Warner. His voice is still coming to me underwater. My brain feels fuzzy, like I'm processing everything in slow motion. Like I'm drunk, but fully aware of how incapacitated I am. I feel like I'm losing my mind. Warner and Coyle don't know why I'm laughing, and I can't get my mouth to articulate my thoughts. Not that now is the time to explain the joke. My emotions tumble around in my head, and I suddenly feel like crying. I really am losing my shit, going from laughing to crying in the span of four seconds.

"It might be shock. Let's get her some rest. CPD should be here soon. We can proceed without her. Ms. Langley, perhaps you should lie down."

"Come on, baby. I'll take you to bed." Strong arms lift me, and I'm enveloped in Warner's warm, comforting scent. Whispered words I can't quite make out skitter across my skin as I'm laid onto Warner's heavenly bed. I sink in, letting the fluffy comforter and pillows pull me under.

When I wake, I feel groggy and disoriented. A lack of light filtering through the curtains in Warner's bedroom indicates it's nighttime, but it can't be that late. His side of the bed is empty. I drag a hand down my face as the events from earlier come rushing back to me. Fuck. Another letter. Murmured voices carry softly to me when I open the bedroom door. When I reach the dining room, Warner stands immediately and sweeps me into his arms.

"How are you doing, baby? Did we wake you?"

"No. How long was I asleep?"

He checks his watch. "About an hour. Not long."

I take in the room. Vincent Coyle's hulking body takes up residence at the head of the table, while two plain-clothed police officers sit on one side, Warner's now-empty chair across from them.

"Lee, these are Detectives Pinal and Gregory." A man with salt and pepper hair and a kind-faced woman nod at me in turn. "They are here to take our statements and collect some evidence. Do you want to sit with us?"

I take the empty chair Warner pulls out for me. As soon as I sit, he retakes his spot, pulling my chair closer to him and grasping my hand tightly in his in one fluid movement.

"How are you feeling, Ms. Langley?" The woman, Detective Gregory, asks gently.

"I'm okay, I guess," I respond unconvincingly. She offers me a small, commiserating smile. "I didn't open the letter yet. I'm probably freaking out over nothing." At her lack of response, my own phony smile drops. She and her partner wouldn't be here looking so serious if it was nothing.

"Lee, do you want to see the letter?" Warner asks me, and I hate the softness in his voice, as if he's afraid showing me the letter will send me spiraling. Which, I guess, isn't that far outside the realm of possibilities since I had a panic attack earlier tonight.

"I need to see it." My response is simple, but I'm hoping the sense of calm infused in my voice will fool my brain into some sort of rationality.

"Ms. Langley, we were called here by Mr. Coyle," the other detective, Pinal, starts. "We were able to open the letter and while we need to take the contents with us as evidence, I think it's important for you to be informed of what's going on. Are you feeling like you can handle it right now?" His words are firm but not unkind. I nod, and it must be convincing, because he continues. "Here are the contents of the letter."

Detective Pinal slides a large, clear evidence bag over to me. Inside, the stalker's letter is unfolded, the large, blocky letters easy to see.

ALICIA,

I'VE BEEN PATIENT LONG ENOUGH. I WILL MAKE YOU MINE AND THERE IS NOTHING WARNER JAMES CAN DO ABOUT IT. GET RID OF HIM OR I WILL DO IT FOR US.

YOURS ALWAYS.

Immediately, bile rises in my throat. I close my eyes and breathe deeply through my nose until the nausea dissipates. When I open them again, Detective Pinal scrutinizes me briefly before sliding another clear evidence bag toward me. These contents are far worse than anything the stalker has sent me before.

The paper is crumpled, as if it had been repeatedly balled up and smoothed back out. A black and white photo is inked across the paper. The edges are roughly cut, bisecting words. It looks like it's a photo printed from a home printer, from a website article. The words are mostly unreadable, but the picture is clear. It's a photo taken of Warner and me at dinner. The bistro chairs and overflowing hanging flowerpots in the corner of the frame tell me it's from a date we went on a week ago at Le Matin, a new French restaurant we decided to try. The photo itself isn't alarming, it's what the stalker has done to it. Warner's whole face is scribbled out in red ink, obscuring his features. I only know it's him because of the rest of the clues in the photo: his hand protectively resting over mine, the closeness of his body to me as we lean in to clink our coffee mugs, the intimate smile on my face I reserve just for him.

The threat against Warner is clear.

CHAPTER THIRTY-EIGHT

Alicia

Tears spring to my eyes as my lunch threatens to make an appearance. Detective Gregory clocks my reaction, dragging the evidence bags back to her side of the table and tucking them away in a portfolio bag. It doesn't matter. I can't unsee the image, I can't unread the words. The scribbles over Warner's perfect face are burned into my retinas.

Warner tugs my chair, pulling me closer and angling me to face him. "It's okay, Lee. I've got you. We're going to figure this out, but I need you to keep breathing for me, baby. Vincent and the detectives are going to handle this, but it's good we involved them. We're going to get to the bottom of this and stop this guy from ever getting close to you again." He pulls me into a crushing hug.

My words come out muffled against his chest. I push off to lift my head but remain close. "And what about you? This is a threat against *you*. I'm not worried about me!"

"Ma'am, with all due respect, this is a threat against both of you," Vincent's voice cuts through my increasingly frantic speech. "We need to be smart and take certain precautions, but now that an actual threat has been made, we can engage with law enforcement further."

Vincent explains that in addition to the increased security measures taken both at the Vandeveer as a whole and specifically at Warner's apartment, he liaised with some contacts in the Chicago Police Department, but limited steps could be taken without more information.

"Yes, this is a threat, but it also means he's giving us more information every time he contacts you." Vincent's firm manner of speaking is oddly calming. I want to believe him. "Mr. James, you said you kept copies of previous notes? May we see them?"

"You kept them?" Thinking back, I don't remember throwing away the last two letters I received. Warner removed them from my sight. I'm not sure how I feel about him keeping them. Logically, I know it will probably be helpful evidence, even if it does nothing but establish a history of contact. Emotionally, I'm overwhelmed. My skin crawls, knowing the letters have been in this apartment with me for weeks, months even. Above all, I know Warner did it out of care and concern for me, and I'm as touched as I am overwhelmed.

He excuses himself and returns within a minute, holding two envelopes. Each has a sticky note with a date attached. I should have known Warner would be systematic and organized in his approach to protecting me. I give him a watery smile; he nods in response.

"Ms. Langley, how long did you say you've been receiving these?" Detective Pinal asks as he slips on a pair of latex gloves and slides the letters out of their envelopes.

"A little more than a year and a half." I shudder when I say it aloud. It's different when I received the letters initially. They were so few and far between that they were easy to brush off or ignore completely. "They come at irregular times. Sometimes, I'll go more than a month without hearing anything."

"She received them at her old apartment, too. She's been living here since the end of January, but he somehow found her here." Gregory nods in response to Warner's words, but her eyes are focused on the photo from one of the old envelopes.

"This is you?" she confirms, holding the photo so I can see it. I don't need to look to know that it is.

"Yes."

"Is this the first time you've contacted CPD about this case yourself? Aside from Mr. Coyle's contact a few weeks ago?" My cheeks grow hot, as if I'm being scolded for not coming to the police sooner.

"I didn't think it was worth doing. It wasn't a threat, so I didn't think there was anything you could do."

Detective Gregory's face softens, her sad smile not quite reaching her eyes. "Ms. Langley, we're not judging you. I ask because if you had brought it to us earlier, I would want to ensure we combined the case notes. You're right, though. There's limited action we could have taken with this information alone."

"I must admit, his approach is unusual. Nowadays, you typically see more cyberstalking, more involvement with digital contact, rather than snail mail. Not that this is coming through the mail," Pinal acknowledges. "The long periods between contact are interesting, too."

"This is clearly taken from the web, though," Warner points out. "Isn't this some sort of cyberstalking?"

"Technically, no. Cyberstalking involves digital contact, like emails or messaging through social media apps. It's about electronic communication. Just looking someone up online repeatedly doesn't fall under cyberstalking," Pinal explains.

"We're going to take these to the crime lab and get them fingerprinted. I'm sure they'll want to do a lot more analysis as well," Gregory says, sliding each envelope into its own evidence bag. "We'll be in touch with anything we find, but you likely won't hear from us for at least a week, realistically." The timeline is not comforting. As if she can read my thoughts, she adds, "I know, it's not ideal to have no more information than what you started with, but this is a good jumping off point. We have some directions to pursue." She squeezes my hand reassuringly. "In the meantime, please make sure you are cautious. Both of you," she adds with a meaningful glance at Warner.

After the cops leave, Coyle sticks around for another hour to go over additional questions and security protocol. I didn't realize he lives in the Vandeveer; the thought comforts me more than I expected. He advised Warner to update the Foxes' security team and to look into private security for each of us.

"No. Absolutely not. I'm not going to be babysat. I'm tired of this interrupting my life as it is." I almost stomp my foot in frustration.

"What will you do when I'm out of town then, Lee?" Warner gives me a beseeching look. "I need to know you're safe." My eyes fill with tears, partly out of frustration and partly out of care for this man. I don't have a plan. Up until an hour ago, I didn't know I needed one. "Can we call your parents? Ask them to stay here while I'm gone next week?"

I sigh. It's better than being babysat by some poor private security guard. "Okay," I agree. "We can call them later tonight."

After Coyle leaves, Warner saunters back into the dining room and places a cup of tea in front of me. "I'm sure Eden wouldn't mind staying here, too, if you parents aren't able to come. Or Jenny and Amy. Any of the wives. I just can't stomach the thought of you being alone."

The idea of having someone with me twenty-four-seven is daunting. As much as I love socializing with my friends, I've never minded being alone, either. The idea of forcing someone to hang out with me is abhorrent. Besides, what is the mere presence of one other person going to do to deter this psychopath?

Sensing my hesitation, Warner turns to pleading. "Baby, please. For my own peace of mind, please." His eyes are full of imploring desperation.

"Fine, but what about you?" I'm honestly less concerned about myself than I am for Warner. Seeing his face scribbled out in that photo was alarming. My reaction was visceral. The idea of him being put in harm's way because of me is so repellent, I can feel myself recoiling in response.

"Nope, don't even go there," he says quickly. I swear he can read my mind. "I'd happily take any inconvenience in order to be with you." He presses soft kisses to my forehead, temple, cheeks. "I'm not worried about myself. I'll be fine. I'll talk to Eric, and we'll come up with a plan for when I'm with the team. Now, are we going to call your parents together or do you want to do it by yourself?"

It turns out talking to my parents was somewhat easier than I anticipated, but I suspect that's only because they were putting every ounce of their energy into shielding me from how concerned they were, in an effort not to worry me further. They agree to look for flights tonight and plan on arriving in two days. It will give me enough time to set up the guest room and get my emotions under control before Warner has to leave town this weekend.

Having my parents in town is more fun than I thought it would be. I know they are worried for me. The crease lines in my father's forehead deepen every time we leave the apartment, but having them near is a comfort.

The first night in town, the four of us went to a local dive bar. My parents love a good dive bar, but my father was going to give himself whiplash, his head was on such a constant swivel. I swear my mother almost broke the small bones in his hands the way she clutched them so tightly each time someone neared our table. Their nerves made me nervous, so we ended up calling it a night early. Luckily, as the week has worn on, they seem to be relaxing slightly. At least they aren't walking around so stiffly, as if my stalker is going to jump out from behind Warner's kitchen island to yell *Gotcha!*

My mother insisted on accompanying me to the museums each time I physically went in to work. It was ridiculous, but at least I was able to convince her to visit the exhibits while I worked. I think the only reason she finally agreed was because I promised I would always have other people around me. Granted, most of the other people were high schoolers, but she didn't need to know that.

Having my parents around is nice, though. They haven't visited me in Chicago since I originally moved here after college. Instead, I often flew home for the holidays, or we met up at various spots for a long weekend together. It's nice getting to show them the things I love about my adopted city.

"Wake up! I've got bagels!" My dad's voice rings from the front hall. He knows both my mother and I are awake, but he's been saying the same thing since he started the weekend tradition of bagels and coffee on Sunday mornings when my siblings and I were in high school. It was his way of ensuring we all stayed connected even with our busy social calendars growing up.

Dad plops the bag of bagels on the kitchen counter but gently sets the tray of hot coffees next to it. I open the bag while Mom stacks napkins and plates nearby.

"So, Warner gets back early this evening," I say around a bite of my standard blueberry bagel once we're seated together. "He asked if we wanted to go out for dinner." I told my parents about Warner and me dating right before they came to town. They didn't know about the fake dating situation to begin with, so explaining why I was sleeping in Warner's room or the loving looks we shot each other's way was easy. He insisted on taking my parents out the first two nights they were in town to get to know them better. It's no surprise they took to each other like ducks to water.

"That would be lovely." My mom especially loves Warner. How could she not, honestly? He treats me like a queen and has been so devoted, so protective, of me throughout this whole stalker situation that she needs no convincing that Warner is the right man for me.

"I picked this up while I was out, too," Dad says, plopping a white plastic bag on the table. I peek inside and see a handheld dispenser of pepper spray and a sparkly purple unicorn head keychain. The keychain has holes where the eyes should be but is otherwise cute.

"Yeah? You pick this up at Bagels, Bagels, Bagels? They've really upped their inventory since the last time I was there," I joke.

"Smartass," my dad mumbles. "It's for when you go running. I know it's hard to find someone who can run as fast or as long as you, now that you're training again. But at least this will give me a little peace of mind if you do go out by yourself."

I'm touched. My dad is the OG feminist dad: never one to stifle my independence but acutely aware of the dangers I face as a woman. "Thanks, Dad," I say, touching his arm. "Is the unicorn to soften the harshness of pepper spray as a gift?"

"No. The woman behind the counter showed me this is how you hold it when you're out." Dad grasps the head, slipping his middle and ring fingers in the eye holes. The flat plastic of the unicorn face lies flush against his palm, while the sharp horn sticks out like Wolverine's claws. "This way, if you need to stab a bitch, you can." My dad's tone is light, and his word choice causes my mom and me to laugh, lightening the seriousness of the moment. I know he's worried for me, and I appreciate the gifts.

"Thanks, Dad. I promise I'll bring them with me." He nods, eyes slightly shinier than when we began this conversation. My dad is rarely emotional, preferring to joke around or find seriousness in his work. Mom takes the opportunity to pull him out of the spotlight.

"Where was Warner thinking for dinner tonight?"

For the next few hours, we walk by the riverfront and the beach before heading to a bar at North Avenue Beach to watch the Foxes game. The sun is bright, but the breeze wafting off the lake is cooling. My parents leave tomorrow night, but we have plans to go to the Foxes game tomorrow afternoon so they can see Warner in action and have a chance to say goodbye before we take them to the airport.

CHAPTER THIRTY-NINE

Warner

Being away from Alicia for a week shortly after receiving the most recent letter was one of the hardest things I've done. My feet hesitated on every step onto the plane leaving the airport last week. Knowing her parents were around was a comfort, as were my daily communications with Coyle. He informed me that additional cameras were installed outside the elevator banks both in the lobby and the penthouse floor. He shared all the video footage of the man who placed the letter in our mailbox with the police. We still don't know how he was able to get the letter in again after having our mailbox rekeyed, but this guy seems resourceful. Coyle suspects he's quickly picking the locks, which makes me that much more grateful for the heightened security measures we took around our unit. He's been smart enough to hide his identity, too. He looks like an average white guy; the only thing remarkable about this guy is how unremarkable he is. The lack of progress in identifying him is infuriating.

The lack of progress on the whole case, as a matter of fact, is infuriating. I'm feeling the strain, which I'm sure is nothing compared to how Lee is feeling, no matter how much she tries to hide it. She insists she's not going to change anything about her behaviors or routines, emphatically declaring this guy has fucked up her life enough as it is. Her tossing and turning at night, after she thinks I've fallen asleep, tells me that she's not as relaxed about the whole thing as she's portraying. It kills me to see her like this. It destroys me to feel so powerless to help her.

When the midseason break finally arrives, I wonder if we should have left town. We have plans together, but maybe getting away is what Alicia needs. When I suggest we cancel our plans in favor of leaving town, she dismisses them. I know she's trying to pretend like the letters aren't impacting her, but I'm not buying it.

"Please, Warner. I need to feel normal about things. I'm tired of this guy having so much control over my life. I'm tired of looking over my shoulder. I'm not saying I'm going to be reckless. I promise I'm not. But I'm not going to uproot my entire way of living just because some psychopath never learned what a boundary is!"

It's hard to argue with her when she's right, but it doesn't stop my protective side from roaring to life anytime we leave our apartment together. I've always loved touching Alicia. Having her skin touching mine is one of the greatest comforts of our relationship. But now I feel like I have to touch her to remind myself she's safe. I want to comfort her and protect her as much as I can, even from her own emotions. I know she's feeling guilt now that the stalker has turned his attention on me. While I'm not going to be reckless either, I welcome the attention on me if it takes the heat off her.

I can't pretend the added stress isn't taking a toll on our interactions. Alicia seems more on edge lately, not that I blame her, and it's been getting harder to fight off my exhaustion at the end of each day.

I'm suddenly reminded why I don't date. Not because the interactions are tiring–they're not, the stalker is. It's because Alicia shouldn't be shackled to someone with all my baggage. At a time when she needs me to be strong the most, I find myself struggling, too. The unfairness of it all pushes me closer to the yawning pit of my depression.

Tomorrow is our boat cruise with Matteo and everyone else who stayed in town for the break. If I'm going to have the energy for a full day of social interactions when I'm already feeling down, I need to go to bed early to rest up. When I tell Alicia this, she seems almost startled.

"Warner, it's only six thirty. You're going to bed now?"

"Yeah, I'm just really tired and we have the boat thing tomorrow." I can't decipher the look on her face. Sadness, maybe? She scoots closer to where I'm standing near the couch.

"Warn, come here." Reluctantly, I settle on the edge of the couch next to her. "I'm sorry." Confusion etches my features. "I haven't been checking in on you like I should have." I shake my head. She reaches up to touch my cheek and I automatically lean into it. "Baby, tell me what you're feeling."

I sigh. It's so much to get into. I know her intentions are good, but it's hard to muster the energy on nights like this to talk about my emotions. "Lee, I'm sorry I can't support you in the way you need to be supported right now."

Now, the confusion is all hers. "What do you mean?"

"I'm just tired. Can we talk about this later?" I see the moment her anxiety spikes, reading too much into my reluctance to talk. I hurry to settle her nerves. "I'm okay, baby. We're okay. I just need a night to rest up. I want to be able to protect you and support you and this fucking exhaustion is getting in my way."

She gives me an understanding smile. "Warn, you do support me and protect me. Exactly the way I need it. You're doing everything right. I'm sorry it's been so stressful lately."

"You have nothing to be sorry about," I tell her honestly. I grasp her hand in mine, squeezing it to convey my sincerity.

"I'm not the only one who needs support and protection, though. Let me take care of you tonight. I can rub your back, and we can watch a movie in bed. You haven't eaten dinner yet either; let me make you something quickly."

I close my eyes. It's all too much. I should be the one taking care of her, not the other way around. She has a stalker, for Christ's sake! She rubs her hand soothingly across my shoulder blades, but even her touch, normally so comforting, is too much for me to handle. I stand abruptly, putting distance between us. I'm so angry at myself, at my depression, for limiting me yet again in being the person I want to be. Only this time, it affects not just me, but the person I care about most in the world.

In a fit of frustration, I lash out. I know in the moment, it's wrong, yet I can't help it. "Lee, you can't fix me!" My voice comes out louder than I intend. She looks at me and blinks one, two, three times. She fixes me with a kind gaze and my annoyance flares again. Why does she always have to be so kind? I'm being rude; I don't deserve her kindness.

"Do you think you need to be fixed?" she asks gently.

"I–what?"

"You said I can't fix you. Do you think there's something about you that requires fixing?" When I don't respond, she continues. "Do you think *I* think there's something about you that needs fixing?"

I still don't respond. How could she not see that I need fixing? My broken brain can't give her or any other partner what they need, not when I can't take care of myself half the time. Not when I'm so exhausted, so physically pained for no reason, that all I want to do is curl up in bed and sleep for weeks? When I can't stop crying and can't articulate what's upsetting me? Who wants to saddle themselves to that? I've created a carefully curated life. Few people get to see the man behind the curtain. Now that she has, why would she stay? Who would want to?

I escape to our bedroom, desperate to be alone. I've already lashed out at her once and she responded with grace and kindness. I can't expect her to be so patient if I do it again. I pace the bathroom behind the locked door, wringing my hands. The guilt I felt for losing my cool in front of her was immediate and lingering. Out of the corner of my eye, I catch a glimpse of myself in the mirror, my forehead obscured by another one of her daily affirmations.

It's okay to show emotion; people love me for who I am inside.

Fuck. Even when she's not physically next to me, she's looking out for me, providing me comfort. I flip through our recent texts from when I've been on the road. I count the number of times she's checked in on my well-being and realize it's been every day.

Lee

> How was your shower today?

> Did you eat breakfast this morning?

> What was the best part of your morning so far?

> I'm thinking of you.

A wave of emotion so strong crashes into me, threatening to take me under. Tears leak from my eyes as gratitude for her and guilt about my earlier overreaction war within me. From the beginning, Lee has treated me with kindness, respect, and dignity, even when she's seen me at my lowest. She's held me through the night as my tears soaked our shared bed. She's gently pushed me to find my own strength in my most challenging moments. She's shown up for me, day after day. And tonight, she continues to show up, even when I don't deserve it.

By the time I compose myself, splash water on my face, and leave the bathroom, she is propped up in bed, reading a book. When she sees me enter, she sets her book aside and opens her arms wide. I climb into the bed and crawl over to her, depositing myself onto her chest, looping my arms around her waist. Instantly, her fingers brush comforting strokes down my bare back, and I know I'm home.

The next morning, I wake early. I fell asleep quickly last night, nestled on top of Lee while she rubbed my back. I apologized profusely for blowing up, which she insisted I didn't need to do, but I still feel a little guilty. She doesn't stir as I slip out of bed and start the coffee maker. I'm feeling much better this morning, rebounding from my exhaustion faster than I typically do. I'm still tired, but it's nothing that coffee and some sunshine won't fix.

When I return to bed, I watch her sleep for a few minutes while I wait for the coffee to finish brewing. When I'm with her, I'm less worried about crawling back into bed, and I'm struck by another flash of gratitude for all that she brings into my life. Her eyelashes flutter briefly before she rolls over in her sleep, one rosy nipple peeking out from beneath the sheets. Last night, she had removed her shirt during the middle of our cuddle, knowing how much I love skin to skin contact with her. It's one of the million things she does that reminds me how truly lucky I am.

I watch in fascination as her nipple pebbles and she sighs. Her legs stretch but her eyes remain closed. I'm not sure if she's dreaming or starting to wake up, but a soft moan from her, followed by a gentle thrust of her hips, gives me my answer. My girl is having a very enjoyable dream. I debate whether to wake her and continue the fun in person or to leave her sleeping and enjoy the show. I settle further into the bed beside her, propping my head on my elbow. She moves but doesn't wake. Her lips part. Her nipple is hardened to a tiny point. My cock thickens at the sight, my mouth watering. She sucks in a sharp breath, which causes her to cough and wake. She turns her head to see me watching with rapt attention.

"Good dream?" I paste a shit-eating grin on my face so she knows there's no mistaking that I know what kind of dream it was. She shoves me lightly.

"Shut up." Her cheeks tinge pink.

"There's nothing to be embarrassed about. It's been a little bit, huh?" Her parents were here when I came back to town and the stress of everything else has impacted our normally high libidos. She nods. "Want to fix that? We don't have to leave for another hour and a half. There are so many things I could do to this pussy in that amount of time." She moans, spreading her legs. "You're such a good girl. Did you keep this pussy wet for me?" She nods again but I swipe a finger under her sleep shorts to check anyway.

"Yes, Warner." Her words come out breathy as she shimmies her shorts off. I push a finger inside her, pumping slowly.

"Tell me, baby. Did you touch yourself while I was gone? Did you slide your fingers into this perfect, pink pussy and make yourself come, shoving your face in the pillow so Mommy and Daddy didn't hear what a bad girl you were?" When she doesn't respond other than to moan, I plunge another finger inside.

"Oh, God, Warner, you're going to make me come!" She jerks her upper body forward when my thumb circles her clit. The movement brings her breast closer to my mouth and I reward her, swirling my tongue around the pebbled point. She is always responsive to me, but the week and a half without sex has made her especially sensitive. She's already clenching my fingers.

"That's the plan, baby. Over and over." I increase the pace of my fingers, crooking them to tap against her G-spot. Her moans become increasingly erratic, her hips thrusting into the air. I add a third finger and she detonates, her walls squeezing the life out of my fingers. Liquid splashes my cupped palm and my cock bobs in response. It gives me a certain level of pride to know I can make her come so quickly; I can't get enough.

As soon as her legs stop shaking, I toss back the comforter and bury my face between her luscious thighs. She scrabbles against the bed. "Warner!" she cries out. "It's too sensitive!"

"You can take it, baby," I assure her, but move my tongue away from her swollen clit for a few minutes, lapping up her juices below. Her cries subside into pleasured moans as I feast like a man starved. "It's been so long since I've had a taste," I tell her between licks. "I need this."

I resume eating her cunt, stroking my hands up and down her inner thighs, rubbing the bridge of my nose against her clit. When her hand slides down her stomach to press my face deeper, I hum in appreciation. Glancing up, I see her pinching and tugging at her nipples and it spurs me to flatten my tongue, attacking her clit with firm, unrelenting strokes. She's so wet that when I replace two fingers inside her, they glide in easily.

"Warner, wait!" Her cry rings out so urgently, I stop. "I think…I think I'm gonna pee!"

I chuckle against her, resuming my feast. "No, you're not. Work through it, baby. I promise it'll be good."

"What—ohhhhhhhh," she groans loudly, squirting over my mouth, chin, and neck. "Holy shit, holy shit," she pants as she soaks the bed. I greedily lap it up until she settles. I crawl up her perfect body and gaze at her, a sleepy, blissful expression taking over her face.

When she finally opens her eyes, I ask, "Have you ever squirted before?"

She shakes her head, whispering, "Never." Again, a spark of pride flames in my chest.

"Thank you for letting me do the honors." I smirk at her. "You taste incredible." She ducks her head but laughs all the same. "Now that we know you can, we're going to have so much fun replicating that."

She grins, swinging a leg over my hips and lowering herself slowly onto my shaft. She feels like heaven. I love watching myself enter her, over and over. We both look down and watch where her body swallows me. It's so erotic, I feel my cock twitch inside her.

"Do it again," she demands, and I flex my hips, reaching the deepest parts of her. She cries out as I do it repeatedly, edging us slightly closer to the finish. "Don't stop, Warn."

As if I could if I wanted to.

Flipping her onto her back, I drill into her. I hike up her knee, pressing it to her chest. It allows me to half kneel, driving in deep. Her mouth opens into a perfect O, her eyes screwed shut in ecstasy. My hips thrust repeatedly as her nails rake down my back. She's going to leave marks, making it obvious to everyone later today what we did during our morning activities, but I couldn't care less. I'll proudly show off my girl's passion like a badge of honor.

"Warner, I'm close!" Her cries are becoming louder. I don't know if I've ever heard them so loud before. It's like my own personal cheering squad and it does the trick. I'm hanging on the edge of my own pleasure, but I only want to go after her. I force myself deeper, thrusting harder a few more times until we both explode at the same time. I pulse into her in long spurts, over and over. I just keep coming and coming; I want to prolong this feeling forever.

It's only when I pull out that I realize we skipped the condom. "Shit, I'm so fucking sorry, baby. I got so caught up." I watch my cum trickle out of her, pooling at the base of my shaft, as panic trickles into my chest. I'm not ready for kids. I don't know if I'll ever be ready for kids. Fuck, what if Alicia wants kids? We haven't even talked about this yet.

"Easy there, tiger," she soothes, reading the panic on my face. Her voice is raw. "I've got an IUD. Please tell me the panic that is so clearly written on your face is because you're worried about pregnancy, not infecting me with an STD?"

I can't help the laugh that bursts out of me. "I'm clean, sweetheart. We get tested every spring training." I pause, my anxiety suddenly taking a new form.

"I'm clean, too. Don't worry." The panic subsides.

"Do you, um, want kids? Like, eventually?"

She winces. "Actually, I don't. Is that a deal breaker for you?"

"Not at all." The tightness in my chest is immediately loosened. "Fuck, why am I so relieved you said that? I never really thought about it before, but shit, to say it out loud, that I don't think I want to have kids either? It feels good to say that."

Alicia laughs. "My thoughts exactly. I like kids well enough; I just connect better to them once they're in their teenage years. That's why I let Amy handle all the littles at work."

I pull her in for a kiss. "I like Eden's kids. They're the best kids I've ever met, and I'm still happy to send them back to their parents at the end of the weekend." She chuckles, scooting down to rest her cheek against my chest. "What do you say you let me clean you up and bring you some coffee?"

"Want to make it tea instead? My throat is a little sore...you know...from all the screaming." The sparks of pride in my chest conflagrate into an inferno.

CHAPTER FORTY
Alicia

Matteo took it upon himself to rent the largest yacht available and commission an entire staff to cater to our needs. Luckily, our needs aren't that complex and are limited to the captain and crewmates responsible for keeping us afloat, a bartender (keeping us afloat in a very different way), a chef, and a sous chef.

"Here, hook a girl up and get my back and I'll do yours," Amy says, tossing me a bottle of SPF 50. Her pale skin needs as much sun protection as she can get; I'm honestly surprised JJ hasn't already jumped at the chance to put his hands all over her again. Those two are rarely apart. She tugs at the shoulder strap of her red one-piece suit. The neckline plunges, showing off her cleavage in a classic cut. She looks gorgeous.

"Where's your fiancé?" I squirt a giant blob of sunscreen on my hand and grimace at the feeling of it seeping through my fingers and onto my bent leg. Amy perches herself on the edge of my deck chair, pulling her blonde hair over her shoulder and away from the greasy cream.

"With the guys, getting drinks. I told him to bring me something fruity from the bar." We haven't pulled away from port yet, but I already settled myself in prime leisure real estate on the sunny deck, hoping to sunbathe early before it gets too hot. "I wanted to get you alone to talk about Warner before they all come back."

"What's going on with Warner?"

"You tell me." She looks over her shoulder and wiggles her eyebrows at me. "Last I heard, he went all protector-mode after your last letter–not that I can blame him!" she tacks on hastily when I shoot her a look. "I just like living vicariously through the young love phase!" She holds her hands up placatingly. I roll my eyes at her.

"You and JJ have been together a little more than a year. You are still in the *young love* phase, too." Amy's eyes widen. "What?"

"You didn't deny that you're in the young love phase though! Now that you're finally dating for real," I frantically look around, ensuring no one is close enough to overhear our secret, "are you finally acknowledging to others that you love him?" Amy squawks. She can be so dramatic sometimes. I can't fight the small smile creeping onto the corner of my mouth.

"I don't know. I mean, it's so early, right?" Amy shakes her head emphatically. She's now fully turned around on my chair, having given up looking over her shoulder. There are still large white smears over her shoulders from where I haven't rubbed the sunscreen in yet, but her priorities regarding skin care seem to have taken a back seat to my love life. "He's amazing, Ames." I sigh, feeling a little bit cliché in my reaction.

After Warner and I first started hooking up, back when we refused to acknowledge to ourselves or each other what this was, I had so much difficulty separating out and naming the whirlwind of complex emotions I was experiencing regarding him. Now, I can look back and pick apart each feeling in hindsight, and one prevailing emotion stands out amongst all the others, unique in its simplicity, which was perhaps why I struggled to name it for so long: happiness. Pure, simple happiness.

Amy squeals. "I'm *so* happy for you, Leesh. He seems like such a good match for you. A steady, reliable constant. And the way he looks at you?" Her lips pull back into an almost maniacal grin. "I'm just so excited for you to find someone who looks at you the way Jackson looks at me. It's magic."

"Yeah..." I scoot back further in my chair, reclining myself. "Sit with me for a sec. I just want to close my eyes and soak in the moment. Just in case you are right about the young love phase thing."

She snuggles up onto the lounge chair with me, despite several unoccupied chairs available in the near vicinity. She lies on her side, tucking her head against my shoulder and under the wide brim of my oversized hat. She throws her arm around my stomach, and we sit for several minutes, just breathing and letting the sun and our emotions sink in.

A few minutes pass by, during which I feel the initial lurch of the boat followed by an uptick in the breeze, indicating we finally start moving. When Amy and I end our mini snuggle, seeming to sense each other's increased movements and coming back to reality at the same time, she leans her face back far enough to make eye contact.

"So?" she asks patiently.

"Yeah," I respond, nodding.

"Are you going to tell him? Wait for him to tell you? That'll be any day now, honestly. I'm telling you, the way he looks at you. I know. So, you should tell him first or he can tell you, but I'm betting both of you will say something in the next couple of days. Especially with the break, you'll be spending so much time together, it'll be impossible for you not to tell him how you feel!" Amy tends to ramble when she's anxious or excited. Her squeal at the end of her monologue morphs to shock when JJ walks over, dripping condensation from a pink cocktail in a hurricane glass onto her legs. Warner arrives seconds later, handing me a beer bottle in a koozie. Both men sit in chairs on opposite sides of the one Amy and I share.

"What's the plan, ladies?" JJ asks, spreading his arms wide to display our options. "The chef said lunch will be ready in about an hour. We should make it to The Playpen in no time. We can hang here, hit the hot tub...Cota's got a poker game going below deck. I won't be doing that, obviously."

"I need to finish lathering up before we hit The Playpen," Amy says, coming to sit between JJ's spread legs. He instantly picks up where I left off, slathering his fiancée with sun protection.

"What's The Playpen?" I ask.

"It's the best spot in the lake to drop anchor and swim. We're heading out there early enough in the day, so we can hopefully beat a lot of the competition for parking," JJ explains.

Sitting up, I hand my own bottle of sunscreen to Warner, silently asking him to follow suit and get my back. His large hands scatter goosebumps across the surface of my skin, despite the humid temperatures. He spreads the sunscreen liberally across my back while we listen to JJ and Amy debate whether parking in the middle or on the outskirts of The Playpen is the best strategy. Long after the sunscreen has soaked into my skin, Warner's hands continue moving, adding slight pressure and becoming a massage. It feels like heaven; I have to actively suppress a moan. My head falls forward, my chin slumping toward my chest, giving him access to the back of my neck. His strong hands knead the muscles there, relieving an ache I didn't even know I had. When he finishes, he taps my shoulders lightly before standing and removing his T-shirt.

He chuckles as he catches me blatantly staring at his chest and abs. He presses two fingers gently against my chin, closing my mouth. I hadn't even realized my jaw had dropped. I see him all the time, and I'm no stranger to the shirtless landscape of his body. Yet every time, I'm momentarily awed at its presence. He turns around and settles onto my chair so I can put the sunscreen on his shoulders and back. I'm busy squeezing it onto my hands when JJ starts laughing loudly.

"Holy shit. Guess you guys had a fun morning!" His laugh booms loudly, attracting the attention of some of the other guys who were climbing the stairs to join us on the deck.

"What are you–" I slam my mouth shut, confusion clearing when I follow Amy's point to Warner's back. His beautiful, muscular, *scratched to shit* back. "Oh my god, Warner. I am *so* fucking sorry."

Warner peeks back over his shoulder just as Kyle Crawford approaches, clearly trying to suppress his own laughter.

"James, do you by chance own a cat?"

"A cat?" Warner is the only one in the dark about what's going on. "No, we don't have a cat. I'm allergic." After a pause in which he suspiciously eyes his starting pitcher, he asks, "Why? What's going on?"

"Ah, so this is *Alicia's* handiwork up and down your back!" I have no doubt my cheeks are redder than Amy's swimsuit right now. Warner joins in everyone else's laughter, slinging his arm around my shoulder and pulling me into his side. He plants a kiss on my cheek, continuing to laugh at the situation and my embarrassment.

"What can I say? My girl likes to sign her work." He winks at me, and I know with such solid conviction that if I didn't love him already, I would now.

CHAPTER FORTY-ONE

Warner

Going back to work after four days wrapped around my girlfriend suddenly feels harder than it should be. Alicia was able to rearrange her work schedule so she was minimally pulled away from me during that time. We ate good food, indulged in the best of Chicago summer activities, and ended each night (and sometimes each midday) with mind-blowing sex. I left for the ballpark an hour ago for our whole team workout and already I'm missing Alicia like a phantom limb. We play tomorrow in Milwaukee, so we will bus there this evening after our workout wraps up. Normally, we fly a chartered plane everywhere, but with Milwaukee only being a ninety-minute drive, it's the only desti-nation we travel to via bus–not that traveling by bus is a hardship when we have a police escort to the Wisconsin state line. That means no stopping for red lights, stop signs, or anything else that could slow us down. It's a little ridiculous, the treatment we get, but who am I to complain? The expedited travel means I get to spend more time at home, which equates to more time wrapped up in Lee in all senses of the term.

By the time I finally board the bus, I'm itching to get to the hotel and videochat with her. She's staying at JJ and Amy's tonight. We're still not taking any chances now that the stalker is seemingly emboldened. I'm relieved she can get away from our apartment; I hate having her feeling trapped, especially now that her parents have gone home and I'm on the road. I offered to ask Eden to fly in for our three-game road trip to stay with her, but she assured me she'd stay with Amy for the long weekend. I may have also made her promise me that if she and Amy went out, they'd take JJ's giant rottweiler, Bruno, with them. He's a big baby, but he looks intimidating, and since Alicia turned down my repeated offers for a security detail, it's as good as I'm going to get. I know I'm being overprotective, but is it overprotective if the threat is real?

As I reflect on the very real danger she could be in, I decide to check in with Coyle. He responds to my text right away, informing me there are no major updates. He told me after reviewing his notes and the security videos, there's a small potential pattern developing as to when this fucker contacts Alicia, usually every three to four weeks. He stressed there wasn't a lot to go off, since Coyle himself has only been involved in the case recently, which means he only has about three data points to consider, but it could be something. He promises to check back with the detectives and get back to me once he knows more.

My stomach rumbles so loudly, Soji raises his eyes at me across the aisle. I didn't have a chance to grab dinner after the workout. I wanted to get in a few more reps with my strength coach and between that and my treatment for a slightly tweaked left hamstring, by the time I finished my shower, I had about four minutes to make it onto the bus. I'm sure they wouldn't leave without me, but I'd hate to be that asshole that holds everyone else up.

Digging in my backpack for a pack of trail mix I swore I threw in there on the last homestand, my fingers graze a bound black book. Normally, I'm very particular about how I keep my backpack organized: I know where everything is at every moment. Things are easy to find and by keeping it organized, I can reduce any clutter that builds up over time. A long time ago, Roy taught me that a cluttered environment leads to a cluttered mind. Now, my backpack tidiness is just another one of the rules I keep to stave off some of the more devastating effects of my depression. The presence of a foreign item in my bag is surprising.

Tugging the book out, I take in the nondescript cover. The whole thing is about ten inches by ten inches, a large, thick square. It's encased in textured black leather with no title to hint at its contents. Frowning in confusion, I flip it open to a random page in the middle, then immediately slam it shut. I swivel my head in all directions to ensure no one else sees what is surely meant for my eyes only.

Lee.

Not just Lee, but Lee in the strappiest, sexiest piece of lingerie I've ever laid eyes on.

I shift sideways in my seat, pressing my back against the window and pulling the book to rest on my breastbone. Holding it close so the front and back covers shield their contents to anyone sitting in front of or behind me, I peek at the inner cover. It was printed to be a blank, smokey gray, the exact shade of Alicia's eyes, but her loopy handwriting covers the left-hand corner.

Warn,

Something to help you feel a little less lonely on your road trips.

Love,

Lee

Love, Lee.

Love, Lee.

Lovely.

I'm sure I'm reading into the "love" signature a little too much. Wishful thinking. But something *has* shifted between us in the last few weeks, and it feels a lot like love. Is it possible that I'm not the only one feeling it? Or did Lee just sign her note with that inscription because she's a kind person and I'm, once again, reading too much into things? I probably am.

I almost told her I loved her this week. It would have been so easy to let the words slide out, but I worried it would have been too much, too fast, for her. Shoving my nerves about the depth of her feelings out of my mind before I begin to spiral, I turn the page to the inner cover and am met with a closeup of her silver-gray eyes, rimmed in smokey black and green eyeshadow. The photo is a strip of just her eyes, but the effect is as immediate as if it was a fully nude centerfold. I shift my legs, giving my thickening dick a little more breathing room. What is it about this picture? Normally, she doesn't wear a lot of makeup, allowing the light smattering of freckles across the bridge of her nose to show. Her clear skin is even and perfect; she doesn't need makeup. But somehow this? This is making me hard and it's literally just her eyes. Perhaps it's the note of promise in them, the seduction clear in those expressive orbs, that has me salivating as I turn the page.

Fuck.

I am not prepared for the next page. It's taken from behind, in black and white. She is wearing a loose sweater and a pair of cheeky panties that ride up her ass as she fixes her chestnut waves in the mirror. It's tame compared to the first photo, when I allowed the book to open to a random page and saw that strappy getup, but it's sending a heavy flow of blood to my cock all the same. I snap the book shut, trying to surreptitiously adjust myself in my pants. I can't be sporting a boner in the middle of the bus, surrounded by my teammates. I'm supposed to be a professional here.

Suddenly this bus, police escort and all, is not moving fast enough. I need to be at the hotel and on a video chat with my girl immediately.

Chapter Forty-Two

Alicia

Suffice it to say, Warner enjoyed the surprise I left in his backpack. I'm a little surprised he didn't find it sooner, with how particular he is about organizing his bag every morning. I carefully slid it behind his iPad this morning while he was packing his clothes for the road trip.

He sent me a text on the bus, presumably when he discovered the book, telling me he was going to video chat as soon as he got back to the hotel and that I better be ready for him. I responded with a string of angel emojis and told him I might be busy at that time. I swear, I could hear his growl of frustration all the way from the state line. He pulled out his bossiest tone in response and told me he didn't care, that unless my friends want an eyeful of what I do to him, that I'd make myself available. I imagined his deep, dominant voice sliding through my texts, and my blood heated in anticipation.

Warner and I have never had phone (or video) sex before. The idea crossed my mind, many times, when he was on the road, but my concern for his mental state often won out. Now, however, as I'm lying in JJ and Amy's guest bedroom, sated after Warner talked me through two orgasms, I wonder if we should have been doing this all along. Seeing long ropes of cum shoot across his abdomen when he finally sought his own release was so hot, and he looks so satisfied and at peace, that I joke about making this a regular thing. He vehemently agrees and after he cleans himself up, we lean our respective phones against our pillows, allowing us to whisper praises to each other before falling asleep.

When I wake Saturday morning, Amy and I head to her yoga studio. On the walk there, I briefly wonder if Warner would be upset that we're technically out in public without Bruno, but I justify to myself that it's fine because even when he is in town, I still go running by myself. He's just worried about what he can't control, but he's no more in control when he's at the ballpark and I'm at home, even though we're in the same city.

Ever since the last note, an undercurrent of anxiety has been rippling through my body, right under the surface of my skin. Sometimes, like when I convince myself someone is watching me, the anxiety is almost tangible, like you could scratch off the top layer of my skin and see it pulsing there. I mostly shove the worry down, which is uncharacteristic of me. It's just too much right now, and I don't have the bandwidth to deal with it.

When class wraps up, Amy and I head next door to Green Jungle for smoothies. She convinces me to take our smoothies to go, since we don't have Bruno with us. Apparently, Amy is taking Warner's concerns seriously, too. I roll my eyes at the suggestion but don't fight her. Secretly, I'm relieved to be heading back. As much as I won't admit it out loud, I am nervous, and my brain is falling into the same pitfalls as Warner's, thinking that because he's out of town, I'm somehow more vulnerable.

We place our orders, hers a lot more complicated than mine. As I stretch forward to hand the cashier my credit card, an arm reaches toward the cashier from behind me, slicing through the air between Amy and me.

"Ladies, it would be my pleasure to pay for your drinks," the man behind us says.

"Oh, no, you don't have to do that," I tell him politely. The last thing I want right now is a guy hitting on us. I just want to get back home, drink my smoothie on JJ and Amy's rooftop, and shower off the dried sweat from class.

"I insist," the man says. I glance at Amy, wondering if she's feeling the awkwardness of the moment, too. At least she has a giant honking ring to indicate her lack of interest in the public dating pool; I have nothing to hide behind.

The guy is roughly our age, with red hair and a kind-looking face. There's something unreadable in his eyes and I prepare for him to insert himself into our conversation. The cashier slowly takes his card, glancing at me to make sure it's okay. I shrug; I'm on a limited budget. I won't say no to someone else picking up the tab as long as there is no expectation of anything more.

"Thanks," Amy says brightly, but she takes a protective step closer to me as we stand off to the side, waiting for our order to be filled. The man says nothing as he stands nearby, scrolling on his phone.

I breathe a sigh of relief. I'm just overly paranoid because of the stalker thing. It's not like this is the first time a guy has offered to buy me a drink. He's clearly not making a big deal out of this, but still, I can't help but notice a fresh trickle of sweat down my spine that has nothing to do with the class we just took.

"Banana-mango with oat milk and pea protein and a berry cooler with spirulina, oat milk, pea protein, and sea moss!" the barista calls out, placing two large styrofoam cups on the counter. In unison, Amy and I each grab them and move toward the exit. I glance at the man, ready to nod at him in thanks, but his eyes are still glued to his phone. Did he even order anything himself? Now I know I'm being paranoid; I'm sure he did.

Just as we push against the door, I hear his quiet murmur. Given the way Amy stiffens beside me, she hears it too.

"See you later, Alicia, Amy."

The door swings closed behind us, shutting out the sounds of blenders whirring and customers chatting to be replaced by city noises. Cars roll by. Somewhere in the distance, a dog barks. The wind rustles through a nearby tree. I hear it all, but somehow, I don't. Amy grips my elbow tightly, grounding me.

"Don't react," she mutters, walking quickly, half dragging me away from the smoothie shop. "Don't react. Just walk. Keep moving, keep moving." She's talking out of the corner of her mouth, an oddly bright smile plastered on her face. I feel like I'm registering everything in slow motion. My yoga mat, rolled in a bag slung across my shoulders, bangs clunkily against the back of my legs as Amy urges me down the street.

We turn the corner and pick up our pace. I'm pretty sure I'm moving on autopilot because my brain isn't taking in information now.

"Amy," I say, unable to form more words.

"I know. We'll talk about it when we get home." Her voice is firm, deeply at odds with the false sunshine she's affixed to her face. She rapidly glances over her shoulder but doesn't slow her pace. "He's not following us," she assures me, but I'm not convinced. I whip my head around, too, but she's right. There's no one behind us.

Amy and JJ live about seven city blocks from her yoga studio. There's a shortcut through an alley we could take that would cut down our journey, and although it's a bright, cloudless day, our feet carry us past it swiftly, opting to stick to main, populated streets. Just in case.

My breathing picks up. Just in case what? He follows us? Was that guy my stalker? My chest is rising and falling quickly now. My yoga clothes are clingy, but they're suddenly too tight, restricting my breathing. Why the fuck did I think it was okay to leave Amy's place? Out of the corner of my eye, I see her looking at me in concern.

"No. Not right now. Just a few more blocks. Come on, Leesh. I know you can do it. We're almost there." She tugs on me harder. If my brain was functioning even at half capacity, I'm sure I'd wonder if she was bruising the soft flesh of my inner arm, but I barely register her touch.

When we reach the entrance of their condo building, she keys in a code to get us through the front gate. She releases her hold on me as the gate clangs behind us, enclosing us in the front garden area. I follow her up the few stairs to the front door, tripping slightly on one of the steps. I notice her hand shakes as she slides the key into the lock. She flings the front door open and practically shoves me in front of her and into the brightly lit hallway.

"Keep moving. Elevator." Her words are clipped, coming to me in an echo. There's a slight ringing in my ears as the elevator doors shut behind us. They barely close before Amy is crouching next to me. How did I get on the floor?

"Breathe, Leesh. You've got to breathe." She cradles my face in her hands. They're wet. Why are her hands wet? "Come on, love. Breathe in and out slowly." I barely register the movement, but she places my hand on her chest. Her heartbeat is erratic, but her chest rises and falls slowly as she models deep breathing. "Breathe with me. That's it. Good job. Tell me two things you hear." When I don't respond, she jostles my leg with her foot. "Two things you hear."

"The elevator ding, your voice." My words are stilted, but my surroundings start to become a little more focused.

"Good job," Amy praises. "Tell me four things you see."

"Your eyes. My smoothie." Oh. It spilled, orange blended drink spreading out across the elevator floor. "Your keys on my leg. My chipped nail polish."

"So good. Two things you feel?" she prompts again as I feel my breathing regulate.

"Smoothie on my pants. Your sweaty sports bra." Amy tips her head back and laughs, helping me to my feet. She reaches up and wipes tears from my eyes before bending to scoop most of my smoothie up. Whipping a towel from her yoga bag, she mops up the rest of my drink while I uselessly stand by. The doors to the elevator had opened twice during my panic attack, but they are closed now. I press the door open button with a shaky finger. Amy snakes her arm around my waist and squeezes, resting her head on my shoulder as we walk together down the hallway and into her unit.

Immediately, Bruno bounds toward us and leans his butt against my legs while Amy smooshes his face and gives him kisses and pets in greeting. The pressure of the dog's giant body against me feels good, and I absentmindedly reach down to scratch his rear. He presses further into me, leaning heavily against my legs. It's amazing to me that he knew what I needed, coming down from my anxiety attack. Normally, Bruno saves his heavy butt leans for Amy, but I'm touched he allowed me the honors today.

Amy looks up at me from where she is crouched by his massive head. "How are you feeling?"

I shrug. "I'm okay, I guess. Not okay. I don't know?" Tears prick my eyes.

"Come on, let's get some fresh air in you and we can relax. Come on, boy." She pats her leg and Bruno trots alongside us. We make our way up the stairs in her kitchen and onto the roof of the building.

Even before Amy moved in, JJ had the roof tricked out for entertaining. The portion of the roof he owns is loosely divided into three areas: an island for food and drinks; an open area for games like ping pong, darts, and bags; and a comfortable seating area with a movie projector screen. Amy steers me toward the couches and tosses a linen blanket at me. I wrap myself in it, suddenly aware of my shivers despite the warm summer temperatures. Bruno shoves his way between Amy and me. There's no lack of seating in this area, and the couch is enormous, but Bruno gets what Bruno wants. And right now, he apparently wants to sit on my lap. He's obviously not done ensuring I'm grounded. The clumsy action brings more tears to my eyes.

For several minutes, Amy and I say nothing, interrupting small sips of smoothies with our deep breaths. Bruno moves his blocky head to my shoulder, and I let out a watery laugh.

"So, are we going to talk about it?"

"There's not much to say," I tell her honestly. She experienced the same thing I did; I'm not sure there's anything else I could comment about it.

"Do you want me to call Warner?"

"Absolutely not!" She eyes me suspiciously, as if she's biting her tongue and wants to tell me I'm being stupid. "There's nothing he can do from a hundred miles away. He's only going to worry."

"I think he deserves to know," she tells me gently, her face softening.

"There's nothing to know! For all we know, the guy was a fan who recognized us from Foxy Fanatixxx or something!" Even as I say the words, I know it's not likely. But I have to cling to the hope that he is just an overzealous fan, just a creep, and not a potentially dangerous psychopathic stalker.

"Can I at least invite Danny and Tim over?" I wave my hand at her, as if to say *it's your house, do what you want.* Her fingers fly across her screen. I take another long sip of what's left of my smoothie, reaching the bottom of the cup in no time thanks to its earlier spill. I take the lid off and allow Bruno to lick the inside. Amy rolls her eyes but doesn't stop me. Apparently, I haven't angled the cup correctly, because Bruno pulls it from me gently, stands, and hops off the couch, carrying it to his outdoor dog bed to clean it more thoroughly.

"They'll be here in an hour," Amy announces. She gives my knee a squeeze. My body has returned to its normal temperature, and I've convinced myself that we both totally overreacted to some stranger knowing both our names at a smoothie shop. Because he knew *both* our names. The likelihood that he was my stalker, instead of just a random Foxes fan, is becoming less probable in my mind. Blowing out a breath, I stand, announcing I'm going to take a shower.

"Tell Danny and Tim they don't have to come because of me. I'm fine. That guy was just a socially awkward fan who wanted to be able to say he bought JJ Jeffers' fiancée a smoothie." Amy makes no effort to hide her disbelief, but she doesn't argue with me.

"I still think you need to tell Warner."

"Later. When he gets home, I will." By then, I hopefully will have forgotten this whole thing, and there will be no need to stress him out or to inconvenience him any further.

CHAPTER FORTY-THREE

Warner

"Hey, James, you got a sec?" JJ approaches me, towel firmly affixed to his waist. We won today's game in a landslide, so I'm sure everyone will want to go out to celebrate. Tomorrow night is a rare Sunday night game. It is being nationally broadcast, which accounts for the later than usual start. That means most of the team will be out in the city tonight, knowing they can sleep in tomorrow morning.

"Yeah, what's up?" I finished showering already and am half-dressed. I pull my polo from my locker and tug it over my head.

"Stick around after the buses leave. We can grab an Uber or something back to the hotel." I eye him suspiciously. After each road game, the buses take us back to the hotel, leaving half an hour and an hour after the end of each game. There's no reason not to take the bus back, especially if our destination is the hotel. There's not a lot to do around the ballpark in Milwaukee, so it makes more sense to regroup at the hotel first before we all go out, so my radar for whatever JJ wants to say is a little off. He clearly doesn't want to talk in front of other people though. I raise my eyebrows at him, urging him to give me more information.

"Shit, Lee. Is she okay?" The panic sets in. JJ and I aren't particularly close, although we've been hanging out more because of Alicia and Amy's relationship. If JJ knows something I don't, it's likely because of Amy.

"Everything's fine," he reassures me, holding up his hands in a placating gesture. It does little to ease my anxiety. When I lift my phone, I see Lee texted me a photo of Bruno sleeping on her lap eight minutes ago. I breathe a sigh of relief.

Time ticks by slowly as we wait for the locker room to empty. An hour after the game ends, the last of the coaches trickle out, heading for the buses, leaving JJ and me alone except for the local clubhouse attendants.

"Let's walk outside," JJ suggests. I know whatever he tells me, he doesn't want to be overheard. My anxiety ratchets up another notch. While the clubhouse attendants are employed by the home team, I'm sure every attendant in the league has heard their fair share of sensitive information. I wouldn't be surprised if they're required to sign non-disclosure agreements as a condition of their employment, so JJ's sudden need for additional privacy has my skin crawling with impatience.

We make our way to the underground players' parking lot. Both our cars are obviously back in Chicago, but it affords us added privacy from any fans who might be lingering outside after the game.

"Okay, before you freak out, you need to know Alicia is safe." I stop walking and JJ turns to face me. His eyes hold sincerity, while I just hold my breath. "She's unharmed. She's at the condo with Amy, Danny, and Tim. She's *fine*."

JJ talking me off the ledge before I even get there isn't helping. I know he means well, but I need him to spit it out.

"Just tell me," I say, trying to keep the annoyance out of my tone.

"Alicia and Amy went to yoga this morning."

"Okay..." I drag out the second syllable, waiting for the other shoe to drop.

"Apparently after, they went next door to get smoothies to bring home." JJ pauses, as if he's giving me time to ask a question or say something else. My irritation flashes; he must pick up on it because he stops pussyfooting around. "Some guy offered to buy their smoothies. Amy said they didn't realize it at the time, but I guess he didn't even buy anything himself. As they grabbed their drinks to leave, he addressed them by name."

"Who was the guy?" I'm trying to force my breathing to remain regular, to slow the pulse of the blood in my veins.

"They don't know. A stranger."

"And he knew their names?"

"Yeah. Apparently, he didn't follow them, but it really freaked them both out. Amy said Alicia had a panic attack when they got home." My hands ball into tight fists of their own accord. He puts his hands on my shoulders, looking me in the eye. "She's *okay,* Warner. But Amy said Alicia has convinced herself it was just some overzealous fan who knew their names because of their relation to us, not because it was the stalker. I don't know if that's right or not, but apparently Alicia was adamant about not telling you for that reason."

My head is spinning so fast, I'm surprised JJ can't hear the gears turning. Flashes of anger spark in my chest. Emotions swirl through me quickly, whizzing in front of my eyes like I'm on a Tilt-A-Whirl. How dare someone scare my girl? Why wouldn't she tell me? Is she safe without me there? Worry, anger, and terror all churn through my gut.

I turn and punch a key box attached to the garage wall. It clangs and rattles with the force of its reverberations, echoing throughout the cavernous garage. JJ says nothing but steps in front of me as I pull my fist back to hit it again.

"Come on, man. Let's go back to the hotel so you can call her. We'll figure everything out." I appreciate that he doesn't tell me it's going to be okay, because, quite frankly, it's not. I'm ready to go on a rampage to protect Alicia, but I can't do it from ninety miles away.

I allow him to lead me towards an exit and into the sunshine. The bright weather clashes with the storm brewing inside me. When our rideshare pulls up, JJ slides in after me. He doesn't force conversation, for which I'm grateful, because I spend the ride to the hotel texting Coyle and giving him an update. I'm sure I'll have more to share after I talk to Lee, but I need him to get started with the latest information right away. He agrees that it could be nothing but promises to look into it immediately.

In the elevator up to our rooms, JJ turns to me. "Look, I know you're doing everything you can to protect her. I promise she'll be safe at my place. Danny and Tim promised to stay till we get home too, so I'm sure they'll be having fun together." I'm sure he's right. I know having her closest friends nearby will lighten any tension she is feeling, but it doesn't stop guilt from flooding through my body that I couldn't be there to protect her when she needed me most. "James, you got to hear me, man. You can't be there for Alicia if you don't take care of yourself first."

He pauses, leveling me with a meaningful look. I wonder what he's not saying with his words but trying to convey with his eyes. He's clearly waiting for me to say something, to divulge my thoughts. I press my lips together as we step off the elevator. JJ's room is further down the hall than mine. He pauses at my door as I slam my key card against the reader, prepared to barrel into my room in my haste to connect with Lee.

JJ's hand shoots out and snags my wrist before I can let go of the door handle. "I know you need to talk to your girl. But when you're done, you should come to my room. We can have a drink, we can talk, we can not talk, but you need to get your head right tonight. And you don't need to do it alone." His eyes bore into mine, conveying the seriousness of his request. I nod curtly before walking into my room, letting the door close behind me.

"Baby," I breathe when Lee answers my video call. "Tell me about yourself." Her smile is overly bright. It confirms what JJ told me: she's not planning on telling me what happened today. I'll have to bring it up myself.

"It was good," she lies. God, she's a terrible liar. "Danny and Tim are over here, too. We just finished making cookie dough and we're going to watch a movie." I can see her walking down a hallway, away from the noise. She calls out over her shoulder for her friends to start without her.

"Is your cookie dough full of salmonella?" I tease. She shifts the camera, jostling my view, before holding up a bowl of raw dough. Chocolate chips and pink sprinkles dot the mixture, and I suppress a gag, imagining the raw egg she inevitably included.

"It's actually all salmonella, no cookie dough at all. I decided I'd mix it up and use only raw eggs. No flour, no butter, just eggs." She laughs as I try and fail to suppress another gag. She theatrically shoves an overlarge bite of dough into her mouth. Laughing with her feels so good. I needed some levity before I Hulk-smashed any more inanimate objects.

"What else did you do today?" Alicia settles against a pillow. I can just make out an upholstered headboard behind her; I assume she's in Amy and JJ's guest bedroom.

"Not a whole lot. Went to yoga this morning and got smoothies."

"Mmmhmm," I hum, waiting for her to tell me more. When she doesn't, I try a gentle approach. "Baby. I know."

"You know what?" she teases, but I don't bite. I can't be playful with her right now, not when I feel like my heart is going to pound out of my chest. When I don't respond, she visibly deflates. "Did Amy tell you?"

"No, JJ did. Baby, why didn't you tell me?" Her eyes fill with tears.

"I didn't want to worry you. I've inconvenienced you enough with all of this. And it's probably nothing." She heaves a sigh. Her teary eyes look scared, and I've never hated the sight of it more. "Are you mad at me?"

"Lee, how could I be mad at you? You didn't do anything wrong." Her spoon clatters as she sets aside her bowl.

"We went out in public without Bruno, and I just thought it wouldn't be a big deal, because it's not like we were hanging out in public. We just walked to class and got a smoothie on the way home. We weren't planning on staying at the cafe or anything." Her gaze drops off screen, likely to her own lap.

"Lee, sweetheart. I need you to look at me." I wait until she flicks her eyes to the screen. "I wanted Bruno there to protect you, but this could have happened even with him there. I'm not your warden—you never have to do what I say if you don't want to. I just want to protect you."

A tear leaks from the corner of her eye where it had slowly been building as I began talking. Once the first one falls, it seems to open the floodgates. Tear after tear pours down her cheeks as I start dying a slow death, knowing I'm not there to comfort her right now.

"Lee, I need you to listen to me. Are you listening?" She nods and sniffles, tears still falling. "It is my job to worry about you. It is not an inconvenience to worry about you. You have never—not once—inconvenienced me. So I'm going to need you to stop saying that to me, and to stop saying it to yourself. One of my favorite things in the world is to take care of you. It might be my new kink," I joke, and she gives me a watery smile. It's not much, but I'll take it. "I want to know about the things that scare you, even if you think they're no big deal. Even if you're trying to convince yourself that they're not a big deal."

I raise my eyebrows and she gives me a guilty look. Busted. That's the real reason she didn't tell me. It's not because she thinks the guy was an enthusiastic Foxes fan; it's because she doesn't want to admit to herself how serious the issue has become. When it was some nameless, faceless, vague possibility, the stalker seemed hardly a threat. Now that there's a potential face attached, someone she interacted with, she's rightfully terrified. My brave girl is trying to hold it together for her friends, for me, and most importantly, for herself. She heaves a shuddering sigh.

"I'm scared, Warn." Her voice is so quiet, so unlike her normal self. I press a hand to my breastbone, worried I will feel a part of my chest caving in.

"I know you are, baby. I am, too. But I promise you, however we move forward, we do it together. Maybe this was nothing, but maybe it was something. I already informed Coyle, and he said he'll work on it. But until we know more, there's no harm in trying to relax. JJ said Danny and Tim are staying the night?" She nods. I still have Danny's phone number from the auction; I'll make sure to check in with him tonight and thank him for keeping an eye out for my girl. "Tell me what your plans are for the rest of the weekend with them."

Lee smiles. It's small, but it's genuine. "You should have seen the amount of food they brought over. They insisted on making brunch tomorrow. Amy suggested we do rooftop yoga here before brunch and day drinking. On the roof," she adds. I wonder if she's reiterating that she's staying away from the public for my benefit or for her own.

"You going to be a sloppy drunk by the time I come get you?" I tease, pleased to see her smile widen in response.

"Maybe. We're planning on watching the game on the roof too, if it's not too hot. Amy said JJ put in a new keg at the end of the midseason break."

"Oh boy," I say, rolling my eyes dramatically. "You really are gonna be a mess by the time I get to you." She giggles. Honestly, I hope she does get drunk and cut loose. She deserves some carefree time with her friends. She needs to get her mind off things where she can feel safe, surrounded by the people who love her most. I shake my head, knowing the person who loves her most is almost a hundred miles away from her tonight.

Ever since I met Lee, I've been enchanted by her. Her delicate features are beautiful, sure, but they pale in comparison to the beauty of her soul. I always thought she was a queen, but I was wrong. She is nothing short of a goddess, and I'm the lucky fool who gets to worship at her feet.

We talk for a little longer before I remind her she should get back to her movie night. I'm sad to see her go, but a text from Vincent Coyle just popped on my screen with two words: "Call me." I school my face into neutrality while saying goodnight to Lee, before disconnecting the call and clicking on Coyle's contact information. He answers on the first ring.

"Mr. James," he says by way of greeting. I barely say hello before he starts talking again, getting straight to the point. Maybe he can give JJ some pointers. "I was able to stop by the Green Jungle location you told me Ms. Langley visited earlier today." I stupidly nod, like he can see me. "The manager allowed me to view the security tape from this morning, so long as I agreed I could not take it from the premises without a police warrant." He takes a deep breath, and in that moment, I know he's going to tell me something I won't like. I brace myself for impact. "It appears the man from this morning bears a resemblance to the man from the Vandeveer lobby security footage."

Fuck.

CHAPTER FORTY-FOUR

Warner

"One moment," I manage before muting my phone and running to the bathroom. I throw up, heaving up the postgame meal. Rage courses through my veins. At this point, I'm not sure my body is even running on blood anymore. I subsist on rage alone.

He talked to my girl. He bought her a smoothie. He interacted with my technicolor girl and dulled her shine today. I want to hurt him. I've never identified so hard with vigilantism than I do right now. I've never been a violent person, but I want to tear him limb from limb. I want to haunt his every waking moment like he's been doing to Alicia.

"Mr. James, are you there?" Coyle's voice sounds from my phone as I spit into the toilet, wiping my mouth with a tissue before flushing.

"I'm here. What do we do now? Who is he?" I demand.

"They wouldn't release the credit card information to me, but I've passed everything along to Gregory and Pinal. They said they'd work on it, but they won't be able to do anything until the cafe opens again tomorrow morning." I sigh. I knew we would be limited on what we could do in the immediate aftermath, but I didn't count on feeling so helpless. I need this resolved. Now.

"So then what? We're just supposed to sit around and wait for him to follow her again?" I realize my voice is louder than necessary, echoing in the hotel bathroom. Coyle seems unfazed.

"Ms. Langley is staying with friends this weekend? She's away from the Vandeveer?"

"Yes. I'll pick her up late tomorrow night. Maybe we should stay in a hotel instead?"

"That's at your discretion, Mr. James, but I can assure you we're beefing up the surveillance at home as well. I plan on personally manning the front desk overnight until we get more traction on this case."

"I appreciate that." I probably won't advertise that to Lee unless she asks; she's already worried enough about "inconveniencing" everyone else. I roll my eyes at the thought that her safety is anything other than convenient. Necessary.

"I can put a security detail outside the current residence, if you'd like." I don't even hesitate before I agree. Alicia will hate this, too, but I need peace of mind when I can't be there to ensure her safety myself.

"I'll text you the address in a few minutes." I click to speakerphone and tap out a text to JJ, asking for his address. He responds almost immediately. I copy it into my ongoing texts with Coyle.

"Mr. James, I know this is frightening for you and Ms. Langley, but getting more information will help us make progress. I know today's interaction wasn't...ideal...but it's allowed us to get a look at his face, which we haven't been able to do so far. Hopefully in a few days, we'll have a name, and we can go forward from there."

I sigh. It shouldn't take traumatizing Lee this morning to move forward. I want to rage at the universe for the injustice of it all. I want to curl up around Alicia and make sure no harm ever comes to her. I know neither are realistic thoughts, but it's what I want. I thank Coyle and disconnect after he promises, yet again, to keep me informed.

Did my involvement with Alicia make things worse? Maybe I should have put my foot down when she suggested her fake dating idea. For all we know, that could have triggered this psycho further. Maybe he would have kept his distance if he perceived she was romantically available? I must admit, things certainly are escalated now compared to the earlier letters.

While guilt is threatening to swallow me whole, I realize that Lee and I may not have started dating for real without the fake dating scheme first–or at least we might not have done anything about our feelings for each other as soon as we did without it. Maybe this guy would have been triggered by something else, even if I wasn't in the picture. What if things escalated and I wasn't there to protect her? Worse, what if I didn't even know her at all? The thought causes my stomach to bottom out.

My worrisome thoughts are interrupted by a knock on the door. I'm distracted enough that I don't even look through the peephole before pulling the door open, something I've never done on the road. You always hear stories about wannabe WAGs and cleat chasers figuring out where visiting teams stay and making their way onto our floors. Luckily, the person waiting on the other side of my door is broad shouldered and familiar. JJ shoves his way into my room, pushing a six-pack of beer into my chest as he saunters by.

I'm forced to follow him as he walks further into the room. He pauses before sitting at the desk chair, pulling a can of beer from the pack I still have clutched to my chest. He cracks it open, raising it and his eyebrows at the same time in a silent salute. He leans back in the chair, stretching his long legs out in front of him, apparently settling himself in. I guess he got tired of waiting for me to check in with him tonight.

In baseball, team captains aren't common. The few teams that do appoint captains usually do so in name only, rather than assigning any sort of leadership responsibilities to the holder. The Foxes do not have a team captain, but JJ has made himself a strong candidate if the position were to be created. He eyes me over the top of his beer.

"How's Alicia?" I sigh deeply, taking a seat on the edge of the adjacent loveseat. I put the beer on top of the small table in front of me, giving JJ access to it. I pull my own can out and pop the top, taking a long pull before responding.

"She's shaken up. She's pretending this morning wasn't a big deal because that would mean admitting it's realer than she'd like it to be." He nods wisely. I look down at my hands, the knuckles on my right slightly inflamed. I pick at some loose skin on the middle knuckle.

"You going to ice that?" He gestures with his beer toward my hand.

"Nah," I say at the same time I press my cold beer against it. I'm sure I'll have some additional club dues to pay tomorrow to cover the replacement cost for the key box.

"Warner, Alicia is in good hands this weekend. Amy, Tim, and Danny will keep an eye on her. Keep her safe. Apparently, Bruno has barely left her side, so even he knows something is up."

"Yeah, I know. I've got a private security guy who is setting up a detail outside your place this weekend." I wince, realizing I never actually asked him if that was okay with him. He nods.

"Good idea."

"The security guy said the guy from the cafe this morning is the same one who's been leaving her the letters. He reviewed the footage from Green Jungle today," I blurt out, unable to hold it in any longer. I need to tell someone.

"Fuck," JJ says softly. He furrows his brow, lost in thought.

"I know. I haven't told Alicia yet. You can't say anything to Amy." JJ looks at me in alarm, as if keeping a secret from his fiancée is outside the realm of possibilities. "Look, it won't do any good to tell her right now. It's only going to make them panic. Like you said, they're safe this weekend. Alicia already had a panic attack today. I can't stand the thought of her having another one. I can't imagine she's going to react well to hearing the news and I need to do it when I can make sure she's okay. Please, JJ. Promise me you won't tell Amy yet."

He cracks his neck side to side, thinking. "You're right," he finally agrees. "Amy will spiral into her own anxiety, too." He points at me in warning. "I don't like keeping things from her, though."

"I know. I don't want to keep Lee in the dark either, but she doesn't need to know this right now. I'll tell her when I see her in person." He nods in understanding. "I wish I didn't have to tell her at all. She's had such a shit year, between her job and all this stalker stuff. She lost her apartment, too, for Christ's sake. She still manages to be happy and vibrant and so fucking grounded. I don't know how she does it." I shake my head. JJ reaches for another beer.

"She's not doing it alone, you know," he points out. "Maybe she's happy and vibrant and grounded *because* she has people to depend on. Maybe she's able to be all those wonderful qualities because you and Amy and everyone else help her to tackle her challenges."

I'm quiet as I contemplate his words. It's a nice thought. I'm not sure how true it is–

"No, don't do that." I look at him in confusion. He gives me a hard stare. "I know you're trying to talk yourself out of what I just said. I can see it on your face. Warner, you have allowed Alicia to thrive. I knew her before you and I know her now that she's with you. She's always been vibrant, as you say. But I guarantee she wouldn't be shining as bright if you didn't help shoulder some of her load." I open my mouth to respond but he cuts me off. "You need to give yourself more credit, James. I'm not going to pretend to know what you've got going on in your life, but I do know you don't give yourself enough credit. I see it." When I look down, he says it again more forcefully. "I see it."

We don't say anything for a long time, silently drinking our beer. The silence isn't stifling, and I'm surprised to find that I'm not in my head about what to say or when I can leave this interaction. JJ brings a quiet comfort with him, an automatic acceptance of who you are. He puts his unquestioning faith in his people. I owe him my truth.

"I have depression." He doesn't say anything, just nods. He doesn't try to give me advice, ask if I've tried medication, or tell me about some person he knows somewhere who cured his incurable depression by eating right and exercising, or by going to some cave somewhere and meditating. Most helpful of all, though, he never asks me why I'm depressed.

We slide back into comfortable silence. After a few minutes, I feel like I should say something. Maybe reassure JJ he doesn't need to pity me, or take care of me, or treat me any different. I want to tell him he doesn't need to worry about me, that I'm not suicidal or self-harming. I open my mouth to form the words, but my voice catches.

"I know, Warner." He nods again, and with that small gesture, I know he respects and cares for me enough to know he won't change his interactions with me. He won't treat me like I'm some fragile thing. He won't walk on eggshells around me, afraid to hurt my feelings in the off chance it will send me on a self-destructive spiral. Somehow, he does know. He knows I'm still me and I don't need to be handled with kid gloves. He clears his throat. "Want to watch Sports Center? See if your diving catch in the fourth made the Top Ten list?"

He leans over the coffee table, snatching the television remote and turning on ESPN. We watch the rest of the broadcast together, commenting on the most and least athletic plays of the night across sports. When he gets up an hour later to return to his room for the night, he claps me on the shoulder and murmurs, "Anything you need."

I nod, walking him to the door and locking it behind him. Nothing else needed to be said.

CHAPTER FORTY-FIVE

Alicia

Most of Sunday night's game was a shutout until Caleb scored on a blooper RBI from Tyler Edwards in the eighth inning. When limited runs are scored in a game, it tends to go by quickly, which makes me happy. I'm ready for Warner to get home. I'm ready to go home myself, but not without him. I don't know when I started thinking of Warner's place as "home," but it undeniably is. The only thing is, now that the stalker has potentially made his presence bolder, home feels less like home without Warner's comforting, steady presence.

Warner was right, too. By the time he made it home to Chicago, we were all a little worse for wear. We started drinking around noon, then again during the game. The festivities were briefly interrupted by naps in the middle of the day. Luckily, I had the foresight to stop drinking in the eighth inning after Caleb finally scored, realizing the game would be over sooner rather than later. I was mostly sober by the time JJ and Warner arrived several hours later, where we all crashed out on the couch in JJ's living room.

"Hey, Lee," Warner tells me gently as he swipes the hair out of my face. I had fallen asleep on a pillow in Amy's lap. She is tilted sideways, using Bruno for support. Danny and Tim had made their way into one of JJ's guest rooms hours ago.

"Hey, pretty girl," JJ coos at Amy. I stifle a laugh as she and Bruno give JJ the same bleary-eyed blinks from their positions on the couch. Warner helps me to my feet as JJ scoops Amy into his arms. I watch him carry my best friend down the hallway to their bedroom.

"Ready to go home?" I nod, rubbing sleep from my eyes. He pulls me to his chest. "God, I've missed you. How can I miss you so much when I just saw you on Thursday?"

"I missed you, too, my love." He twines his fingers into my hair at the nape of my neck, tugging gently to pull my head back. He plants a soft kiss on my lips.

"Go home and do that at your own house," JJ teases, reappearing with Bruno's leash. The dog groans as he stretches and hops off the couch, as if JJ taking him outside to relieve himself is a huge chore. I laugh.

Warner's car is parked outside but within the confines of JJ's property gate. He loads my luggage in the back, tucking it next to his, and seeing our two mismatched suitcases nestled into each other in the back of his car oddly warms my heart. There is something so domestic, so normal, about the sight that I find myself a little choked up. Chalking it up to stress and a lack of sleep, I allow him to buckle me into the front seat. I smile at the way he takes care of me, even in the simplest of actions. I allow him to tuck me under his shoulder as we ride up the elevator to the penthouse floor. And I allow him to settle me into bed, wrapping his large body around me as we both tumble off to sleep.

When I wake the next morning, there's already a steaming mug of coffee on my nightstand. The coaster the mug is settled on is electric, and I realize the solid green light indicates the warming feature is turned on. Warner bought me a mug warmer. I choke up again.

What is wrong with me? The stress must really be getting to me. I find nothing wrong with being sensitive, but even I am thrown off by how easily I'm brought to tears these days. I accept it for what it is though: appreciation for his thoughtful gesture. Humming at the taste of Eden's secret coconut creamer in my coffee, I settle back into my pillow. I've propped it upright a bit more so I can leisurely sip my hot drink. Somewhere in the apartment, I can hear Warner's deep voice but can't make out what he's saying. He must be on the phone.

Scrolling through my phone, I flip through photos from this weekend. Aside from Saturday morning's scare, which I'm pretty sure was just an overreaction on my part anyway, it was a good weekend. It's been a while since the four of us could hang out like old times. I hover over the picture of Tim dangling a barbequed carrot above Amy's head as she jumps to take a bite out of it. She was convinced that barbequed carrots were a passable vegetarian substitute for hot dogs. She was wrong, of course, but that didn't stop us from having fun.

"Hey, did I wake you?" Warner's deep voice reaches me from the doorway.

"Not at all. But it felt good to sleep in." I pull back the covers on his side of the bed and pat the mattress, inviting him to settle back in with me. It's Monday morning, but he's got an off day. It's a nice way to ease back in from vacation–working four days before another off day.

Being away from him this weekend gave me clarity about our relationship. Sure, some of it started on the yacht with everyone when Amy asked if I loved him over the midseason break, but I didn't say anything. Now, the words are ready to burst out of my mouth. A few days ago, I was worried I would be jumping the gun, telling him so early into our relationship. I was nervous if he didn't feel the same way, he'd have this weird sense of obligation to keep protecting me, living with me, being with me. Which is ridiculous, because even if he doesn't love me back, he still deserves to know how I feel about him. Besides, it's not like he's going to kick me out if the feelings aren't reciprocated. Shaking my head at myself, I fold my legs underneath me, angling my body towards him.

"Hey," I start, pulling his hand into my lap. "Thank you for always taking good care of me. And I know I overreacted this weekend. I'm like ninety-nine percent sure the smoothie guy was just a rabid Foxes fan." Warner opens his mouth to say something, but I interrupt him. I need to get all my thoughts out before I blurt everything out in a less eloquent way. "Anyway, you never invalidated my feelings. You didn't tell me I was crazy for feeling worried. You didn't get mad at me even though we should have taken Bruno with us. I just wanted you to know that your unending support means so much to me." Deep breath. "And I love you, Warner."

For a brief, terrifying moment, my world stands still. Then, Warner's face cracks into a wide smile and I forget to breathe for an entirely different reason. He's stunning.

"Lee." He cups my face in his hands, pulling me towards him and pressing a soft, lingering kiss to my mouth. "I love you. I think a part of me fell in love with you the moment you stood up to the racist at the taco joint after JJ's gala. You were a tigress, protecting the ones you cared about." He pauses, pressing another kiss to my lips, which are pulled into a soft smile. "My tigress." Another kiss. "My queen." Kiss. "My goddess."

The next kiss is the deepest yet. He imprints a bit of himself on my soul, and I know for a fact that I will never be the same. There was life before knowing Warner James, and there is life after. Without a doubt, life after Warner James is a richer, bolder, amplified kind of life. The only kind of life worth living.

CHAPTER FORTY-SIX

Warner

I hang up the phone and find Alicia on the terrace, an almost empty glass of water in front of her as she taps away at her keyboard. I don't pretend to understand what she's doing on her laptop, but the tiny divot between her eyebrows tells me she's locked into her work. I cringe, knowing I'll have to interrupt her.

Sitting next to her on the outdoor loveseat, she flicks her eyes over to me and gives me a bright smile. With that radiant smile, she shines some of her goodness on me. I hate what I'm about to do to her.

"Let me know when you're at a point where you can stop for the night."

"Okay. Gimme like ten minutes." She's cheerful and it makes me feel even worse that I'm about to burst her happy little bubble. Fuck.

She continues typing as I try to force calm into my body. I nervously rub my fingers over my right knuckles. They're still a little sore, but the swelling has gone down and no bruising is visible. The skin is a little cracked, but not obviously so. I sneak glances at her out of the corner of my eye, wanting to remember her this way. When she finally closes her laptop and places it on the table in front of her, I breathe in deeply through my nose. Time to rip the Band-Aid off.

She tucks her feet underneath her as she shifts to face me. Her features are soft, relaxed. I commit the sight to memory, knowing I'm about to destroy it.

"Alicia. You know I love you," I start, and I immediately regret my word choice. She recoils at my use of her full name. The furrow between her eyebrows returns.

Shit, I'm already fucking this up. It sounds like a breakup speech.

"Let me start over, Lee. Baby, I love you." She relaxes only slightly, her eyes wary. I pull her hands into mine and scoot closer to her. "I have something serious to talk to you about though, and I want you to know that I love you and I'm going to take care of you." She inhales sharply. I don't know if she knows where I'm going with this or not, but still, I forge ahead. "I just got off the phone with Detective Pinal. They asked that I bring you to the local station because they have someone in custody."

I hate this moment. I knew I would hate it, but I had to do it anyway. The second I said Pinal's name, Alicia's face morphed from relaxed to pinched. She pulls her fingers from my hands to push her hair behind her ears. It's slightly poofier than usual due to the humidity and I'm disheartened to see her fingers shake as she does so. I pull her into my chest, hugging her against me, as if I could squeeze the anxiety out of her.

"I've got you, Lee. I'll be with you the whole time. If it's terrible, we leave. No questions asked."

She pushes off my chest and squares her shoulders. "I'll get changed." What she's wearing, khaki linen wide legged pants and a black tank top, is perfectly appropriate. I suspect, however, she needs some time to compose herself.

"Of course," I murmur. "Let me know when you're ready to go." I pace the veranda while I wait for her to get ready. Pinal already informed me there was little we could do to avoid having her come down to the station, but he assured me there would be no interaction between Lee and the suspect. He promised the suspect wouldn't even see her, but if I so much as catch a hint of compromised safety for Lee, I'm whisking her out of there. She's been through enough already.

When we get to the station, Detective Gregory meets us in the lobby. The lobby itself is large, containing benches and chairs scattered around small tables. Uniformed officers sit behind a desk, a glass partition separating them from the public. If it weren't for what I assume is bulletproof glass, the lobby would remind me of a hospital waiting room. Gregory leans against the front counter, waiting. As soon as she sees us, she makes quick, efficient strides towards us.

"Thank you for coming in. Please come with me." I place my hand on the small of Alicia's back, guiding her in front of me as Detective Gregory leads us behind a locked door and through a maze of desks. Fingers tap against keyboards, phones ring, and a low hum of incessant chatter fill my ears.

"Please have a seat." Gregory gestures to two chairs in front of a desk in the corner of the room. "I'll grab Detective Pinal, and we can get started."

Alicia lowers herself slowly into a chair. I slide the empty chair closer to hers before taking my own seat.

"Look at me, Lee." When her eyes finally meet mine, my chest crumbles a bit. Gone is the confident gleam normally housed there. In its wake, fear and anxiety take up residence. Pressing my forehead against hers, she softly closes her eyes and breathes me in. "Whatever happens, we do this together. You are not alone. We're going to get through this, and you are going to be safer and stronger than you've ever been. You hear me?" My voice cracks at the end, the result of seeing her small and scared.

We pull back when a deep voice clears his throat; as promised, Gregory brought Pinal, and, from the looks of it, several files. He sets the files on the desk where Gregory has already seated herself. Dragging a roller chair from a nearby desk, he sits heavily across from us.

"Thanks for coming in, Ms. Langley, Mr. James. I know this isn't what you wanted to do with your Monday evening." Alicia gives a weak smile but doesn't say anything. "Ms. Langley–"

"Alicia," she says quietly but firmly.

"Alicia." Pinal smiles. "I need to record this for documentation purposes. Is that okay?" She nods, and Gregory clicks a button on a small recorder on her desk. "I'd like you to look at some photos and tell me if you recognize anyone. If you don't recognize anyone, that's okay, too. It is just as important to exclude innocent persons as it is to identify a perpetrator."

He lays a photo lineup in front of her. We both lean forward in our chairs to inspect the photos. The men in them look similar in a general sense, in that they are all heavyset adult men with red or blonde hair. A cursory glance through them shows me I don't recognize any of them, but I inspect each photo again more carefully just in case. Next to me, Alicia seems to be doing the same. I don't miss her gasp, a sharp intake of breath.

"Do you recognize anyone, Alicia?" Gregory asks gently. Her pen hovers over a paper, ready to document anything Lee says or does.

"I don't know who he is, but this guy–" she taps her finger twice against the second to last photo– "he was the smoothie guy."

"Tell me what that means, the smoothie guy," Gregory prods.

"He bought Amy and me our smoothies on Saturday. He knew our names." Her eyes slowly fill with tears as realization sets in. I see the exact moment when she realizes if that man really was an overzealous fan, his photo wouldn't be in a police lineup. Gregory furiously scribbles as Pinal asks clarifying questions.

"Number seven, is that the man you're talking about?" She nods. "Alicia, for the recording, I'm going to need you to provide a verbal response please."

"Yes, number seven." She tugs her shirt sleeves closer to her body, crossing her arms across her stomach. She's literally folding in on herself. Her oversized shirt is actually mine. When she requested time to change, she came out of my bedroom wearing the same outfit, except she pulled one of my white button-down shirts over herself, tying it at the waist. I had little time to marvel how she somehow managed to make a men's oversized shirt look both incredibly sexy and completely appropriate for public wear.

"You're sure about that?"

"Yes."

I grasp her hand and find myself subconsciously rubbing small circles with my thumb across the back of her hand, as she so often does for me.

"Thank you, Alicia." Pinal stops the recording. Gregory slides her paper and a black pen towards her. "Please read what I've written and make sure it's accurate. Once you're sure, sign below under 'witness.'"

It's very official and clinical and cold. Once Alicia finishes reading Detective Gregory's notes, she signs her name at the bottom of the page. As soon as she releases the pen, I take her hand back in mine. Gregory whisks the paper away and slides it into a manila file folder before closing it and setting it aside.

"Alicia, you're doing great. I'm sorry we couldn't give you any information before the photo lineup. We have to ensure things are done following protocol. I'm sure you understand." She gives a tight smile and Alicia nods.

"Can you just tell us what's going on?" My voice is laced with impatience. "Do you have this guy or not? Who is he?"

"The man you identified, Alicia, is the man we picked up following a review of credit card records and security footage from Green Jungle. He also appears to be the man from Mr. Coyle's security videos of the Vandeveer. His name is Brian Joseph. Do you know him?" Pinal looks to Alicia, then me, to see if there's any recognition of the name. We both shake our heads.

"When we went to question him at his apartment, he was very cooperative. He answered all our questions and even willingly accompanied us to the station this morning."

Great. So, because he's a nice guy they're going to tell us there's nothing they can do. I fight the urge to roll my eyes. Instead, I squeeze Alicia's hand in what I hope is a reassuring gesture.

Pinal reaches across Gregory and pulls another file towards him. He opens it and looks at it but does not display it for us.

"When did you say you first started receiving his letters?"

"Probably about two years ago? Maybe a little less than that. I threw them all away as soon as I got them." Pinal nods.

"Ms. Langley–Alicia–I need to show you some photos, but I want you to prepare yourself, because they may be distressing for you to look at." I feel myself stiffen beside her as she straightens. "Are you ready?" She nods, but neither of us are prepared to see the photos in the file.

Pinal spreads page after page of photo printouts across the desk. The photographs are of a cramped apartment, the entire wall in one room covered with photos, drawings, and random words written on scraps of paper. Pinal slides more photos onto the desk, this time, they are close-ups of the wall.

The close-ups reveal photos of Alicia, some grainier than others, clearly taken at a distance. Alicia grocery shopping, walking into The Field Museum, standing on a crowded L platform. Lee going for a run, scrolling through her phone, filling up her gas tank. Alicia drinking a beer in the window of a dimly lit bar, putting a cardboard box in the trunk of her car, laughing at something outside of the frame. Interspersed between all these random moments of Lee's daily life are sticky notes and taped up pieces of paper with "ALICIA," "AL + BJ," and "DREAM GIRL" scrawled across them. A few pieces of paper that look like they are printed from online news sources are tacked up as well.

What. The. Fuck.

I want to throw up. Alicia looks ashen. She emits a soft sob, and I grip her hand tighter.

"You can't remember meeting this man?" Gregory's voice is soft, nonjudgmental. Lee continues staring at the photos, her eyes rapidly flicking from one image to the next. This Brian Joseph psychopath has cropped every other person out of the photos, so it's just her. I want to rip up every shred of the papers on the desk, if only to get them out of Alicia's sight. Gregory must pick up on her visual overload, because she sweeps the evidence into a tidy pile, scoops it into a folder, and places it in her desk drawer, eliminating it from sight. She repeats her question again.

"No, I've never met him." Lee continues staring at the empty desk.

Pinal and Gregory take turns filling us in on the information they gathered from the apparently very loquacious Brian Joseph. The man is convinced that he and Alicia are deeply in love and have been dating for two years. He told the detectives they first met when Brian's cousin, Chris, brought him to work one day. Chris, apparently, works at the planetarium, where Alicia's office is housed.

"Chris Jasper?" Alicia's mouth hangs open.

"You know him?" Pinal raises an eyebrow.

"Yeah, Chris is one of our security guards at the planetarium. He works the daytime shift. He tends to go out of his way to talk to me, but I just thought he struggled a little socially." She pauses, frowning. "Did he talk to me because he knew his cousin was stalking me?" Her voice rises on the last word, both in volume and in pitch. I feel my blood pressure rise with it.

"I'm not sure. We haven't had a chance to talk to him yet," Gregory admits. "We brought you in pretty quickly, given how urgently and frequently both Mr. James and Mr. Coyle have requested this case take priority."

Pinal leans forward. "We're still putting a lot of pieces together. What I can tell you is that Mr. Joseph is in our custody and he has been arrested for stalking and harassment. He will be arraigned tomorrow or Wednesday. In the meantime, we will continue talking with him and gathering more information for as long as he is cooperating."

"Arraigned? What does that mean exactly?" I interrupt.

"It's when he goes before a judge and is formally charged. He will enter a plea at that time. After that, court dates are set for a trial to begin."

I feel Alicia sway in her seat beside me. It's a lot to take in and I know I haven't fully wrapped my brain around it.

"A trial? Will I have to testify?" Gregory and Pinal share a look.

"Unfortunately, that will likely be necessary. Without your testimony, Joseph and his attorneys could argue that you were a willing participant, and this all is a misunderstanding," Pinal is gentle in his delivery, but we both still feel the blow.

"I think we're getting a little ahead of ourselves right now," Gregory acknowledges. "We still have a lot more evidence to gather. I can't share a lot of information right now, but I can tell you from my interactions with him, Mr. Joseph seems mentally unwell. He will remain in our custody until arraignment, possibly after as well if he is unable to make bail." Alicia tenses next to me and Gregory must sense it, because she hurriedly amends, "Right now, we must gather more evidence. I know it's a lot to ask, but if you think of any interactions you might have had with Mr. Joseph or anything with his cousin that might be helpful, please let us know."

"What if he pleads guilty at arraignment?" Alicia's voice trembles, but she seems to be following everything she's been told so far.

"That's more of a question for the state's attorney's office, but usually, when a perpetrator pleads guilty, a plea deal is arranged. A trial, where you could be asked to testify, is no longer necessary, but he will usually have to admit to his crimes in court prior to sentencing. We're not there yet, Alicia. I know it's hard to hear all of this and for me to ask you to take it one day at a time, but that's what we must do. A lot can happen moving forward, but we're going to do everything we can to help you get justice."

"We threw a lot at you in a very short period of time," Pinal agrees. "What's most important now is that you rest, take care of yourself, and call us if you think of anything that could be helpful.

Even if you think it's not important, it's good just to let us know and we can worry about whether it's relevant to the case or not."

"Okay," Alicia agrees, nodding. We all stand at once, our meeting clearly over. I place my palm on Lee's lower back, guiding her out in front of me. I slip my hat and sunglasses on before we exit the station, on the off-chance photographers are hanging outside. It's an occupational hazard that never bothered me too much before, but now, I'd give anything to have a quiet, boring profession that keeps Lee out of the spotlight. Fortunately, the sidewalk is empty as we walk to the car. She settles into the passenger seat, her normally graceful movements stilted and awkward. She's clearly reeling from the information.

"Do you want me to swing by Sal's drive thru on the way home?" Something tells me a greasy burger and fries might help her temporarily forget about our meeting. I'd give anything to take away some of her fear, even just for a few minutes. Her responding shrug gives me little to go off.

"Alicia is the mentally healthiest person I've ever met. And to see this, to see *him,* break her...I don't know what to do!" Amy collapses against JJ's chest and he rubs soothing circles against her back. Tim and Danny look on silently, helplessly, from the corner of my living room couch.

When Lee came home and climbed, fully clothed, into bed and stopped responding to my questions or suggestions, I turned the lights in our bedroom off, pulled closed the curtains, and walked out of the room, shutting the door behind me. Then, I called in the cavalry. Now, the people who love her most, apart from her family on the West Coast, are standing in my living room trying to make sense of everything.

I feel like exploding. I feel like imploding. I feel so out of control in this situation when all I want to do is to take control for her. Make it better. Make *her* better. I can't, and it kills me.

"Let me call Sean. I'll see if he has any advice," JJ offers. I nod. His brother is both of our agent but a lawyer by training. While his background certainly isn't criminal law, I'm not in any position to turn down help from anyone.

"She needs a restraining order," Tim says firmly from the couch. I've taken to pacing the room. Danny watches me nervously, his eyes ping ponging to follow my movements.

"Definitely," Amy agrees.

"He's in custody for now, so we'll have some time to get that set up, but I'll talk to Coyle about it. I want more security around her at all times if this guy ever gets out."

"Is him getting out a possibility?" Danny asks anxiously.

"They didn't really give us a ton of information. I guess a lot will be determined through the state's attorney's office, but if he makes bail, he could get out, yeah." My pacing increases.

"We're going to do everything we can to make sure that doesn't happen, okay?" JJ puts his hands firmly on my shoulders, forcing eye contact and making me stop my rapid pacing. "We're family. We're doing this all together."

My shoulders sag. The intercom buzzes. When I answer, Manny's voice fills the front hallway.

"I have a Mr. Caleb Andrews here to see you."

"Thanks, Manny. You can send him up." Most of my teammates haven't been to my apartment; I haven't had a lot of energy to socialize with them in the past, so I haven't put them on a list or given out the penthouse floor elevator code. I guess I'll need to start doing that.

When Caleb and Jenny arrive with trays of food, the seven of us work together on a plan. Sean calls JJ back and advises us on the next steps to obtain a restraining order, which mirrors what Coyle had texted me already. Sean fills us in on a few more legal procedures. Amy disappears for a while, saying she is going to lie with Alicia. When she returns, she says she got her to eat a little bit. I want to kiss Amy, knowing she was able to fill a hole that I couldn't.

By the time the night is through, we are all feeling better. We don't have any more information than we did when the night started, but the presence of our Chicago family and a little food seem to do wonders for our spirits. Amy elects to stay over, sleeping in our bed with Alicia. I am never going to fight her on that; Lee needs her friend, and I am the last one to stand in the way of that. JJ kisses Amy on the nose, promising to pick her up in the morning.

I trudge to Lee's old bedroom, face planting into her bed. She hasn't slept here in months, but the room still smells of her. If I can't be next to her while she sleeps, then at least I can drift off, surrounded by her scent.

We're going to get through this. I just hope we don't lose too much along the way.

CHapTer Forty-seven

Alicia

The weeks drag on both slowly and at lightning speed. My parents again came out to stay with me, this time while Warner was still in town. It wasn't entirely necessary, but sometimes a girl needs her parents. After they left, a week later, Warner's parents arrived. They were just as lovely as I imagined them to be, and I'm confident I gained several pounds after a long weekend of eating Anita James' excellent cooking. The visitors are great, but each night, the lingering fear that Brian Joseph will somehow get away with everything, avoiding jail time and picking back up where he left off keeps me from easily falling asleep.

I've been attending a stalking support group that meets in the library every other week. It's been helpful to know that I'm not alone. Some of the women in the group have been through the trial process, each with varying results, which is both comforting and terrifying at the same time.

The same thoughts cycle through my brain on a regular basis: what if he isn't found guilty? What if the jury doesn't believe this is bad enough? He technically didn't directly threaten me; what if that's not enough to "count?" What if he is found guilty but is let off with a slap on the wrist? What if he starts stalking me again?

I know I need to get a handle on my own anxiety, before it develops into something worse. Meditation is helpful, but when Amy slid Connie's contact information to me one day over lunch, I decided her therapist might be helpful. It's been nice to be able to voice my fears to an impartial person. I've tried to avoid doing so to Warner and Amy because I know they'll just worry more than they already do.

There are so many delays to the trial. Joseph pled not guilty at arraignment and apparently, he can't make bail, so for now, I know I'm physically safe from him. His lawyers requested a psychological hearing, which angered Warner to no end. He's having difficulty finding compassion for him.

"Why should I have compassion for someone who terrorizes others? I'm depressed as shit, but I'm not harming others with my mental health!" he had said when we were told about the psych hearing. In a way, he has a point, but I also understand that you might *have* to be delusional to believe you're in a relationship with someone for two years without having had a conversation with them. I'm not sure if Joseph potentially meeting the legal definition of insanity is a comforting thought or not.

Sandi Llewellyn, the assistant state's attorney who will be prosecuting Joseph, has been incredibly helpful in helping us to understand the legal proceedings and potential next steps. She explained that in Illinois, the legal definition of insanity means that Joseph could have been too mentally unwell to know that the stalking and harassment was wrong. Warner didn't want to hear it, but I'm afraid Sandi might have a point, especially when she pointed out that many of Brian's letters came near the end of the month, likely when his monthly prescription medication ran out. She hasn't told me what he was diagnosed with to get placed on medication, but she did tell me that Brian has been hospitalized for it before.

Sandi then explained about the Baker Act in Illinois, which allows patients to be held involuntarily at a mental health facility if they are a danger to themselves or others. She didn't outright tell me the issues surrounding his hospital stay, but she heavily alluded to him being "Baker Acted" for his own protection, which happened shortly before the threats against Warner were made.

When she told me that, I felt a flash of guilt. Maybe our fake-turned-real dating act pushed this man over the edge? Was his sanity hanging by a thread, and seeing me with Warner the final act to make him snap? Amy told me I was being ridiculous when I brought it up to her. Connie, however, was less dismissive of my concerns. She, however, stressed that even if my relationship caused Joseph to go off the deep end, it was not my responsibility to ensure others—especially strangers—were stable before making any of my own decisions. She also challenged me to recognize that even if my actions at that moment didn't cause a mental break, there's nothing that says something else totally unrelated to Warner and me didn't cause the fracture.

Either way, my head has been swimming the last few weeks, and I'm not sure I'll ever get the answers I seek. Can we ever truly know what another person is thinking?

I'm jolted from my thoughts by Warner walking through the front door. He kisses my head when he finds me in the dining room, laptop open to an empty lesson plan template. I've been staring at it for the last hour, hoping the tables will populate themselves with ideas for next month's field trip programs.

"How long have you been sitting here?" he asks when I roll my stiff neck. He stands behind me, gently kneading my neck and working out a knot at the connection between my neck and right shoulder.

"Long enough to know I should have given up half an hour ago. How was the game?" I didn't watch, hoping to catch up on some work, but I got the alerts on my phone in real time.

"It was good. Another win." He presses a kiss to the knot he's been working on. I tilt my neck to give him greater access.

"Mmm," I respond, distracted by his tongue swirling. He drags it up the column of my neck and lightly bites my earlobe.

"Tell me, Lee. If I slid my hand between your perfect thighs, would you be wet for me?" A large hand slides down my collarbone to cup my breast while his mouth continues its exploration of my neck.

"Only one way to find out," I say breathlessly and his hand creeps lower, skating across my belly and into the waistband of my leggings. I widen my legs. We're interrupted by the shrill ringing of my phone; normally, I keep it on vibrate, but I wanted to make sure I heard every update from today's game. Warner's hand stills as we both glance at the name on the screen. Sandi Llewellyn.

"Shit, you should take that," Warner says, withdrawing his hand. The cold dread I experienced upon seeing an otherwise lovely woman's name on my phone doused all flames of desire from Warner's roaming hands. I answer the call, turning it on speaker.

"Hi, Alicia," she greets warmly. "Do you have a few minutes to talk?"

"Yeah, go ahead. You're on speaker with Warner, too."

"Hi Warner. I'm going to get right to it. Brian Joseph's lawyers have reached out to our office, looking for a plea deal. I've been working with them today about the details and he's tentatively agreed to them, but I didn't want to go ahead with anything without running it by you."

"A plea deal? Meaning we can avoid a trial?" Warner voices the thoughts I'm too stunned to articulate.

"It seems that he's resumed taking his medication in the last two weeks, which has afforded him some...mental clarity," Sandi tells us. "His lawyers report he is still dealing with a lot of side effects from the medication, but in addition, he is apparently finally able to acknowledge the harm he caused you. He allegedly is experiencing a lot of guilt and wants to rectify the situation, which has allowed for us to structure an agreement I'm hoping you will find favorable." She pauses, waiting for questions.

"Go on," I encourage. I wasn't expecting a phone call like this, not when, as far as I know, the psychological testing hasn't even been conducted. Did I miss that?

"He has agreed to a stay in a secure mental health facility for at least two years, or until his symptoms resolve, whichever is later. Which means he will get treatment for *at least* two years," she stresses. "He will pay a twelve thousand dollar fine and will be responsible for restitution in the form of any therapy bills you or Mr. James will incur as a result of the emotional trauma inflicted by his actions."

That's a lot of money for someone who can't afford to pay bail.

"He has also agreed to restricted internet access, all correspondence–written or telecommunications–to be monitored, and probation for three years following dismissal from the facility. Those things are all standard, of course, but they are still a part of the agreement. Of course, he will have a criminal record as well." When Warner and I remain silent, Sandi continues. "Mr. Joseph is aware of the restraining order filed against him, which will, obviously, remain in place. He will still be barred from contacting you in any way, including physically approaching you, cyberstalking and cyber communications, and the old-fashioned way of snail mail." Detectives Pinal and Gregory finally figured out how Joseph was getting the letters into my mailbox. It was never a nefarious plot involving stealing or duplicating mailbox keys. He apparently is very good, and very quick, at picking locks.

I nod, even though Sandi can't see me. "Okay."

"Okay, meaning you're in agreement with this? Is there anything you would like to see added or changed? Apparently, Mr. Joseph is open to making additional concessions should you request them."

CHAPTER FORTY-EIGHT

Warner

Remember when I said Alicia was a tigress, a goddess? She's so much more than that. She is power and grace incarnate. A warrior goddess. A true Athena. Apparently, she still can shock me with her goodness, as evidenced by her next comment to Sandi.

"Um, yes. I would like the fine removed from the agreement."

"Excuse me, can you repeat that?"

"The twelve thousand dollar fine. I would like to remove that from the plea deal, if possible."

Since I arrived home twenty minutes ago, I have been standing behind Alicia. Now, I crouch at her side, needing to see her face, to make sure I'm hearing her correctly. Apparently, Sandi is struggling with the same issue.

"I don't understand, Alicia. With the plea deal, everything can be wrapped up. You avoid the time and emotional expense of a trial, and we can move forward with ensuring Joseph no longer has access to you."

"Yes, I understand that," Alicia says, making eye contact with me. "But without a job for at least two years, how is he going to make enough money to pay a huge fine, in addition to restitution, when he can't even afford his own bail money right now? He's never going to be able to get back on his feet."

I can't believe I'm hearing this. Alicia has been through hell and back over a period of two years, and she's worried about her stalker's quality of life after he serves his punishment? If ever there was a moment when I knew Alicia was too good for me, it's now.

"I don't want to speak for Warner," she continues. "But so far, my therapy bills have been covered by insurance, so restitution is not needed by me. I don't know what sort of mental illness he's dealing with, and I'm not an expert on psychology, but I can't imagine he's had an easy life or will have an easy life from this point on, especially with a criminal record. If you feel there are enough stipulations in the plea agreement to prevent him from doing this again–to *anyone*–I'm okay with it. I'm not looking for revenge here. I'm looking to move on."

I know my mouth is hanging open. If it wasn't attached by skin and ligaments, I'm sure my jaw would be on the dining room floor. If anyone has a right to seek vengeance, it's Lee. Yet here she is, sitting in our dining room, calmly saying she doesn't need or want it. My brain can't make sense of it.

"I understand," Sandi is saying, as my lagging brain tries to catch up. Alicia and I talked about potential outcomes to a trial. We even briefly discussed our wish for the possibility of a plea deal, but we dismissed that early on, not wanting to get our hopes up. Not only had we not really considered the reality of a plea deal, but we also certainly hadn't considered the details a deal could possibly contain.

"Mr. James?"

"Huh?" I respond. It's clearly not the first time she's said my name. "Sorry, this is a lot to process right now. Can you repeat that?"

"Of course. I was asking, since Alicia requested that her restitution be removed from the plea deal, if you wanted us to continue including yours? As a threat was made against you, you have a right to restitution as well."

I look at Alicia. She shrugs, and I know she'll let me make my own decision without judgment.

"I don't need anyone's money," I say firmly. My resistance to Joseph paying for my therapy is multifactored. I don't want him to realize how much he affected me. Honestly, my stress from our situation was more a result of how he impacted Alicia rather than any threat he made toward me. I also recognize that if I have lingering trauma for his actions against me, it likely is so wrapped up in my current need for therapy for my depression, and asking him to pay for my therapy related to that hardly seems fair. Fuck, maybe Alicia is rubbing off on me.

Last week, JJ texted me the name of his therapist. He told me he doesn't see him often these days, aside from semi-regular check-ins, but noted that therapy was necessary for him in dealing with his past traumas. I bet it was, seeing as his own mother shot him last year.

"Okay, I'll make those changes and submit them to Mr. Joseph's legal team. Do you have any additional questions before we hang up?" Sandi is still talking while I'm lost in my own thoughts.

"No, thank you." Alicia answers for both of us before hanging up.

I rock back on my heels. She pushes back from her chair and sits next to me on the floor.

"Fuck, you're such a good person, you know that?" I tell her earnestly. She shrugs modestly.

"I just want to close this chapter of my life and move on." I can understand that, I just know that if I were in her shoes, I would have done it with a little less human decency.

"I love you, Lee." I squeeze her hand, hoping to impress upon her just what her goodness means to me.

"I love you, too." She squeezes my hand back. "Now, can we pick back up where we left off before we were so rudely interrupted by that phone call?"

My desperation for Alicia is physical, sure. I crave her touch—*need* her touch—like an addict looking for his next hit. There is some-thing about the way she touches me, the circles she rubs on the back of my hand, the gentle squeezes she gives me when I need reassurance, that grounds me. Don't get me started on the skin-to-skin contact after a night of making love–and make no mistake, that's what we're doing now. We still fuck hard and intensely, but the undercurrent of love is still at the center, even when we're not fucking slow and deep.

But my desperation for Alicia goes far beyond the physical. She's my lighthouse in a storm, the first drop of rain after years of drought, the first gasping breath taken after being underwater for far too long. My body knew Alicia was home long before my heart did. But now that my soul is involved, I know Alicia is endgame. My desperation for her isn't want. It's need. It's survival. It's salvation.

CHAPTER FORTY-NINE
Alicia

"I swear, with everything that's gone on the last two seasons, we're going to need to expand the support of the family program!" Deb, the director of the Foxes family program, jokingly tells Amy and me as we place cupcakes on little tiered stands.

"Yeah, I'd say we brought the drama. But that hopefully means we aren't due for more drama–or police involvement–for a long time." Amy smirks at me. Between JJ's "drama" with his estranged mother last year and my stalker, I'd say the universal karmic payments we've been making should more than tide us over for a long time.

"Do you want the banner on this wall?" Hailey McClintock asks, pointing to the blue accent wall behind her.

"That would be great," Deb tells her. We're in the Foxes corporate offices, in a large event room on one of the top floors. In the basement below us, the boys are showering and finishing up their post-game workouts in the clubhouse. We have a few more finishing touches before the guest of honor arrives.

I shoot a text off to Warner, asking when everyone will be finishing up, and he promises me Caleb has already completed his workout and left to pick up Jenny. The guys are slowly filtering upstairs. Hailey slaps away her husband's hand as he surreptitiously tries to steal a cupcake.

"Don't even think about it, Eli," she warns.

"I'm hungry! I just finished three hours of baseball!" he whines, but Hailey isn't fooled.

"It's too bad the Foxes don't provide you with, like, nine square meals a day," she rolls her eyes and mimes playing a tiny violin.

"Wow, it looks great in here," Warner says, stepping into the room from the elevator bank. Pinks and purples splash across the room, clashing violently with the permanent orange accents of the room, but everyone ignores that. A large balloon structure forms a champagne bottle pouring into silver sparkly balloon bubbles at a photo station. Across the room, a large pink banner with purple lettering spells out "NO MORE CANCER!" in bold font. An oversized pinata hangs in an otherwise empty corner of the room, shaped to look like an angry, malignant cell–of course, matching the pink and purple theme.

The entire team is here, even the players without wives or girlfriends, all ready to support Caleb and Jenny. Even staff members arrive. Benny, Warner's manager, is standing in the corner, talking to Hayden Oliver and a coach I don't recognize. Deb and some other front office staff members are chatting next to the cupcakes.

JJ steps off the elevator and announces Caleb is walking in the building several floors below us. Voices hush immediately and when we hear the ding of the elevator a few minutes later, we stand ready. The lights are on, but I know Jenny will still be surprised. When Caleb and Jenny step into the room, we cheer for her.

She looks adorable, her bob wig looking cute and stylish, with her yellow sundress and flat green sandals. When she takes us all in, she bursts into tears, crying harder when her eyes flick to the banner announcing her good health.

She's had a long journey fighting breast cancer. At times, it felt like there were more downs than ups, more valleys than peaks, but through it all, she maintained a positive attitude and Caleb's support never wavered. They put their wedding on hold for her treatments. No one deserves a break more than them; this party was the least we could do for our friends.

Caleb and Jenny make the rounds, hugging and thanking everyone. We pose for pictures in front of the champagne bubbles and Jenny bursts open the pinata, which contains candy and little plastic bottles of liquor. We eat and laugh and cry and love, because that's what a family does.

"Now batting, right fielder, Warner James." The announcement booms across the loudspeaker and the crowd cheers, myself included. It's a tense moment in the game. The Foxes are down by two runs with the bases loaded in the bottom of the ninth inning. It's the last game of the first round of playoffs; whoever wins advances to the next round of the postseason, getting one step closer to the World Series. Whoever loses goes home.

My fingers find Amy's and I grip them tightly, pulling her hand onto my lap. I can talk about statistics all I want, but it doesn't help me feel better. Statistically, there is no one better to take this at-bat than Warner James. He has the highest batting average on the team this series. He's not easily flustered by high-pressure situations; he's been in a thousand of them over the course of his career. That doesn't matter to me. I want to cover my eyes and peek through my fingers. Warner might be able to handle the pressure, but I cannot. Amy's strangled fingers are proof. She grits her teeth at the pain but doesn't pull her hand away.

The first pitch is a ball, low and outside the bottom right corner of the plate. Warner watches it sail by before stepping out of the batter's box to take another practice swing. He adjusts the strap on his batting gloves and resumes his stance in the box. The second pitch is delivered, and his swing is half a second too late, fouling the ball back behind him and into the backstop, dribbling down the netting and rolling away. A ball boy sprints to remove it, and the third pitch is delivered.

Crack!

I'm out of my seat at noise, leaping to my feet, yanking Amy's hand with me, and leaning my upper body toward center field, as if leaning can make the ball travel further. It sails deep to center, the outfielder below it careening full speed toward the wall. It's no use though; the ball plops itself squarely in the glove of a fan sitting three rows back. A walk off grand slam.

The roar of the crowd engulfs us. Tears stream down my face as Amy's screams drown out my own. We watch, jumping up and down, as Warner jogs around the bases, pumping his fist in the air. The stadium blares celebratory music as the team streams out of the dugout to meet him at home plate, leaping and grabbing at him as he crosses it, officially ending the game, giving the Foxes the win and advancing them to the next round of the playoffs.

CHAPTER FIFTY

Warner

M y postgame interviews last longer than I'd like. I'm dying to get out of here. Lee and I have important dinner plans. Don't get me wrong, I'm thrilled that the Foxes have advanced in the playoffs. We play Philadelphia next week, giving us a few days with no games. We still have team workouts and meetings, but the reprieve on our bodies is welcome.

I disregard the fourth beer someone presses into my hands. I've been setting them on the bench behind me, which apparently serves as an invitation for JJ to hand me another one, despite refraining from drinking the previous ones. Giving up, I finally accept the fifth beer and take a sip. It's cold and refreshing, but I'd like to get out of here and get some rest. Alicia has an important day tomorrow; I've got to get her home.

Standing on the bench, I address the clubhouse. "Alright you fuckers, go celebrate. But," I point my finger at the room. "Every single one of you better be up at mile twenty tomorrow."

Someone yells "Hell yeah!" followed by a chorus of whistles and shouts of agreement. Shaking my head at my teammates, I hop down and head to the showers. It's not late, but I want Alicia to be well rested. The Chicago Marathon starts tomorrow; Lee must be there at an ungodly hour to get into her corral, which means she must be up even earlier for breakfast. She made me promise to go back to bed for a few hours after dropping her off, but I doubt that'll happen.

By the time I make it upstairs and meet up with Lee, who is waiting with the other WAGs, it's several hours after the game. She leaps into my arms, congratulating me again on the game. I saw her on the field after the game, but at that point, I was covered in sticky orange sports drink, so I didn't want to hold her too closely.

"Thanks, baby. Ready to go home? I'm going to make you the biggest pasta dinner. You'll be sweating garlic all through mile sixteen." She tips her head back and laughs. I set her back onto her feet before taking her hand in mine and walking towards the exit.

"Tomorrow, everybody better be there," I point back at the WAGs and a few of their husbands who have trickled upstairs. They all nod or give me some sort of verbal confirmation. When I look down at Alicia, she's shaking her head.

"You're ridiculous, you know that, right?"

"You love it." I tap her nose and pull her outside.

"She's got a neon green beanie on," I tell Jenny, who cranes her neck through the crowd. If Lee is maintaining her pace, she should be nearing us in the next few minutes. I caught her just after mile marker four and again at thirteen. I was hoping to see her between thirteen and twenty, but navigating anywhere in the city right now is hopeless. I'm just glad I found our crew at our agreed-upon meeting spot. It's a madhouse out here.

I look around at my friends, in awe of their creativity. They line the street carrying homemade signs of varying artistry, but everyone is decked out in a way that supports my girl.

"Do you like them?" Amy asks. "Everyone came over after the game last night to make them." She holds up her sign emblazoned with *Alicia Langley is my hero!* I smile. Next to her, Jenny displays hers, proudly announcing *On a scale of 1 to 10, Alicia is a 26.2!* Tim and Danny have Alicia's name and bib numbers written on their cheeks in what I hope is not permanent marker. I laugh, catching a glimpse of Carter's sign: *Never trust a fart during a run. Toilets, up ahead!*

"There better actually be restrooms up ahead," I joke.

"Don't worry, I checked. They're right around the bend," he assures me.

"Guys, there she is!" Hailey squeals from her seat on Elijah's shoulders. Sure enough, Lee's neon beanie allows us to locate her easily. I don't know how she can run for twenty miles and look stunning doing it, but chalk it up to one more way she amazes me.

Our section cheers loudly and Lee smiles widely. She thought mile twenty would be the most difficult for her, which is why I planned for everyone to meet here, cheering her on to get through the last six miles.

JJ clangs a cowbell while Tim whistles through his fingers. Everyone else is shouting and cheering all at once; I'm sure Alicia can't make out what anyone is saying, but she gets the picture: we love her.

She passes by us, grinning wide, maintaining a steady pace. I refresh her tracking page through the marathon website, but it hasn't been updated since I last looked at it. We remain at mile twenty a little longer, giving out high fives and cheering on random runners. They are all incredible athletes, and I couldn't be prouder of my girl for joining their ranks.

"Alright, come on, we only have like twenty minutes if we want to make it to the finish line to see her cross!" Amy voices my own anxiety. Luckily, we're only a block away from the L station. We easily hop on and head to Grant Park, where the finish line and post-race party is being held.

We time the transport perfectly and make it to the finish line with time to spare. It's packed; there's no way she will be able to see us. The throngs of people waiting near the finish line are dozens deep. Hailey climbs on Elijah's shoulders again, serving as our lookout. I hit refresh on the tracking page, but reception is terrible here, likely because everyone around me is doing the same thing.

"There!" Hailey's cry screeches above the din of everyone else's cheering. I hand her my phone with instructions not to drop it. I don't care if my phone breaks, but I'm not missing capturing these moments. I promised Lee's parents I'd send them the video of her crossing the finish line. Eden may have also threatened me with bodily harm if I didn't do the same for her.

Alicia comes into view, the runner in front of her moving slightly to the side, allowing an unobstructed view of the most beautiful runner on the course. Her feet pound heavily against the pavement, her mouth open and breathing heavily. The relieved look on her face when she nears the finish line makes me want to break onto the course and run the last tenth of a mile with her.

"Go, baby, go!" I cheer, knowing she can't hear me, but not caring either way. I will always cheer for my girl.

She crosses the finish line and continues jogging, gradually slowing her pace so those behind her don't crash into her. Her chest is heaving and I swear I see tears stream down her face, but I'm too far away from her. Large metal barricades separate the runners and the course from the crowd. I snatch my phone back from Hailey and turn.

Feeling like a salmon swimming upstream, I fight my way through the crowd, yelling at Matteo over my shoulder to meet me at our prearranged spot later. He nods and is swallowed up in the crowd as I keep moving. I know if she's hurt, there are medic tents she can visit lining the path she'll walk to meet up with us. She'll be in good hands, but since I don't know the cause of her tears, I'm ready to start shoving the crowd forcibly to get to her.

Breathing deeply, I try to calm myself. My publicist's voice rings in my ears, urging me to let cooler heads prevail. Luckily, I'm a few inches taller than most people around here, so I can navigate myself to less crowded areas a little easier. When the crowd finally breaks up, I catch a glimpse of Lee's beanie and pink tank top. We're walking parallel to each other, but there's so much distance between us, she won't be able to hear me if I shout for her.

A large medal rests against her torso. I lose sight of her as she walks between a sea of tents. I start jogging, looping my way back toward her and waiting near the mouth of the tents. I scan the area frantically, worried I got the timing wrong and missed her exit already. A flash of pink and green catches my eye.

"Langley!" Alicia whips her head around, trying to find where my shouts are coming from, but I'm already on the move. She spots me and grins, no longer teary. She starts slowly making her way towards me, limping slightly. I pick up my pace as I stand in front of her, throwing my arms around her.

"I'm so gross!" Her protests are swallowed by my chest as I envelop her. Her arms are full of an assortment of snacks and drinks; they squash against my stomach, but I continue holding her tightly.

"I'm so proud of you, baby!" She pulls her head back to look at me and I see her eyes fill with tears. "Tell me these are happy tears,"

I implore, as one escapes the confines of her lash line and trickles down her cheek. I swipe it away with the pad of my thumb.

"Yeah, they're happy…It's just…it's been a long year." Her lower lip trembles as I pull her close again. I'm not fooled for an instant. Some of those might be happy tears, but I know some are holdouts from when she didn't know if she'd be able to train and run due to Brian fucking Joseph stalking her. She's come such a long way, but she's right. It's been a long year.

"To Alicia!" We toast for perhaps the eighth time at brunch after we all meet up following the race. Alicia changed into the sweats and long-sleeved shirt I brought her, and we all walked from Grant Park to The Waffle Wagon, where I reserved the back room for Lee and her adoring fans.

It was a decent walk from the finish line to brunch, but Alicia insisted she needed the movement to cool down her muscles. She declined my offers for a piggyback ride and a fireman's carry. Matteo offered too, which Lee also declined, reminding us that we have postseason baseball to play in a few days. That's when Danny offered to carry her, which she also declined. My stubborn girl.

As we were walking, I pulled out my phone and made an online reservation at the spa for Lee for two days from now. She deserves a little pampering after what her body went through. JJ caught my eye and looked at my phone.

"Make it for two if you're not going with her. Amy will kill me if Alicia gets a spa day without her." Laughing, I adjusted the reservation and checked out.

Alicia looks at me, clinking her mimosa glass to mine, accepting yet another toast in her honor. I swipe my thumb at the droplet of syrup in the corner of her mouth and bring my thumb to my lips, tasting the sticky sweetness. She ducks her head and stifles a yawn. I'm not surprised she's getting tired, now that the adrenaline and excitement have worn off.

"We can get the check," I offer.

"I've got it," JJ interjects from my side. "You get her home before she falls asleep at the table." Alicia shoots him an appreciative glance before pushing off the table to stand. She winces as she does so.

"It's just blisters, I promise. My feet are just tired." Luckily, home is a block away.

"Lucky for you, your boyfriend is a big strong athlete who can carry you." She rolls her eyes but agrees to hop on my back when we get outside the restaurant.

She lets me carry her home and into the shower, where I plop her on the bench and wash her, massaging her legs in the process. She doesn't fight me when I wrap her in a heated towel and carry her off to bed, lying her gently down and pressing a lingering kiss against her lips.

"I'm so proud of you, Lee. For everything you've been through. You never once lost your shine throughout everything this past year. Thank you for letting me be by your side for it all. I love you."

I sit on the bed next to her, gently rubbing her back as her eyes drift closed. She's the picture of contentment. I smile, knowing that it may have taken more than a marathon's worth of obstacles for us to get here, but we're finally where we're meant to be: in each other's arms.

Epilogue: Alicia

"Here you are, Mr. and Mrs. James." The flight attendant brings us to a door in the interior of the front of the plane. "I have your reserve elite cabin in here." She holds the door open, allowing us to walk through in front of her. My eyes practically bug out of my head. When Warner told me he was going to splurge for our honeymoon, I was expecting luxury, but I was not expecting this.

A queen-sized bed sits at the center of the room, across from the door we just walked through. A small table sits in the corner, upon which a tiny bud vase with a single flower rests. A large television is mounted on the wall next to the door. There's not a lot of space to walk around, but it's a room! On an airplane! Just for us!

"As you can see," the flight attendant gestures to the bed, "we have the room configured for sleeping arrangements, as it is nearly bedtime in Morocco. We suggest if you are staying in North Africa, that you get your body used to the time zone as soon as possible." Warner nods. I continue gaping at the room.

"I have showers reserved for you approximately two hours before we are scheduled to land in Casablanca. Is that to your liking?"

"That's amazing, thank you so much," I gush. The flight attendant nods and performs a small bow before continuing.

"We will be around with warm towels and dinner shortly after departure. In the meantime, can I bring you some champagne? Tea? Something to eat?"

"Champagne would be great," Warner answers for me. When she leaves, giving us another small bow, I gape at him.

"Warner James. I didn't know *this* is what you meant by 'taking care of the honeymoon plans.'" He shoots me a wink and shrugs.

"You know I like to take care of you."

"Yes, but we could have flown regularly…or even first class! You didn't need to get us a whole freaking apartment!"

"You deserve a whole freaking apartment, though."

I should be used to this by now. Warner is good about saving money and investing in diverse opportunities. He makes his money work for him. But I swear he really does get off on taking care of me. At first, it made me uncomfortable, but now I don't fight it as much; I never win anyway. Besides, when Warner sets his mind to "taking care of me," he doesn't let anything hold him back.

He proposed to me on a hot air balloon ride over Napa Valley last midseason break. It was perfect, but I was so scared one of us would drop the ring, never to see it again. I should have known it would fit perfectly; Warner does nothing by halves. The marquise diamond glittered in the evening sun as he fed me wine and cheese and whispered how much better his life is with me in it.

We all know, though, that my life is better with him in mine. It's not just the way we look at each other; it's the way we look after each other. We lift each other up. We recognize that our relationship will rarely ever be fifty-fifty. There are days when Warner's only able to give me twenty percent, and I happily put in eighty percent of the effort. There are days when I can't manage a full fifty percent either, and he gladly picks up the slack. That's why we work; we take care of each other.

Warner's depression is obviously still present, but better managed now that he's regularly attending sessions with the therapist JJ recommended. He's still on the fence about medication, but he's open to revisiting the topic if he feels he can no longer manage on his own. I stopped seeing Connie after a few months, feeling able to manage things on my own, but therapy helped me get over the hump of my trauma related to the stalking.

Even the wedding planning wasn't stressful. Amy and JJ got married last year and seeing her go through all the meticulous details made me realize I just didn't care about that too much, as long as I got to marry my best friend at the end of the day. Warner, it turns out, did care about the details, so we hired a woman named Tekia to do the hard work for us. It turned out to be a great idea, because once we settled on his mother's restaurant as the reception venue, Tekia took the reins and made everything smooth not only for us, but for Anita and the staff at Squash Blossom as well.

The ceremony and reception were exquisite. All I cared about was my dress and my guests having a good time. Anita crafted an entirely unique menu for us that I know I'll dream about for the rest of my life. Warner got an ice cream sundae bar, complete with his mother's banana pudding ice cream and two kinds of hot fudge toppings. He claims he's been hooked on hot fudge sundaes since our adventures together in his kitchen.

Our friends all flew into Atlanta for the wedding. My parents and I went a week early to finalize our plans and for them to meet Warner's parents. Of course they got along well; Anita and my mom now swap cross-stitch patterns, of all things. When my parents finally walked me down the aisle, I'd never felt surer of anything in my life. Seeing Warner at the end of that aisle, across my very own finish line, he never looked more handsome. His suit was perfectly tailored, and his wide smile made the breath catch in my throat.

Now, two days after the wedding, he smiles the same grin at me, and I'm once again reminded how lucky I am. Not only have I found my person, my protector, but he happens to be the kindest, most thoughtful man I've ever met.

The flight attendant returns with our champagne. Warner plucks them off the tray and hands one to me. The attendant informs us we will be taking off soon and shows us how to watch the safety briefing on our television screen and how to lock the door to our room. As soon as she leaves, Warner flips the lock and gives me a predatory grin.

"How many times do you think I can get you off before we reach cruising altitude?" He sets his flute down next to the side of the bed; I follow suit. Placing his palm on the center of my chest, he presses into me slowly, pushing me onto the bed. The gold of his wedding ring glints in the recessed lighting as he slides my pants down my legs.

"I haven't tasted you since this morning. I'm dying here, Lee." I laugh, tossing a pillow at him from behind my head.

"You went down on me like three hours ago," I say. My laugh is cut short when Warner licks a long line up my center.

"Exactly. Three hours too long." He tosses the pillow back at me. "You better be quiet, Lee. Can't let everyone know what we're doing in here. You can scream into the pillow when you come."

I clutch the pillow tightly in my hands, knowing I'll need it. Warner resumes feasting as if he really was dying. His enthusiasm for eating me out is only matched by his desire to see me come in any way possible. He throws my legs over his shoulders and attacks my clit with his tongue, sliding a thick finger inside me.

"Warner," I moan, trying to stifle it and failing spectacularly. He chuckles against me, and the vibrations feel incredible.

"Baby, I don't care if this whole plane knows how delicious my wife's pussy is or how good I am at making her come." He crooks his finger and sucks my clit into his mouth, and just like that, my legs start to shake. I'm on the precipice again. "But I have a feeling *you* might be a little embarrassed if everyone on this flight finds out just how much I make you scream."

I press the pillow down over my mouth right before I shatter against Warner's tongue.

"Mmm," he groans, pressing his mouth harder against me as I ride wave after wave of pleasure. When my tremors die down, he finally pulls his mouth from me, licking his lips. "That was one, and we haven't even left the runway yet. Are you ready for more?"

The End

Acknowledgements

My first acknowledgement is to you, dear reader. When I first decided to share my writing with the world, it was a terrifying experience. Thanks for taking a chance on a new romance author. Thank you to the Booktok and Bookstagram communities for liking, sharing, and interacting with my work. You are an incredible, supportive, community, and I wouldn't be here without you.

My alpha readers, Alexa, Aleshia, and Jill: I could spend forever singing your praises. Your thoughtful feedback made Alicia and Warner who they evolved to be. You've jumped int each of my chapters with care and enthusiasm and made me a better writer in the process. Chelsea: thanks.

Emmily – you've always been talented, but too see my ideas and characters come to life at your hand has been incredible. And the vines you drew for my scene breaks? Iconic. Thank you for the gorgeous sketches. Warner and Alicia have never looked better!

Neil – once again, you knocked it out of the park (pun intended) with you cover design. Thanks for sharing your talents with me on book two!

To my friends and family who have supported this crazy journey of late night writing sprees, decision fatigue, character development, and the dreaded editing caves. Most especially, thank you to Mr. French, the OG baseball boyfriend-turned-husband, who takes a very personal interest in my hydration levels while I'm writing and doing everything book-related. You ensure I'm fed, watered, and, most importantly, loved. You've never doubted my dream for a second, and I can't tell you what that means to me. To my brother, Andrew...thanks for deciding to become an intellectual property attorney; it's been wildly convenient for me! Thank you for your support and talking me off the ledge.

To Erica and the Wonder Women/Tuesday Tea ladies (you know who you are): I joined your ranks right as I finished writing book one, and there was never any hesitation in the way you embraced not only me, but my writing persona and my spicy little books. I'm so lucky to have a group of supportive women at my fingertips.

I started this book with a dedication to my dog, and I'm going to end it speaking his praises once more. A Postsecret postcard once said "I only believe in heaven because I can accept nothing less for my dog." Truer words have never been written. Gryff, you were my boy for eleven wonderful years, and it's been so hard without you. You helped me sift through the imposter syndrome plaguing me after the publication of my first book. Your head was next to me on the couch for every word I wrote in books one through four, and beside mine when I laid down at night. Losing you has had a profound impact on me, and I'll never be the same. Thank you for your goodness, your constant companionship, your unending love, your ceaseless hugs, and the frequent but necessary reminders to release my anxiety and find my joy. You, my sweet boy, were my joy. Thank you for being everything and more.

About the author

Meghan French is a romance author who loves writing about strong female characters and the swoonworthy, dirty-talking men who love them. A self-professed foodie and yogini, she lives in Arizona with her husband. When she's not in a writing cave, she spends her time as a school psychologist, cooking, hiking, and reading all the romance novels she can get her hands on.

Join Meghan's Facebook group, Meghan's Francophiles!

*Scan here to
join the Facebook
group!*

Also by Meghan French

Casual Now
Book 1 of the Chicago Foxes Series

I'll Look After You
Book 2 of the Chicago Foxes Series

Book 3 of the Chicago Foxes Series
(Coming Soon!)

Book 4 of the Chicago Foxes Series
(Coming Soon!)

Billionaire Spinoff Series

(Coming Soon!)